Girl in a Box

Also by Sujata Massey

The Typhoon Lover
The Pearl Diver
The Samurai's Daughter
The Bride's Kimono
The Floating Girl
The Flower Master
Zen Attitude
The Salaryman's Wife

Girl
in
a Box

Sujata Massey

HarperCollins*Publishers*

HarperCollins books may be purchased for educational, business, or sales promotional use. For information, please write: Special Markets Department, HarperCollins Publishers, 10 East 53rd Street, New York, NY 10022.

FIRST EDITION

Designed by Nancy B. Field

Library of Congress Cataloging-in-Publication Data

Massey, Sujata.
  Girl in a box / Sujata Massey.—1st ed.
    p. cm.
  ISBN-10: 0-06-076514-3
  ISBN-13: 978-0-06-076514-9
  1. Shimura, Rei (Fictitious character)—Fiction. 2. Japanese American women—Fiction. 3. Women spies—Fiction. 4. Tokyo (Japan)—Fiction. 5. Department stores—Japan—Fiction. I. Title.
  PS3563.A79965G57 2006
  813'.54—dc22   2006041085

06 07 08 09 10   ❖/RRD 10 9 8 7 6 5 4 3 2 1

Acknowledgments

My heartfelt gratitude rests with the many people around the world who answered all my odd questions about Japanese fashion, espionage, banking, and international financial crimes.

In Japan, I am grateful to: John Adair Jr., Hidetomo Hirayama, Koichi Hyogo, Akiko Kashiwagi, Kenichi Masuda, Satoshi Mizushima, Rei Mori, Akemi Narita, Atsuko Noda, the staff of Osawa Onsen, Ken Tashiro, Yosuke Umano, and Miko Yamanouchi.

Friends outside Japan who helped greatly with the manuscript include John Antweiler, Richard Dellheim, Ann Gunter, Rob Kresge, Ryohei Omori, Ayumi Sawa, Rob Serjeant, and my Sisters in Crime writing group: Karen Diegmueller, John Mann, Janice McLane and Marcia Talley. I remain indebted to my longtime publisher, Harper-Collins, especially my brilliant editor, Carolyn Marino; her crackerjack assistant Jennifer Civiletto; and Clare McMahon, a creative and hard-working publicist.

And to my family—thank you for your continued love, and also for your tolerance of the many times when I disappear from our world, figuratively and literally.

Cast of Characters

REI SHIMURA, a young Japanese-American woman working as a special informant to the Organization for Cultural Intelligence (OCI), an elite governmental spy agency.

MICHAEL HENDRICKS, chief of OCI's Japan bureau.

MRS. IKUKO TAKI, a native Japanese translator working for OCI.

NORIE SHIMURA, Rei's beloved aunt, who lives in Yokohama with her banker husband, HIROSHI; son, DR. TSUTOMU "TOM" SHIMURA; and daughter, CHIKA, a recent college graduate.

MASAHIRO MITSUYAMA, elderly chairman of Mitsutan, Japan's most successful department store, founded and still owned by the Mitsuyama family. His son, ENOBU MITSUYAMA, is general manager of the Ginza flagship store.

MS. AOKI, director of personnel at the store; her assistant is MS. SEIKO YAMADA.

MRS. OKUMA, head of Mitsutan's K Team foreign shoppers assistance program; her assistant is MIYO HAN, a young woman of Korean ethnic heritage.

MR. FUJIWARA, director of customer service at Mitsutan.

MR. YOSHINO, director of Accessories.

MR. KITAGAWA, director of Young Fashion.

MRS. ONO, director of Alterations.

WARREN KRAVITZ, head of investment banking in Japan for the famous American firm Winston Brothers. His wife, MELANIE, makes his life run smoothly in Tokyo. Among his employees are two young bankers: ARCHIE WEINSTOCK and RAVI SHAH.

JIMMY DELONE, American retail magnate and owner of Supermart, a giant national chain of discount warehouses.

BRIAN JONES, a trusted aide of Michael Hendricks.

Also: shop clerks and shopping addicts, friends, soldiers, and spies.

1

It's taken me almost a whole lifetime to become a decent liar.

I still endure stabs of good-girl guilt about it, even though lying has started a brilliant second career for me. I tell stories easily, rarely missing a step as I switch between English and Japanese. But I often wonder how I ever got to this crazy place in life, and where I will go next.

This day had been like all the others: a cool winter day in Monterey, with eight hours of classes at the Defense Language Institute, followed by my usual routine—a run out to Lover of Jesus Point in Pacific Grove. On days like this one, I felt that the Pacific was my constant friend. The water was the divider between me and Japan, between my old life and the new one. I'd have to cross it to go home.

It was odd that I felt this way, I thought as I ran along the dirt trail that paralleled the coast. California was my birthplace—San Francisco, to be exact, about two hours to the north, where my parents still lived. But Japan, where I'd lived so briefly but happily teaching English and selling antiques, always beckoned. The sensation had been stronger on this day than at any time so far in the two months I'd been studying at DLI, preparing for the kind of career in which you couldn't tell anyone what you did, but that could get me back to Japan.

Good things are worth waiting for. I reminded myself of this truth as I ran, dressed for the winter in a long-sleeved black shirt really meant for bikers, and shorts, because I was too vain to wear sensible running tights. The wind on my legs didn't bother me; but on my way back, my knee started throbbing, and I thought about how much I wanted to replace the Nike Airs. In Monterey, there were a few places to buy running shoes, but nothing with the vast array of choices that a thirty-year-old with fading knees required. Of course, I could go up to San Francisco and easily get my favorite Asics style, but I wasn't in the mood. I'd been there at my family home for Christmas and New Year's, a time when I found myself fending off a combination of unhealthy foods and intrusive questions. As much as I loved my parents, I couldn't tell them about the Organization for Cultural Intelligence—OCI—the supersecret spy agency where I'd been hired as a special informant. I also couldn't explain why Hugh Glendinning, the man to whom I'd once been semi-engaged, had thrown me out of his life and Washington, D.C., apartment forever. But I wouldn't lie to my parents—that would be completely against my internal code. So I chose not to talk.

I actually liked the solitude of the Monterey coast, with its jagged rocks set against the turbulent, frigid Pacific: home of sardines, surfers, seals, and whales. Now I glanced toward the ocean, just to make sure I wasn't going to miss the sunset. Another great blessing of my posting in Monterey was my proximity to sunsets over the Pacific: performance art in vivid shades of red, orange, and purple, each sunset unique, like the kanji characters I was studying.

The sun took its leisurely time slipping down to the horizon, but as closely as I looked, I missed the green flash. I always seemed to miss it, even on the days when I'd been with Hugh, vacationing in beautiful parts of Japan and Thailand, and he took pains to point it out. I never saw the same things he did. Perhaps that had been the problem.

I shifted my gaze forward in the direction I was running, coming close to the Hopkins Marine Station, a research outpost connected to Stanford University. It had a beautiful rocky lookout point, but I'd never gone out because the station had a high wire fence and many signs saying "keep out." I was getting quite used to barriers, fences, and warning signs; usually, the Department of Defense identification card that I carried would get me in most places, but I had no business at the station.

Someone else did, though; a solitary sightseer, who was out on the rocks with field glasses close to his face.

I had noticed the same man half an hour earlier, because of what he was wearing: a business suit, which was a rarity in Monterey. I assumed he had to be some muckety-muck, though in my experience, marine scientists were more likely to wear jeans than gray flannel. Not that I could tell what the suit was made of: I was much too far away to make out those details, let alone the guy's face. I imagined for a minute that he was a spy, watching the coast for his contact to come in. He was probably an out-of-control tourist who just wanted to take pictures—though why he wasn't looking seaward rather than at the recreation trail didn't make sense.

It took me a couple of minutes to pass the rocky outcropping, then the rest of the fenced station, and then its exit. My knee was really bothering me, so I moved to the side and tightened my shoelaces— anything for more support. As I finished tying the knot, I turned around to look for bikers, always a liability on the trail, and I was stunned to see the man in the business suit running out of the marine station's parking lot. Now I knew that what I'd sensed earlier had been correct; the field glasses had been trained on me, not on any form of sea life.

I was fairly breathless because I'd already been running for about half an hour, but I mustered an extra bit of power and began running toward the American Tin Cannery Outlets. The first place I saw was a Reebok outlet, but I ran on, figuring I wouldn't get much sympathy there when I was wearing Nikes. I also passed by Isotoner and Geoffrey Beene, on the assumption that these were not brands that would draw a young, fit crowd ready to aid in my defense. The students at DLI, mostly young enlisted men, were certainly buff enough to help me out against an assailant, but I was the last woman they'd want to help. I don't know whether I'd ticked them off by screwing up the academic curve, or because I'd refused any and all romantic propositions. It was impossible to know—and actually of no consequence at a time like this.

Damn, I thought, after glancing backward. He was gaining on me, and the glasses were now hanging around his neck, hitting his chest as he ran. No normal jogger ran in a business suit; he was a lunatic. I broke into a full-throttle sprint. He was still so far away that I couldn't see his face, but from what I'd seen, he had gray hair. This fact—that he was significantly older than I—should have made me calm down, but did not.

There was a little restaurant at the end of the outlet strip brightly painted red, white, and blue, probably in an attempt to cater to both Monterey's military population and foreign tourists. I jogged up the steps and burst inside, finding the place absolutely empty; of course, it was before the dinner hour.

At the far end of the room, a couple of young men in T-shirts and jeans were sitting together conversing in Spanish. They looked at the runner in their restaurant and said nothing. I didn't know if it was because I looked so disheveled, or because there was a language barrier.

"I have a problem. Can you call the police?" I said between heavy breaths.

The two men hesitated a moment, glancing each other. Then they ran back through the kitchen.

"It's a misunderstanding, I didn't mean—" I called out, wishing I had spoken in Spanish the first time. Spanish was the first language of Monterey, I should have thought to speak it right away and not use a trigger word like "police."

A banging sound told me they'd gone out the back door. Now I was all alone. I quickly threaded my way through the restaurant, looking for a telephone. The man had obviously seen me go in; there was no point in hiding. I'd just be on the phone with the cops when my stalker arrived.

I found a phone at last, and as I pressed "talk," I finally got a close-up view of my pursuer through the window. And shakily I put the phone down. I had been right when I'd briefly daydreamed about the figure on the rocks. He was a spy—a spymaster, to be exact. The man I'd run from was the chief of OCI's Japan desk: Michael Hendricks, my boss of the last three months.

"Michael! What a surprise," I said, striving for normality as he stepped through the door.

Michael Hendricks must have become extremely bored with his duties in Washington, because he'd been e-mailing me jokes almost daily, silly lightbulb riddles like *How many spies does it take to screw in a lightbulb?* Answer: *Twenty. One to do it, and nineteen to develop a distraction.*

However, in Michael's numerous e-mails, he'd never once mentioned that he was planning a cross-country trip to California.

"Why were you running away?" Michael was breathing hard and pulling his tie out of his shirt collar as he spoke. Michael was not a conventionally handsome man; he was too thin, and although his features may have started out patrician, he looked as if he'd had his nose broken somewhere along the line. But his salt-and-pepper hair was cut well, in a classic military buzz, and his ice-blue eyes were so appealing that I often had to look away.

I decided to answer honestly. "I was scared. Wouldn't you be, if someone watched you with field glasses and then started running after you?"

"I was looking for you." His breath was gradually slowing. "When I made the positive ID, I decided to catch up with you. By the way, did you know that you pronate when you run?"

"Yes. The shoes make it worse." I flushed, embarrassed that I'd been seen not only running away, but running away with bad form.

"You mentioned once that you ran in this area, so that's why I came, after I found you weren't at your apartment. I picked that point, on the rocks, just to make sure I'd see you before you went home, or into town, or wherever." Michael tugged off his suit jacket. I looked for huge sweat stains on his oxford shirt, but it was crisp and dry. Either he was a very cool customer or he wore an undershirt.

Michael spoke again. "Actually, I've been trying to catch up with you all day. There's something we have to discuss, as soon as possible."

"What could it be?" I asked grimly, because I was sure I knew. He had learned the results of my embarrassing polygraph test a few days earlier, and come to tell me that my very short career in government intelligence was over.

"It looks like there's nobody here to take an order, so let's talk about it back at your apartment." Michael reached into his jacket pocket and pulled out a car key with a rental company tag. "There's plenty of room in the Impala they gave me."

A Chevy Impala? "No, thanks. I'd prefer to finish my run. It's barely a half mile back to the apartment. And then I've got to shower."

"Of course," Michael said smoothly. "Hey, I'll get us some take-out food, and meet you over there. That'll give you enough time, I hope."

An Impala was a ridiculous car for a man not yet forty to be driving, I thought as I jogged up Spaghetti Hill to my apartment. I had a feeling that Michael was going to beat me in the car, but I needed the time to clear my head.

But he wasn't there after all. I unlocked the back door to the Spanish-style bungalow on Larkin Street with the key I'd tucked into the inner pocket of my shorts. I went immediately into the small bathroom, took a superfast shower, and dressed, this time in a pair of jeans and a silk kurta I'd bought in one of the little boutiques downtown. I decided against putting on makeup and blow-drying my hair—I rarely bothered with those things these days—but I did attempt to straighten up the apartment a bit before he arrived. The apartment had been converted out of the back end of a modest two-bedroom bungalow built in the twenties. At one time it must have been lovely, but now the stucco walls were crumbling, and the landlord had covered the old terra-cotta tiles with vinyl and had provided only cheap wicker garden furniture. I was rearranging the cushions on the love seat and chairs that made up my living room suite when I heard a knock on the door. I checked the peephole, identified Michael, and opened up.

He was carrying a bag from the Paris Bakery, one of my favorite haunts, and two cups of coffee. But behind him, lying against the small porch railing, were more than a dozen large, flat cardboard boxes—moving boxes, I realized with a start. After handing the food to me, he began hauling the boxes into the room.

"You brought—cookies? What kind of a dinner is that?" I asked as I looked at the enticing mixture of checkerboard cookies and raspberry butter cookies. I was trying to figure out both the meal and the moving boxes.

"There's not enough time for a sit-down meal. But I thought the sugar could carry us both through what we need to do tonight." Michael cleared his throat. "You're probably wondering why I came all the way to see you."

"Yes, I'd say Monterey is a little out of the way from D.C.," I said.

"I took a military hop. Nonstop, on a Learjet. Really a pleasure. "

"So it's urgent." I sipped the coffee and winced. He had added plenty of sugar, but no milk.

"You wanted milk?" Michael's gaze was keen.

"Yes. A latte with just two sugars would have been perfect, but you'll know that for next time." I caught myself. "Actually, I guess there won't be a next time, from the boxes you've brought. Something's wrong, isn't it?"

"I wouldn't say wrong." Michael paused. "And I am sorry to pull you out before the academic course is over. Your instructor told me that you were doing really well, the top of the class."

"Little else to do around here except study." But I was secretly pleased that he'd heard how well I'd done.

"Well, maybe you can come back to Monterey later in the year." He paused. "I need you in D.C. I came out to explain the situation personally, because you have the option to accept or decline."

Obviously he expected me to accept, because he'd brought moving boxes. Carefully I asked, "Do you mean it's an OCI job?"

He nodded. "We have about a month to prepare for the mission. Then it's back to Tokyo for you."

"Excellent." My spirits rose for the first time in weeks. I didn't mind leaving Monterey if it was for Japan. I knew where I was going to find my replacement running shoes—in Shinjuku!

"I'm going to explain as we pack, because you've got to be out of here, on my flight, tomorrow at ODT."

"What does *that* mean?" I'd noticed that Michael's years in the Navy and then the federal government had resulted in his speaking a language of abbreviations that was as complex as Japanese.

"Oh-dark-thirty. It means very early, before daylight." He paused. "Our flight to Langley leaves at six-thirty. You've got to be packed tonight, and we'll leave everything here for one of our people to move out tomorrow. Your personal shipment will be airmailed space-A after we go."

Another one of his abbreviations, which I'd learned meant "Space available," probably later than sooner. I glanced around my untidy apartment. "How can I possibly . . ."

"I'll help you." Michael was starting to fold and assemble the first box. "I've done this kind of pack-out many times, and yours should be a snap. All you've got are clothes and books, correct?"

"And music. And cooking stuff, and . . ."

"No problem," Michael said, pulling a thick roll of tape from his jacket. "As we pack, I'll tell you everything."

2

It was all about a store—a Japanese department store, Mitsutan. This was the place where I'd shopped with my Japanese relatives for as long as I could remember, mostly at its Yokohama branch, but for special occasions, at its huge flagship location on Ginza-dori, Tokyo's historically high-class shopping district. At the Ginza store, my Japanese grandmother had bought me an expensive kimono to celebrate my turning three and seven years old, landmarks in a girl's life. Eighteen years later, when I'd returned to Japan to teach, I was stunned to discover that the clothes at Mitsutan—and nearly every other department store and boutique in Japan—fit me as if they'd been custom-made.

At first I'd gone a little crazy buying Agnes B skirts and Lucky jeans. Within weeks, though, I figured out that an English teacher's salary couldn't stretch to cover the cost of these wonderful clothes. I gave up shopping for clothes at Mitsutan and firmly adjusted myself to wearing the designer hand-me-downs that my mother mailed in lavender-scented boxes from San Francisco.

"The Treasury Department has received some complaints," Michael said, jolting me from fashion nostalgia. "Treasury thinks—given the current state of Japanese retail sales—that Mitsutan's profits, especially those from the Ginza store, fly in the face of all logic."

I put down the stack of towels I'd been about to dump into a box. "Come on, doesn't our government understand that most Japanese companies fudge their profit statements? There's an art to writing those financial reports to please the stockholders and save face with their competitors. Of course they're going to look like they're doing better than the reality."

"There's a great difference between juggling numbers on paper to protect an image and actually profiting because of illegal activity." As Michael spoke, his long fingers stretched packing tape across the top of the fourth box of my possessions.

"So what has Mitsutan done that's illegal?" I nestled towels around my trusty Panasonic boom box, another relic of my youth. "Sell Anna Sui at too steep a discount?"

"I don't know what Anaswee means," Michael said, "but to answer the former question, our bosses have a special interest in the store."

"Do you mean there's some perceived threat?"

"Let's hope it's actually nothing," Michael said. "It'll be easier all around, if it's nothing. But there's been this—concern—raised, and I actually think it's a compliment to our little agency that we're given the chance to handle it."

"But I'm not knowledgeable about modern retail. Antiques are my thing." The previous job Michael had assigned me had tied into American military efforts to recover an antiquity stolen from a museum in Iraq. It had been a difficult job that called not only on my training in art history but on skills I had never realized I had. The job had been one of the most meaningful experiences of my life, though it had also caused me heartbreak.

Michael sat back on his heels and looked at me. "I know that you have both the guts and talent to handle this thing. Not just anybody can do the job; the last person who attempted it was killed."

"What?" I exclaimed.

"It was a Caucasian male agent who went over, undercover."

"How was he killed?"

"The official story was drowning. The reality was that he was beaten to death, and his body was found floating in the Sumida River."

A chill ran through me. "Do you mean Tyler Farraday? I read a story about an American male model working in Tokyo who supposedly did too much cocaine one night and tumbled in the river."

"Tyler Farraday—not his real name—was our boy." Michael's expression was sober. "Actually, he was technically another spy agency's boy, but I was forced to use him in the new spirit of joint agency cooperation. I was hesitant about him from the start, Rei. I had a feeling he wasn't strong enough."

And you think I am? I thought to myself gloomily. Aloud, I said, "Well, knowing what you know, why don't you just press charges against the store owners?"

"The Japanese police have to do that, and remember—we can't do anything. Our organization doesn't even exist, as you know."

"Oh, right," I said.

"Anyway, there's no evidence linking anyone at Mitsutan with his death, and it may actually turn out to be a straightforward *yakuza* murder, as it appeared to us, based on the autopsy. But don't worry about trying to figure out what happened to him. All I want you to do is get a picture of what's going on within the store culture. Just come up with some evidence of irregularities, and I can take it from there."

I looked at Michael's closed expression, suspecting there was something more, but knowing that I wasn't going to get a bit of what it was—at least, not yet.

"How can I figure out the store culture, though?" I asked, absent-mindedly folding a DLI T-shirt into thirds, the way Hugh did it—and then quickly undoing the folds. This was my own T-shirt; I should fold it differently, perhaps Japanese-style. "Do you want me to make a series of shopping trips at all its branches, or something like that?"

"It's a bit more sophisticated than that." Michael went on to explain that I'd be based at the main store, where I'd collect information from written records, computers, and employee conversations. Most of this was work that I hadn't been trained for, but would be first thing on my arrival in Washington.

"People take years to learn those espionage methods," I protested. "I should have at least a year or two to prepare."

"CIA case officers do, yes. But you're not a case officer; you're an informant. And OCI is a small, street-smart agency; we aren't budgeted for prolonged training." Michael hauled a taped-up box to the apartment's entryway, then returned. "Don't worry another moment, Rei. I'll personally oversee your training in D.C. You'll learn the most important tools of the trade, which I'm sure you'll have no problem with, given your demonstrated skill with a putty knife. At the same time, you'll start the application process for your job at the store."

"Wait a minute! I'm going to work for Mitsutan? Isn't that a conflict of interest?"

"It's the perfect setup. You will be on the scene in uniform, with an ID card granting you access to many areas of the store."

"Michael, there's another problem. You may not understand how hard it is for a foreigner to get hired by a Japanese company, but I do. I've tried."

"You're not a foreigner this time around." Michael's eyes swept over me, disheveled in my running gear. "Nor are you half Japanese. You're a foreign-returned Japanese—a young woman who graduated from Waseda University and who's worked in San Francisco and Tokyo, doing things like wholesaling Japanese textiles to American department stores, buying Japanese antiques for private clients, and styling a Japanese restaurant."

"Hmmm," I said, thinking. It was a pretty realistic cover. "I've done everything you mentioned except for graduating from Waseda. I was there my junior year, though."

"I know. We'll put together a transcript showing that you were there four years," Michael said. "And you'll be operating under your own name. That way, if you run into acquaintances shopping in the store, there'll be no chance of blowing your cover."

"Don't you think I'm slightly notorious?" I handed Michael a new box to put together. He was much faster at it than I could ever be.

"Well, you've got a common enough Japanese name—I don't think it's going to raise any red flags."

"But I've had my photo in the papers."

"Yes, but who cares?" Michael ripped off a length of tape and pressed it along the box's edge. "I think it's great that you have a backstory in Japan. The problem with Tyler Farraday was that he veered too dramatically from his natural identity, and he knew shit about Japan. Anyone who stumbles across evidence of your life before will fixate on a few paparazzi shots of a young woman out on the town with her various well-connected boyfriends. At a glamorous store like Mitsutan, those kinds of connections are going to be considered more of a help than a hindrance."

"The nail that sticks up must be hammered down." I repeated a cliché about Japan, because I wasn't above using clichés when I wanted to make a point.

"Nobody could hammer you down," Michael said. "Ever. This is the reason why, out of the half-dozen or so special informants who were considered for this job, you are the chosen one."

3

I thought about Michael's words in the long hours after midnight, when the boxes had been packed and my boss had driven back to the postgraduate school for a night in the bachelor officers' quarters. A trained professional had tried to do the job; he'd been recognized and murdered. And now it was the rookie's turn, the rookie who was supposed to be able to succeed just because she could pass for Japanese and she was, as Michael had said, *connected*.

I twisted between the uncomfortable poly-cotton-blend sheets that came with the apartment—the sheets that I wouldn't even have to launder the next morning, because OCI would pay for the cost of cleaning the vacated apartment. I'd never show up in class again; my classmates would assume I had given up.

Michael clearly hadn't trusted me to awaken in time, because he was at my door at ten minutes to five. I wasn't completely ready, of course; I scampered about for twenty minutes collecting things, while he repeatedly checked his watch. For him, it was easy; a good three hours later in the morning, EST. Michael looked as though he'd had plenty of time to shower, shave, and dress. He was crisp in a dark blue business suit, a white shirt, and tie with a tiny pattern that hurt my eyes when I looked at it.

"So, does everyone dress up for the plane?" I asked, feeling uneasy. I had gone for cozy: a beloved pair of faded, patched Levis and a ribbed thermal undershirt. Over it all was a vintage Persian lamb jacket, in anticipation of the cold when we landed.

"Not exactly. You'll see lots of uniforms, because mostly military people fly on these planes." He looked me over with a sober expression. "You do look casual for a DOD employee traveling on business. If anyone pushes you for more information about who you are, just pull out your ID card. Officially, you're a linguist on orders to transfer to D.C."—he pulled a folded paper out of a briefcase he was carrying—"that's all they need to know."

"A linguist," I said as we rode along the coastline, watching the sky slowly lighten over the water. "If you only knew how badly I did in linguistics at Waseda."

"You're not much of a joker," Michael said. "That's about the only verbal impairment I've noticed."

"That's not true!" I loved comedy in all its forms—movies, fiction, live theater.

"How many spies does it take to screw in a lightbulb?"

"I mean really funny stuff, okay, not lightbulb jokes."

"Come on, Rei, how many spies does it take to screw in a lightbulb?"

"Do tell," I said sourly.

"Damn, do you mean that lightbulb was one of *ours*?"

I couldn't help snickering, but I didn't want to dismiss the serious subject at hand: languages. "I suppose you must have a decent grounding in Japanese to be chief of the OCI Japan desk. *Nihongo ga joozu desho*." I'd sarcastically used *You must be skilled at Japanese*, the stock phrase Japanese offered to foreigners, whether the foreigners knew two words or two thousand.

"I'm not *joozu* at all. I went to DLI ten years ago, but that was to learn how to speak and write Hangul, because my old beats were North and South Korea. If you have any concerns with Japanese, you'll get help from Mrs. Ikuko Taki. She's the Japanese translator who's going to fabricate your Waseda transcript. Later on, she'll translate the recordings you send back."

"Great. I can't wait to meet her."

"I hope you like the bureau. It's a pretty small office, because I'm the only person there, day in and out, but there is some extra space for Mrs. Taki, and a few others like you who work with us on a temporary basis."

I felt a tinge of nausea at having an office in Washington, the city of my failed romance. It was one of the reasons I'd so readily agreed to go to Monterey. "Where is the bureau exactly—did you tell me Foggy Bottom?"

"That's the seat of the State Department, OCI's cover address," Michael said. "We really work in Pentagon City. You'll be staying at one of the furnished condo units we have in a building a few blocks away. I figured if you were close by, I could work you harder. You know, late nights, weekends . . ."

"Ha," I said as we parked the car at the rental drop-off. Then, after a quick trip through security, it was a walk out on the tarmac to an alarmingly small dark gray plane decorated with a number, but no name. Everyone on the plane except Michael and myself was in uniform.

"Where did those guys in camouflage come from? I've never seen them at DLI," I muttered as Michael steered me toward the remaining vacant seats near the tail end of the military jet.

"They're marines based at Camp Pendleton, and I imagine that their facial expressions have something to do with the fact they were detoured here just to pick the two of us up." He held out a Dunkin' Donuts bag to me and said in a louder voice, "Have one!"

I took a plain sugar doughnut—reluctantly, because the last thing I'd eaten was cookies the night before. I don't care for empty calories, especially in the morning. I whispered back in his ear, "I can't believe you dressed up for this."

Michael finished chewing his own selected doughnut—raspberry jelly—before answering. "Rumor had it that the secretary of the navy, who's in the Bay Area, might have been flying back east today. If that had been the case, the hop could have been on that Learjet I came out on yesterday. This C-140 is a very safe plane, but the seating's not the greatest."

Yes, it was a shame about the seating, and also about the toilet smell, which gradually began to seep out after about thirty minutes' flying time. But most of all, I was slaughtered by the noise—a roaring sound of engines barreling straight out of Hades. Even my iPod playing Death Cab for Cutie couldn't completely drown out the racket the plane was making.

"You know," I said loudly into Michael's ear, "we could talk about our business and nobody would hear anything."

"Including me," he shouted back, hitting my ear with a light shower of sugar. "But I'm glad you're in the mood to work. I brought some reading for you. Maybe it'll take your mind off the discomfort."

Michael reached into his briefcase and drew out a thick folder, which I took reluctantly. So much for the John le Carré novel I'd hoped to spend my time reading.

The first page said "secret," and I felt a slight thrill to realize that I was authorized to turn the page. "Secret" didn't carry as much weight as "top secret," but still, for somebody as new to spying as I was, this binder had a lot of spiritual, as well as physical, significance. My government trusted me with this material. And I knew that once I turned the page, I would be venturing into a world as foreign as Japan had been for me, so many years ago.

Michael's face disappeared behind a copy of *Foreign Affairs*, which was shielding something completely different that he was reading, so I started in on the binder. Section one was a description of a complaint that Treasury had received from one Warren Kravitz, a senior partner at the Asian headquarters of Winston Brothers, an American investment banking firm. A copy of a letter from Warren Kravitz outlined his theory that there was no reason for Mitsutan to be worth more than its competitors, based on a numbing array of facts and figures, most of which were buried in fine print in fifty pages of attached material.

"What is Warren Kravitz's problem? Does he want to be a PI or something?" I asked Michael.

"There's no problem. He just made a complaint. It's every citizen's right to do that." Michael said right into my ear, "From this point on, no real names spoken in public, please."

"The last time I complained to Treasury about anything, I was nine years old. They didn't make my dad raise my allowance."

Michael cracked a small smile, but put his finger to his lips. Apparently, as loud as the background noise was on the plane, the topic was still too classified for discussion. I turned with more interest to a second set of documents: a history of retailing in Japan. I learned that although Mitsutan had formally opened for business as a department store in 1911, it actually had a much longer history. Its founders had opened a kimono shop in Tokyo in the late 1700s, during the prosperous Edo period. Mitsutan's elegant silk robes for men, women, and children had been popular enough to bring the shop owners considerable fame and the capital needed, in the early twentieth century, for the expansion into the store that I knew. Mitsutan was not the first *depaato* on the Ginza; it was built on the heels of Mitsukoshi, Matsuya, Isetan, and Matsuzakaya, all famous kimono makers who were blazing new trails. Japanese women were starting to wear *yofuku*—Western dress— and retailers were developing ambitions eight stories high.

Business dropped off during the war. Mitsutan and its neighbors went into sleep mode and then emerged in the postwar reconstruction, selling the luxuries for which people longed after having spent years in near-starvation. But the original department stores faced competition from a new group: upstart department stores started by companies that owned railway lines. These transportation conglomerates were tight with the new Japanese government and managed to get the zoning to build massive stores next to busy train stations throughout Tokyo, Osaka, Nagoya, and other major cities. The new stores—which included Parco, Tokyu, and Seiyu—were full of luxury goods, sometimes at cheaper prices. In my family's opinion they lacked the centuries-old knowledge of customer sales and ritual.

Both types of store—kimono-descended and railway-descended— flourished as Japan rebuilt itself, especially during the prosperous 1980s. But in the 1990s, the ever-stretching bubble burst. The economy tanked and Japanese consumers stopped shopping. Instead, they funneled most of their yen into savings accounts at the Japanese post office.

There followed several pages of graphs illustrating profit-and-loss statements for Japan's twelve major department store chains. Mitsutan followed the same highs and lows as everyone else—until 2003. Then, its numbers started tracking upward. The store's reported inventory holdings, cash reserves in its private bank, and reported profits were huge. And unlike many other department stores, Mitsutan paid out generously to its stockholders. It seemed like a glorious situation for all.

I closed the folder. Still, I was wondering why a complaint from an American banker had received such serious attention from the U.S. government in the first place. Michael had said it was because of suspected malfeasance on the part of the store, but I just didn't buy that a successful exception to a retail trend mattered.

Would Michael keep a secret from me? I glanced at him. He was bent over his own folder, which was marked "top secret."

Of course he knew things he wouldn't tell me. But I hoped to God he wasn't withholding something of vital importance, something that might lead to my making a monumental mistake that would send me to the same place Tyler Farraday had gone.

4

Arlington in late winter was chilly, but it was less windy than Monterey.

This became the mantra I silently repeated to myself as I hustled the seven blocks to work early each morning, the Persian lamb collar pulled up around my ears. Everywhere there was ice, the remnants of past snowstorms. And on my arrival, it snowed again, though as Michael had said, with my apartment's proximity to the OCI office, there was no reason to take a snow day. The federal government closed for two days, but Michael steadfastly went in, leaving me no choice but to join him.

The fact was that I liked going to work, because I hadn't experienced being in an office routine for so long. I arrived at eight; Michael was already there, with my double skim latte and his triple-sugar espresso, carried out from a nearby Starbucks. The first hour was spent reading—briefs that had come in, by e-mail or fax, from various intelligence agencies, as well as the U.S. embassy in Japan, and the State Department a few miles away in Foggy Bottom. We also reviewed the daily newspapers. Michael brought the *New York Times*, and the Asian and American versions of the *Wall Street Journal*. I picked up the *Post*, *USA Today*, and once a month the *Washingtonian*, because I always had my eye on the party page, looking for a face I would be better off forgetting. It was all a matter of strategy; if I could pretend that this was a normal office, with a normal colleague, I could almost forget that the next step in the process might result in death.

Throughout the day, Michael met with visitors whom I'd learned not to ask about—special informants, like myself, who delved into the mysteries of Japan and other parts of the Pacific Rim for OCI. They always talked with Michael in a back room; and even if I strained my ears to hear what was going on, I couldn't catch a word—the place was annoyingly soundproof. At some time during the day, I worked in another private back room, or I went over to the Pentagon for tutorials with various technicians who were training me in the nuts and bolts of bugging.

Quickly, I found out that it wasn't very hard to drill a listening device into a table. The challenge was that the drill itself was often concealed as something else, such as a fountain pen, and pulling the pen apart to put a working drill together was sometimes more of a challenge than installing the bug. And bug sweepers—devices that were designed to ascertain whether my own environment and telephone were secure from listeners—were harder to operate than even the most confusing TV remote.

But computer hacking was the hardest task of all. Because I'd gotten my first laptop eight years after the rest of the world, I found it very difficult to install spyware, let alone cover my tracks. I had no idea what I was doing on the computer even if all the commands and codes were available to me in English—so I could imagine how impenetrable things would seem in Japanese.

"There's a story about Supermart in today's *Journal* that I want you to read," Michael said, interrupting me from my attempts to hack into a dummy account one of the agency trainers had set up on my computer. It was late morning, and I'd finished with my newspapers, so I figured I should try to accomplish by myself what I had been able to do with intense guidance the previous afternoon.

"Supermart? But that's an American store."

"American as Wal-Mart and Target, but there are rumors that its founder, Jimmy DeLone, wants to buy a Japanese department store. His acquisitions manager is said to be considering Mitsukoshi, Wako, and Mitsutan."

"No kidding!" I swung myself out of the chair and came over to the couch, Michael's preferred reading spot. I settled in cozily next to him and took the paper. Jimmy DeLone, a sixty-six-year-old discount tycoon who'd transformed Supermart from a small chain in Oklahoma into 310 discount warehouses, had "gone ahunting" in

my favorite city. DeLone credited high anime video sales at Supermart outlets with bringing his attention to the potentially profitable
interface between Japanese and American retail.

I shook my head after reading all this. "Department stores aren't
where kids go to buy anime. Something's off in this commentary."

"Smoke and mirrors," Michael said, taking the paper from me over
to his desk, where he picked up scissors and began cutting it out.
This was a serious sign, I thought—anything that Michael cut out he
photocopied for each of us, and the facts were generally supposed to
be committed to memory.

"Well, let's say the comment about anime is meaningless, and he
just wants, for some reason, to buy up Japanese stores. I can understand his wanting to buy Tokyu or Seiyu—he knows about that kind
of middle-class mass-market selling—but I can't imagine how Supermart could handle a classy Ginza department store. And what could
they take from Japan to sell at a profit here? They certainly couldn't
carry Mitsutan clothing in their stores—nobody would be small
enough to wear it! And as for other consumer goods, anything they'd
bring over to sell in the United States would be five times more expensive than if it was manufactured in China."

Michael shrugged. "Mitsutan certainly would add glamour to
their holdings. Supermart owns a lot more than just its own stores."

"Yes, the article was talking about DeLone's owning the Seaways
motel chain, Ryan Beer, and . . . what was the last thing?"

"Power companies in six states. He's nicely diversified," Michael
said, dropping the newspaper scraps into the office's paper shredder.

"Well, if he's smart, he'd want to buy a distressed store that could
be turned around, not one with such high stock values that it would
cost him a lot," I said, turning over the situation in my mind.

"Econ 101." Michael started up the photocopier. One of the things I
liked about Michael was that he never asked me to do his photocopy-
ing—something that, as my employer, in an office with no secretary,
he probably had the right to do.

"When we take into account the Treasury Department's interest in
Mitsutan—you know I think it's strange," I added when Michael shot
me an annoyed look. "If we pull together the information showing
that Mitsutan is worth less than they say they are—well, that would be
helpful for Jimmy DeLone, when he finally pulls out his checkbook."

Michael wasn't facing me, because he was placing the clipping on the photocopier's glass plate, but I could see his shoulders stiffen under the striped oxford shirt he was wearing.

"Rei, who do you work for?"

"You?" Was this a trick question?

"No, you don't work for me." Michael sounded exasperated. "Yes, I'm your supervisor, but you work for a greater entity: OCI, and beyond that, the CIA. I don't believe anyone would think that you sound like a loyal employee at the moment." Michael picked up the photocopied papers and slapped them both down on my desk.

"Just because I asked a question?" I wrinkled my nose at Michael. "Come on, you've got to have some of these questions in the back of your mind, too."

"Agreed," Michael said evenly. "Every good officer should ask questions. But I can tell you that our government is not in the habit of using tightly stretched funds to help a billionaire retail magnate get a better shopping deal. For some reason, we've been ordered to investigate Mitsutan. It's our job to collect data for analysis, not to answer riddles."

"But how about a lightbulb joke, like how many spies does it take to figure out we have a trade deficit in lightbulbs?" I shot back. "Obviously, this country would be better off if Americans were making the cheapest lightbulbs in the world rather than buying them from suppliers in Asia."

"Econ 200," Michael said, his tight expression finally relaxing into a smile. "What exactly did you learn in Monterey?"

I laughed. "You'll never know."

"Just like today, I'll never know what you and Mrs. Taki will do, exactly. But I'm really looking forward to seeing the results of your appearance modification."

"That nonsense is happening today? Why didn't you warn me?" I was annoyed. Mrs. Taki, the sixty-something, very bossy translator who worked with us, was the Defense Department's self-proclaimed expert on Japanese appearance. She had taken me on a shopping trip that had lasted three days: a hunt for the perfect suit, shoes, and bag for the interview at Mitsutan. After we'd finally found the right things at Escada, she'd made me buy a second suit from Jil Sander, just in case there was a second interview. German designers in Japan!

I didn't quite understand her enthusiasm for German couture, but then again, I was a bit younger, and not native-born.

"Remember, we talked about it before? She called when I came in this morning to make sure you were free to go over. It seems the salon finally has a four-hour block available for you."

"Michael, you said to me that I'm not going over with an assumed identity. If I'm going back to Japan as Rei Shimura—why would I want to change the way I look?"

"You're trying to be hired at a very glamorous department store. In order for you to accomplish that, you need to resemble an ideal Japanese twenty-three-year-old woman. Consider this." Michael picked up a copy of *An-an* that had been lying on my desk.

"I'd need multiple surgeries to look like that." I looked down at the indescribably lovely girl—poreless skin, eyebrows as delicate as birds' wings headed upward for flight, and limpid dark brown eyes that opened innocently under rose-tinted eyelids.

"Mrs. Taki says that the salon owner used to do theatrical makeup, so she knows how to create the illusion of an epicanthic eyelid. I believe it's possible, given that I myself have passed for Korean in the past." Michael narrowed his eyes at me in a way that he must have thought mysterious but that made me laugh out loud.

"Sometime I'll show you pictures." Michael laughed, too. "Anyway, I'd like to take an earlier lunch, so I can get out while you're still here. Okay?"

"Sure. I've got some e-mail to answer." Another part of our work routine was that we both exercised at lunch, taking turns, because we were the only regulars in the place, full time, and the office phone needed to be answered at all times, just in case Michael's boss called in. Typically, Michael would change into his old Naval Academy sweats in the office's small, full bathroom and run over to Virginia Highlands Park, returning sweaty but holding a bag of Vietnamese summer rolls, or *pad thai*, or something else delicious from the numerous Asian restaurants that dotted the neighborhood. I was happy to chip in for an Asian take-out lunch every day, but the only thing I remained militantly against was his favorite Korean cuisine. I'd found, after two experiences, that I could not concentrate on much during the afternoon if the taste of kimchi lingered in my mouth.

Despite what Michael had said about my being a runner, I'd decided that I preferred to spin the wheels of a stationary bicycle and lift weights at Bally rather than test my luck on the icy sidewalks of Pentagon City. Today, as I worked my triceps to the point of exhaustion, my thoughts turned to the Japanese makeover Michael wanted me to undergo. If Michael didn't want people to know that I ran, weight lifting might be a problem as well. Japanese girls were slim, but very few had muscular arms.

I thought about asking Michael whether my strength training was a risk, then shook myself. No way would it matter, when Mitsutan's uniform was a slim, long-sleeved black jacket and matching straight-leg pants. Nothing of my body would show; I could even have carried a weapon, except for the fact nobody in OCI was allowed to carry weapons, concealed or otherwise. I was in favor of gun control, so this fact should have relieved me; but every time I thought of Tyler Farraday, I felt sick. How I wished I'd studied a martial art for years instead of dabbling at the gym. The best I could do was learn to kick-box, but that class was already filled.

Mrs. Taki honked the horn of her black BMW outside the office at eleven-thirty, and I hurried down, slipping into my coat as I went.

"Rei-chan, ikaga desu ka?" She asked me how I was doing in Japanese, as she always did. During our private meetings, Mrs. Taki spoke to me only in Japanese; and because she'd left Japan thirty years ago, she seemed to be missing a lot of the lingo.

"I'm fine, Taki-san," I answered in Japanese. "You're very kind to try to help me out with my appearance. I worry that I won't live up to your expectations."

"Don't worry, Rei-chan. It's actually a Korean place on Wilson Boulevard. Very pleasant, good prices. I have my hair done there." Mrs. Taki proudly touched her Doris Day–style bubble, dyed the typical purplish-black of older Japanese women.

"But—I'm supposed to look Japanese."

"This isn't California, Rei-chan. Unfortunately, there's no Japanese-owned beauty salon in this area. But her place is quite good. They have all the Japanese things: hair straightening, special skin creams and waxes. Her sister has a salon in Tokyo. They used to do makeup for Takarazuka Revue, the girl actresses who perform as boys. They are good at changing identity, I think."

Despite her fancy car and impeccable, tailored work suits, Mrs. Taki apparently didn't run in the mannered, pretentious crowd; the salon was nothing like what I was used to, but more of what I'd expect in the back streets of Tokyo's Kabuki-cho, where gangsters and hookers roamed. At the salon, I was made to stand in the middle of the room while Dora, the redheaded owner, and her three Korean assistants with various auburn and blond hair colors, all dressed in low-cut tank tops or blouses, circled me, picking up strands of my shoulder-length hair, which I was in the process of growing out after a disastrous coloring job. They also prodded at my skin and tugged my eyelids and, for some reason, my earlobes. Numerous unkind remarks were made about my flyaway hair, oily forehead, and overly dry lips.

The only thing the beauticians agreed on was my body. My figure was excellent, although I had what Mrs. Taki disparagingly described as *binyu*—small breasts. The women conversed about underwire bras for a while, and a couple of the girls raised their shirts to show off their own specific models, which could make Asian women look a bit more fashionably voluptuous. I was greatly relieved when the topic turned to shoes. I should be wearing high heels, not flats, so that I wouldn't look like such an overgrown schoolgirl. Well, the makeup would take care of that.

But first, the hair. A great deal of discussion took place, and everyone agreed that my hair would be straightened and then cut into a pageboy. Dora brought out a long piece of cardboard to which swatches of hair were attached, in different shades from the blackest black to an almost red-blond.

"Why not go with basic black?" I suggested, thinking that if I was going to look like a *kokeshi* doll, I might as well look like a traditional one. But my idea was quickly shot down. Not fashionable enough! Nobody in Asia had black hair anymore.

"Who am I to complain? It's only my head," I grumbled as I was shampooed and towel-dried and the color process began. While I sat under an old-fashioned stationary dryer, one of the girls gave me an excruciatingly tickly pedicure, selecting a delicate pearl pink for the nail color, while another girl worked on my hands. The colored nails weren't going to last more than a week—and I had several weeks left before traveling—but I decided not to argue this point. I hadn't had my nails polished for as long as I could remember, and the result was pretty good.

I was out of the dryer, but still not ready to have my hair straightened and cut. My head was wrapped in a towel, and another towel was handed to me as I was ushered into a back room.

"Please undress," Mrs. Taki said. "I will wait outside, for your privacy."

"What's next, a massage?" I asked, half hopeful and half worried, in case the expense might qualify as something for the Defense Department's waste, fraud, and abuse hotline.

"Something different, I think."

Something different turned out to be waxing. Dora shouted directions at an underling who waxed my brows, my cheeks, my chin, and my arms. I didn't argue, because I'd never seen a fashionable Japanese woman with so much as peach fuzz on her arms.

Dora ordered the assistant to pull the towel from my hips, and she gasped aloud.

"It's been a while since my last bikini wax. Sorry!" I didn't know why I was apologizing, but she was making me embarrassed.

"No problem, we take care of that. But—that thing! Those beads!"

Dora had been undone by my navel ring.

"They're pearls, actually. I can take the ring out, if it bothers you."

"No, no, let everyone see. I want to show them the pretty little beads. Real pearl? How you get them in there? Maybe we can do this as a new service here!"

While Dora's lackeys ripped the remaining hair from my body, I tried to explain that navel rings had been popular for about the last decade, and that there were plenty of piercing salons around already.

After I'd gotten into my clothes again and been resuscitated with a cup of green tea, the women applied the straightening gel and sat me under a bubble dryer again. Then the solution was rinsed out, and my hair was washed and painted again with the highlights that Dora thought appropriate. After half an hour, I was placed before a mirror while Dora cut my hair at the exact point where neck met shoulder. The true test came at blow-dry time, and I was amazed to see my hair hanging perfectly straight in the Louise Brooks mode, and glinting like a piece of rare red-black silk.

I'd doubted that anything short of surgery could be done to change the shape of my eyelids, but I was amazed to see what Dora could do with a bit of concealer, four eye shadows, and both liquid and pencil eyeliners. My eyelid crease hadn't totally vanished, but it seemed to have receded under a wash of light golden color. The reshaped eyebrows enhanced the illusion; Dora had understood about the delicate, bird-wing eyebrows that Japanese women favored. In fact, the only thing I truly disliked about the makeup job was that I had to wear heavy foundation to make me look as if I had a paler complexion—something that was highly valued in Japan.

"The minute I wash my face, the illusion's gone," I said as Dora's assistant wiped off the makeup with a damp cloth at the end.

"Ah, but you will always appear socially with makeup, from this day on," Mrs. Taki said. "I think, for the sake of learning, you should do this every day in Washington. I will check you."

It seemed like a lot of trouble to totally transform to the Japanese me while I was still in Washington. Still, recalling what Michael had said about cementing my cover, I didn't argue with her, and in fact made myself up again, in full. It took twenty minutes and didn't look quite as good as Dora's work; in fact, she redid my eyes, clucking as she worked.

I was expecting the bill to be high, but I still flinched at $480 at checkout time. "Includes all the cosmetics, such a bargain," said Dora. Mrs. Taki, according to our prearrangement, paid for it all with her Visa card, as Michael had suggested. Dora and her staff believed that I was Mrs. Taki's American-raised niece being groomed for a return trip to meet the family in Japan.

"You are a great customer, Mrs. Taki. You bring me business all the time," Dora said. "This beauty job, for this niece of yours, it is my honor. She looks cute now."

"Well, not so bad," said Mrs. Taki disparagingly, as any Japanese auntie would do when a junior relative was praised.

The two ladies bowed, and I bowed, too. Alone in the car with Mrs. Taki, heading back to Pentagon City via Washington Boulevard, I turned on the cell phone that I had silenced during the salon appointment. I was intending to phone Michael to let him know we were finally on the way back.

The phone's tiny screen lit up with a notice that I had a text message waiting. I pushed a few buttons and read something that could have come only from Michael.

EMRGNCY, it said in the terse shorthand he liked to use. CALL ASAP. SAY NTHNG 2 T, SEND HR HOME.

5

I read the emergency communication a second time, with a growing sense of dread. While I had been getting sheared and waxed and painted, something terrible had happened with our forthcoming campaign.

"Taki-san," I said, deleting the message, "it seems as if Michael wants me to go to a meeting with him somewhere out of the office today. He suggests that you take the rest of the day off."

"But today we were going to work on the application form. My plan was to help you get your photograph taken, since you look so nice today, and then we would finally complete the writing of the form."

"Well, I guess we're going to have to postpone. What time are you coming in tomorrow?" I asked as Mrs. Taki turned the corner to Fifteenth Street. Thank God I'd checked the phone for messages before we'd both gone up.

"I arrive at one o'clock, just as usual." Mrs. Taki seemed miffed.

"Great, I'll see you then. Oh, why don't you just stop here at the end of the block, it's rather congested at the entrance." It was—but not with the usual emergency vehicles, like fire engines and police cars. There were four plain black sedans lined up, each with a male driver waiting inside.

Mrs. Taki let me out, and I hurried to the vestibule of the building, where a man in camouflage, with a long-range rifle strapped across his body, halted me.

"But I'm supposed to go upstairs. My boss is waiting for me," I said, flashing my Department of Defense identification card. It didn't say OCI, but what it did say should have made him take notice.

"It's a secured zone," he said like an automaton.

"Okay, okay." I glared at him as I made my phone call, hoping that whatever the emergency state was upstairs, Michael's cell phone would still work.

He answered after the first ring. "Is Taki-san downstairs?"

"No, I sent her home. What happened?"

"I'll tell you when you get upstairs."

"But they won't let me upstairs—"

"I'll come down, then. We should go out anyway to talk."

When Michael arrived, he glanced at me shortly and said, "You look great."

I'd almost forgotten my Japanese makeover. "Thank you."

Michael walked in long, fast strides, his head down, so I had to both hustle and lean in to hear what he said. "There was a break-in when you were gone."

"I was thinking something like that, when I saw that commando guarding the place. What happened?"

"You let someone in." Michael started to cross Fifteenth.

I stopped short in the middle of traffic, outraged at the accusation. "No, I didn't. How can you say—"

"Come on, you'll get hit by a car." He motioned me to follow him across the street, and there, in the shadow of another office building, with our breath frosting the air, he continued. "I'm sure it was accidental. Let me explain what probably happened."

"Can we do it inside Starbucks or somewhere?" I was freezing.

"No," he said shortly. "As you know, back at the office, we swipe our ID cards over the device on the right of the door frame in order for the door to open—and we're the only two people, save my boss at headquarters, with the cards."

I nodded, following so far.

"When you went out to meet Mrs. Taki, someone was waiting in the hallway—most likely behind that file cabinet." He was talking about an empty file cabinet that had appeared in the hall about a week ago; I hadn't thought much about it then, but now I was wondering. Our suite of offices took up the whole third floor. Who could have put the file cabinet there in the first place?

Michael continued, "You passed by, and as the door began to close, our lurker placed a small object between the door and the frame to keep it from completely closing."

"That's a pretty detailed hypothesis."

"I found a wadded-up paper in the door, just as I was heading out to pick up lunch," Michael said shortly. "Right now it's been taken as evidence, and it will be undergoing a fingerprint and substance analysis. After that, you can see it for yourself."

"I—I don't know what to say. I'm sorry. I really thought I was alone in the hallway, I mean, we're the only tenants up here . . ." I trailed off, feeling miserable.

"You know how the office is set up—the waiting room with the bathroom off it, and then our workroom, and the two back offices behind it?"

I nodded.

"Whoever came in probably started planting bugs in the waiting room while I was working in the back. When I went into the restroom, he or she took the opportunity to do the same thing in our workroom and possibly some of the back offices."

"But it takes a while to figure out where to install a bug and then plant it." At least it took me, a novice at the process, a while. "How long were you in the bathroom?"

"About fifteen minutes." Michael's face pinkened. "I brought in a couple of the papers."

Why men enjoy reading on the toilet is incomprehensible to me. But I wasn't going to push the issue with Michael, not on a day like today.

"Did they run past or something like that when you came out? I can't imagine you wouldn't have caught them—"

"I heard a scraping sound: the window going up. When I finally reached the workroom, the window was open. And you know we have that balcony." He shook his head. "I hate balconies, they're like a carte blanche for entering and exiting."

"What did the burglars take?"

"Not sure yet. Your computer was turned off—bravo. Mine was turned on, but after three minutes of idle time, it locks. So I don't know whether they got to it quickly enough to see anything. The guys working inside now are running all kinds of spyware sweeps."

"What about all the stuff on paper?" I thought about my binder loaded with information about the store's profits, the various company executives, and the store layout.

"Your binder's still on your desk. You can examine it after security's finished sweeping for bugs."

"My bugs?" I was momentarily confused, thinking about my drawerful of listening devices.

"Their bugs. Like I said before, it's likely that whoever came in intended to install spyware, cameras, and listening devices."

"Jesus, Michael, how could Mitsutan know about us already? I haven't even applied for the job!" I felt helpless, angry, invaded.

"It might not be them." Michael's voice was grim. "Look where we are, smack in the middle of the real world. Anyone with half a brain could have figured out we're more than a government think tank. And as you've seen, other agents come in to meet with me. People involved in other cases I'm handling might have reason to want to eavesdrop."

"Your message to me said that you didn't want Mrs. Taki to come upstairs. Do you suspect her in this?"

"Not really." Michael sighed, his breath rising like a plume in the cold air. "She's worked for the government for twenty-seven years. Still, there's no need for her to know what happened this afternoon."

I felt some gratitude for what he'd just said; that I was the one, out of his total of two employees involved in the assignment, whom he trusted enough to give the details. "What are we going to do now? Can we ever talk to each other in the office again?"

"Not today. While I'm waiting for the techs to finish, I suggest you go somewhere in the neighborhood and have passport photos taken while that face is still perfect. You'll need one for the application, which we've absolutely got to get in the mail this week."

I looked down at my Persian lamb jacket, which revealed a sliver of black T-shirt studded with silver beads. It was a great top, but not for an employment photograph. "I'll run home and change into a proper blouse first. But do you mean—you still want me to go to Japan?" I wrapped my arms around myself, shivering at both the cold of the late afternoon and my uncertain status.

"Of course." Michael looked at me closely. "Unless this has spooked you, and you've changed your mind."

"Yes!" Then I realized that this sounded wrong. "I mean, yes, I'm prepared to go. I haven't changed my mind."

• • •

The experts determined that an attempt had been made to hack into the computers, but whoever had tried had left without getting anything. However, there were three bugs, all located in the areas where Michael and I worked together.

Michael phoned me with the news just as I was leaving the photo shop with a bag containing a sheet of tiny, identical images of an unsmiling, Japanese-looking me wearing a plain white blouse and pearls. The bugs were out, but he wanted me to come back to see where they'd been—and then to look through my folders.

My papers didn't look as if they'd been touched, though fingerprint analysis would tell for sure. The bugs had been placed in Michael's phone, but not mine; and in the chair rail near the conference table where we sometimes worked on translations with Mrs. Taki; and under the sofa where Michael and I read the daily papers.

"Pop quiz. What does the placement of the bugs tell you?" Michael asked

I thought for a minute. "Well, they're interested in who you're talking to on the phone, what we talk about together during our recap of the morning media, and what we're learning from Mrs. Taki's translations." I thought some more. "Whoever bugged us must be interested in the Mitsutan project—not anything else you're working on."

"It would seem that way, although I do use my phone to speak about those other areas of interest."

"Doesn't the fact that we removed the bugs prove we know we're under attack? I mean, we could have kept them in place and spoken to each other in a way that didn't reveal anything—"

"Rei, I'm going to be at a meeting tomorrow morning at Langley about our security crisis, so I may have some answers for you by the afternoon. But what I'm thinking is that the folks who came in—there probably were at least two, to get as far as they did so fast—were a bit sloppy. They should have expected us to figure out they'd been there, because of that rapid departure through the office window." Michael sighed heavily. "Anyway, I doubt it will happen again. We've got a guard, from this point on."

"You mean, someone guarding us all the time?" I was unsettled by the idea of facing a gun-wielding Special Forces type before having my morning coffee—and dealing with his presence in what had been such a cozy little world.

"Outside our door only," Michael said as if he'd read my mind. "Our work will remain confidential."

"Whoever thought the finances of a Japanese department store would be a matter of national security?" I shook my head. "What a world. What a day."

"At least you have your disguise in place. Did you manage to get your photos done?"

"Yes. They're not great." I pulled out the sheet of tiny color pictures.

"That's because you didn't smile."

"Japanese people aren't supposed to smile in official photographs. You should see my cousins' school graduation pictures, not to mention my aunt and uncle's wedding pictures—"

"Another thing that you know that I don't." Michael paused. "Rei, I'm sorry I snapped at you about not watching the door. It was the kind of unfortunate event that could happen to anyone. I'm going to bat for you tomorrow; I don't want you to tear yourself up anymore over this."

"Thank you," I said, relief washing over me. "I'm just glad this day is coming to an end. After we're done tonight, I was thinking about going for a pint at the Irish pub over at Pentagon Row—have you been there?"

Michael shook his head. "I haven't. But there's no need to wait around. I'll release you now, if you want to go. It's almost six o'clock."

"I meant," I said carefully, "that I thought you might like to have a beer with me, at that place."

"Rei, I thought you knew that I cannot fraternize with you outside the office."

Michael's response was so severe that I found myself blushing. "How is having a beer after a hard day fraternizing?"

"If we see each other socially outside of work, I have to report the contact. Given our current situation—even though one contact is allowable without reporting—I'd feel duty-bound to report it."

"But it's not—I didn't mean it to be—" I was aghast. My boss thought I was trying to pick him up! How could he think a thing like that, when I still recovering from a broken heart and was also ideologically opposed to sexual harassment, especially in the workplace?

I must have started sputtering some of the things that I was thinking, because Michael cut me off.

"I understand your intentions are well-meaning," he said. "But the fact remains, if you and I—develop a friendship, things are going to be very, very difficult."

"But we are already friends. Or so I thought—" I flashed back to all the mornings reading together, the shared lunches, the jokes mixed between the serious lessons in espionage. Michael was one of the sharpest yet kindest men I'd met, definitely the best boss I'd ever had. I ranked him with my mentor, the legendary antiques dealer Mr. Ishida, who was almost eighty, and someone with whom I'd often drank sake, without an eyebrow being raised by anyone.

"I won't deny that I like you," Michael said, sounding awkward. "But if I were to declare I had a social relationship with you, any of the decisions I make regarding your housing overseas, your mode of travel, and certainly your financial compensation would be regarded with suspicion. Our masters might even reassign us away from each other. Permanently."

I swallowed hard, not liking the turn of the conversation.

Michael spoke again. "I know it sounds strict, but there are sensible reasons for these rules."

"I'm well aware of most agency regulations about social life." I couldn't help feeling a flash of anger—the kind of anger I hadn't felt since all the personal questions I'd endured during my polygraph test. "Apparently, case officers can sleep with prostitutes and not have to report it."

"But not the same prostitute more than once," Michael said, holding up a cautionary finger. "The rules are archaic, but they're really there to protect officers from intimacy that could jeopardize them and their colleagues. I'm sorry, Rei."

"Forget it. It's not your fault," I said grumpily.

"Let's not talk about faults anymore." He ran a hand across his brow, and for a split second, with his mostly silver hair, he looked ten years older than his actual age, thirty-eight. "Take care of yourself. And be careful."

6

I didn't go out for a drink after all. Drinking alone in bars wasn't the kind of thing I was ready to do in the United States. In Japan, maybe—after I'd put an ocean between myself and the unknown person who'd invaded my office to find out what Michael and I were doing; the person, maybe, who had masterminded Tyler Farraday's killing.

There were other alternatives, of course. As I puttered around my apartment, I thought of OCI's überbosses; the "Masters of Langley," as Michael privately referred to them. The invasion of our office might have been part of an internal investigation, but why? Michael was the straightest arrow I knew—I had never seen him carry as much as a government-issued pen out of the office; he always, in fact, used his own Waterman. The exercise break we each took fell within forty-five minutes. Eating was done on the clock, while we were working.

No, I thought. The only one under observation could be me, because I was new and maybe also because of what I'd said about the Treasury Department, Supermart, and Warren Kravitz. I was far too vocal—and obviously skeptical—to be a decent spy; that was the problem. Michael had talked about my doing other work for OCI after this job was done, but I now thought this first assignment might be my only one. I'd do my best, but it would be a single engagement.

I thought about the situation long into the night. In the wee hours I gave up on getting any rest, turned on my bedside light, and began to rough out the final draft of the answers that I had been carefully constructing for the Japanese employment application.

The best thing about the application was that it was a standard national form available at any Japanese convenience store; an agent in Tokyo had picked one up and mailed it to Michael. After I'd filled it out and glued my photo to the correct spot, Michael would mail it back to the agent, who in turn would mail it to Mitsutan's personnel department. There would be a Japanese stamp and postmark on the envelope, and a phone number with the most common Tokyo cell phone area code, 090, as its prefix. The number matched my new Au brand cell phone, sent over courtesy of the same agent; it was a phone I hadn't used yet and wasn't looking forward to using, given that all the commands in the menu were in Japanese.

I still wasn't comfortable with kanji, I thought as I painstakingly fumbled my way across my scratch pad, searching for the right words to state my intent regarding employment. *I have thoroughly enjoyed my experience as the founder and sole proprietor of a personal shopping business devoted to high-end antique textiles and furniture. After that business became too large for me to serve private customers individually, I grew my business into a wholesale operation to overseas retail clients in California and Washington, D.C.*

I stopped myself. There was no verb in Japanese that would correspond to "grew" in business English. I had the sense that using the verb this way might be incorrect in ordinary English too. I scratched out "grew" and substituted "expanded." Then I chewed on my pencil and worried about whether I should describe myself as the proprietor of a business. Yes, I was a one-woman operation, but would that sound pathetic to a Japanese department store? Would they think I worked alone because nobody would hire me, which was absolutely true?

I had to stress who my clients were and raise my own prestige by association. The restaurant I'd decorated in D.C. had been short-lived, but the chef who worked there was famous in Japan, so I would drop his name. Also, they probably had heard of Gump's, an elegant, California-based department store and mail-order business, which had sold vintage textiles that I'd supplied to them. I would leave out mentioning all the various museum consulting jobs that I'd done; they were irrelevant.

I worked on the employment intention statement, and another statement about why I wanted to work at Mitsutan in particular. Before long, it was eight o'clock in the morning, yet I was still in my pajamas. I was going to be late for work, the first time ever.

I dressed quickly, not even bothering to shower, and raced the eight blocks to the office. There I showed my identification card to a new, surly-looking man who sat outside our office, and slipped inside with the key Michael had left him, in a sealed envelope.

Michael was obviously at his appointment in Langley, so I'd have to do the office security check myself. Fortunately, we'd practiced it a few times.

After I'd opened the door and deactivated the alarm, I ran my eyes around the room, looking for any signs of a new invasion. There was something different about Michael's desk: a rearrangement. I studied it for a minute and realized that a silver-framed photograph had joined the few neat supplies on the shelf over the computer terminal.

The color photo showed a close-up of a couple on a sailboat—a laughing couple, a young man hugging a beautiful girl wearing a slightly outdated neoprene bikini. The man was Michael, looking a little bit younger, his hair as close-cropped as ever, but dark brown, without any silver. The woman was a blond—a stunning, long-haired model type in her late twenties, with high cheekbones and emerald-green eyes. She wasn't posing for the camera, but had tilted her face up to Michael and was showing him an expression of outright adoration.

The picture made sense, I thought grimly as I turned away. He was so worried about my invitation the night before that he'd brought in a photograph of a sexy girlfriend as ammunition.

"What kind of picture is that?" Mrs. Taki clucked disapprovingly when she arrived a few hours later, bearing a cardboard box with Styrofoam cups of green tea from a restaurant around the corner.

"Oh, thank you, but you shouldn't have. I could have brewed green tea here for you, Taki-san!" The truth was that I had the real, leaf form of green tea, and it was better.

"Never mind. Where is Michael? What does he say about this picture?" Taki-san drew closer, her eyes opening in wonder.

"He's at the Pentagon this morning." The lie came easily to me; it wasn't as if Michael had said I couldn't tell Mrs. Taki that he was going out to CIA headquarters, but I'd decided not to let her know, to further the idea that absolutely nothing was wrong at the office. "I haven't had a chance to ask him about the picture, but I'm sure it's a girlfriend. I'm surprised you didn't know—you've worked together for years, right?"

"He never mentioned any girl at any time," Mrs. Taki said, turning on me now, with a frown. "That woman's bikini is out of fashion. Rei-san, where's your makeup?"

I clapped my hands to my cheeks. "I didn't think of putting it on. Actually, it doesn't match my government ID photo, so I thought it would be better to avoid using it, just so the guard downstairs doesn't become wary."

"You should practice. You'll be going there any day now, so that face must become second nature. I know. I was undercover myself many times."

"Really? Who as?"

"A Chinese." Mrs. Taki cleared her throat. "And as you mentioned, there is a new guard outside the office door who asked me for identification—me, when I've worked in this office for so many years! What is going on?"

"Apparently it's a new security directive from our masters," I said.

"Homeland security." Mrs. Taki shook her head. "It almost makes me want to return to my homeland."

"I've wondered about that," I said. "It must have been pretty brave and unconventional for you, to leave Japan as a young girl for this kind of life."

"Oh, well, I did it for love."

I was surprised—I'd thought Mrs. Taki would have said that she did it for adventure, or because she was sick of a sexist society and wanted to have a meaningful job.

"How's your application?" Mrs. Taki changed the subject, as if sensing that I'd been surprised.

"Actually, I've been working pretty hard on it. Will you look at what I've drafted so far?"

Mrs. Taki settled down at the conference table. At the end of her reading, she looked up at me gravely. Her verdict was: not modest enough. The job was for a salesgirl, not a CEO. I had not presented myself as the kind of person whose goal in life was to offer customer service at the greatest department store in Japan.

"Okay," I said, writing down the line that Mrs. Taki suggested I use for my statement of personality. "My family and friends call me reliable. I value punctuality and kindness to others, and I delight in helping people of all ages."

We went through the whole application like that. By three o'clock, we had all the words in place in Japanese. I began to painstakingly write the answers in Japanese on a photocopy of the master form, but Mrs. Taki stopped me. "I'm sorry, Rei-san, but your handwriting, it still is a little like a schoolchild's."

"I don't know what I can do about it at this late date," I said as I heard the slight click of the front door opening. Michael had arrived. "I mean, I would have loved to stay longer at Monterey to work on writing, but I had to leave."

"How about if I write out the application? What do you think, Michael-san?" Mrs. Taki asked as he entered the room.

Michael came over to where we were working, looked at the application for a minute, and frowned. "What if she has to write something down while she's at the store? I worry about a discrepancy in the handwriting and somebody accusing her of forging her application."

"The application will be filed away at personnel. She'll be on the sales floor. She won't write anything at all—she'll just be punching codes into a computer," Mrs. Taki said.

I turned to my boss. "Perhaps it is better if Taki-san does the actual writing. The Japanese consider handwriting a mirror of the soul."

"That's what we'll do, then," Michael said. "And Taki-san, if you don't mind, I'll let you take the work home. May I drop by at five to pick it up?"

"Five o'clock? It'll be ready in less than an hour. I'll do it here."

So Taki-san worked while Michael punched furiously at his computer and shot me glances from time to time. He clearly had something important to say, in private.

Taki-san finally left, satisfied with the look of the paperwork. When the elevator doors had closed behind her, and both of us had double-checked that the office door was locked, Michael got down to business. He unpacked a good-smelling shopping bag that held two super-long rectangular boxes. I opened mine and found the largest, thinnest golden-brown crepe I'd ever seen.

"Wow. What is it?"

"*Dosa* from Woodlands. It's a really great Indian restaurant out in the suburbs, and I was coming through, on my way back."

"It's great," I said, between bites. There was potato and green pea curry inside, a true vegetarian delight.

"Would have been even better right off the griddle," Michael said.

"Well, anyway, the pause while Mrs. Taki remained here gave me time to think."

"About what happened at Langley?" I was hoping against hope that I was still in.

"You want to know what they said?" Michael paused. "Well, to sum things up, they're more annoyed with me than you, which is the way it should be."

"But what did you do wrong—other than stay too long in the powder room reading the *New York Times*?" I couldn't resist getting in a dig.

"When a ship runs aground, it's always the captain's fault." Michael's voice was somber. "A principle to live by that my father hammered into me since I was old enough to handle an oar."

"Does that mean they're going to fire you?" I asked.

"No, although you can imagine I'm going to be under a microscope for the rest of my career. But we deleted the bugs before anything dangerous was leaked; there's no known loss of information. And I'm happy to say that you're still going to Japan."

"Great." I hadn't realized I'd been holding my breath; now I let it out in relief.

"The break-in's goosed them enough to want you out there faster than before. It's a good time for hiring in Japan, too, as you know."

I nodded. Because of the January sales, there had been a slight increase in department stores' want ads in *Recruit* magazine. I doubted that the demand would hold through February, though.

"They want you out there before the end of the month, which means I'm going to send this paperwork as soon as you and Mrs. Taki say it's good to go."

"Well, my application will be ready to go today—but it's up to Mitsutan whether I even get an interview. And the way the application looks now, it's rather underwhelming." I showed him a copy of the final draft, translated by me back to English.

"It looks okay," Michael said after he'd read it. "But it seems like something's missing. Why didn't you include your work with Gump's?"

"Well, Taki-san pointed out that department stores are so competitive. Someone might resent Gump's, and feel I wasn't a good candidate because of that."

"But what you did there was so Japanese. You wholesaled kimono and obis."

"Used clothes," I said, repeating the words Taki-san had used. "She said if they thought I trafficked in dirty used clothes it would ruin my image before I had a chance to impress them with my clean good looks." I said the last sarcastically.

"You'll impress them," Michael said. "The application's good. You come off like a well-educated but not particularly ambitious woman. Someone who would be easy to train and would follow the hierarchical rules without question."

"Oh, Michael, I don't know!" All the stress came rushing back. "I've screwed up so many times here in the last day alone—how could I even handle an interview there? I won't have Taki-san whispering into a hidden microphone in my ear."

"Yeah, it's not like the last presidential debate."

"Michael!" I mock-reprimanded my boss, who had always been exquisitely nonpartisan.

"They'll call," Michael repeated. "I'm sure."

7

Michael was right. The application traveled to Japan on a Wednesday and was mailed to the store from the Hiroo post office on Friday. By Tuesday of the next week, a message was tucked into voice mail on my Au cell phone. Mrs. Taki helped me retrieve it and cheered when she heard the words. The deputy director of personnel, Ms. Aoki, wanted to know if I was still available for employment, and if so, asked me to please call to schedule an interview.

"Oh my God," I said to Mrs. Taki. "This is really it!"

"You need coaching," Taki-san fretted. "We need you to rehearse a good explanation of what you've been doing with yourself while waiting for this job of a lifetime. Michael-san, please you go out and give us some peace and quiet. We have much work."

"I have much work, too," Michael said drily. "I need to get Rei some kind of flight fast. Supposing the recruiter wants to see you as soon as Friday?"

"Friday here is Saturday there," I pointed out. "So that would be impossible. And why shouldn't I ask to have my interview next week?"

"You'd better call her immediately to find out when she wants to see you," Michael said. "I don't want you losing the job because another applicant was quicker on the draw."

"Right. Well"—I looked up at the wall of clocks—"right now it's midnight in Tokyo. I'd say I have a few hours to kill before Aoki-san gets to work."

"No time for killing. Time for practicing!" said Mrs. Taki. So we did.

Since I wanted to make sure the call was perfectly clear, I was going to use the landline at the office, from which it was possible to dial without revealing the number of origin—a necessity, since I was supposed to be living in Tokyo, not Arlington, Virginia. I knew the time I wanted to make my call—ten in the morning in Japan. That meant eight in the evening EST. I'd stay a bit later than usual—no problem with the guard outside. Michael had offered to stay as well, but I'd turned this offer down flat—although I'd happily accepted his offer to run out and get me dinner at seven. I hadn't asked for anything in particular, and he came back with spinach cannelloni, a mini-bottle of red wine, and tiramisu for dessert.

"Smells good," I said, opening the plastic container and taking a whiff. "I'm a little surprised about the wine, though."

"It's nonalcoholic. I don't know whether you normally drink wine with dinner or not, but since you're staying late, I thought you might as well have something to perk up the evening." Michael twisted the paper bag, then let it drop into the trash. "You're still sure you don't want me to stay? It could be late when you get out."

"No, thanks. And whatever the time, I'll call a cab," I said after I'd swallowed my first bite. The pasta was as good as it looked.

"Save your receipt," Michael said. "And will you promise me you'll really do it?"

"I won't even go downstairs until they've honked."

Michael stood silently for a minute, and I imagined he was thinking about what had happened to me last spring in Washington, when I'd taken a chance at night. I hadn't been working for him then, but he knew my personal history. He'd made it his business to know everything, before he even approached me for the tryout job in the fall.

"What if the cab doesn't show up?" he asked. "What will you do then?"

"Then I'll stay put and phone you," I said. "But if I do all this, there's one thing I have to ask of you. Actually, I've been wanting to ask it for a while."

"Go ahead." His face flushed, and I realized he thought I was going to ask him out again.

Crisply, I said, "I want to see the file on Tyler Farraday."

"What?" Michael responded as if my question had caught him off guard.

"I want the daily report of what he was doing, and whom he was seeing, before he was killed. For my own information, so I don't end up in the same bad place."

After a long pause, Michael nodded. "I understand your point. The problem is that it's not an OCI file. It's CIA. I certainly don't have it here—I don't have it at all."

"Well, can you get it for me?"

Michael nodded again. "I'll do my best."

After Michael left, there were twenty minutes till call time. I placed the call promptly at 8:01, and an assistant answered, saying in elaborately polite language that the store was in the process of opening, so Aoki-san wasn't at her desk. Suddenly, I remembered that department stores opened at ten, and that the opening itself was an elaborate ritual with store managers lining the aisles bowing to the first incoming customers. I apologized for causing trouble, and told the assistant I was a job applicant returning Aoki-san's call. Could she kindly take a message for me? Her voice was slightly less polite, probably because she realized that I was the lowest of the low—a future sales trainee. Still, she agreed to take my name and the number of the Japanese cell phone.

I was worried about having to leave a callback number. Although the Au phone had international calling ability, I'd found through some experimental phone calls I'd made to my aunt in Yokohama that the quality of reception was poor.

I adjusted the cell phone's ringer volume to high and set it down on the coffee table. I curled up where Michael used to sit, and decided to open the bottle of mock Chianti. Of course there were no wineglasses in the office; I had to make do with a paper cup left over from the day's Japanese lunch. I sipped the wine, deciding that it wasn't bad, though I'd harbored no great expectations. As I drank, I leafed through the latest dossier of documents that had been sent to me; it was a flowchart of the management structure at Mitsutan. A store that had 2,000 employees in the Ginza location alone had plenty of managers—more than 100. I needed to be able to match the names and faces of the executives Michael was most interested in—and there were twenty-five of those, all men save for three. Some of the documents had been translated by Taki-san, some not. At least the office was totally quiet and I could concentrate.

I began my work at the top of the pyramid: the Mitsuyama family who owned the store. Masahiro Mitsuyama, age eighty, was the patriarch of the family and chairman of the board of directors. He would be easy to recognize because he was completely bald, with thick glasses, and his suits looked as if they had been bought back in the 1980s. Well, he didn't have to dress to impress. His son, Enobu, was fifty-five, still had hair, and wore better-looking glasses than his father. Enobu had studied accounting at my supposed alma mater, Waseda University. He'd started his career at the store in the accounting department, and had risen in responsibility to ultimately oversee the credit division. He'd been appointed in 2003 as the *shacho,* or chief operating officer, of the five stores that made up the Mitsutan chain. In that year, 2003, the profits had started to climb. Although he visited all stores at least once a week, his headquarters were at the Ginza location.

What did that mean, exactly: Ginza location? I flipped through my folder until I found the brochure with a full store map. Mitsutan had eight floors, but nowhere was there any marking of administrative areas. I hoped the executive offices were in the store itself; if they were in a different building in the Ginza, I'd have to go through all kinds of hell to get inside and plant my bug. Of course, the personnel department might be in that building, and it could be my excuse to get in.

The phone rang, startling me. But it wasn't the Japanese cell phone, it was the landline on my desk. I picked it up and heard Michael's voice.

"You're still in the office." He sounded accusatory.

"Ms. Aoki wasn't in when I called. I'm waiting for her to call back."

"You could do that at home. It's nine o'clock. And by the way, tomorrow morning I'll have what you asked me for. Though you can't keep it around. You're going to have to return it to me—"

"I understand. Thanks. And, well, the reason I'm here is that I'm working on memorizing the names and faces of Mitsutan executives. And I know you don't want me to take those papers out of the office."

"That's fine, but you have a full day tomorrow. Do you realize that?"

"Of course I do. That's why I've got to get this done." I tried to hide my irritation. "You're very nice to encourage me to go home, but I'm sorry, I'd rather kill two birds with one stone—handle the phone call here and get the paperwork finished."

After I hung up, I decided to check the messages on the Japanese cell phone, just in case there was something. I bit my lip when I saw that a call had come in from Mitsutan. My phone had let me down, not even ringing.

I shook my head and used the cell phone to dial Mitsuan's personnel office, where I spoke to Ms. Aoki's assistant. She told me Aoki-san had gone into a training meeting and wouldn't be available until six o'clock that evening.

I scrunched my eyes shut. Damn, but I'd screwed up. Now I would have to wait until four in the morning to call.

The next call I made was to Michael, at home. "I can't call for a few more hours. Aoki-san's at a training conference. Also, it turns out that my Japanese phone won't even ring here—I can call out on it, and it'll take voice mail, but I can't just answer it."

"Could there be a chance you just have the ringer off?"

"Nope. I checked already."

"Damn it," Michael said. "So did you leave them the exchange for the landline?"

"Of course not! That would be an overseas call, which not only would confuse them but would simply cost too much for them to call. I think I'll just keep calling, trying to get lucky."

"Hmm. Do you want to grab a quick nap and have me give you a wake-up call in a few hours?"

The last thing I wanted Michael to know was that I planned to hang out in the office all night. "No, thank you. My watch has its own alarm. I'll be fine. Good night, and sorry for the trouble."

I had learned everything about the Mitsuyama family by midnight. By one o'clock, I could spell the names and match them to the faces of two-thirds of the executive board. But I was tired. I tested the alarm on the inexpensive Timex that I'd recently bought for its stopwatch feature, to help time my cycling and running sprints—and then set it for three forty-five. I wasn't going to let Aoki-san slip by me this time—even if it meant phoning the personnel office every five minutes. And I'd start early, because I wasn't sure if the assistant had meant that Aoki-san would come back at six, pick up her coat, and leave—or settle in for a final hour or two of work. Women in Japan didn't typically work as long as the men did—women's usual time for leaving was somewhere between six and eight in the evening, whereas men often were in the office until ten, unless they had to go out for a company drinking party.

I was having a nonalcoholic after-work drinking party of one, and it was no fun at all. I chucked the empty mini-bottle into the trash, then turned on my computer, fiddling around with the sound until I got an alternative rock radio station from Towson, Maryland, that I liked. I double-checked the door and the locks on the office's few windows, because I still had some residual nervousness about the break-in. Everything was set. Then I settled down on the love seat, arranging my pleated wool skirt like a blanket over my calves. Tracy Chapman's voice washed over me like a lullaby, and I closed my eyes.

The buzzing sound in my ear made me jump. I opened my eyes, shut them again, and squinted at my watch. Yes, three forty-five. I was on schedule for my call.

I drank a glass of water to get rid of the early-morning croak in my voice and dialed. It was five minutes to six. Of course, Aoki-san wasn't there.

"She says your cell phone isn't working," said the assistant. "She called it again during her lunch break."

Damn it, but I was going to lose the job. I knew it. I was not only unreachable but lax in checking my phone messages.

"Is there another number where she can reach you?" the assistant asked.

"Not really, I'm so terribly sorry to cause all this trouble—"

"Just a minute. She's walked in."

Miss Aoki came on the line. "Aoki here. Who is it, please?"

"Shimura Rei," I said, croaking a bit as I gave my name in the proper backward sequence.

"Who is it? I cannot hear you—" Her voice was curt.

"Shimura Rei," I repeated, pitching my voice in the correct, high register that I'd worked on, ceaselessly, with Mrs. Taki. "Excuse me for not returning your earlier calls promptly. The circumstances were difficult."

"I saw your résumé," Ms. Aoki said. "The fact is our regular positions are full."

Regular positions full. To think she'd called me just to turn me down—what a disappointment.

"Oh, I'm sorry to hear that. I was really, really hoping." My voice broke off. I wanted to cry.

"What we can offer girls with your experience, these days, is contract work. It's on a six-month basis and doesn't include benefits, outside the shopping discount."

"Oh! But I'm interested in that!" I said, stumbling over my Japanese in excitement.

"Do you really think so?" Ms. Aoki sounded doubtful. "Well, I suppose you should come in for an interview, though I should warn you there is a group of fifty we're looking at, and only five positions, at least for the Ginza store."

"I'd be honored to interview. Is there anything I should bring with me, please?"

"We have your application, so there's really nothing more needed. We just want to see and talk to you. Friday is our scheduled day. What hour are you available to come in?"

"Afternoon. Late afternoon, if you don't mind." I prayed that this wouldn't make me sound slothful, but flights from the United States typically arrived at noon or later. If I couldn't get a flight on Wednesday night and had to go on Thursday, I'd still have a few hours' cushion to reach the store, but I didn't like to take chances.

"Four o'clock, then." She paused. "We'll see you then. Please be punctual, because others will be waiting."

I thanked her profusely and rang off. It was too late to go home, by this point; and besides, I had plenty of things to do.

8

Something soft was tickling my lower back. It was a delicious, sexy feeling, like a cashmere massage. Every nerve ending on my body awoke, slowly and deliciously. I savored the feeling, wondering why I'd been so freaked out by the Korean beauty salon. Whatever Dora and her friends were doing to my back was really nice.

Blearily, I opened my eyes and found myself staring at a nubby beige sofa armrest. I was crashed out on the sofa in the OCI office, and Michael Hendricks was laying his cashmere overcoat over me like a blanket.

"Sorry." He jumped back, looking guilty. "I didn't mean to wake you. I just thought you might be cold."

"I meant to take a catnap." I sat up and rubbed my eyes. "I have so much to do!"

"You never went home?" Michael's expression darkened. "Next time you're going to do something crazy, clear it with me first."

"I got the interview," I said.

Michael caught his breath, then said, "When?"

"Friday, which means I have to leave this afternoon or evening, if I'm going to have a day before the meeting. Do you think I'll be able to fly on such short notice?"

"Certainly. I'll drive you to Dulles myself. You go home and get your passport and the rest. I don't know when you're going to have time to look at this file—" He held a manila folder labeled "Farraday," and I grabbed it.

"I'll do it in the car. Oh, God, I don't know if I can do a whirlwind pack-out like last time—"

"Travel light! Remember, you'll take nothing with you that seems like it was bought outside Japan, from the bag itself down to your socks and underwear." He reddened slightly after the last sentence, as if he'd forgotten whom he was speaking to.

"I don't wear socks, Michael. I wear stockings." I stretched out my legs, which happened to be covered in fashionable, flesh-tone fishnet.

"So you'll be able to pack yourself up while I take care of your ticket?" Michael was looking at my legs as if seeing them for the first time.

"Yes, but I don't know what I'm going to do about the apartment and my mail and everything like that." Now that I was fully awake, the fact that I'd agreed to leave for Japan in a few hours stunned me.

"Don't worry about the apartment, I'll keep the rent payments going. After I get things set with the travel agent, I'll run by the post office and pick up the paperwork to get your mail forwarded to the office. You can sign on the way to the airport."

"Thank you," I said to Michael, but he was no longer looking at my legs, or any part of me. He was on his cell phone to the travel agent, asking about a plane to Tokyo.

"I wish I could have said good-bye to Taki-san," I fretted. I was in the passenger seat of Michael's Audi. Blue Merle was crooning "Burning in the Sun" from the Bose speakers, and the sun in fact had come out during our last few minutes on the Dulles Toll Road. I'd finished reading the file on the man everyone called Tyler Farraday, which had struck me as more pathetic than insightful. He'd worked a few places around town as a male model; and on an accessories shoot for Mitsutan, he had attempted to get the photography director to introduce him to the big honchos in corporate. That kind of thing just wasn't done, and as Tyler had made some outrageous attempts to make himself visible to store management, he'd wound up getting cut out of the ad campaign. He'd been doing cocaine in the men's room at Gas Panic the last time anyone had seen him alive. The Tokyo police had ruled his death a drowning, which was the story I'd read in the papers; but a CIA medical officer who'd performed the autopsy, once the body had been returned to Virginia, confirmed that Farraday had received so many physical blows that he was very likely dead before he touched the water.

"Mrs. Taki did give you her best regards by phone. She was very pleased that the application succeeded," Michael said, bringing me back from the gruesome past to the present.

"It all happened so quickly," I said. "Everything, from the application to the packing. Thanks for helping me again."

"No problem," Michael said. "You've got both passports, right?"

"I double-checked. The American one is in my carry-on and the Japanese one in the suitcase." The bright red Japanese passport was a forgery, a document giving details of the birth of Rei Shimura on the same day in September that I was born—but seven years later. I also had a new address book in the carry-on, a book that was practically bare but did contain the names of my supposed parents and our family address, an apartment in a good building in the upscale Hiroo section of southwest Tokyo. I'd already memorized the facts about my father: he was an investment banker, frequently out of the country; in fact, he'd brought my mother and me to California for many of my school years. My mother was a housewife who enjoyed making shopping expeditions wherever her husband worked. I'd grown up in a culture of international shopping—which was one of the reasons I'd always wanted to work in a department store.

So many things to remember! I pushed them to the back of my mind as Michael turned into the airport parking lot and started cruising to find a spot.

"Why don't you drop me on the sidewalk outside the terminal? It'll save time." I was jumpy, because the flight departure time was an hour and a half away, and who knew if the check-in people would pull rank on me for not being on the scene two hours before my international flight? Stranger things had happened to me in airports.

"Okay." Michael said reluctantly. "I'll say good-bye to you now, and good luck, but I'll meet you at the departure gate."

"But you don't have a boarding pass. They won't let you through." I looked at him, utterly confused.

"My name is on a list of people allowed access to the airport, at all times."

"How convenient." I stepped out of the passenger seat and around to the car's trunk. He came out to join me. I'd started to lift the suitcase, but he took it right out of my hands.

"Thanks for the help," I said. "But really, I don't get it. I'm under-cover now. I can't be seen hanging around with you. I mean, there's a very slight chance there would be someone on the plane who could notice and might tell the wrong people in Japan—"

"I won't talk to you at the gate," Michael said tightly. "I just want to see for myself that you get out in a safe and timely fashion."

"But why would they let you through, without a ticket?"

"I have a special pass issued by TSA. It works in all the American airports."

"How nice for you. But really, there are better uses for your time," I said, starting to wheel my suitcase away.

I passed through security easily, and made it to the gate with an hour to spare. As I sat there, restless, I felt a slight pang of guilt. Michael had done so much for me, over the last month, and the last words I'd said to him had been snippy. I regretted them, just as I regretted not having the chance to look into his ice-blue eyes one last time and say a proper good-bye.

Michael had urged me to use a taxi from Narita Airport, but the fact was that I'd been too rushed to remember to get some yen before my departure, and at the late hour we arrived, the currency exchange window was closed. Most Japanese taxis didn't take Visa. I was hesitant to take Friendly Limousine, a round-the-city hotel bus that would be likely to stop at more than two dozen places before getting to Hiroo.

My only option was the train. The Keisei Flyer was a bit of a mis-nomer, because it took over an hour to get from Narita to Ueno-Okamachi Station, from which point I'd have to travel forty minutes on the Hibiya line to wind up at Hiroo, where I would disembark and follow the handwritten map Michael had given me to find the apartment. He'd stayed there before; many other operatives had as well. But it had been waiting vacant for me the last two months.

Usually, I didn't mind getting into a train after a trans-Pacific flight—I was always so excited to be back in Japan, among Japanese people. But this flight had been eight hours longer than the route I typically took from San Francisco, and we'd had to wait on the run-way for almost two hours before taking off.

Good going, Rei, I said to myself. I'd been sick, my suitcase was heavy, and I was heading not toward the bosom of my real Japanese family, but to an unknown apartment belonging to my fake family on a street I could only hope to find.

On the train, there were plenty of seats, given the late hour. I sank into a bench and let the silence surround me. People were busy with their cell phones, clicking them to send text messages. It was impolite to speak on your cell phone on the train, let alone to allow it to ring. Signs all over the train instructed passengers to switch their phones to *mana modo*, an expression that translated literally to "manner mode," what Americans simply called "ringer off."

Feeling chastened by the quiet text-messagers, I retrieved my Au phone out of the Japanese carry-on bag. I pushed it into silent mode and scrolled through the menu to check for messages. There was one, from Ms. Aoki, who, owing to scheduling changes, had shifted our interview time to Thursday at five.

Thursday at five? That was hours ago, I thought with panic. I'd missed the interview, but it was too late to cry. Too late to do anything but lug my suitcase up the gargantuan staircase at Ueno past the drunken salarymen, the gravely quiet homeless, and pretty office ladies laughing too loud to the other section of the station, where I took a train to the main Ueno Station, where I caught the subway to Hiroo. And then, up another steep flight of stairs, past a closed bakery and, after the Mitsubishi bank, the next left to a little street where a small stucco apartment house called Ambassador House stood.

I stepped into the empty vestibule and glanced around. No doorman, just an elevator with a keypad next to it. I pressed in the code Michael had taught me, and the doors parted and I rode up to the third floor. The apartment, which looked as if it had been furnished within the last year, was nothing special. But it was clean, and the central heat was on. I made a quick sweep of a bedroom with a double mattress resting on a low teak platform; a study with a fax machine with a short stack of papers lying in the tray before it, and a kitchenette. The fridge held milk, bread, juice, jam, and peanut butter. The thought flashed through me that this might have been Tyler Farraday's food, if he had lived here before. The milk had not been opened; I sniffed it, came away with nothing odious, and decided it was worth risking a good, long drink.

I crawled into bed just as the telephone on the nightstand started ringing. Briefly, I entertained a fantasy of yanking it out of the wall, but reason won out and I picked up, saying a weary *moshi-moshi*.

"You're there." A male voice speaking English, as clear and crisp as if he were in the next building. Michael had to be on the landline at the office, the one that was supposed to be "secured," however secure anything really could be.

"Yes, Brooks." I was never supposed to use Michael's name over the phone with him or anyone else, so I'd created a fitting, private code name—Brooks, as in Brooks Brothers. He'd laughed when I'd christened him, and he'd decided that I would be "Sis." I suspected that he'd chosen this name because he regarded me as either a little sibling or a girlish coward—neither of which was particularly flattering.

"Why didn't you call me right away? I've been waiting."

"We came in very late. And then my trip by train took two hours." I yawned, to emphasize my exhaustion.

"I know you took off late. I'd read all of *Le Figaro* by the time your plane took off, and that's really saying something, because French is not an easy language for me—"

I interrupted. "You mean you were inside the airport?"

"Yes, the next gate over. I wanted to make sure your flight took off okay. Remember, I told you what I was going to do."

But I'd never seen him. I'd made a thorough visual inspection, and noticed only an elderly man with glasses and a ratty black beret reading a newspaper at the next gate. Now I realized that this had to have been Michael, working in deep disguise.

"Michael, you're amazing," I said. "Now, can you tell me something? Did the infamous Tyler Farraday live in this apartment? It's got strange vibes."

"Briefly. He wound up moving to a place in Shibuya that he told us would help him maintain cover."

"The fridge still has food in it."

"Stocked earlier in the day by one of our people. Relax, it's all new stuff for you."

Feeling relieved that I was not living in the land of the dead, I went on to tell Michael about the text message Aoki-san had sent, telling me to come for my interview a whole day earlier.

"A slight derailment," Michael said, after a pause. "But you'll still go to the personnel department on Friday."

"How can I show up if the appointment was changed? She's probably got somebody else slotted in for that time—or for all I know, they'll be done with their hiring decisions."

"I suggest that you play—unaware," he said, and I suspected he'd been about to say "dumb," but changed his word. "The personnel director already knows that your phone has some problems, so you could conceivably not have received the message. If you're there in person, dressed to the nines and speaking politely, you'll get the chance to talk to someone."

"I guess it's my only option."

"There's never just one option," Michael said. "An operative always has a plan B, C, and D and even E. If there's anything you take away from this mission, I want it to be this. Let it become so ingrained that you never permit yourself to be defeated."

"Right, Brooks," I said, trying to sound more enthusiastic than I felt.

9

My journey had been long and hard enough that I broke with my usual tradition of awakening many hours too early. Instead, my eyes fluttered open at seven, when it was light beyond the blinds, and I could hear the gentle sounds of morning traffic beneath my window. I stretched, feeling unusually refreshed as I lay in the comfortable though unfamiliar bed—the resting spot of so many agents before me, including Michael. Today, as my bare toes touched the polished wood floor, I knew I had big shoes to fill. But I already had large feet: size eight and a half narrow. It was fortunate that I'd bought my new Celine pumps in the United States, because I was almost certain that size wouldn't have been available in Japan.

I took a long, luxurious shower and went to look at the clothes in my suitcase. I hadn't unpacked the night before, so the Escada suit had some deep creases. But I found an electric iron in the bathroom and a mini-ironing board in a drawer, which also contained a variety of oddments that included false eyelashes, mustaches, eyeglasses with non-prescription lenses, spirit gum, pancake makeup, and toupees. The drawer gave me the feeling that most of the agents who'd come before me were men; still, I was glad for the resources. I added my own stash of makeup to the drawer. It had been a few days since I'd done the full Asian eyelid maquillage, but I had a diagram, and it wasn't that hard to duplicate—almost as good as Dora's work, I decided. I was going to test it this morning, just to see what happened.

By ten, I was out the door. Even though there was food in the fridge, I was tempted by the memory of something I'd glimpsed the night before: an Italian cappuccino bar. It made sense that a well-off girl of twenty-three who wasn't an office lady would have the time for a cappuccino or latte in the morning; and spending some time near a window, gazing outward, would give me a chance to get my bearings in my new neighborhood.

Hiroo was a mystery to me. I had lived all over the city, from Minami-Senju in the northeast to the central Shitamachi neighborhood of Yanaka and in the southwest in Roppongi. Hiroo was close to Roppongi but was more staid: a land of fur coats and Volvo wagons, art galleries and patisserie shops—perfect for bankers and foreigners on expense accounts who wanted to send their children to the neighborhood's English-medium private schools. Even if I could have afforded it, it wasn't my speed.

I stopped first at a nearby Citibank cash machine to withdraw some yen, then made my way into Giulia's, a beautiful little shop with an interior of what looked like aged wood and small, marble-topped tables.

The first sip of delicious coffee mixed with perfectly frothy milk jolted me into the present. Hiroo wasn't half bad if I could have this every morning. I would save my receipts, mindful that I could spend up to $200 a day, not including my rent-free apartment. When I found and purchased a new pair of Asics running shoes at the sports emporium near the station, I was still happily under budget. I was beginning to enjoy the perks of spying, although there was a lot of hard work ahead—starting with my attempt to get the job interview.

I laid my cell phone on the table in front of me, thinking about how it was supposed to be my excuse. This was all so pathetic—like saying that the dog had eaten my homework. But I had an idea. Michael had mentioned that he'd wanted me to change cell phones as we went along, for our security. Maybe I should get a new one sooner than later.

I rode the subway seven minutes to Roppongi, my old stomping ground, because I remembered that the last time around, I had seen a lot of cell phone shops there. As I began to browse around Roppongi Crossing, I was overwhelmed with options: private companies like Au and DoCoMo, where you took a phone and paid the bill later; or prepaid phones that could actually be discarded after they were used up. The second idea seemed somehow wasteful, but I liked the anonymity of it. After getting a guarantee in writing that the phone was capable of making overseas calls, I bought a pale pink one for 10,000 yen—about $100. I'd noticed, while at the coffee shop, that most young women had little hang-tag things dangling from their phones, so on my way back to the subway, I bought a cell phone charm from a kiosk that I liked: a tiny replica of Tokyo Tower, which itself was a copy of the Eiffel Tower—just as I was a copy of a Japanese woman, down to the cell phone charm.

It was one-thirty, high time for lunch; but having gotten up so late, I wasn't hungry enough for a restaurant meal. A woman was roasting sweet potatoes in a little brazier set up on a truck on Gaien Higashi-dori, the street that was a main artery in and out of Roppongi. For 100 yen, I sank my teeth into the soft, sweet *yakiimo*. The vendor looked at me anxiously when a tender chunk dropped on the lapel of my blue interview suit; I accepted a paper napkin with gratitude and cleaned myself up.

The truth was, I thought as I went belowground to the subway to catch the Hibiya line to Ginza Station, I didn't love the suit that Mrs. Taki had insisted that I buy. We'd bought it in a hurry, finding it in the overwhelmingly characterless Tyson's II Mall, filled with endless boutiques and salesgirls who'd ignored us. Maybe they'd thought that we couldn't speak English or that, because I'd come in dressed in jeans and a T-shirt, I wasn't going to be a big spender. I was accustomed to such reactions, all the time, in America.

The suit was a mixture of silk and wool, in a color called French blue—a slightly brighter, prettier color than navy, but still dark enough to mean business. The cut was close to the body, though, and the jacket had an asymmetrical closure that was fashionable. Still, I regretted that the skirt hung a few inches below my knees, because it was a standard size 4; no petite had been available.

Mrs. Taki had warned me in advance that my trademark fishnet stockings, even in a conservative color like nude, would appear shockingly risqué in Japan, so I wore regular sheer pantyhose, in which I felt mightily uncomfortable, with the Celine pumps that had a cute strap across the front and a two-inch heel. I was carrying a matching purse, another Japanese touch. To jazz things up a bit—after all, most girls here changed their handbags as often as their cell phones, and right now the trend for phones and handbags was pink and beige—I'd tied a red-and-pink Hermès scarf of 1980s vintage onto the strap. I'd already made sure my new cell phone was on manner mode, though I didn't expect anyone to know the number yet and call me. The phone was going to be a key prop in my excuse.

When I got out at Ginza Station, I studied the complicated map, looking for the best way to Mitsutan. The customary way to reach one of the department stores was to trek along an underground tunnel that in turn led to a specific exit with a short flight of steps into the store's basement. Entering a store through a basement—even a basement packed with mouthwatering food displays—did not strike me as the proper way to begin my adventure. So I took another exit, which brought me up a short flight of stairs to the great outdoors.

It was ironic that Ginza-dori had been named using the kanji character meaning silver or money, because the street itself was plain gray: a respectable, businesslike gray that was a reflection on the weather, the constant flow of traffic, and time. I stood on the sidewalk, surveying the great temples of retail that I'd read so much about and now was seeing through different eyes. Matsuya, Matsuzakaya, and Mitsukoshi were as big as the largest department stores in New York City. This made sense, given the prewar timing of their construction. And while most of the buildings had redesigned their facades to look up to the minute, one hadn't.

Right on the corner, across from Mitsutan, was Wako, half the height and width of its competitors, but architecturally charming. Wako was one of the Japanese department stores that Supermart was contemplating buying. I couldn't imagine it, I thought as I gazed upward at its historic clock tower, which looked like a bigger version of the diamond-circled face of a Wako watch. What would Jimmy DeLone suggest replacing it with, Timex or Swatch?

Right now it was two-thirty, Wako time: for me, it was eleven-thirty at night. I rubbed my eyes, then regretted the action. Now I'd have to check my makeup. To be on the safe side, I went into Matsuya, not Mitsutan—up to the young women's floor, past a delicious display of beribboned Tocca spring dresses and into the ladies' room, where I decided to freshen not only the eye makeup but the blush and lip color. During my short sprint through the store, I'd been impressed by the exquisite appearance of the dozens of salesgirls in blue-skirted uniforms who had bowed toward me, breathing a gentle *irasshaimase,* or welcome.

I was not on par with these girls; if they were so perfect at Matsuya, I could only imagine how they'd be at Mitsutan. Ms. Aoki could probably handpick Miss Japan runners-up to sell makeup or handbags or evening dresses. It was that kind of store.

I went down to the first floor, where a giant midsection of the store—the exhibition hall—had been set up for a "World Chocolate Fair." Forty specialty chocolatiers from Switzerland, France, Belgium, and Germany were selling their wares in special boxed sets for the Japanese Valentine's Day. The average going rate seemed to be 3,100 yen for twelve chocolates; but there were cut-up chocolates at each counter available for sampling. I picked up a tiny sixth of a bonbon from Jean-Paul Hevin, relishing the tiny jolt of sweetness and energy.

I'd whiled away more than an hour; it was finally time to make my approach to Mitsutan. I left Matsuya and crossed the street when the traffic light chirped green. I was doing everything by the book, from this point forward.

A pretty girl in a pearl-gray suit smiled when I asked her where the personnel department was located. Gently she said, "I'm so sorry, but it's not in this building."

Not in the building? How stupid I'd been not to check it out beforehand. What if the personnel department was in the Asakusa store or even out in Yokohama?

"It's located in the annex, directly behind us. You'll need to go around the corner, enter the alley, and then you'll see it. There's a guard outside the door, and just tell him you have an appointment in Personnel."

"Thank you," I said, breathless with relief. I didn't have far to go, and I still had fifteen minutes.

"*Gambatte,*" she said as I headed out the door.

Work hard; give it your best shot.

The same thing Michael had said.

10

I straightened my back as I went down the alley, which really was a small, busy road that led to the loading docks and parking garage. Parking at Mitsutan's garage was free if you spent 50 within two hours.

The parking guard directed me to the annex building, which turned out to be dimly lit and cold. As I stood gazing around this place that seemed the opposite of the bright, well-heated department store, workers trundled racks of clothes into storage areas, women sped unsmilingly into the ladies' locker room, and employees of both genders started lighting cigarettes as they headed into a cavernous, grimly decorated cafeteria. Apparently smiles, light, warmth, and glamour were commodities to be offered to customers only. Feeling slightly disturbed, I entered a battered-looking door marked with the kanji character for personnel.

A girl in the black Mitsutan uniform was seated at a small desk with a phone glued to her ear. She motioned for me to sit down on one of two chairs upholstered in purple-and-black-striped fabric. While she talked on the phone, I decoded the kanji on her name tag. Her family name was Yamada, an easy name made up of the kanji characters for mountain and rice field. Her given name was a bit harder—Seiko, made up of the kanji characters for sacred and child. Now that I was back in Japan, everywhere I went could be a living language lab.

"Hello, Shimura-san," Miss Yamada said after she'd hung up the phone.

I couldn't hide my surprise that she knew me by name. I nodded, still speechless.

"Your picture was on the application. I recognized you. Actually, Aoki-san, our director, was expecting you yesterday. Did something happen?"

"Really? I'm so sorry. I must have had the time confused, because I wrote down Friday at four."

"That was the original time, yes. She wanted to change times, because the circumstances changed."

I liked Yamada-san; she was presenting lots of information, obviously without being aware of it.

"She called!" I tried to sound hysterically upset. "I'm so sorry, I didn't know."

"I left a text message about the change on your voice mail."

"My phone is awful!" I cried. "Actually, I've given up on it and bought a new one, so I hope this kind of thing never happens again." I whipped out the pink phone to show her.

"That's a cute charm. Is it Tokyo Tower?"

"That's right. See, you can light it up by pressing the back."

We were playing with the charm when a door in the back of the office suddenly opened. I realized I should have been working harder on convincing Seiko to rebook my interview than on showing off a phone charm. The phone clattered to Seiko's desk between us, and she looked as distraught as I. She jumped to her feet and said, "Aoki-san, may I present Shimura Rei, one of yesterday's applicants!"

"You didn't come yesterday. Or call either." Ms. Aoki, wraith-thin and exactly my height, was about ten years older than I. As she spoke, she was unabashedly inspecting me from head to toe, her gaze lingering on the clothes. After I'd really had a chance to look at her, I realized why: she was wearing Escada, too, one of the other suits that I'd seen in the little video of the designer's collection that had been playing in the boutique where I shopped. But her suit fit her, hitting just at the knee. Obviously, it had been sewn for the Japanese market.

I bowed deeply, thinking to myself what this meant. She liked Escada. Was it a good thing that we both wore the same line, or would it make me seem to be overstepping?

Blessedly, Seiko Yamada interrupted. "She was just telling me, medical emergency. And her telephone wasn't working in the hospital."

"I didn't see you mention any medical conditions in your application." Miss Aoki pressed her lips together.

"It—it was my aunt, and normally my mother would help her, but
she happened to be traveling away from the city that day." I prayed
I wouldn't forget these details. "And, yes, I'm so sorry, it's true that
my telephone wasn't ringing. Not just because we were in the hospital, but because—it was poor quality. So today I bought a new phone.
I regret missing out on my greatest employment possibility because I
was careless enough to have owned faulty equipment."

It had been quite a speech; much more talk, in one go, than Taki-
san had advised. I hung my head humbly after I was done, looking
at my new shoes, which were starting to hurt like hell. If only I could
have broken them in first. If only—

"I have a few minutes. Follow me." Taki-san was using the com-
mand form of Japanese, as befit her status. I, on the other hand, had
thrown myself into using *keigo*, a kind of old-fashioned, superpolite
Japanese spoken at tea ceremonies and in department stores, at least
by salesclerks to customers.

I proceeded behind the personnel director into her office, which
was large by Japanese office standards, although it was window-
less, and stacked almost to the ceiling with file cabinets. There was
no computer terminal, perhaps because working at a computer was
Seiko Yamada's job. I noticed she'd had a PC on her desk.

Miss Aoki—who I'd decided was probably a miss, because there
was no ring on her left hand—motioned for me to sit in a stiff chair
facing her desk. She settled back into a luxuriously padded regular
office chair. "You sounded different when you were speaking with
the secretary, just before I came out. Why is that?"

"Well, ah, I have always thought that in a department store, one
would speak formal polite Japanese, so that is why I'm speaking it
now—"

"That's correct. You don't ever shift into casual form with another
employee, even if there are no customers around." She paused. "But
your formal Japanese, it's a bit strange—almost antiquated, like kabuki."

"I'm sorry," I said. "I'll try to do better."

"Perhaps it comes from—working with antiques."

I paused, not knowing whether this was an invitation for me to
protest or to make some kind of comment. So I did neither.

"Or perhaps it comes from living abroad for a while, then coming back here." Before I had a chance to figure out a nonanswer to that, Miss Aoki launched into a staccato barrage of questions that corresponded, roughly, to the kind of questions asked everywhere at interview. Why did I want to work at Mitsutan? Answer: to combine my love of fashion, sales, and hospitality in the greatest department store in Japan. What was my greatest weakness? *A tendency to exaggerate*, I thought privately, but said instead, with a rueful smile, that I shopped too much. My greatest strength? I'd thought about this one hard, because I had to be careful not to sound boastful. Then I remembered my whole reason for being at Mitsutan.

"Listening. I think if you listen to people carefully, you can resolve almost any conflict."

"The thing that marks you out from the other applicants I've seen is your time abroad."

Damn. She wanted to know about America. Well, I'd do my best with the story that Michael, Taki-san, and I had concocted.

"My father's work—he is an investment banker—brought us there, to California. I went to a girls' school in San Francisco." My school, actually.

"The one in *The Princess Diaries*?"

So Miss Aoki was a fan of adolescent romantic comedies. I looked at her with new hope.

"No, I'm not sure where that was filmed—I mean, when it came out I was already back here at Waseda University, studying art history."

"What do you think of foreigners?" she demanded.

This had to be a trick question. Had she seen through my makeup? She'd already detected that my use of *keigo* had a theatrical bent.

"The foreigners were very kind to us," I said. "It was no problem for me and my family to get along. Of course, we missed Japan very much, which is why we returned."

"Do you have foreign friends?"

Again, I hesitated. "Yes, I made several good friends at Waseda. It's so nice for me to have the opportunity to keep up my English."

She put her head to one side. "How's your English?"

"Not too bad. I had some kind teachers in San Francisco, and I enjoyed keeping up my English at Waseda."

"Ah, then you are a *kokusaijin*," she said, her voice slowing as she appraised me.

A *kokusaijin* was a term for a Japanese person who was comfortable with foreigners; who wasn't shy about speaking with them, at least. Miss Aoki was so stern that I couldn't tell if this was a compliment or a complaint. So I just looked at her, waiting.

She folded her arms and looked at me. "The fact is, I think I have settled already on the two girls I want to hire for the sales floor. Those positions are no longer available."

"I understand." But Michael and Taki-san wouldn't; they'd be horrified that I'd managed, in fifteen minutes, to completely shut myself out of the position we all wanted so badly.

"But you strike me as a *kokusaijin*, and we have an opening for one of those as well."

"Really?" I knew Japanese stores were staffed with many more people than American stores, but I was stunned to think that they actually had a staff position for a *kokusaijin*; it was the strangest thing I'd ever heard.

"Do you know of our K Team?" Miss Aoki continued.

"I'm sorry, but I don't."

"Well, perhaps you wouldn't, because a Japanese person wouldn't need to use the service. But we have a personal shopping service for foreigners, known as the Kokusaijin Team. That team is called to interpret and to assist in currency exchange, processing tax rebates, and, of course, gift and clothing selection. The foreigners who can prove residency in Japan get a K Team card, which allows them a five percent discount on everything, and free parking."

"How nice for them," I said. "Does the K Team only work with English speakers, then?"

"The team is supposed to be able to help any international customer, but unfortunately, we are not the United Nations. Okuma-san, who oversees currency exchange as well as the K Team, speaks Chinese as well as English and Japanese. Han-san is half Korean, so her languages are Korean, Japanese, and English. There was another employee, Marcelle, who spoke French, Japanese, and English, but she recently repatriated to France. It would have been better if you spoke French or German as well, but English will do." She raised a cautionary finger. "That is, if your English is truly fluent. I can't promise anything until you take your written and oral language tests."

The wheels in my mind were spinning. This was better than I had dreamed. If I worked for the K Team, my stomping ground would be the financial services section of the store. I would be able to plant bugs in the area where currency exchange was happening, and I'd have a good excuse to make my way around the store's various departments—that is, if I wasn't constantly busy.

"I speak a little bit of Spanish," I said. "I'm not fluent, but I'd be willing to help any Spanish-speaking shoppers to the best of my ability."

For the first time, Aoki-san's mouth edged into a slight smile. "Really? Why didn't you put it on your application?"

"I'm sorry that I didn't. Since this is a Japanese department store, I didn't ever think it would be useful."

Aoki-san shook her head, as if dismayed at my ignorance. "I'll ask Yamada-san to administer both tests in the waiting area. That is, if you think you are ready."

"I'd be honored to take the test," I said, not daring to smile fully, because that could appear too cocky. "Thank you so much, Aoki-sama, for this tremendous opportunity."

"One last thing, regarding your application." Her eyes bored into me. "Where are you living, exactly?"

"In an apartment in Hiroo with my parents. It's only fourteen minutes by subway to Ginza Station."

"Yes, I saw the address on the application form, but you only listed the cell number. Do your parents know you want to work here? Do they approve?"

"Oh, very much so. I'm sorry, I should have listed the home phone, and I'll do so now," I answered hastily. "There is an answering machine there, in case I or my parents are not there to answer. A regular telephone is much easier to deal with than a cellular phone, anyway."

"I noticed you brought your cell phone into the office." She shook her head. "We don't allow our salespeople to speak on cell phones while working."

"Of course. I'm sorry that I didn't think of that." I hung my head.

"Well, now you understand. And nothing's final, anyway, until you pass your tests."

I wound up with a score of 80 percent in Spanish, and 98 percent in English. I wondered if I'd really flubbed an English answer, or whether the answer sheet was incorrect. Ultimately, it didn't matter. Miss Aoki offered me a job, with the contract to be reconsidered after six successful months. My starting pay was 1,000 yen an hour, but that was offset with a generous ten percent discount, and two free custom-fitted uniforms. The uniforms would be fitted on Monday. I was to join the rest of the incoming class of salespeople at Mitsutan's manners-training program, which lasted through Wednesday. Then I would be introduced to my new boss, Mrs. Okuma; and the Korean-Japanese saleswoman already on the K Team, Miyo Han.

"Congratulations, although I knew you'd pull it off," Michael said when I telephoned him afterward with the good news. It was six-thirty on Friday night in Tokyo, which meant eight-thirty on Friday morning in Washington.

"Plan B worked," I said, realizing that all I'd done was follow the directions he'd given me.

"Great. I just hope you don't wind up working there the full six months," Michael said. "By the way, do you know how many spies it takes to change a lightbulb?"

"Tell me."

"Only one, but it took three senior advisers to agree that it was broken in the first place."

I laughed. "You're getting better, Brooks."

"I'm shocked. You know, it's pretty quiet around here, without you criticizing my jokes."

"If you miss having another person in the office, you should give Mrs. Taki more to do," I said crisply, to hide how pleased I was by his comment.

"I will, just as soon as you start sending back some recordings."

"I hope you don't expect me to get anything out next week. I'll just be getting started, and I'm sure my manager will be watching me like a hawk."

"Of course. Don't take any risks, and don't worry about me twid-dling my thumbs with nothing to do. I have important things to do, like eat as much Korean food as I want, now that you and your sensi-tive nose are gone."

"My new colleague is supposed to be Korean," I said. "I'm very sorry you can't be on-site to impress her with your good taste."

"Mmm," Michael said. "She's probably one of those very tall and beautiful Koreans. I know the type."

I bet he did—before he'd hooked up with the blond woman I'd

seen in the photo at his desk. I decided to return the conversation to safer ground by telling him about my new cell phone.

"Call me back right away so we can make sure it works. Or better yet, text-message me. I can't answer the phone on the subway or while I'm at work. But I can easily sneak a look at messages."

"Are you sure you want me to bother you any more tonight? After the last three days, you deserve a good night's sleep."

"Oh, no chance of that. I just stopped in to call you on the landline, and change my clothes. I'm going out."

"With whom?"

"What do you mean, with whom? It's Friday night, and I'm just hanging out with some friends."

"Old friends, new friends, who? I need more information," Michael said. "I don't want you to wind up in the river with our departed friend."

"All right, Brooks, you'll be relieved that I'm not going to Gas Panic, but Salsa Salsa, where I intend to catch up with Richard Randall, my former apartment mate. I can't promise we'll be there all night, though, or say who else might wind up tagging along with us—"

"Don't drink," Michael said. "The last thing you want to do is accidentally give away your reason for being here."

"But I'm supposed to tell people I work at a department store. And if I drink nothing, people will be suspicious—"

"Stick to bottled beer and the salesgirl story, but only if someone asks. Nothing further."

11

Later on, I was to think that this weekend marked my last real time of freedom. After Michael signed off with a disapproving good night—as if he recently sensed I was going to drink caipirinhas instead of Kirin—I pulled on my favorite vintage Levis, a purple-and-red-flowered Betsey Johnson tank top, and my boots. Since the night was cool, I threw my vintage Persian lamb swing coat over it all and took the subway to Roppongi, where I walked a few blocks to Salsa Salsa. Richard and Simone were there already, so absorbed in the rhythms of the Brazilian band that they never even asked why I was back in Tokyo. It was enough that we were together, dancing. Nobody even noticed my sleek, red-toned hairstyle or the intense eye makeup—I sweated the makeup off within minutes, anyway.

At the back of the club, there was a bulletin board papered with signs for upcoming dance nights, sublet apartments, and so on. There was even a paper with a picture of a gorgeous blue-eyed blond guy—a dead ringer for Jude Law. But the message below the smiling face said "Have you seen Tyler Farraday?" first in English and then in Japanese.

"What's that about?" I asked Richard when he emerged from the men's room.

"That's an old lost-person flyer," Richard said, jabbing a finger-nail painted with black polish into the paper. "Tyler Farraday was an idiot gaijin who drowned, but that was almost four months ago. That thing should be torn down."

"Why do you call him that?" I felt a rush of sympathy for Tyler, my poor dead colleague. I studied the phone number below the message; it was a Tokyo exchange, with no name listed. I wondered who would have answered the call; just a friend, or perhaps another spy?

"He was a total fake, Rei. A straight pretending to be gay. As if he thought nobody in Japan has gaydar!" Richard ripped the paper off the board, and I took it from him, tucking it into my handbag.

"Don't litter," I said, studying Richard. "So you met him?"

"He was everywhere. Crashing parties, dancing on tables, winding up in the back of cabs. Big spender who picked up the tab for lots of people, but that was the only good thing about him."

"You sound awfully vehement. Did you have some kind of, uh, interaction?" Richard was between boyfriends, just like me.

"No," Richard said. "He was after middle-aged Japanese business-men, although not really *after* them, of course. Why do you care?"

"I was just wondering whether there was some kind of sweeping social change afoot, that a guy could openly go after men here."

"You're right, people are pretty much still in the closet, and speaking of that—who are you doing these days?"

"Doing?" I repeated Richard's word in disbelief. "I'm not doing anything, let alone anyone."

"It's been, what, a year since your night of skin? I mean, sin." Richard laughed.

"Four months. That's not such a long dry spell."

Richard studied me and said, "I suppose I should tell you about Hugh."

"Oh?" My stomach lurched.

"He swung through on business last month and I spotted him at a wine bar in Roppongi Hills."

"You're kidding." I knew which bar he was talking about, but Hugh was supposedly not drinking. This was really bad news.

"I hate to be the one to tell you, honey, but Huge had a girl with him."

"Really." This was even worse news than I'd imagined.

"Because she was Asian, I assumed she was a local, but he actually flew her in with him, on his business trip. Guess where she's from."

"Washington, D.C.?"

"China. Born in Shanghai, now living in Hong Kong, where she stars in a prime-time soap opera." As my face fell, Richard pressed

his lips together. "I wouldn't have expected it, because the thing between the two of you seemed so—sincere—but it looks like Huge
turned out to have an Asian babe fetish, all along."

Richard was a kidder, I reminded myself. I couldn't trust anything
he said. But I looked up the girl's name on Google, and sure enough,
found pages and pages of fan sites devoted to her, though almost all in
Chinese. She looked like me—well, the way I used to look, when my
hair was short—only she was bosomy, with long legs. Heart thumping, I typed her name plus Hugh's into the search engine. Bingo. Six-
teen different links to pictures shot at their engagement party at the
Mandarin Hotel in Hong Kong.

The plot thickened when I had dinner at Nelja, a hip hideaway
of a bar, with my cousin Tom the next evening, after he'd finished
his shift at the emergency room at St. Luke's Hospital. During our
second round of Ebisu beers, he confessed that Hugh had recently
telephoned to see if Tom could help him get access to his old favorite
golf club, just for the afternoon. Tom hadn't been available to golf on
the day Hugh wanted to go, but he'd set up the arrangements—not
just for Hugh, but for a second golfer, whom another friend had spotted: a beautiful, tall Chinese.

"The question I have is whether he's still in the country," Tom said
in English, the second language he loved to practice with me. "If he's
still here, well, maybe the two of you could see each other and work
things out. If only I'd known you were coming back to Japan when I
spoke to him!"

"The situation couldn't possibly work out," I said to Tom. "Even
if he hadn't moved on to another woman, I know that the union was
futile."

"But I like him," Tom said, looking at me. "Frankly, I don't know
everything that happened in the end, but I have a suspicion that you
put him through, how do you say, the ring?"

"The wringer," I said. Yes, I'd been bad. But I had begun to wonder, over the last month or so, whether I'd done something heinous
because I'd wanted to force an ending. And I could never have made
the first move—I needed to be thrown out.

"Love is not enough," I said to Tom. "I have a new lease on life, I
enjoy standing alone—"

"I disagree with your thoughts about love," Tom said. "If I could find a woman to love, that would mean everything to me."

We sat in silence for a while after that, and when it was time for my cousin to catch the last train back to Yokohama, I took advantage of my per diem money and hopped a cab back to Hiroo. I deserved the comfort of a cab to cry in, despite what I'd said.

I was up at five on Sunday morning, so I wound up fixing myself a good breakfast with the provisions I'd bought at the Meidi-ya supermarket the day before. Meidi-ya, which had a stunning array of foreign foods and equally stunning prices, was no longer no-man's-land for me. I'd casually bought Guatemalan coffee, locally baked croissants, and juicy tangerines from Shizuoka, just as if I had as much money as everyone else. But I still had the soul of a bargain hunter. After my breakfast, I took the subway to Togo Shrine for my favorite of all the Sunday morning flea markets.

The flea market was busier than usual, even at eight in the morning. I found myself, for the first time, fighting to take possession of a particularly stunning red and purple ikat kimono. There was a lot of competition now, which ran contrary to everything Taki-san had said about how the Japanese abhorred used clothing. How I longed to call her when, around lunchtime in the nearby trendy shopping district of Harajuku, I spotted six girls wearing vintage kimono as they strolled along, leaving enthralled male spectators in their wake. Japan had come full circle, from *wafuku* to *yofuku* and back. I couldn't wait to tell Mrs. Taki that used kimono were no longer poor-people's clothing but rather an ultrafeminine youth costume.

Monday, my first day of the training segment at Mitsutan, was all about new clothes.

At the uniform fitting, where six other incoming workers and I stood in our underwear, eyes everywhere but on each other, we were circled by Ono-san, a tiny, sharp-eyed woman of about sixty, wearing the store uniform of black jacket and slacks, and wielding a measuring tape that she occasionally flicked out for a quick, painful measurement of someone's shoulder or hip span.

Thank God I had thought ahead and was wearing waist-high, stomach-flattening panties that covered my navel ring. If I had been in the lacy bikini or hip-hugger panties the other girls favored, my secret would have been revealed. And the employee manual, which I'd studied over the weekend with the assistance of a few emergency e-mail clarifications from Mrs. Taki, laid things out clearly. Female Mitsutan staff members could have no piercings except at the ear— just one hole per lobe.

"Your uniform is a privilege!" Mrs. Ono announced, her gaze sweeping over everyone as if she was looking for someone, like me, who was inwardly rebellious. "You will be issued two uniforms, and you are responsible for dry cleaning them and keeping them in immaculate condition. If you have any problems—broken buttons, dropped hems, and so on—please see me before a small problem becomes a huge disaster. My regular office is close to the kimono section on the third floor."

I was spared the snap of the measuring tape, because it took only a few seconds of visual inspection for Mrs. Ono to proclaim loudly that I would wear *saizu* L; I was not only the oldest but the biggest girl in our freshman class. It was true, I realized after covertly inspecting the others, that I was different. Not fatter, exactly, but I had wider shoulders, and more developed upper arms and thighs. Weight lifting and spinning had done me in.

Once we were all dressed, Mrs. Ono reminded us of the other sartorial rules. No necklaces or scarves were allowed; the only accessories were an all-black purse and all-black pumps with a heel not higher than three and three-quarters inches. One ring was permitted on each hand, and stud earrings of either gold, silver, or pearl could be worn—unless one was working at a specific jewelry counter, in which case wearing store merchandise already purchased or on layaway was encouraged.

During our afternoon tour of the store, I learned the reason that about half the sales staff did not wear uniforms. Male employees didn't have to wear uniforms, for reasons of sexist privilege; there was also a large minority of female salesclerks who could get away with beribboned Tocca dresses and Comme des Garçons strap-and-buckle pants. It turned out that these women worked in individual designer sections within the store that were completely owned and operated by the designers themselves. It was a true consignment system, whereby the vendor paid Mitsutan a commission ranging from ten to thirty percent for every item sold. The vendor also paid the salesclerks' salaries and paid for the cost of constructing the in-store boutique, and took back every garment that didn't sell.

It seemed like a sweet deal for Mitsutan, to be able to spend so little on merchandise or staff. But I realized that the same operating agreement was in place at most Japanese department stores; consignment couldn't be the reason Mitsutan was doing too well. There had to be something else.

As the tour continued, I turned my attention toward the best places to plant my bugs. My first thought was to go for the highest-grossing departments and boutiques within the categories of accessories and fashion. But as we wound our way along, stopping to bow to every department manager and floor manager, I began to realize that the hottest spots were the cashier stations. Salespeople rang up sales not in their individual departments, but rather by going to designated cashiers' desks, two or three of which were located on each floor.

The process of selling something was much lengthier and more convoluted than I'd ever realized, even though I'd shopped at Mitsutan many times before. It was briefly explained by Mr. Fujiwara, the store's customer service manager, a stylish man in his fifties. He wore a different dark gray suit every day of the training session, but instead of the standard boring tie, he would wear something individual: an ascot one day, a bow tie the next. There was always a tie, but it was out of the mainstream, a little bit exciting; it made him seem a little more approachable, and that made sense for his position.

Mr. Fujiwara had a different style from Mrs. Ono. Instead of being stern, he was perky—more like one of the motivational direct-sales people who appeared on late-night American cable TV hawking juicers or exercise machines.

"The most important reason a shopper chooses a store is what?" he shouted encouragingly toward us.

"Good-quality merchandise?" the girl next to me ventured.

"No! Please try harder!"

"Price?" someone else ventured.

"No! Guess again!" He was positively chortling.

I raised a tentative hand, and when he called on me, I said, "A relationship with a salesclerk?"

Somebody snickered, and I realized that I'd sounded as if I were talking about people having affairs. But Mr. Fujiwara understood and was smiling.

"Exactly right! Customer service, the sense that customers will always be treated with grace, is exactly what has kept our department store number one. As my wife says, she and her friends would never again return to a shop where she was treated rudely. Retention of customers is entirely contingent on you! A joyful sales experience will result in great customer loyalty. One unpleasant moment, and the customer is lost. You are the most important link in the chain that makes up the Mitsutan empire. It is up to you to keep our customers happy."

Mr. Fujiwara went on to explain, in minute detail, the selling process. When a customer announced that she wanted to buy a particular garment, my job as a salesperson would be to bow, offer heartfelt thanks, and carry the garment, plus the customer's payment, to the cashier's station, where the sale would be rung up under the supervision of cashier directors. There, a designated gift-wrap clerk would carefully pack the garment into a tissue-paper-lined box, which in turn would be wrapped in the store's distinctive green-and-white paper, and ultimately placed in a shopping bag. The original salesclerk would give the receipt and the credit card or any change back to the shopper. The last step was to hand the consumer the shopping bag, and to remain in a humble bow, attention focused on the customer, until she was gone from sight.

During the tour I'd gotten some good ideas about places for eavesdropping. In addition to getting computer spyware into a PC at a cashier station, I hoped to plant listening devices in the highest-grossing accessories boutiques, which were Vuitton, Versace, and Coach. Among Mitsutan's regular departments, I had already pinpointed Young Fashion—since supposedly the freest-spending people in Japan were women between ages fifteen and thirty—and Gifts, the spot where shoppers went to buy "duty presents" for their friends and colleagues during the December and July gift seasons, typically spending between $700 and $1,200 per holiday.

Now, as we followed Mr. Fujiwara downstairs into the food basement, which was thronged with more shoppers per square foot than any other section in the store, I had a new consideration. The women who came to buy bread or chocolates or marinated squid engaged in direct cash or credit transactions with a counter clerk; there was no cashier station. I wondered whether it would be possible to bug these places, and if so, whether there was a good likelihood I'd pick up something of value. The more bugs I planted, the greater my risk of being caught.

"We have at present eighty-eight food shops on this floor!" Mr. Fujiwara called out, interrupting my worries. Now I became aware of other sounds: the din of vendors hawking fresh fish, steamed Chinese buns, and chocolate croissants. With their kerchief-covered heads and aprons, and their wider range of ages, the employees in the food basement looked more like a cross section of traditional Japan than the fashionable, black-clad crew who worked upstairs. My nose twitched at the delicious aromas of grilled onion in one area, rich miso in another, and perfectly ripe strawberries across the aisle. Some shoppers were doing more than just smelling. A backpacker with unwashed red hair who looked as if she hadn't eaten since she'd left Bali was devouring sample after sample of *gyoza,* held on a tray by a man wearing a white chef's toque and a very anxious expression. Japanese onlookers were nudging each other, snickering a little at the out-of-control foreigner. I looked away, feeling sorry. I knew what it felt like to be really hungry, with no money.

"Eighty-eight food shops, all staffed by Mitsutan employees who have completed our food specialty program. Remember, your ten percent discount applies here when you shop in uniform, but that is only for food to take home. No eating at any time on the sales floor!"

"Which food counter is the most successful?" I asked, coming up close to Mr. Fujiwara so that he could hear me.

"It's hard to make one choice, but I believe Lady Beautiful cakes is a consistent high performer in the sweets section; and in the Japanese food section, Country Bento is extremely popular. Can you see it, with the royal blue canopy overhead? Ah, my goodness, the *kaicho* is right here, taking a walk around. Look smart, everyone! I will see if he is willing to inspect you."

Mr. Fujiwara threaded his way ahead of us and over to the Country Bento counter, where I recognized Masahiro Mitsuyama, the chain's *kaicho,* or chairman. He looked older than he had in the photos I'd studied from the board reports—here again, I thought, was another instance of the store putting its best face forward. In the pictures, Mr. Mitsuyama had looked about sixty; but in the flesh, stooped over with a cane and with a deeply creased face and bottle-thick glasses, he looked somewhere in his eighties. How impressive that he was on the floor, tending to business! I watched him point from dish to dish, asking questions of the Country Bento salesclerks, two men and one woman, lined up at attention with their hands clasped in front and heads bowed.

Mr. Fujiwara ran up, bowing deeply himself. I could see his lips moving, and he gestured back to our group. Mr. Mitsuyama nodded; and, bowing again, Mr. Fujiwara made his way back to us. "He will greet you. Have you had your Physical Hospitality Seminar yet?"

We all shook our heads.

"*Ah so desu ka.* Well, remember that the most important part of Physical Hospitality is the bow. I will say '*Rei*' very quietly, then all bow together. Try your best."

For a moment, I jumped at the sound of my name, feeling singled out. Then I recalled that *rei* was the word for bow.

I bowed along with the others, hoping to give Masahiro Mitsuyama the impression that we were the most obedient, focused class of trainees to ever come through the building.

"How do you do?" he intoned in a delicate, reedy voice. "So pleased to see you."

I'd wondered if Mr. Fujiwara would introduce us, because we did have our name tags on, but he didn't. And indeed, the warmth he'd shown us seemed to have vanished as he made a few general comments to the chairman. "This group seems a bit rough, but with concentration they may prevail," Mr. Fujiwara said. "It is a great privilege for them to meet you, the one who has led Mitsutan for the last forty years."

"Forty-four," corrected Mr. Mitsuyama.

"Yes, of course! Excuse me," Mr. Fujiwara said.

"Forty-four years, and I visit each store at least once a week," Mr. Mitsuyama intoned. "Currently, I'd like to check the temperature of the *bento*."

"Please do, *Kaicho*. The temperature is meeting regulations, I hope," the manager said, pulling a thermometer out of the case.

"The number on the thermometer is one thing, but how about that rice?" Mr. Mitsuyama pointed at a glistening square of rice, topped with a purple plum—part of a fish-and-vegetable *bento* box lunch at the front of the counter. "That rice looks hard. I shall sample it to check."

Masahiro Mitsuyama chewed. "Too hard," he announced, speaking with his mouth full of half-chewed rice and tuna.

"Oh, I'm very sorry!" The manager hung his head as I glanced into the case at the fish-topped rice, which looked okay to me.

"Don't let it happen again."

"Yes, yes. I will try harder to improve."

Mr. Mitsuyama looked at us. "Your first week, you are learning an important lesson. There will always be a challenge to follow the rules set for you, but understand that the rules do not guarantee perfection. Perfection is up to you entirely—to your own hard work."

We bowed again, and following everyone else's lead, I remained silent. Mr. Fujiwara burbled his thanks, and we remained at attention, then fell into bows again until Mr. Mitsuyama had moved away and could no longer be seen.

When I stood up, I rubbed my lower back and looked at the Country Bento counter staff. Their faces were grave.

"I don't need to tell you what you need to do," Mr. Fujiwara said. "You know yourself. "

"My sincere apologies for our poor example!" The counterman's voice squeaked with emotion.

"Don't worry." Mr. Fujiwara reached out to take a sample rice ball set out in a tiny paper cup on the counter. He munched it quickly, his face softening into pleasure. "This isn't bad at all. And as the *kakaricho* said, you and your staff have provided an important lesson for our trainees. Customer satisfaction occasionally means going *beyond the rules*. Never forget."

12

Beyond the rules: this was the situation that my government feared was Mitsutan's standard business practice. And if the culture of pleasing people was so entrenched throughout the store, my job of digging up proof of corruption was going to be pretty straightforward.

When I finished my first day at Mitsutan and rode the subway home, I wondered, as I had fleetingly before, about why the United States was so threatened by the success of an old-line Japanese department store that it had sent Tyler Farraday over to investigate. There had to be a link to American interests, somehow.

What if the U.S. government thought Mitsutan was trying to take over an American retail giant like Macy's? I'd read *Rising Sun* back when I was in junior high school—and I'd gotten into trouble with my father for doing it, too—and I now recalled that the famous thriller was all about the threat of Japanese takeovers of American businesses. The book reflected a certain paranoia that flashed through America in the 1980s, when Japan's bubble economy expanded to many real estate holdings worldwide. No matter that the British and Canadians owned more buildings and companies on American soil—it was Sony's ownership of Rockefeller Center that scared everyone.

No, I reminded myself, any takeovers going on in retail were supposed to be in reverse. I remembered an article in the *Wall Street Journal* about Jimmy DeLone and Supermart possibly going after Mitsutan. DeLone was an out-of-control foreigner, a blunt speaker who wouldn't get along in Japan. But he was important enough that nobody would dare throw him into the Sumida River.

When I reached my apartment, I kicked off the pointy-toed pumps that were killing my feet, poured a glass of Chilean wine, and dialed the United States. It was five in the morning in D.C., so I'd be getting Michael out of bed, and I hoped he wouldn't be cranky.

"I hope I didn't wake you," I apologized when he picked up.

"No, I've been up for a while. How was the first day?" Michael's voice didn't have the slightest sleepy edge to it; I wondered if he always woke up this way.

"Quite interesting." I told him about Mr. Mitsuyama's involvement with the store's minute details, including the temperature of rice at a food counter. But Michael seemed less impressed than I'd been by this; instead, he wanted to know if I'd been personally presented to Mr. Mitsuyama.

"Not exactly. I was part of the group of trainees and our leader—the customer service director I mentioned, Mr. Fujiwara—was keeping us on a pretty tight leash."

"Good," Michael said. "You want to be unremarkable in case he sees you again, which he very well might when you're up around the boardroom."

"Oh, I doubt they'll be sending me to the boardroom for any reason. Now, one of the reasons I was calling was that I was hoping you might still have that article about Supermart? I wanted to read it again."

"Sure, I'll fax it right over. But about the boardroom, Sis—I know it's a little early in the game for you to explore the whole store, but within the space of three or four weeks, I'd like you to get something in place there." Michael was talking about bugging, but he'd never use the word over the phone.

"But I have much better access to other places in the main building: cashier stations, food counters, Young Fashion—"

"But we need to hear what goes on at stockholders' meetings," Michael said. "The annual one is set for June. And before that, there might be private conferences between high-level executives, which we'd love to know about."

"I'm doubtful the boardroom's even in the main building," I said. "Personnel and the locker rooms and cafeteria and all the other backstage areas are in an annex—"

"Well, it sounds like you have a reason to be in that building as well," Michael said. "Don't worry—you'll find your way. Now, what about your boss on the K Team? What's he like?"

"It's a she, a Mrs. Okuma, and I haven't met her yet. Supposedly I will soon."

"Well, you don't need to report back until then, unless something's urgent." Michael's tone was as dismissive as his words.

After we hung up, the fax came through. I read it slowly this time, pondering the meaning behind each of the involved entities: Jimmy DeLone, Supermart, Mitsutan. What was the connection, and could they have been somehow involved in Tyler Farraday's death?

The next day at Mitsutan was completely devoted to a course called "Physical Hospitality." I learned the correct way to give directions, with the thumb tucked against the palm, and a flat hand extended; and the importance of personally guiding shoppers, whenever possible, to what they were looking for. I bowed so much that my lower back ached; but at least I'd gotten the correct, flat-back movement right.

I also learned that under no circumstances could I use the pretty public restrooms; if I had to go to a restroom, it would be on my break and over at the annex building, where a grim, unheated women's room stood next to an equally dismal employees' cafeteria. There was a locker room where women employees were to report no later than nine; we had up to half an hour to change into our uniforms and apply makeup, and go over to the store for *cho-rei*, the motivational lecture conducted by a senior manager every day and broadcast over the store's PA system. After that, when the store opened at ten o'clock, we were all to be standing at attention at the fringes of our departments, bowing deeply and ready to offer a heartfelt *irrasshaimase*—"welcome"—to the first customers of the day.

This Wednesday was the first semi-workday, because it was time for me to begin going through the processes rehearsed during the first two days of training. At eight-thirty, I caught a subway to the Ginza; at seven minutes to nine I made it to the annex building, where I went to my assigned locker and unlocked it with the key I'd gotten during training. Because I was a new girl, I felt hesitant to break into the conversations of the happily chattering saleswomen flinging off their fashionable street clothes. But I didn't need to say anything, because I was noticed right away.

"So you're Shimura." A voice came from the left, that of a tall, slim girl next to me, who was already dressed and was brushing the long, silky curtain of midnight-black hair that fell to her elbow.

"Yes, how do you do?" I said, as I finished pinning my name tag onto the left side of my jacket.

"You aren't supposed to take your uniform home," she said.

"*Ah so desu ka*! Thanks for the information. I had to take it home to—fix a button." I'd taken both suits home because I needed to sew my equipment into each outfit, one listening device per jacket cuff. I had also sewn my tiny drill and a tube of putty into the jacket lapels. My aim was to always have my equipment handy, because purses weren't allowed on the sales floor.

"Ono-san can do the alterations. But usually, there is no need. Why did you burst a button—did you eat too much at lunch?" The saleswoman looked me over with a superior smile, that of a *sempai*—a senior student.

"I must have. The curry rice in the cafeteria is really delicious." I was aiming for a laugh, but my comment was met with dead silence. "Oh, I'm sorry. I know nothing, this is my first real day." I now shifted into the role of *kohai*—junior student. Now a second girl came over to look at me; she had a perfect pageboy and a cupid's-bow mouth painted a perfect pale pink. I was suddenly conscious that I had no lipstick on, because I'd left the correct choice from Dora's salon at the apartment.

"Didn't someone talk to you about your hair?" the second girl asked.

"What about my hair?" I shifted over to the mirror to take a look. I had carefully blown dry the style Dora had cut for me just a week and a half earlier. It looked fine.

"There are color rules at Mitsutan. You can't have hair that's too light."

It was true that Mrs. Ono had pulled out a sheet of cardboard which had five little colored swatches of synthetic hair on it, ranging from the blackest black to a subtle red-tinted dark brown, just like the color Dora had mixed for me.

"Thanks for the warning, but nobody has remarked on my hair so far." I prepared to exit; I didn't want to spend another minute with these sadists. Next time I was going to choose a locker as far away as possible.

"Maybe you colored it last night? Looks like an at-home job." There was undisguised malice in the girl's laughter, and I wondered what she would scrutinize next. I hoped not my eye makeup, which I'd spent half an hour on in the apartment bathroom that morning.

"Thanks for your welcome," I said. "But I must be joining my class." In fact, I'd seen another one of the girls in our freshman group glance over at what was happening to me before she slipped out the locker room door.

Out on the main floor, I tried to push away the sense of awkwardness the girls had worked so hard to instill in me. Hazing was a fact of life in Japan, from elementary school onward. I should have expected it to happen in the store as well, but still—in such a mannered world—it came as a shock.

I stood silently with the women from my training group as the personnel director who'd interviewed me, Miss Aoki, spoke. "You are lucky, for today the *cho-rei* will be led by our *shacho*, Mitsuyama-san. Hush, it's time to listen now."

For a moment I started in confusion, because the voice booming over the speaker system was strong and youthful, not thin and wavering like that of the old gentleman I'd seen the day before. Then I remembered that Chairman Masahiro Mitsuyama's only child, Enobu Mitsuyama, had become the store's chief operating officer three years earlier. And on my first day, he'd lead the *cho-rei*.

"Today is the first day of the rest of your life." A dramatic pause. "It's an old piece of wisdom that I came across recently, while reading. I thought about it for a while, and how in retail it's also true, especially at this store. Kindly allow me to explain."

I listened closely as Enobu Mitsuyama's lecture continued to describe the great responsibility to treat all those who came into the store with respect, for it was they who truly paid our salaries.

"What can we do to extend life?" Enobu Mitsuyama asked, then answered himself. "Work beyond the best of one's abilities. Reach out to help a colleague in need. Remember to counsel one's family and friends to think of Mitsutan as the best place to fulfill their shopping needs. Shop here yourself."

There was a pause. "As you know, our employee discount is ten percent, standard for the industry. Now, we are proud to announce a new initiative—a fifteen percent discount, available to all store employees who shop using their Mitsutan credit card."

Excitement rippled through the women around me. Fifteen percent!

"As part of the process, we will phase out the point cards used in the past, whereby one pays cash for an item and has the points recorded. Credit is much more convenient, I'm sure you will find. I am delighted to offer this gift to you. It is my personal gesture of thanks for your hard work and loyalty."

As the words died away, people around me sank into deep bows, and I joined them, realizing belatedly that Enobu Mitsuyama was on the premises—in fact, walking down the aisle toward the front of the store, where we were. He was a tall, good-looking man somewhere in his thirties, with a strong gaze; a full head of black hair, cut modishly short; and a black-and-charcoal-pinstripe suit. I had to hand it to him; increasing the employee discount would obviously encourage the sales staff to buy, especially the young women who still lived with their parents and thus had no food and housing expenses. And a rise in the use of credit would enrich Mitsutan's private banking division; most Japanese used cash, not credit, so this was a clever way to encourage borrowing among people who hated to borrow money.

"It's the big moment; time to report to your departments," Miss Aoki said after *cho-rei* was officially over and all the employees had left the aisles for their workstations. "Please hurry, because in five minutes the store doors open. You must not be late!"

I nodded, and hurried up the escalator to level four. The K Team office was adjacent to the cashier's station here, on a floor devoted to middle-aged women's fashion. Not my ideal fashion scene—but highly convenient for the bulk of K Team's customers, foreign women accompanying their executive husbands on business trips to Japan. Quickly, I passed the "Rose" section devoted to fuller-sized fashion—garments that were even more fully cut than the size L suit I wore, but with labels that were more discreet—sizes like 0, 1, 2 and 3. Then it was "Daisy," the section for small sizes—women under four feet ten inches, and generally less than ninety-five pounds. I passed the coat section and the formal suit section, tracking along the path to a sign hanging from the ceiling with both a dollar symbol and a yen symbol. There, just as Miss Aoki had said, was a glass door marked K Team, and an office beyond it.

A middle-aged woman who had to be Mrs. Okuma, director of the K Team shopping service, was standing outside the door, eyes set expectantly on the aisle. Next to her, arms folded and looking bored, stood one of the beautiful but mean girls from the locker room—specifically, the one who'd faulted me for taking my uniform home.

As Muzak began pouring over the PA system and a melodious woman's voice began welcoming customers to Mitsutan, the girl narrowed her already catlike eyes at me.

13

"So, you're the English-speaking one. Welcome, Shimoda-san. I am glad to have you with the K Team. I will be your supervisor. My name is Okuma."

Mrs. Okuma bowed slightly, more of a shoulder shrug than anything else, her silver-streaked bouffant hairstyle remaining in place. Lots of hair spray, I guessed; she was heavily made up, and she wore the same black pantsuit as the other women employees. She wore a wedding ring and appeared to be somewhere in her fifties, but didn't look like a typical woman of that age in Japan. She was too thin—thin like Miss Aoki—and she didn't seem relaxed and happy; I could imagine that when a woman worked sixty-hour weeks in a high-pressure environment for over three decades, the situation could wear one out.

However, there was no time for a psychological analysis of my boss. I was faced with my first crisis, whether I should correct her about the mistake she'd made with my name.

Miyo Han—I'd ascertained her identity from the name tag on her uniform—seemed to be watching me for a reaction. I made an extra low bow and said, "I'm honored to meet you, Kakaricho." I was using the word for section head, which I had gathered, after listening to Mr. Fujiwara, was the correct honorific to use. "And please pardon me, my family name is actually Shimura. Shimura Rei."

"Shimura? Are you in the correct department?" Mrs. Okuma's smile remained fixed in place.

"I believe so. I was hired because I can speak English and Spanish." It had seemed strange to me that the boss of the K Team hadn't been the one to interview applicants—everything had been done by the personnel department. So now, here I was, and she was hesitant to accept me.

"Did you bring your paperwork?" Miyo asked in a fake-helpful voice.

"Paperwork?" I repeated.

"Your temporary service contract," Miyo said.

"I'm sorry, I have that at home. I didn't know I needed to bring it today."

"She doesn't need it, Han-san," Mrs. Okuma said. "If she has those language abilities, she must be our employee. Let's not fuss anymore, because some customers are coming."

I couldn't see a customer, but I could see a movement of bows slowly rippling through all the employees stationed in different departments. It was like a more subtle version of the body wave of American sports fans, though the event spurring on the movement was significantly less exciting than a home run. It was the arrival of a trio of Japanese women in their fifties, dressed in good wool coats and holding status handbags. They walked forward, smiling vaguely like royalty at the commoners, and disappeared down the aisle, in search of something other than language assistance from the K Team.

I snapped down into my bow a half second after Miyo Han and Mrs. Okuma. I paused for a fraction longer before coming up, because I wanted to assure Mrs. Okuma that I had the proper humility to work in her department. When I came up, I saw that she was looking troubled.

"There's a lot to learn today." She paused. "You really do speak English, *neh*?"

"*Hai, ossharu tori desu.*" Yes, I answered her as politely as I know how.

"Then why don't you speak it?" Miyo interjected in stilted English.

"What do you want me to say?" I asked her back in English, rapid-fire. "I enjoy speaking English."

The girl's eyes flared, and Mrs. Okuma nodded. "Well, it sounds as if your conversational skills are adequate. I hope you also can use the computer?"

"I learned some basic skills during the training, although I understand K Team work is somewhat different. Mr. Fujiwara said that I would do best if I learned it directly from you."

"I apologize that I cannot teach you much this morning, but Han-san will show you what to do this morning. I need to prepare the agenda for the expansion conference."

"What kind of expansion?" I asked, switching back to Japanese.

"We're opening a new store in Osaka. Both our chairman and our general manager have invited the top-producing departments to the retreat, where we'll talk about how to translate the success of this store to Osaka."

"Oh, that's very impressive. Which other departments are participating in the conference?" I asked.

"Young Fashion and Ladies' Accessories."

I nodded. That sounded right, on the basis of what I'd researched. And if the K Team was truly one of the most profitable—and therefore most suspicious—segments of Mitsutan's business, it was a blessing to be right in the center of it.

"I have a question," I said. "Those departments you mention have a lot of consigners, don't they? Are those vendors treated like part of the Mitsutan team?"

"We all work together for the greater good of the company," Miss Okuma said piously. "And about the consigners, our K Team customers aren't particularly interested. Because these customers are international, they usually already own Vuitton or Fendi bought overseas at a lower price. When they come here, they are looking for Japanese luxuries they cannot find elsewhere. So you will do well to familiarize yourself with store brands, especially traditional goods, first."

"Yes, you may need to work on your Japanese a bit," Miyo said softly as Mrs. Okuma's attention was distracted by a male manager who had appeared in the department. I looked back at Miyo steadily, reminding myself that I was registered as a Japanese employee, not a foreigner. There was no way she could know I was American.

Our tense tête-à-tête was broken up by the arrival of a customer—an Australian woman in her fifties who was looking for a suit for a formal luncheon. I remained silent, watching Miyo handle the transaction, because the cheery hello I'd offered right away in English had been rebuked by Mrs. Okuma, who reminded me that for the time being, I was to shadow them in their work with the customers, not take it on myself.

So I remained quiet as Miyo tripped through a conversation with Mrs. Robinson, asking both her height and her weight. I watched

Mrs. Robinson's face flush with embarrassment as Miyo politely explained that foreign-size people often found a perfect fit in the Rose section. Of course, I thought, but why rub salt into the wound? It was tough enough for me to be identified as size large—I could imagine how a woman six sizes larger than I would feel.

I walked behind Miyo and Mrs. Robinson as we trekked to the Rose section, and Miyo continued her awkward patter of questions about Mrs. Robinson's taste in colors. Mrs. Robinson asked a question about the fiber content of a suit Miyo held up to her, and I could tell Miyo hadn't understood the question, because she didn't answer it. She just talked about the softness of the fabric and its appropriateness for the coming spring months.

As Mrs. Robinson disappeared behind the curtain of the changing room, Miyo said to me in Japanese, "Shimura, did you notice what I'm doing?"

"You're helping guide her choice," I answered, holding myself back from commenting on the fact she was neither speaking to me in *keigo* nor using the honorific that was supposed to come naturally to the Japanese.

"This is a Hanae Mori suit. If you look at the label"—she picked up another suit and showed me a number code—"you'll see that this came in a month ago. It's part of a spring group that needs to sell out. The Rose department manager let me know."

"Really?" I had seen the department manager, a woman who was appropriately stout and of a certain age, wave her hand in a curious way when Miyo had entered the department. It was not a hand motion I'd learned in the Mitsutan etiquette class, where we had been told never to point with an index finger—just to hold out the hand, thumb tucked in, to gesture politely.

"If I sell this suit, the manager will be pleased," Miyo said.

"But what if the customer doesn't"—I broke off as Mrs. Robinson peeked out from the curtain.

"Does this come in a larger size?" Mrs. Robinson asked.

"Get one," Miyo said, and I did.

Fortunately, the size 2 worked, and perhaps the low number made Mrs. Robinson psychologically comfortable, because she decided that yes, the Hanae Mori suit—which cost a whopping 70,000 yen, or $700, would do. Even though, I thought darkly to myself, the flower print did nothing to flatter Mrs. Robinson, who I could have more easily envisioned in something tailored from Eileen Fisher or Liz Claiborne. It was all so new to me—who was I to suggest anything? I felt insecure as Miyo performed a series of bows and thank-yous as gracefully as the etiquette teacher had done in class earlier that week.

Miyo proffered the suit like a papal robe for a salesclerk in the Rose department to wrap, and then she led Mrs. Robinson to a cashier's station, where she took the customer's Mitsutan charge card on a small lacquered tray, bowing profusely again, then handed it to the cashier, who waved the card in front of an electronic reader. This was something I'd noticed earlier about my combination ID and credit card; it had no magnetic strip like the cards I was used to in the United States. Newfangled technology, Mr. Fujiwara had told us; it was more secure for the customer, because she was the only one who received a printed receipt showing the purchase and account number. The reader captured the data and sent it directly into the computer, bypassing the clerk completely.

Miyo sent me back to the Rose department to pick up the shopping bag with the suit, which had been placed in a gift-wrapped box, telling me to meet them back at the K Team, where she'd be issuing Mrs. Robinson's tax refund—a perk available to nonresident foreigners that gave them five percent back on all purchases over 10,000 yen. Mrs. Robinson was a former longtime resident of Japan—that was why she had the Mitsutan charge card—but she was currently based in the United States again and was back visiting, so she was entitled to the refund. The proof she needed was the disembarkation card in her passport, which I saw had several tax rebate slips from other Japanese department stores stapled within.

Miyo placed the rebate—three crisp 1,000-yen notes and a 500-yen coin—on the tray. She bowed as she handed the tray to Mrs. Robinson. "It has truly been a pleasure to serve you."

"The pleasure's been all mine! Really, I adore shopping in Japan." Mrs. Robinson beamed back. She stood up to go, and following Miyo's lead, I bowed and smiled until she was out of sight.

The whole transaction had taken an hour, I realized, looking at my watch. And there were other customers at the K Team desk—a German woman, for whom Mrs. Okuma was issuing a rebate; and an Asian husband and wife who I deduced were Korean, from the language the Mitsutan brochure they were studying was printed in.

"I need a little bit of help," Mrs. Okuma said to us in Japanese. "Can you assist this couple? They want to look for some gifts for colleagues. I suggest the gift department or maybe items from the Tohoku wood products fair."

"Of course," Miyo said, bobbing her head. I smiled at the waiting couple, who I could clearly see had been bored by their wait. As Miyo walked around the desk where they were waiting, the door pushed open and a tall, blue-eyed businessman walked in. "Is this the place where someone can help me?" he asked in Midwestern English.

"Certainly," Miyo answered. "Please make yourself comfortable. I'm delighted to help you."

Mrs. Okuma nodded at me and said in Japanese, "All right, Shimura, we're extremely busy, so this is your chance. Get started with the Koreans, and once Miyo has finished with this new customer, she will join you to finish the transaction."

"I don't speak Korean, I'm sorry—" I was stunned that Miyo, who was half-Korean and reputedly fluent, hadn't taken on the couple, but was turning instead to the person who spoke my native language.

"Do it in English or Japanese, it doesn't matter! It will be all right," Mrs. Okuma assured me.

I took a deep breath and said in slow Japanese to the couple, whose expressions had changed from bored to angry, "I'm sorry for your wait. *Irrashaimase!*"

No reaction. I switched to English. "Welcome to Mitsutan."

A glimmer of recognition. We were off.

It was like the blind leading the blind. My trip to the gift department with Mr. and Mrs. Lee had been a trial by fire, Daniel in the lion's den, and every other cliché you could think of for the situation. A new employee had to find the needle in the haystack that would be just the right present for the Lees to take home to their friends in Seoul. Mrs. Okuma had told me they wouldn't spend much, but on gentle questioning from me, it turned out they were not penny-pinchers. And they didn't want a tea set or bath salts or any of the customary smaller items that were popular with the Japanese as gifts. Eventually, they found themselves enthralled by the linens department, where soft towels were available in a myriad of colors and details. I actually found myself getting excited about the weaves and cotton content of the different towels; ultimately, the Lees selected fifteen thick towels in a rainbow of hues, then followed me to the eighth floor, to buy a suitcase to hold their purchases.

Mrs. Okuma handled the rebate for the Lees, once we'd returned; I hung over her shoulder, trying to learn, and was astonished to see her make a mistake, listing their purchase as 69,000 rather than 60,000. I hesitated a moment before whispering in her ear that the receipt said something different. She just had butterfingers, not criminal intentions, I decided when I saw her fumble over her keyboard a minute later. All in all, my boss struck me as rather confused and disorganized; though that, in itself, was not going to hurt my own purposes.

I couldn't watch Mrs. Okuma any longer after the next customer came in, this time from South Africa. Then there were two separate groups of Germans, who wanted, of all things, to find the Escada collection—as if the selection would be better here than at home. Mrs. Okuma stayed in the K Team office, so it was never left unattended; and Miyo remained as busy as I did circling the store with foreign customers. I noticed she spent a longer time with the customers if they were male and western.

I was given my lunch break after Miyo had taken hers. In the chilly, dank annex building, I took my long-awaited toilet break and then dashed into a side street for a baked sweet potato, which I ate hastily, before running back inside Mitsutan to prowl the store. I had so much to learn about merchandise, not knowing who would wind up at my desk after the break.

I was happy when I landed two Frenchwomen looking for gifts for men; they pooh-poohed the men's handbag collection, because their husbands already carried nice bags, but were very interested in the idea of traditional Japanese game sets. I started them off with a tour of an exhibition of antique Japanese games in Musée Mitsutan on the sixth floor. Despite the slight language gap, I was able to communicate a lot about the games, because I'd studied old Japanese games when I was in the antiques business. We looked at fabulous old wood and stone game sets of *go* and *ban sugoroku* and then examined memory and matching games similar to a modern card game called snap. In old Japan the pieces for these games were exquisite shells painted underneath with the famous sayings that needed to be finished, or verses of haiku poems. By the end of the tour, the women were thrilled to buy handmade lacquered go sets when I led them into the sales area just past all the genuine antiques. Because they had convinced me that they were interested in antiques as well, I gave them directions to a Sunday flea market where I knew that vintage dolls could be bought for a fraction of the usual price. They thanked me profusely and asked me to join them for coffee in one of the restaurants on the eighth floor; regretfully, I declined. Somehow, I had the feeling that socializing with customers during work hours would be frowned on. But back at the K Team office, I was stunned when Mrs. Okuma said that I should have taken them to whichever restaurant they liked.

"You should have gone and put the charge on the house," Mrs. Okuma said. "We have a special fund for cultivating customers. If you had cultivated those customers, they would have certainly returned to this store, and no other."

"I'm sorry. I didn't hear about house charges in the training class—"

"You wouldn't have heard it there; I'm sorry I didn't mention it to you myself. You and Miyo are among the very few salesclerks in the store with that privilege. It's because you deal with foreigners, not regular people."

Many hours later, I had a chance to tell Michael about the customer entertainment fund. He'd gotten excited. "I want you to put it in writing," he said. "Because you didn't get it on tape, I bet."

"No, it was my first day, and I didn't want to attempt anything that could cause notice. But surely—customer entertainment would be a way of draining store finances, not enriching them. Right?"

"Don't know yet. There are many parts to the picture. This employee discount thing you mention—that's interesting, too."

"It gives me a good reason to lurk around the various departments, doesn't it? A zealous interest in shopping."

"Your day starts at nine. When are you through, five or six?"

"Actually, I work till seven. Then there's only an hour or two until closing, depending on what day of the week it is. I stayed until closing tonight, trying to learn more about the different departments."

"If it's not too draining for you, that's a good idea—staying late a few nights per week."

"Okay. The store's really crowded then, so there actually is more cover," I admitted.

"Really? I'd think people would want to go home after a long day in an exhausting Japanese office environment."

"Not if they're female. Office ladies start coming in around six, and they like to meet their friends to get makeovers, eat in the food basement, and get in a bit of shopping before going out that night."

"And you're the same age, which makes things perfect. You'll blend right in." He paused. "You are always prepared, right?"

"Like the proverbial Boy Scout. I'm wearing the full Mata Hari eye makeup, and my tools of destruction are sewn into my two work suits."

"Are you taking the suits home every night?"

"I have to keep them in the locker room," I admitted. "I already got into trouble for taking the suits home. I can't do it again."

"But you've got to keep the bugs with you, not leave them where they could be discovered." Michael paused. "Here's an idea. Bring them in and out of the store not in your jacket, but in another garment that stays on the whole time."

"You mean—my underwear?"

"Yes. I was a little hesitant to spell it out, but that's what I was thinking."

I would have to spend a long time in the ladies' locker room toilet after work, doing a transfer from my suit pocket to the lining of my bra. And I hated the idea of tearing apart my relatively new wardrobe of Japanese lingerie, which really could not be replaced.

"Brooks, will I be reimbursed for these clothing expenses, I mean, if I have to cut up my new Japanese bras, which cost about fifty dollars each?"

Michael had a coughing fit, and I imagined I'd embarrassed him. At the end he said, "You can buy new ones at the store. Save the receipts. And remember, don't under any circumstances leave these garments lying around in the wrong place."

Was there a double entendre in that comment? I wondered as I was drifting off to sleep. Did he think I was likely to jump out of my clothes, now that I was back in my beloved Tokyo?

With my work schedule, flirting with handsome strangers at Salsa Salsa was nothing I had the energy for. And as unhappy as I was about the aridity of my sex life, I couldn't imagine who was going to help me change the situation.

14

By Thursday morning, I couldn't remember why I had ever thought it would be fun to work in a department store. My toes were blistered and my lower back ached. I walked around a lot, trying to concentrate on maintaining the correct posture: tummy sucked in and buttocks clenched. How I longed to run or cycle or lie down—activities my life as a dilettante antiques dealer had permitted throughout the day—and in clothes more comfortable than a poly-cotton pantsuit.

My suit had been worth its weight in gold, though. Early Thursday morning, while I was waiting for a Spanish ballet dancer to try on ten different Comme des Garçons skirts and tops, the area salesclerk had wandered off with another customer to the cashier's station, and I'd had a chance to pull out and plant a listening device right in the mouthpiece of the boutique's central telephone. I was delighted that I'd been able to pull it off.

Michael would also be pleased, because I was getting the first bug in much earlier than we'd expected. I resolved that I would plant devices this way when I was certain that no other employees were around to catch me; and as I became more comfortable with the computer system, I'd be able to work from the K Team desk, planting the spyware that was most likely to collect the information needed. Already, I'd noticed that the three of us were not always in the office at the same time; and with Mrs. Okuma's somewhat scattered attention, I would certainly get my chance.

I still thought, from time to time, about Mrs. Okuma's error the first time I'd watched her: miscalculating the amount of a purchase.

The mistake surely would have been caught by the customers, I thought—almost all of them were aware of the five percent tax rebate. In fact, I couldn't recall that a customer had ever come to us without the passport necessary to obtain this little bonanza. So, I decided, Mrs. Okuma wasn't intentionally cheating anyone. I saw her make plenty of mistakes, of all kinds.

Miyo knew that our boss was an airhead, and clearly took advantage of this. For instance, although both of us were supposed to work a fifty-hour schedule that included most weekend days, Miyo had ensured that she had either a Saturday or a Sunday off for the next month. My weekly days off were to be Tuesday and the half day, Monday—although I did have the forthcoming Saturday free, because if I didn't get the break, I'd be scheduled to work eight days in a row, in violation of the store's labor laws. Already, I had plans for the day; I'd put in my hours listening to audio recordings, then go for a long run through Ueno Park. I could hardly wait.

Miyo had actually complained to Mrs. Okuma about the fact I was working a shorter week; Mrs. Okuma told me privately that in the future, I was to negotiate the schedule with Miyo to find times mutually convenient to both of us. She herself would be spending the weekend at the famous old Okamura Onsen on the Izu Peninsula; it was not for pleasure, but the Mitsutan retreat for top-producing departments she'd mentioned. Mrs. Okuma fretted to us that everything would have to be perfect because the Mitsuyamas would be there—Masahiro, the picky old chairman of the board; and his son, Enobu, the store's general manager.

"I wish I could help you there, be your assistant."

"*Ara*, that wouldn't be a bad idea, to have someone hold my graphs and distribute papers—but Saturday is your time off, and you are scheduled to be here on Sunday, *neh*?"

I nodded. I knew I couldn't switch my days around, not when the person I had to deal with was Miyo Han.

"So, that's our problem. We don't have enough staff," Mrs. Okuma continued. "We had a full group of six employees in the K Team three years ago, but now it looks like three is what we must manage with. So we work together, a little harder."

Reduced staff. I thought about whether this might be a reason Mitsutan's profits were higher these days. If staffing was cut fifty percent in many of the store's departments, the savings would be significant. And from what I'd noticed walking around the other department stores in the Ginza during the day and evening, Mitsutan was no busier than any other place. And while the store dazzled the eye with a seemingly endless array of cosmetics, jewelry, accessories, and clothes, it didn't offer a greater amount of these goods than what I saw at the other stores while walking around on my lunch break.

Despite Mrs. Okuma's talk of teamwork on Thursday morning, she soon left us to go to an administrative meeting in Shinagawa. Shinagawa, a decidedly unglamorous section of town, was where the Mitsutan boardroom was, in a privately owned building that also held offices for the planning department—the group that planned new investments and expansion. It would have been great to bug both the boardroom and the planning department, but I knew I had no credible reason whatsoever to be as far away from the Ginza as Shinagawa. The only way I could get there would be if Mrs. Okuma became attached to me and saw me as a kind of errand girl—something I'd have to cultivate, but it would be difficult with competitive Miyo nearby.

"Han-san, you must be looking forward to your weekend. What are you planning to do?" I asked in *keigo* Japanese after Mrs. Okuma had departed.

"Oh, enjoy some late nights dancing." She looked at me loftily, as if she saw me as the kind of girl who stayed home on weekend evenings.

"Where do you like to go?"

"Gas Panic. Why?"

"Just curious." That was the place where Tyler Farraday had been last seen alive. I wondered if Miyo, with her penchant for English-speaking males, would have known him.

"You're curious about a lot of things, aren't you?" Miyo retorted.

"Isn't it the place where that cute *gaijin* model died?"

"What are you talking about?" Miyo blinked.

"A cute male model. His first name was Tyler. I think he did some work for the store."

"Oh, yes. Tyler Farraday was American, and he was in a photo portfolio of fall men's bags. They pulled it, because he died."

"Did you ever meet him?"

"Well, I saw him a lot around here. He used to come up and try to get shopping help sometimes. But he was *okama*, you know?" She wiggled her hand.

She was using the Japanese word for the rice that has scorched on the bottom of the pot. For reasons that were not obvious to me, it was also a slang expression meaning a gay man. It was a silly word, and belittling—but also mysterious.

"How did you know him?" Miyo looked at me.

"Well, there was a time I was considering modeling as a career, and he gave me a few words of wisdom—"

Miyo interrupted me, sputtering with laughter. "You? Modeling?"

"Of course he discouraged me—I'm simply too short. I decided that since I love clothing, I should try to work inside a department store, though unfortunately I haven't had the advantage of all the experience you've had here. How many years is it again, Miyo-san, eight or ten?" I could dig back just as hard.

"Five," she said crisply. "I would be in retail management by now, if the job wasn't just a year-by-year contract position."

I shot a sideways glance at her. She was frowning. Carefully I said, "Do you believe we're discriminated against?"

"Of course! This is Japan, and you're a half, and I'm a full-blooded Korean, no matter that I'm the second generation in my family born here."

"But there are other contract workers here, one hundred percent Japanese, who are in the same economic situation."

"I understand that, but they don't care." Miyo's voice had an edge to it that went even beyond her usual nastiness.

"Why?"

She looked at me as if I were incredibly stupid. "This is something you do for a little while, and then you get married. Some girls work here entirely because of the discount."

"So do you think the rise in discount percentage is going to be really popular?" I was skillfully, slowly drawing Miyo out, so that when a tall westerner with limpid brown eyes and dark curly hair approached our desks, I was annoyed.

"Irrashaimase!" In one smooth movement, we jumped to our feet and bowed. It was the first time Miyo and I had ever done anything in harmony.

"I'll take him," Miyo murmured, her lips already curving into a smile.

"I'm searching for a present for my daughter," the man announced in a lovely burr. "Do you reckon you could help me find the right size kimono for a six-year-old?"

My gaze shot to his right hand, because that was where the Irish were supposed to wear their wedding rings. There was a silver band there. I saw Miyo looking at it, too.

Miyo said in her stiff English, "What a nice gift. Rei-san knows a lot about kimono." In Japanese she added to me, "Okuma-san asked me to go through a list of all our past customers and telephone the ones who haven't come in lately. I'll work on that here, and why don't you assist our honorable customer."

Miyo had no interest in married men with children, I thought as I led the attractive father up to the seventh floor, where traditional Japanese goods were sold. Miyo was out for someone unattached, someone who could become more than a boyfriend. Figuring out Miyo's psyche cheered me; it made me feel that I had something to use sometime, though I wasn't sure how.

My time looking at kimono with Mr. O'Connell, as he turned out to be called, started off quite well. I learned all about his daughter, a fairy princess of a girl who lived with his wife in Dublin. Together, we chose a lavender kimono patterned with cherry blossoms, because he'd said her favorite colors were purple and pink. Mrs. Ono, the lady who'd been in charge of outfitting the new hires, came out of the nearby alterations department and unsmilingly watched me attempt to choose the correct size.

"Is she about this tall?" I put my hand at my waist.

"No, here." He laid his hand flat in the air, but close enough to my body that it accidentally brushed my breasts. "Sorry." He grinned, and I caught my breath in shock. The touch apparently wasn't accidental; I had my own ideas about what I would have done to the guy if we were outside the department store, but I needed to keep my job.

Mrs. Ono, who was suddenly between us, said, "The average Japanese six-year-old is about as tall as that girl in the corner, looking at the dolls' dresses. Is your daughter about that size?"

I was surprised at the facility of Mrs. Ono's English, and also at the way she'd stepped in to help. When Mr. O'Connell was gone, I thanked her profusely.

"He was trouble, neh." Mrs. Ono's disapproving mouth was pinched as tightly as the pickled plum on the rice Mr. Mitsuyama had decided to spot-check a few days earlier.

"Thank you for taking over with him. I don't know what I would have done if you hadn't been close by."

She nodded. "The other morning, your coworker Han-san mentioned that you have many troubles."

"How so?" I asked apprehensively.

"You found trouble with your uniform and took it home to mend." Her pursed lips dropped into a grievous frown.

How bitchy of Miyo to tattle on me to the alterations czar! "I know it's not supposed to be done, ordinarily, but I know a little about sewing—"

"*Ah so, desu ka,*" Ono said. "That's good. Not many young women know how to sew anymore."

"Well, I need to because I collect vintage—" I'd been about to say kimono, but I remembered that Mrs. Taki had said they were considered dirty and déclassé. "I collect vintage textiles and often must make small repairs by hand."

"Hand sewing. Very good, fine work." Mrs. Ono nodded. "Tell me, what are your plans next Tuesday?"

"It's my day off, actually. I have nothing planned."

"Why don't you come with me to Asakusa for *harikuyo*." Her words sounded more like an order than an invitation; the only problem was that I had no idea what I was being invited to.

"I'm sorry, but I'm so new here I'm not yet familiar with *harikuyo*." How I hoped this was not a simple thing every Japanese woman should know!

"It's got nothing to do with Mitsutan, exactly—it's the broken needle festival, celebrated all over the country." She shook her head. "Of course, the younger generation doesn't necessarily know about it. But if you sew, you should. During this day, all seamstresses bring their worn-out needles to rest peacefully at the temple. There, we will show respect to our needles for their hard work of the last year, and pray for the power and energy to persevere in this new year."

"It sounds remarkable. Yes, I'd love to go." Even though I wasn't a real seamstress, I would take all the spiritual help possible to get through the next few weeks. And I was touched that this prickly older woman had invited me out—she was my first colleague at Mitsutan to do so.

Mrs. Ono nodded, looking satisfied. "Let's meet at the Asakusa Kannon bell at eleven. I recommend that you wear kimono. I'll be wearing mine."

15

The rest of the week sped by. I'd never worked harder, and at night I had no energy left for Tokyo's high life. I supposed that it was just as well. Thursday night, instead of going out with Richard for happy hour, I stayed home to fiddle with the listening station. Despite my having installed a bug at Comme des Garçons, the listening station was not spilling forth conversations about fashion, financial transactions, or even what the salesgirls were going to do that weekend. All I heard was static.

By nine, I was feeling frustrated enough to phone Michael. Seven in the morning in Washington, and he wasn't at home or at the office. Now that I was gone, he was taking it easy, probably breakfasting in bed with the gorgeous blond girlfriend, showing up at the office at nine.

My annoyed thoughts were interrupted by my own phone trilling in the classic Japanese double-beep. I picked it up on the second ring, answering in the higher-pitched voice that I'd adopted since coming to Mitsutan.

There was no sound.

"Brooks?" I asked.

Michael drew in his breath sharply. "You didn't sound like yourself!"

"I guess my cover's becoming reality," I said, realizing that this was the first time I'd spoken English since my embarrassment with Mr. O'Connell. The words came a fraction more slowly, and I realized, for the first time, how sharp-edged English sounded.

"So, what's new?"

"Well, as I e-mailed you earlier, my first device is in place. But I can't seem to pick up any sound on my receiver."

"Really." Michael sounded almost blasé. "And what's the situation at the store right now? Is anyone working?"

"No, the doors closed at eight."

"So what you're hearing is the sound of silence."

"But I'm supposed to be able to hear things that were said *earlier*!"

"Look at the left side of the machine. Is the green light on?"

It turned out that I'd never activated the record feature. Michael told me I could leave it on, or start it up the next morning, before I left for work. I opted to leave it on, because chances were I'd forget the next morning.

"I'm such an amateur," I said.

"Don't feel bad. This is your first experience with devices, and everybody takes a while getting used to them. And it's good you've got the hang of it early. You know, the store's board of directors is probably going to discuss the proposal from Supermart in the next few days."

"How do you know that?"

"Well, I don't really know. I'm guessing it's likely, because a story in the Asian *Wall Street Journal* reported that Jimmy DeLone is veering away from Wako and Mitsukoshi. I'd like you to get a listening device into the Mitsutan boardroom next."

"I'd like to as well. The only problem is that the boardroom is in a privately owned building somewhere in Shinagawa. I can't possibly come up with an excuse to get over there." I paused. "Mrs. Okuma went there today, so she probably will go again sometime. And she's so absentminded, it's possible that I could send a bug over with her and let her leave it there by mistake."

"It's an idea," Michael said. "But they probably clean up papers after each meeting. On the other hand, if you could get a bug on any of the store big shots, say the Mitsuyamas, your idea would work."

"But I can't see how—"

"Be creative."

I thought for a minute, and said, "Maybe I could get close enough to plant something. Masahiro Mitsuyama goes around the food basement, tasting food and raising hell. And it's a crowded environment, I could drop something into his pocket—though there'd be no chance to sew it in."

"He'd find it," Michael said. "You need time to work on his clothing, if you're going for that idea. Does he—or his son, for that matter—tend to take his jacket off?"

"Never," I said. "It's important for them to preserve formality and show how powerful they are. For all I know, those suits never come off until they undress to take their nightly bath—but . . . but . . . hold on." A germ of an idea was growing. "There's a senior management retreat at a hot spring this weekend." I told Michael that Mrs. Okuma was going to the hot spring resort in Izu.

"I have Saturday off. Theoretically, I could hop the bullet train and get down there within a couple of hours. But how could I be there?" I wondered aloud. "I have no reason to follow Mrs. Okuma. I hinted already that I'd like to help her, but she dismissed the idea."

"You don't have to be seen," Michael said. "You spent a week studying how to get around without being noticed. I remember it well."

"The Mitsuyamas wouldn't recognize me, but Mrs. Okuma certainly would. I don't know about the others. What should my story be?"

"Before we run around in circles frustrating ourselves, let's outline whether there even is a logical way to plant a bug down there. You're facing the same challenges you have in Tokyo, except that once you're there, I won't be able to help you much. I've never been to a hot spring; I don't know how they're set up."

"Maybe Okamura Onsen has a website." Already I was tapping the Mac's keyboard, getting into the Japanese Yahoo! site. Bingo. Okamura Onsen came up, with both English and Japanese versions of the page available. I told Michael the web address of the English version, and within a few seconds, the two of us were looking at a picture of the sun setting over a rocky beach.

"Looks like a gorgeous part of Japan. Nice tiled roof on the place, too. But we need to see floor plans. It doesn't look as if there are any."

"There are floor plans on the Japanese-language website," I interrupted Michael. "Hold on, I'll give you the link." I walked him through the picture, telling him which rooms were which. The baths were obvious—they were represented as blue boxes attached to most of the rooms. There was also a communal bath, partly indoors, with the bulk outdoors. The drawing was so detailed I could even see the location of the men's and women's dressing rooms.

"Chances are that at some point in the evening, the men are going to bathe communally," I said. "That's when the real business talk will start."

"So, you're thinking of going for their clothes in the locker room?"

"Too risky. I thought I could circumvent the whole problem by going for their shoes. They'll have to leave them in the *ryokan* entryway. It's just going to be a matter of knowing which shoes belong to whom—and getting a quiet moment, like bath time, to go for it."

"So you're thinking of planting something in the shoes?"

"The heel. That's the easiest, least detectable place."

Michael was quiet for a moment. "I like it. The beauty of it is, they'll keep wearing their shoes. We can pick up conversations for months—maybe even a year."

Suddenly I was alarmed. "The pay is great, and so is the apartment, but . . . I'm not going to have to spend a year working at Mitsutan, am I?"

"Nope. If you can bug the big guys—and we actually get good stuff on tape—I can have you out of Japan within the next month. We'll just have the listening station in your apartment moved to that of another of our colleagues in the area."

"I'll be sure the listening station's working properly," I promised. "I won't make a mistake like leaving the record feature off."

"Don't worry about that," Michael said. "The heel bug is a brilliant idea. But now we have to figure out a good excuse for you to be in Izu, a day and a half from now."

A good excuse. I thought about it for most of the night, but the answer finally came when I was drinking cappuccino the next morning at Giulia's. Unfortunately, I couldn't call Michael right away—I had to go to work. And Friday was projected to be one of the busiest shopping days of the week; I and the other Mitsutan employees were reminded of this again during the morning lecture.

Enobu Mitsuyama, wearing another elegant charcoal-striped suit and polished black brogues, talked about how the end of this week was very important. We would have more office lady shoppers in the time frame from five to eight o'clock in the evening, because they would be killing time in the city before going to nightclubs. This meant they would eat casual dinners in the store's restaurants and from the counters in the food basement; many others would sample free chocolates at the Happy Valentine Chocolate Fair set up on the main floor near Accessories. And as for shopping—well, chocolate was scientifically known to stimulate blood flow and create euphoria, and a shopper in a euphoric state was more likely to stretch herself financially. Cosmetics, Young Fashion, and Accessories were the departments that were expected to double their profits this evening.

"It is our duty to create a state of joy," Enobu Mitsuyama boomed into his microphone as he strolled around the first floor. "We are always smiling, always available with an extra size and a kind compliment for our honored customer."

After we'd dispersed and gone to our workstations, I asked Mrs. Okuma about how we managed to stay so busy in the evening with the pre-nightclub business, when there were so few nightclubs in the Ginza that appealed to young people.

"Is that so?" My boss turned from me to look at Miyo. "I'm afraid I don't know much about nightclubs. Han-san, what do you think?"

"Shibuya has more clubs, yes, but you can reach it on a straight subway connection. It's not a great distance."

Mrs. Okuma said, "I think we're close to many good employers, and that's our advantage. There are some very big companies based around Ginza-dori; they have plenty of office ladies, as well as foreign workers. Which reminds me, Han-san, how are things coming along with the telephone calls to the resident international shoppers?"

Over the last couple of days, in the rare moments when I'd been at my desk instead of out on the floor with customers, I'd watched Miyo working her way through the call list. I'd grown annoyed by the sound of her flirtatious broken English: "Mr. Johnson? This is Miyo Han calling from Mitsutan K Team. It has been a long time. How about coming back to Mitsutan to say hello to me and buy somethings nice for yourself?"

Now Miyo said to Mrs. Okuma, "Since yesterday I've called seventy customers, and several have made shopping appointments. Mr. Martinson agreed to come at noon today to look for a suit."

"Well done, Han-san. Shimura-san, while she's gone you can pick up the rest of the list, starting with the English speakers. Let me explain it to you."

Blessedly, this list was typed in English, because so many of the customers were westerners. The only Japanese reference points were the headings: for example, "place of employment," "number of K

Team visits," "departments of interest," and "sales total to date." I goggled at the amount of money some customers had spent; they were easily earning the five percent thank-you discount. Well, it wouldn't be hard if you had the funds, and you were shown the best that Mitsutan could offer. I myself had spent $600 on clothing as I tooled around the store over my last few lunch breaks—and I had yet to receive my first Mitsutan paycheck to pay for it.

I was glad to be in the office, going over the list, with Mrs. Okuma nearby. I had noticed the folder she was carrying around, labeled "Izu Retreat," and I was ready to make a move toward it the first chance I could get. But in the meantime, I went through the list, noticing the starred names that Miyo had called. Atkinson, Barrett, Chambers, Cudahy . . . almost all of them western, and male. There were many more female customers—but Miyo hadn't bothered with them.

I continued through the list, realizing that there were some names I recognized—people like Winifred Clancy, a snobbish embassy wife who might, potentially, embarrass me with questions about Hugh if she ever came in.

I continued down the column of names and stopped at one I'd never heard before: Melanie Kravitz. I knew the name Kravitz, of course. Warren Kravitz was the banker who had raised the red flag about Mitsutan with Treasury. There were loads of Kravitzes in America, but not so many in Japan. Could this Melanie Kravitz be Warren's wife?

I read through Melanie Kravitz's profile. Native language, English. Employer, Winston Brothers (husband). Departments of interest: designer women's clothing, designer men's, accessories, jewelry, cosmetics, traditional Japanese handicrafts. Number of shopping trips to Mitsutan: sixty-five. Amount spent: 13.5 million yen.

This was Warren's wife, without a doubt. But why had Warren complained to Treasury about Mitsutan if it was a place he liked enough to let his wife spend $135,000 there? I glanced down the list to see the year-to-date spending of other resident international customers. Most of the sales were between $500 and $10,000; a few were in the high five figures; but the Kravitzes were the highest.

I felt my fingers itching to pick up the phone and call Melanie Kravitz; this was one person I'd like to take around. But common sense told me that since she was Mitsutan's number one foreign customer, she'd probably come in spontaneously on her own. I turned a few more pages and came to a printout for client entertainment. I blinked at the sums spent: 20,000 and 30,000 yen per meal. Either Mrs. Okuma and Miyo Han had taken out plenty of customers each time at the store's restaurants or everyone had eaten like a horse, because the prices at Mitsutan weren't outrageous by Japanese standards. In a couple of the in-store cafés that I'd glanced into, a cup of coffee was 600 yen, a little under six dollars; cake was only 400 yen; and a sandwich and soup cost 800 yen. Of course, the fancy Chinese and Japanese restaurants on the dining floor would cost more—maybe this was where they'd taken the customers.

A group of Chinese schoolgirls interrupted my thoughts. They were happy but frantic, with only two hours to shop before their teacher took them down the street to Kabuki-za. They had tiny budgets and huge shopping lists. To my surprise, Mrs. Okuma smilingly offered to take them; but then I remembered that one of her languages was Mandarin. It was amazing to see how smoothly she switched to it. Over her shoulder she said to me, "Don't leave till I come back."

Excellent. I waited till she was out of sight, then slid the folder on the Izu retreat in front of me. I didn't bother trying to decode the kanji on most of the papers, which looked like reports of sales totals. I wanted directions to the hot spring, the agenda for the meeting, and the six pages of graphs and flowcharts relating to the K Team's progress.

Quickly, I photocopied the papers with the directions and agenda, putting the originals back. Then I removed two of the flowchart pages; these would be the "lost" pages. I slid the two pages along with the photocopies of directions into a plastic page protector that I'd tucked into my handbag the night before.

Mrs. Okuma's folder was back where she'd left it just as Miyo Han swung back into the office with a self-satisfied smile.

"Are you finished with Mr. Martinson?" I was determined to keep my normal demeanor, no matter how much she tried to rattle me.

"Yes," she answered shortly.

"But you didn't bring him back here, for the tax rebate?"

"Mr. Martinson doesn't qualify for a tax rebate, because he's a resident alien." Miyo looked at me as if I were the biggest idiot on earth.

"Thanks for reminding me. So I guess all the people in this book can't get a rebate?" I gestured toward the K Team's registry book.

"No, but some of them get discounts, because of the credit card. That's what we always tell them. So, who did you call?"

I hesitated to reply. I'd had just five minutes to myself, and I'd been too busy with covert activity to get to the phone calls.

"Who did you call?" Miyo demanded.

I admitted, "I wasn't sure where I should start, so I wanted to ask you for advice. I'd like to know about the personality of some of these people first."

"Don't waste time on that!" Miyo said sharply. "Customers will be coming in all day, and with Okuma-san so—distracted—over her conference, we have very little time. You'll be busy all day, and I'll have to deal with making more calls on Saturday when you're not working. I am shocked that in all the time I was gone, you have nothing to show for yourself."

Oh, but I did.

I smiled at my rival, then went back to the K Team's book.

16

Saturday morning, I awoke a few minutes before my five o'clock alarm went off.

I was so excited that I actually jumped out of bed. This was the day I was going to breeze down to Izu and fix everything. The night before, I'd stayed up watching television and sewing new pockets into the interior of my brand-new white crinkle-cotton Issey Miyake jacket. Today I was wearing that jacket with stone-colored Agnes B cargo pants I'd bought because of the multiple small pockets, which would handily hide the various pieces of equipment used in bugging shoes. I'd practiced last night, on my own shoes, just to refresh myself, and made a trip to the coffeehouse. Sure enough, when I'd come home and checked the recording running on the transmitter, I'd heard myself, and the clerk who drew my latte, in exquisite detail. I could do it. The only question was whether I'd get the chance.

As I waited in line at the JR booth to buy my ticket to Atami, I mulled over the first challenge: explaining my presence. If I told Mrs. Okuma that I'd received a morning phone call from Miyo mentioning a paper found lying on the floor, Miyo would never support my story. So I came up with something a little shakier: I'd say that at the last minute, the night before, I had found Okuma-san's missing pages and, not knowing how to contact the boss at her home, decided to travel straight to Izu.

No employee would do such a thing, Michael had opined when I'd described my plan to him. A Japanese employee might, I said, reminding him that duty was everything.

The greatest challenge was timing. The retreat activities were to start at noon, which meant that people would be traveling in the morning. To be on the safe side, I took a train from Tokyo Station at six in the morning; it would put me into Izu's biggest transfer city, Atami, at around seven o'clock. With luck, I'd be at the *ryokan* by eight, and things would still be quiet enough there for me to discreetly locate a surveillance position. If I had visual access to the *ryokan*'s entry, the *genkan*, I'd see the Mitsuyama men arrive. In the *genkan*, they'd exchange their shoes for slippers. When the time was right, I'd slip in, remove the shoes for a few minutes to my hiding place, then replace them.

"Theoretically, the missing papers are your insurance policy," Michael had said during our last phone conversation. "You shouldn't try to make yourself known to anyone in the party. Just bring up the papers in a worst-case scenario, if one of the managers spots you."

"But Mrs. Okuma needs the document I have. How can she give a good presentation without it? She's the only female employee there, I'd hate to see her fail in front of all the guys—"

Michael sighed heavily. "If only you were as loyal to me as you are to this boss of two whole days."

"Three—and don't be ridiculous." But it was true; I was starting to feel that I really was part of a team at Mitsutan. I felt a great deal of sympathy for Mrs. Okuma, and I admired the store's general manager, Enobu Mitsuyama, for his ambitious vision and personable style. Mr. Fujiwara, the customer service czar, had been very nice to me; and Mrs. Ono, the alterations director, was turning out to be a surprising ally. It was only Miyo Han who remained a thorn, but I wasn't going to take that personally. All of the K Team interpreters before me had quit, no doubt because of Miyo's fierce sense of competition.

As I boarded the train, carefully putting the ticket away in one of my many pockets, I thought about how I could help Mrs. Okuma yet satisfy Michael's desire for secrecy. If all went well with bugging the shoes and I was able to escape without detection by lunchtime, I'd simply fax Mrs. Okuma the missing pages from a convenience store, or a similar place back in Tokyo, and hope that it wouldn't be too late.

The bullet train tracks ran right past Fujisan—a mountain that, for once, was free of cloud cover. I took this as an auspicious sign, though the bright weather would make my own attempt at concealment, in the garden at Okamura Onsen, a little harder. I stretched back against the soft chair, wishing it were one o'clock and my mission were accomplished. But it was six forty-five in the morning. I had plenty of time to kill.

The train raced close to the rocky black coast, where seagulls circled over the choppy waves. A few fishermen were setting up on the beach, getting ready for a day's work. As we neared towns, the smoke from outdoor baths rose skyward. Normally, these scenes of relaxed country life would have charmed me, but I was too tightly wound to enjoy them.

I disembarked at Atami Station. Here, the local women wore unpretentious warm down coats and sensible boots; but still, each held a Louis Vuitton handbag. I had brought a white nylon Coach backpack, wanting to look like a young vacationer, but because it came from Mitsutan's accessories department, it cost fifty percent more than it would have in the United States. I wished I'd thought ahead and bought one in Washington, but I hadn't known, until I'd reached Tokyo, that this was the backpack of the moment: a must-have, if I wanted to appear like a fashionable twenty-three-year-old.

A shuttle bus to the *ryokan* was available, but to arrive so visibly would wreck my strategy. I drank a can of hot Georgia coffee and studied the map at the station exit, which showed a Prince Hotel half a mile up the river from Okamura Onsen. I'd decided that the Prince was large and anonymous enough to make it the perfect starting point for my expedition.

The taxi ride to the hotel took me away from a city loaded with touristy *kissaten* coffee shops and *pachinko* parlors and deep into the country, through tiny hamlets of tile-roofed houses and wild groves of mikan trees, the delicious, uniquely Japanese tangerines that were famous in Izu. The town of Okamura, with its small stucco houses, had signs everywhere pointing to various spas and hotels. Not many people were about at this hour—I saw only locals cycling or walking to their jobs. At the hotel, a boxy modern spa complex, I paid the 2,000-yen cab fare and stepped inside the hotel to visit the women's restroom. I went out by another entrance, being careful to load my backpack with two liters of water and a bag of salty-sweet *sembei* rice crackers, remembering something Michael had once said about being prepared for surveillance that could go on for hours without breaks for food or drink.

I strolled by the river, which had an English-language sign reading, *Keep a River Clean. Don't Throw the Trash.* Little need to worry, I thought, because there was zero evidence of garbage or any other detritus in the clear stream flowing over black rocks. A fisherman and his son waded through the shallow river, scooping for fish with nets, oblivious of my presence as I continued along a dusty path, river on one side and small vegetable plots planted with cabbage and daikon on the other. A farmer had set out bags of tangerines on a rock, with a little can next to them for payment. I dropped 300 into the can and added three tangerines to my backpack.

A slight bend, and then I saw Okamura Onsen, a stately group of cream-colored stucco villas with beautifully tiled roofs that reminded me of temples. Around them were the gardens full of blooming plum trees and aged storehouse buildings.

When Michael and I had been looking at the *ryokan* website, I'd learned more about it. Okamura Onsen's oldest buildings, the great hall and storage buildings, had been the property of an Edo silk merchant called Nario Okamura. In the 1960s, the Okamura family had sold the land and antiquated buildings to a hotel group who had carefully restored it. With only twenty-five guest rooms, it was a very small inn, not the kind of place you'd expect for a typical corporate retreat, unless the retreat was meant to be very intimate and inner-circle.

From Mrs. Okuma's paperwork, I'd learned about the other Mitsutan executives who'd been invited to this retreat. At the top of the list were Masahiro and Enobu Mitsuyama; Mr. Fujiwara, director of customer service; Mr. Yoshino; and the senior manager of the two floors devoted to Young Fashion, Mr. Kitagawa. I knew everyone except Mr. Kitagawa, though I'd seen him moving through Young Fashion, notebook in one hand and Palm Pilot in the other, taking notes. He was a stylish man, with hair long enough to touch the back of his collar, who wore really good suits—Jil Sander and Giorgio Armani, straight from the rack of what was currently selling in Men's Designer Wear.

Mr. Yoshino, the director of Accessories, was more typical of the store's veteran male managers: a balding man in his fifties who wore conservative suits and thick glasses. He reminded me a little of my Uncle Hiroshi, the banker, so it amused me greatly to think of him poring over designs for handbags and necklaces, figuring out what would sell fabulously for spring.

Mrs. Okuma was the only woman in the group; senior managers

at the store were mostly male. Many women employees left the store when they became mothers. It struck me that I knew Mrs. Okuma was married, because she wore a ring, but I didn't know if she was a parent. Day care was limited in Japan, so I imagined that it would have been very hard for her to work full time while having a child; I decided that she probably was childless.

I wouldn't leave her in the lurch without her papers, I promised myself while settling on the far side of a heavy waterwheel that had been erected in the *ryokan*'s front garden as a decoration. It was the largest thing I could camouflage myself with. Lounging with my back against it, the latest Banana Yoshimoto novel, in Japanese, in hand, I felt that I must be the perfect picture of a relaxed young Japanese tourist. And the position was great, because I could see through the spokes of the wheel to view all the arriving guests.

Things were slow, so I'd text-messaged Michael: IN IZU AND WAITING. ALL SYSTMS GO.

Within minutes, a message had flashed back: SURE U REMBR DRILL?

YESSIR! I answered fliply. IN PANTS PKT ALNG W/EXTRA JST IN CASE.

I WAS REFRNG 2 YR PLNS IN C/O POSSBL SNAFU. ANY QSTNS?

Despite the 8,000 miles between us, I blushed at having so grossly misunderstood the reference. After a pause, I typed back: I'M GDTGO.

I had to be.

The sun was high and I'd been bitten by half a dozen blackflies by the time the Mitsuyama limousine rolled in. I'd already witnessed the arrival of Mrs. Okuma (in the black pumps she always wore to work), Mr. Fujiwara (in tan loafers of indiscriminate origin), and Mr. Kitagawa (in snappy brogues, maybe Paul Smith).

As I'd expected, the boss and heir apparent arrived last. They came in a chauffeured black Mercedes with the kanji characters for "Mitsu-tan" on the passenger doors. Apparently, the Mitsuyamas thought of themselves as royalty.

I peeped over the rim of the waterwheel and focused on the son, Enobu Mitsuyama, who emerged wearing a white polo shirt, white pleated pants, and—once I'd put my camera lens into close-up mode—blindingly white loafers with a gold G firmly affixed to the front. He walked around to the rear, to stand at attention while a black-suited driver opened the door and assisted his father, Masahiro, out of the rear. The conference was taking place over a weekend, yet the elder Mitsuyama had worn a sober dark blue suit and highly polished black wing tips. I wouldn't need to take a photo to identify these shoes in the lineup later on. He would be the first individual out of the thirty-odd people I'd spotted arriving that morning who had worn work shoes to the resort.

The chauffeur hefted the men's bags—Vuitton, the store's best-selling luggage brand—up to the front as Enobu took his father's arm, leading him at a gentle pace toward the door.

But Masahiro Mitsuyama shook off his son's hand. From my hidden position, I smiled at the show of independence. The store's patriarch was staunchly independent, not even allowing his son to treat him like an old man. With that kind of attitude, and on the basis of what I'd noticed in the store, I was looking forward to some lively commentary once the bugs were in place.

17

The problem with long-term surveillance comes down to one thing: the bathroom.

Or, to be more discreet, the honorable hands-washing place. That's where Mrs. Okuma discovered me five hours after my wait in the garden had begun. It was my own fault, because I couldn't hold out any longer.

I'd memorized the *ryokan*'s floor plan, so I'd thought getting in and leaving would be a snap. But that was before I emerged from the toilet, which was a nice one—an electric toilet seat with a built-in bidet wand, and a button you could press to make a constant flushing sound for the ultimate discretion. Maybe it was because I'd been enjoying these privacy features that I hadn't realized there was another person in the restroom: Mrs. Okuma, wearing tweed pants and a matching jacket, washing her hands. She shot a glance at me, nodded, and then looked again—as if she'd realized how incongruous it was that I had infiltrated her company retreat.

"Hello . . . Shimura-san?" Her greeting was partly a question. Well, I did look a little different.

"Okuma-san, hello. I'm sorry to disturb you here, but I've been looking for you everywhere." I spoke loudly, hoping that I sounded urgent rather than scared. I bowed, wondering whether I should start washing my hands now, or wait until the conversation was over.

Mrs. Okuma took a paper towel and began drying her hands. "I'm surprised to see you. Are you on holiday for the day?"

I could say yes, because she didn't seem suspicious, but then she wouldn't get her papers back.

"There's been—I found out—" I stumbled over my words.

"Please, Shimura-san. Why don't you take your time and I'll meet you in the lobby and we can talk there?"

"Yes. But aren't you terribly busy with the conference?" I asked.

"Well, we just finished a seminar and are taking a break before the evening meal."

I looked at my watch. I had been so intent on surveying the scene that I hadn't realized it was already four o'clock. No wonder nature had called me.

"I didn't know. I just hurried from the station, I have something for you—"

"Please, let's talk outside. When you're ready."

Mrs. Okuma was waiting for me in the lobby, which was the grand old reception room of the original Edo period home. The room's walls were supported by heavy wood beams, none of which had been fastened with nails; the floor was tatami, of course, and there was a sunken *irori* fireplace with some cushions around it.

"It's this," I said, opening my bag. "I found something on the floor at work that I thought you needed. Pages from your presentation."

She took the pages I handed her and glanced over them. "Oh, I see. Yes."

"Is it—essential to your presentation?"

"Not exactly; but, yes, they are helpful to have. Where did you find them?"

"I spotted them yesterday evening, when I'd stopped back into the office because I'd forgotten my bag. Miyo had left for the day, so I couldn't ask her for advice. I decided I'd better just bring them!"

She blinked. "You are a hardworking person."

I bowed my head. "Not at all. I didn't get the paper to you in time, I'm afraid—"

"To the contrary. I will speak tomorrow, perhaps. Or perhaps not, depending on what the leaders' plans are."

"Really?"

"So you came all this way, Shimura-san." Mrs. Okuma nodded

approvingly. "I would call that old-fashioned behavior. But you are more of an old-fashioned girl than the others I've hired. More of a *hako-iri-musume*."

She was using a metaphor, girl in a box, which was often applied to describe excessively protected, well-brought-up young women. The term didn't jibe with me at all, except for the fact that my Japanese could lapse into an overly formal mode, something I could blame only on too much time spent with my well-mannered aunt.

"What are your plans now, Shimura-san?"

"I think I'll just go back to Tokyo. I work tomorrow, as you know. But now, since the paper is with you, I can relax." And, I hoped, get my hands on the shoes, when the activity in the lobby quieted down enough that I could enter without being noticed.

"Did you know there is a *rotenburo* here?"

"No," I lied.

"A hot spring bath in a beautiful garden is one of the great pleasures of Izu. I know, why don't we take a bath? I've not had a chance to talk to you about my impressions of your first week. We can do that now."

I blinked. Michael Hendricks had thought it was inappropriate to have a beer after work with me, but Mrs. Okuma thought it perfectly fine to sit together in a hot spring. Naked.

"Thank you, but I couldn't possibly . . ."

"But why not? I really have nothing to do, while the men are at golf."

I thought about it. If I went to the bath with Mrs. Okuma, at least I'd be presenting the appearance that I was a guest with the department store group. And afterward, I could don one of the hotel's *yukata* robes, which would make me look even more natural in the hotel lobby.

"I'd like it. Thank you for the invitation," I said, bowing my head.

"You may go straight ahead to the dressing room, and from there you can find your way into the water. I'll put the papers away in my room, and then I'll join you."

In the empty women's dressing room, I folded my clothes and placed them in a basket, hoping nobody would snoop through it and discover that I had enough tools to be a locksmith in the pocket. I showered and chose a towel from a stack of folded ones on a wooden counter. The towel was only about a foot wide and two feet long—not much surface area, but that was typical of a *tenugui,* or modesty towel, which bathers used to shield their private parts as they entered and left the bath.

Beyond a moon-patterned split cotton *noren* lay the entrance to the bath; it was a damp, warm room paved in granite, with a small section of water from which steam rose. There were a couple of women sitting in this area, but I could see that the roof of the room ended and the bath continued outward, into the open air. I preferred to be outside, rather than claustrophobically close to people I didn't know, so I ventured on and found a place leaning back against a rock support.

The bath was formed in a natural riverbed, so it had an organic, meandering shape; beyond a cluster of scenic rocks topped by a bronze tortoise the bath extended farther than I could see. This was the largest *onsen* I'd ever soaked in, and I found it impressive that so much space was allotted to women.

I lay back in the delicious, naturally hot water, stretching out my legs, thinking that this silky, clean-smelling spring suited me better than the baths I'd been to in Hakone, which smelled strongly of sulfur. This particular spring was rich in potassium, reputedly good for the skin. Perhaps so, but the steamy water was making my elaborate eye makeup run into my eyes. I used a corner of my *tenugui* to clean them off completely. I did it quickly and surreptitiously, because one wasn't supposed to perform any actual cleaning in a public bath.

Mrs. Okuma was taking her time, but I was glad, because I had no idea what I was going to say to her. Dinner started at six—maybe then I'd finally get my chance at the shoes in the entryway. I closed my eyes, letting myself go for a minute. I loved the feeling of the cool February air drifting over my head and shoulders; it kept me from being overheated. And the hot water felt wonderful on my blackfly bites.

I heard an owl hooting somewhere and glanced skyward, looking for it. I saw it fly off with a great beating of wings at the sound of water splashing and men's voices on their side of the bath.

I sank a little deeper under the water, annoyed at the break in the quiet, but knowing that it was inevitable. This was a *ryokan* with twenty-five rooms. Of course other guests would drop in. And I wouldn't have to talk to them, unlike Mrs. Okuma when she joined me.

I listened to the conversation, which was curious—some of the men were speaking very politely, while others spoke in plain-form Japanese.

"Just takes practice. You'll improve." Plain form, older man's voice.

"No, no. I'm really not cut out for golf, I'm afraid." Superpolite, and younger.

I mulled over the voices, wondering if they could belong to the Mitsutan party. After all, some of the men had gone off to play golf. Maybe they were back already. If so, I'd get some excellent eavesdropping, though when Mrs. Okuma joined me, I'd have to pay attention to her.

Two men came wading around the cluster of rocks, directly toward the part of the bath where I was lounging. Quickly, I grabbed the *tenugui* to cover my front as two more men followed them.

"Good evening," old Mr. Mitsuyama said, bowing to me. His flabby upper body drooped with age, decorated only with a few sparse white hairs. I looked away as quickly as I could.

"Good evening," I echoed faintly, contemplating taking a deep breath and swimming underwater all the way back to the indoor bathing area where the women had been peacefully soaking. No wonder I hadn't seen Mrs. Okuma—I'd gone beyond the prescribed point.

"It's very nice to enjoy a warm bath on a cool evening, but isn't it . . ." Mr. Fujiwara waded closer in the waist-high swirling water. "You seem familiar. Were you at the reception desk, earlier?"

"No, I—"

"I know! You were on the trainee tour this week! The one who answered the question correctly about the importance of customer service."

I ducked my head into a bow. "That's so. I apologize for disturbing you, Bucho, I'm going to leave now—"

"I recognize your voice, that unusual *keigo*." Mr. Fujiwara was speaking expansively, and I realized that he was probably drunk.

"A brand-new employee here. My, how surprising!" Mr. Yoshino echoed.

"Wonderful!" Mr. Kitagawa said.

I was surrounded now; the only thing between them and myself was my wet *tenugui*, which barely stretched from my breasts to the top of my thighs.

"Your name again?" Mr. Fujiwara demanded.

"Shimura Rei." I bowed my head. "I'm so sorry about this, Fuji-wara-san, I will excuse myself now—"

"Shimura will not leave without permission!" Masahiro Mit-suyama's voice crackled with the same authority he'd exhibited at the food counter.

What was this? I clutched my *tenugui* closer as the old, wrinkled man waded across to sit on the portion of stone bench that lay be-tween me and the route back to the women's area. The male bathers had placed their *tenugui* in various places; Mr. Yoshino and Mr. Fuji-wara were blessedly covering their own laps, though Mr. Kitagawa had stretched his across his shoulders and Masahiro Mitsuyama was using his to rub his face.

"How was golf?" I asked, trying to break the tension.

"You know we played golf?" Mr. Kitagawa, the young stylish one, laughed lightly.

"I heard from my boss," I said quickly. "Actually, the reason I'm here is I was running an errand for Okuma-san. I was supposed to meet her in the bath, actually, but I think I may have gotten the ladies' location wrong—I've never been to this place, and I'm afraid I just didn't know." I attempted a light laugh; but once it came out, I realized what a mistake it was. They might think that I was enjoying myself, that I was some kind of—entertainer—

"Okuma-san! We should have her join us too, but I'd rather not see her unclothed, *heh, heh!*" Mr. Fujiwara said.

"Kaicho, may I ask who had the lowest golf score?" I asked, as old Mr. Mitsuyama blew his nose in his *tenugui*. I cringed, thinking that I had to figure out plan C, since I'd already whipped through B. What had C been? I hadn't ever imagined this would happen.

"It was Yoshino-san," Mr. Kitagawa said. "Excellent game. As I was saying, I must work hard to improve."

"But you are better at other games," Mr. Yoshino said; and sud-denly, somebody was holding my thigh.

I froze for a second; I had no idea if it was Kitagawa or Yoshino, because they were both on my right, and I was steadfastly refusing to look below the clear water's surface for fear of seeing things even uglier than their facial expressions.

I had to get away, whether or not I would lose my job at Mitsutan. But now, the path back to the curtain, and the area behind it where women had been, was obstructed by Masahiro Mitsuyama. I would run into his body if I tried to get out, staying in the water. The only escape was to jump out to the rocky surface surrounding the bath and make my way back to the dressing room, completely exposed.

Better sooner than later. I turned away from them and, using my arms, hoisted myself out of the bath; once I was clear enough to have a knee on the stone surface surrounding the bath, I grabbed at my *tenugui* with one hand to make sure my hips were covered. I refused to worry about the rest of me. I knew that my breasts were completely average for a Japanese, nothing that they hadn't seen before.

"Shimura-san, please don't go," someone pleaded, while several of them laughed and applauded.

I had risen out of a crouch and was standing up straight, catching a few drops of water glistening on the pearl ring in my belly. I turned and faced them with a posture as straight as if I'd been in my Mitsutan uniform. That was what I was told myself: my skin was my armor. They couldn't see through it.

"It's a bit like one of the vendors said in the food basement the other day," I said with the cool, closed-lips smile that I'd learned from Miyo. "You can look, but don't touch." The tempura chef had actually said something a lot milder, but who cared about manners and accuracy at a time like this?

I walked off, abs tight and head high, feeling the eyes. And something had changed; I wasn't even cold as I walked back wet and unclothed to the curtain, which I lifted gently to one side so I could pass through. I'd done my best, with dignity. They'd hoped to humiliate me, but I'd won.

18

Mrs. Okuma wasn't in the women's dressing room. A brief thought flashed through my mind that she'd set me up to run into the men, but I dismissed it almost immediately. She was no more devious than she was organized. I dressed quickly, slipping on my watch last. Six o'clock. The men would linger in the bath a while longer, I expected, hashing over the incident. I'd bought myself a little extra time.

The passage to the banquet rooms—and there were many rooms, because at a *ryokan* people generally dined only with their traveling companions—was down a hallway to the right of the dressing rooms. I could imagine the men perhaps wearing their robes to dinner, although that might make Mrs. Okuma feel uncomfortable. I wondered if the golf game was a lie they'd told her, so they could just hang out alone together.

Where was she? I thought about that again as I went confidently into the reception area of the hotel, walking as if I had a right to be there. I sat on a low cushion by the sunken fireplace, acting as if I were awaiting someone. I could clearly see Masahiro Mitsuyama's brogues and his son's loafers resting with their toes turned out, ready to go. My shoes were there, facing outward, as if one of the clerks had come along and straightened them for me.

I had wanted to bug all five men's shoes, but my Coach backpack could handle only two pairs, so I went for the main players. It took me twenty seconds of precious time to wrestle Enobu's Gucci loafers and Masahiro's wing tips into the backpack and then shoot outside to my spot behind the waterwheel. The rapidly darkening sky was excellent for privacy, but a challenge in terms of seeing what needed to be done with the shoes. Fortunately, I had a flashlight attachment on my key chain, which I used, in the shelter of my elbow, as I set about examining the heel of Masahiro Mitsuyama's left shoe.

First on the agenda was prying up the U-shaped rubber heel protector. It came off with a flat, spatula-like tool, and I found that the underlying heel was made of a synthetic material—an easy place for my tiny battery-powered screwdriver to drill a quarter-inch diameter hole and slip the bug in, after making sure it was switched on. Then I selected, from a small case I'd been carrying in one of my leg pockets, some black putty that matched the color of the synthetic heel. I filled up the part of the heel that was now open, and nailed the protective heel covering back on. Perfect. Michael had told me that one microphone in one heel was enough to pick up sound.

I'd spent five minutes, total, on the first shoe. I was confident I'd be even faster on Enobu Matsuyama's heel, but after I'd turned his shoe over, my hopes were dashed. This loafer was more expensively made than his father's shoe, so it was going to be trickier to penetrate. The heel was shorter—giving me less room within for the bug—and both the heel and the sole were covered with nailed-down leather, not glued-on rubber, with a horseshoe-shaped metal tap. I worked gently with a nail puller to remove the tap and then the heel covering. It was frustrating; I knew I should work as fast as possible, but if in my haste I tore the heel's cover, it would be noticed. I had a few extra heel covers with me, just in case I needed to make a replacement; but everything in my bag was standard black, dark brown, or white. I didn't have one in the corresponding toast-colored leather.

Finally, I had it open; now the challenge was to drill. A couple had walked into the garden to lean against the waterwheel for a kiss. I waited impatiently for them to leave so that I could use the drill, which was as audible as an electric toothbrush. I remained motionless as the kiss went on, the woman giggling as the man shifted his weight over her.

After my own months of celibacy, being witness to someone's passion felt unseemly, although I now understood that exhibitionism was the way of the world. I thought about my own behavior, the way I'd gotten out of the bath—a snap decision that I thought I had made entirely for my own safety. But as I thought it over, I had to admit that having all the visual attention had not been as humiliating as I'd expected. In fact, I was slightly stoked by the whole event.

I shook myself. I didn't like to think of myself as a narcissist, but maybe I had become one, without even noticing. Perhaps the reason Michael had nicknamed me Sis had more to do with the character out of Greek mythology, Narcissus, who lost track of time staring at his reflection in a pool of water. I'd been looking at myself in mirrors a lot lately, checking my makeup. Obviously, the habit had gone too far.

There was no doubt that my naked boldness could have repercussions. I could be fired on a trumped-up charge. I didn't know whether Masahiro Mitsuyama would take seriously what had happened, but Mr. Fujiwara was Mrs. Okuma's boss, so he could easily force her to fire me. It all depended on how the men had decided to regard the experience. Japan had a cultural history of communal bathing—men, women and children together. The tradition continued, though usually the bath was just for the immediate family, at home.

Things between the lovers were getting hotter. The man was slowly edging the woman around the edge of the wheel, toward greater darkness. For all I knew, they were going to try to consummate their passion against my hideout. Feeling faint, I began to slowly gather up the shoes and tools in the bag and edge backward. I couldn't help rustling as I squeezed my way under a stand of camellias.

"What's was that?" the woman whispered to the man.

"Nothing," he muttered thickly.

"I think someone's out here!" She pulled herself together hastily and began to trek back to the inn's driveway, her high heels making squishy noises in the wet grass until she reached the stone path. The man grunted, clearly frustrated, and after rearranging his clothing, stalked after her.

Well, they had a room where they could finish their business. I didn't feel sorry for being Agent Interruptus.

It took me only five minutes more to finish the shoe bug for Enobu Mitsuyama. I drew closer to the *genkan* and waited to return the shoes until the clerk at the front desk went to the restroom. So my job was done. All I had to do now was pray that sound would come through—something I'd learn for sure on Monday, when the men were back at work, and in the proper radius of the listening post.

Owing to a combination of stress and exhaustion, I fell asleep a few minutes after boarding the bullet train back to Tokyo. Few things are as sleep-inducing as a quiet, smooth, fast train, and I had to be physically awakened at Tokyo Station by one of the car's attendants. Feeling foolish, I stumbled through Tokyo Station and caught the Hibiya line back to Hiroo. I went out at the station, past the Kobeya bakery and a beauty salon advertising "Lovely Hair and Meke." I would probably want to go there, sooner than later, to keep up my strict grooming, but not tonight: I was headed home, to finally curl up in bed.

I unlocked the apartment door. This evening—just as I'd done every evening since I'd arrived in Japan—I turned off the security alarm, and checked the monitor tucked behind the false back of a kitchen cabinet, which had a flashing green light. All systems safe, but I still had to inspect the room's electric outlets and telephones, using a couple of handheld devices, just to be sure. Everything was good to go, as Michael would say. I was so tired that I just wanted to flop between the sheets, but there was a message light blinking on the answering machine.

The answering machine was in the apartment, to make it look like a normal home, although the machine itself was a bit of a risk, because anyone who penetrated the apartment and listened to messages would learn plenty. Therefore, Michael never left recorded messages for me on the house phone; he left cryptic text messages only on my cell. But apparently Mrs. Taki hadn't been clued in on this security proceeding, because she'd blithely left a message requesting that I buy her a Shizuko Natsuki novel she couldn't find in the United States. She'd apparently checked on the Internet and found that there was a copy in Mitsutan's book department, so picking it up wouldn't be too much of an effort. She'd be happy to refund me the cost of the book and postage, when I returned.

I rolled my eyes, glad at least that the message was innocuous and that she'd spoken in Japanese, not English. After erasing the message, I settled down to more serious business; setting up the listening station to turn on two channels, which I hoped would gather sound recordings of conversation from Masahiro and Enobu Mitsuyama.

I flipped up the control panel of the dishwasher to get to the hidden panel that held the listening station. It was an ingenious hiding place, but a bit irritating because it meant that I couldn't actually use the dishwasher and had to wash everything by hand.

Tonight, the light for the listening stations blinked white, which meant that recordings had been made. I could fast-forward until the light blinked green, meaning that I'd reached a chunk of recorded conversation, or some other significant noise. The first recording I listened to was from the device I'd left inside the department telephone in Accessories. The conversations seemed mundane to me: a salesclerk, Miss Oita, had called up to the Yves St. Laurent department, alerting its sales manager that a certain customer was headed for the department—a very good customer, who'd just bought the new Vuitton purse with cherries on it and would be in the market for clothes that went well with it. Very smart, I thought, as I listened to Miss Oita make more calls around the store, advising her colleagues about several big spenders who were still on the premises.

The second recorder had picked up what was going on at the K Team in my absence. A floater had been assigned to help Miyo for the day. Over the recorded phone, I heard this young woman repeatedly call the cashier's office, confused over how to process tax rebates for customers who were shopping without their passports. The answer came back as I'd expected: no can do. The customers, if they returned within the same day with a passport, could get the rebate; but the passport was the essential proof of their temporary status in Japan. The girl whimpered a bit about being afraid of offending the customer, but the cashier's office was firm.

I also heard Miyo Han on the phone, calling her friends in other departments to complain about how this was the fifth Saturday she had been made to work in three months, and it was totally unjust. Miyo also made a few calls to the K Team's clients, trying to coax them in. The ones Miyo phoned were, of course, all male. One shouted at her for waking him up before noon on a Saturday morning; another agreed, somewhat wearily, to a shopping appointment the following week.

As I was listening to Miyo's halting English, the sound of another voice came clearly from position nine on the listening board. One of the shoe bugs, I realized in excitement. One of the Mitsuyamas actually had put on his street shoes and was talking to somebody, despite the fact that it was eleven o'clock at night. I was hearing it live, something I shouldn't have been able to do, because the shoe bugs were too far away from Tokyo—the plan had been for me to be able to hear them later on, when they were back in the city, within fifteen miles of the listening station.

I switched off position three and cranked up the volume on position nine.

"What's the report?" The speaker's voice was gruff, obviously that of Masahiro Mitsuyama.

Mumble, mumble. The other person speaking wasn't close enough to Masahiro Mitsuyama's shoe for the shoe microphone to record the sound clearly.

"Where are you?" Masahiro Mitsuyama spoke in the powerful plain-form Japanese I had heard everywhere—from the Mitsuyama basement to the mineral bath.

More silence, then a reply. "That's not enough. How many times have I told you to take charge? Every time you've failed! What are you, stupid? I should never have given you the power I did."

Maybe he was talking to an underling, or to his son. Although if it was his son, Enobu, the Gucci loafers were not in use. Perhaps Enobu was wearing another pair of shoes, or Masahiro was standing on the stone entryway and his son was still up on the tatami mats.

"You do what needs to be done, or you'll be erased."

Pause.

"I won't tolerate any more excuses or pleas. The situation has too much of a risk, and it's got to—"

There was no more recorded sound after that. I stayed by the listening station for a good hour longer, waiting for more talk, but none came. So I played back the tape again and again, to make sure I understood what had been said.

The big boss had used a verb I'd learned years ago as a student of Japanese. *Kesu* meant "to erase." In the most literal context, it meant cleaning up a chalkboard. But I'd heard it used as slang, and in slang it also meant "kill."

Erase. It was a horrible verb that made me feel sickened and desperate, because I didn't know the identity of the person on the receiving end of the conversation. And to my ear, it sounded as if Masahiro Mitsuyama had been threatening murder.

19

It was midnight now, ten in the morning in Washington. Michael was not at home, but he picked up his cell phone after a few rings. He shouted a greeting over the background of what sounded like cheers.

"You should have called in hours ago! Didn't you catch all the messages I left on your cell?" Michael demanded after I'd identified myself.

"Sorry, I didn't check for a few hours because getting the job done was rather—tricky. But it's all systems go with the listening station, which is why I'm calling—"

"Super. Well, we can talk about the details when I'm out of this circus—"

"Yeah, I was trying to find out where you are."

"Just like I told you, at the circus. Ringling Brothers came to D.C. I'm on a Big Brothers field trip with Jamal. You remember him, right?"

Jamal was a ten-year-old boy whom Michael was mentoring. I'd never met him, but a few times in the office, I'd overheard Michael talking on the phone about reporting to a youth center for some activity or other.

"I do. I hope you have fun at—at the circus—but I need to talk to you ASAP."

"Are you safe?" His voice changed timbre.

"Of course. But I think someone else—isn't."

"Rei, I wish we could talk now, but I won't be in Virginia for hours. By the time I get in, you'll be asleep."

"No, I'll probably be at Mitsutan, and I can't possibly use the phone to chat with you there," I said glumly.

"I wish I could walk out now, but I can't." Michael sounded as frustrated as I felt. "Just call me when you're done with work. I don't care if you wake me up, I want to hear what's going on."

I went to bed after that, sleeping until the brutal alarm clock roused me at eight. Still, I lingered, not getting out of the bed until eight twenty-five. No time to shower; I patted ineffectively at the great bags under my eyes with a Shiseido under-eye toner, which brought things down slightly, so I could cover up what was left with concealer. I realized that I'd discovered the cure for jet lag; it was a mixture of adrenaline and exhaustion. If you could bottle it, the stuff would outsell melatonin.

Try as I might, I couldn't stop brooding about what I'd heard the previous night—the murder threat. The worst part was that I had no idea whose life was at stake. I could only hope that the intended victim was not Mrs. Okuma, who had vanished for absolutely no reason just a few hours before that scary conversation.

The doors to the subway train that I'd wanted to catch closed just as I was sprinting down the steps to the platform, and since it was Sunday, this meant I'd wait seven minutes till the next train. A short time, in the scheme of things, but enough of a lapse for me to arrive at the Mitsutan locker room around nine-twenty, not at five minutes to nine. And this meant, no matter how quickly I tried to change into my uniform in the locker room, I might actually be late.

"Demerit," said the self-important chief of security to me when I attempted to enter the store's back entrance.

"Are you sure? My watch says nine-thirty." Once the words left my mouth, I regretted them. I should have just apologized.

"The instructions are to be in place on the main floor at nine-thirty." He swiped the employee card I had to show when starting my shift. It recorded the start of working time, for purposes of payroll and, I realized now, punishment.

I slipped into the back of a group of workers standing at attention. The good-morning music had already been played, and the weekend manager, a man called Yasuda-san, was talking about the slow start to chocolate sales, despite the teddy bear advertising campaign: how it might be a reflection of a decline in women's feeling duty-bound to buy chocolates for their male coworkers.

I thought to myself about why the store didn't try to get the men shoppers to buy chocolate for themselves. Perhaps because it was emasculating for a man to choose sweets himself. Valentine's Day was about women pleasing men. White Day, which came a month later, was supposed to be the payback; the man you'd given chocolate to would give you something sweet and white in return. If Michael had been Japanese, I would have had to buy him chocolate. And with his sweet tooth, he would have adored it, though he could never admit it.

What would be the best chocolate for his particular taste? Jean Paul Hevin, or something else—

I shook myself out of my fantasy. Someone was about to die. That was all I needed to think about.

Sunday, the biggest shopping day of the week in Japan, forced a different rhythm in the K Team's office. Because it was a Sunday, the foreign customers tended to be bona fide residents, rather than tourists, so few people came in for tax rebates. This was a day when more couples and families shopped, and there was less need for interpretive services.

Miss Ota, the salesclerk who'd been on with Miyo the day before, was on duty today at the K Team's office with me. She seemed hesitant to speak to me beyond saying hello, but I expected that this was because she'd heard bad things from Miyo. I tried to make friendly conversation in between taking people upstairs to buy kimono or toys or shoes, but it was no use.

By the day's end, I was in need of something to take away the bad taste in my mouth. On my break, I'd gone down to the food floor and found some tempura to carry over and eat in the cafeteria, but it had been cold and limp by the time I'd gotten there. I held off from eating any of the chocolates. Instead, I went home and made a cup of cocoa from a tin of Schaffenberger I'd bought at Meidi-ya. With my mouth pleasantly full of the round, dark taste of seventy percent chocolate, I placed the return call to Michael. He picked up, then told me to hang on because he was going to turn on his tape recorder.

"So you're bugging me?" I asked, feeling the words suddenly stick in my throat.

"You are agreeing to be recorded. I want to have a record of every-thing you're going to say, because you said it was a dangerous situation?" He cut off his own question with a yawn, reminding me that it was six in the morning in Washington. "But don't let me put words in your mouth. Tell me what's going on."

I told him how the receiver had crackled to life with the voice of Masahiro Matsuyama; how it meant that the boss had actually left the retreat and had come back to Tokyo to phone a threat to someone.

"I shouldn't have heard it," I said at the end. "If he needed to talk to someone on the phone, surely he would have done it from the retreat and I wouldn't have heard anything. But for some reason, he came back."

"Maybe he couldn't because the inn was in a dead zone. There are mountains around it—I remember seeing that on the *ryokan* website."

"Yes, that's right. But I can't understand why he went so far back to make the call."

"Don't worry about that," Michael said. "We have relay stations in different areas capable of picking up signals that would then trans-mit back to your post. He could have been near a station that one of our guys set up in the past."

"And where's that relay station, exactly? On the Izu Peninsula or more toward Yokohama—"

"Let's not get into specifics now. Just tell me who you think he was talking with."

I flushed, thinking that of course Michael wouldn't divulge the lo-cation of listening stations, even on a telephone line that was secure. "I have no idea. But the words—the words were so severe, about erasing someone—"

"Can you repeat what you remember hearing in Japanese, verba-tim?"

"Sure, but, Brooks, I don't know that you'll understand it—"

"Someone else will."

Mrs. Taki would. Now I understood why he wanted a tape of my account. I told him, as closely as I could remember, what Mr. Mit-suyama had said about asking for a report, then criticizing the person on the other end for not using power well enough, and then finally, making the threat of erasure.

At the end of everything, Michael said, "Thank you. You've done just what I hoped you would."

"The thing is—I don't want to set it up like he's a criminal if he's not. There's another context to erasure that I'm sure Mrs. Taki will mention to you."

"What do you mean?"

"Well, an employee could say to another, 'If I don't get that report finished today and on the boss's desk, I'll be erased.' It can mean that you're just in trouble."

"Passive condition," Michael said. "You just spoke now about being erased, rather than erasing."

I nodded, then remembered he couldn't see me. We'd been talking so intently that I could almost picture him stalking around the office with the phone to his ear. But of course, he was at home. "I understand what you're saying. I've mainly heard the verb used in a passive condition."

"Well, e-mail me a file with the transcript. And why don't you also send all the recordings that you have to date."

I hadn't done it yet, but I knew what I was supposed to do. I was supposed to take the microchip out of the listening station, slip it into my cell phone, and save it as an electronic file. Then I was supposed to send the file, from my laptop computer, to OCI.

It was a little bit cumbersome, but it was a secure way to get the data back to the United States. I thought for a minute about what it would be like to go back to Virginia myself—how theoretically, now that I'd planted the bugs, I should be heading home soon.

But I didn't know when the other shoe was going to drop—and that was enough to make me not want to leave.

20

"Where were you? What happened? I was worried!" Mrs. Okuma descended on me upon my arrival in the K Team's office Monday morning, and immediately, half my worries were gone. She was alive and well, and now I owed her an explanation of why I'd vanished from Okamura Onsen.

"I was so embarrassed," I said, and went on to explain that in the dressing room, I'd been questioned about my status by a staff member and told I was not allowed to be in the bath because I wasn't a registered guest—a rule I'd gleaned from the website. "I wish I could have told you, but I was so ashamed of my behavior that I left immediately. I'm so sorry for any inconvenience I caused."

"But there is no need to apologize. You did a great service to bring the information I'd forgotten—I'm sorry I wasn't there to smooth things for you with the inn staff. The fact is, I was a little late arriving to the bath because the store's general manager noticed me and wanted to discuss a business matter."

"Mitsuyama Enobu-san? The *kencho*?"

As she nodded, my stomach sank. Could she have been the person the senior Mitsuyama had been threatening? It had seemed as if Enobu was supposed to be a go-between for his father and someone else.

Miyo Han was listening with a half frown on her face. She was too smart to say anything while Mrs. Okuma was present. But when our boss went off with a Chinese delegation, the cat unsheathed her claws.

"So, you went to the *ryokan* where they were meeting? You actually crashed the meeting?"

"Yes," I said mildly, "I had to take papers that Okuma-san forgot."

"And she asked you to go there? On your day off?"

"No, it was my idea. I just wanted to help—"

"Sesame seed grinder!" Miyo slung the Japanese equivalent of brownnose at me.

"You would have done the same if you found the papers, I'm sure." I tried to keep my voice mild and even. "And how was your free Sunday?"

"Super," she said between her perfectly straight, white, gritted teeth. "Went out with my boyfriend shopping all day long."

"I didn't know you had a boyfriend," I said, thinking about her propensity to troll for gaijin men on the customer list. This reminded me that I needed to know more about Melanie Kravitz; to figure out why, if she spent so much at Mitsutan, her husband had gone to the effort of creating a lot of trouble for the store. Surely there were easier ways to curtail a spendthrift spouse than by shutting down the operation.

"Yeah, he's English. Investment banker," Miyo added.

He had to be a moneyman, if he took someone like Miyo for an all-day shopping trip. Seizing an opportunity, I said, "Lucky you. Speaking of banking, I notice quite a few of the people on the call list have connections to banks. I was thinking about calling an American woman customer, Melanie Kravitz, whose husband, the list says, works at Winston Brothers. Or do you or Mrs. Okuma prefer to work with her?"

She looked at me, that familiar look of suspicion mixed with distaste. "You want to work with her because you noticed she spent the most."

I exhaled, feeling relieved that she hadn't noticed the serious gaffe. "It couldn't be bad to work with someone who likes to spend, could it? But if she's your favorite client, I'll defer to you, of course."

Miyo breathed deeply. "Often it's the two of them together, and there's nothing I can bear less than a shopping couple. I mean, the guys tell their wives they look bad in their clothes, and the women wind up saying things like the guy's suit costs too much money. Couples should shop separately, whenever possible. No matter how much they spend, ultimately—it's just a headache for me."

"So it's okay if I make the call?" I held my breath.

"There's no need. She comes in every two weeks, at least."

In that case, I'd wait.

It was a busy morning. A group of Ecuadorian embassy wives kept me in the food basement most of the morning. I cringed inwardly when I saw Masahiro Mitsuyama making his rounds, this time tasting an apple tart and making clearly audible comments about pastry that was too crumbly. When Masahiro Mitsuyama glanced in my direction, he frowned. He recognized me, I thought in a panic, and attempted to hide myself behind the largest of the Ecuadorians, but he didn't push the issue—he just moved on, an underling scurrying behind him carrying various wrapped boxes of food.

I wondered where Mr. Mitsuyama ate his lunch. Was it with the other executives, in some special room? Or by himself, in the chauffeured car that must have taken him away from the retreat in the dead of night? I hadn't seen Enobu, his son, that day, I realized suddenly. And that was strange. Enobu was always at the morning pep talk, whether he spoke or not.

After the Ecuadorians had learned the name of each of the eighty-nine pastries for sale in the basement, I wearily made my way back to the K Team's office. I could have used some food myself, but store protocol was not to shop alongside your customers.

As I reached the K Team counter, Mrs. Okuma was issuing a cash rebate for an Englishwoman. She didn't acknowledge me until the customer was gone.

"Before you do anything, you need to return some phone calls."

"I'm so sorry! I never told anyone they could make—a personal call to me here."

"The calls aren't from the outside. The first one was Mr. Yoshino of Accessories, and he said it was urgent. And there was a second call from Mr. Kitagawa, from Young Fashion." She looked searchingly at me, and I dropped my gaze. I couldn't possibly confess what had happened.

"I'm sorry," I said, tucking the paper into my pocket.

"Don't delay! When you get requests from other departments, you must answer them immediately. You know how to dial numbers in the annex, don't you? You may use the desk phone."

With a growing sense of dread, I punched in the numbers for Mr. Yoshino's extension. The call, I knew, was being recorded on the equipment at my apartment, so I would have to explain the situation to Michael and Mrs. Taki.

"Excuse me for disturbing you, Bucho-san, it's Shimura Rei," I said, using the honorific title reserved for upper managers. Mr. Yoshino, Mr. Kitagawa, and Mr. Fujiwara were all called *bucho*.

"Ah, Shimura-san, let's see, ah, thank you for returning the call. You must be very busy." Mr. Yoshino was mumbling, and I realized that he was as nervous as I. "The fact of the matter is, I have a matter to discuss with you."

"Oh?"

"Well, why don't you come see me about it? How about this evening? Or if that's not good, lunch?"

Suddenly, I got it. I was not in trouble; I was being asked out. And for a single Japanese woman to date a married man was, unfortunately, a growing trend. There was even a slang word for this type of infidelity—*furin*.

"I'm so sorry, but my responsibilities today are all-consuming."

"Tomorrow, then?"

"My day off, and I won't even be in town."

"Ah, but what about the evening? I know a wonderful little restaurant in Shinjuku, a very quiet, peaceful place."

I swallowed hard. I couldn't slam down the phone or say anything rash, not with Mrs. Okuma sitting next to me. And Mr. Yoshino had the goods on me, which meant he could get me fired if he wanted. "Perhaps later in the week is more convenient. Would that suit Shacho-san?"

He was quiet for a moment, then said, "How about Thursday?"

After I hung up, I noticed that Mrs. Okuma was looking at me curiously. "What did Yoshino-san ask of you?"

"It seems like he wants to talk to me about encouraging my customers to buy a new accessories line. He thought I should stop by during my break hour, but I know we always get a lot of customers on Mondays."

Mrs. Okuma looked at me thoughtfully. "You are a hard worker."

I blushed. If only she knew that my sole achievement, in his eyes, was walking naked.

"Yes," Mrs. Okuma continued. "In your short time here, I have noticed all the extra effort you have made. I have no choice in the employees I get for my department . . . but this time, I feel quite lucky."

Thank God Mrs. Okuma wasn't around when I returned the second call, to Mr. Kitagawa. This time I was tougher—because Mrs. Okuma wasn't listening, and because I suspected that he'd been the one who'd touched my thigh.

"I'm sorry, I don't think my boyfriend would be comfortable with my meeting you outside the office," I said in response to his invitation for a drink that evening at a wine bar located near Hiroo Station.

"Surely, if a senior executive just wished to . . . talk over your employment situation with you . . . he wouldn't object."

What was he suggesting, blackmail? Would he ruin everything, when I was so close to getting the last few bugs planted?

"I can meet you, but it can't be until later on in the week." I didn't want Mr. Yoshino to catch wind that I'd gone out with Mr. Fujiwara during a time I'd said I was busy.

I hung up, with the date set for Wednesday, wondering which evening was going to be worse. If only there was a way I could channel back the power I'd felt when I'd left the *rotenburo* bath and use the situation to my advantage.

Mrs. Okuma was back. "What did Mr. Kitagawa want?"

I thought quickly because, out of the corner of my eye, I saw that Miyo was heading into the office, purse in hand. She'd come back from lunch. "The fact is," I improvised, "it turned out he'd actually spotted me at the retreat on Saturday, and he wanted to know why I was there."

"*Ah so, desu ka.*" Mrs. Okuma's face was grave. "And did you tell him about how you'd traveled so far, at your own expense, because I forgot a document?"

"Not exactly. I did say I was there helping you, but I made it seem like a planned thing, not a crisis."

"How thoughtful of you," Mrs. Okuma said. "You have a good head, *neh*?"

"Rather a lot of strange coincidences," Miyo said when Mrs. Okuma had picked up the telephone and was deep in conversation with a client. "And a lot of sesame seeds ground, as well."

I looked straight at Miyo and said, "Well, the fact is, I like to cook."

I was busy all day, but not too busy to notice, by day's end, the new message sitting squarely in the center of my desk, written in neat kanji by Miyo, who, Mrs. Okuma said, was out on a run around the store with an energy trader from Houston.

Mr. Fujiwara had called and wanted to hear back from me, as soon as possible.

"Oh. I'm sorry I missed that call," I said to Mrs. Okuma, who was looking at me curiously.

"What do you think it's about? I mean, for so many of them to call you today."

"I'm sure it's the same thing the others wanted," I said, before realizing my mistake. I'd made up separate lies for Kitagawa and Yoshino; I would have to remember to keep those stories straight. "Actually, I have no idea. Is it common for store managers to check up on K Team members like this? If so, our department must be awfully valuable—I'll really do my best to make everyone happy—"

"Fujiwara-san usually communicates his orders through me." Mrs. Okuma looked at me thoughtfully. "This certainly is a policy shift, for executives so high to work with a K Team clerk."

Now her approval of me was turning to suspicion. Damn those men for calling me on the K Team phone! I'd have expected them to be more discreet, because that was how Japanese men hoping to engage in *furin* were said to operate, at least if they wanted their liaisons to be successful.

"I'll make the calls back to them on my lunch hour, I think. I don't want to take time away from my work," I said piously.

"But you never had lunch. And it's almost four." Mrs. Okuma still kept her eyes on me. "You should have reminded me."

I took my lunch then, without calling anyone. I went to the annex and tucked myself into a corner table, with a limp iceberg, corn, and cucumber salad in front of me and a can of hot green tea at my side. Smoke from a table nearby drifted over, surrounding me in a stinky fog that exacerbated my misery.

I left the store at seven without returning Mr. Fujiwara's phone call. I told Mrs. Okuma I'd do it on my way home. The truth was that I was sick of answering to male bosses—at this point, I didn't even want to call Michael.

I had to call him, though. He was going to know about the inappropriate interest of the Mitsutan executives as soon as he heard the recordings of the bugged K Team phone. It was my duty to give him advance warning about the trouble I'd inadvertently created for myself, although I couldn't imagine what he could suggest I do to save myself.

No, I thought, he wouldn't tell me to save myself. He didn't think of me as a girl in a box who needed protection from wolfish older men; he thought of me simply as an agent.

I was no longer in the store, so I didn't have to worry about camouflaging my feelings. I boarded the subway slowly, despite the pushing crowd around me. I didn't care; I had finally given in to my painful pinched toes, and the even more painful realization that the first men I'd be dating, after Hugh, were not of my choosing at all.

21

Tuesday morning—my first genuinely free day since starting at Mitsutan—didn't dawn auspiciously. It was dark and rainy. In this weather, I was going to have venture out to borrow a kimono and all the trappings from my aunt in Yokohama, and make it by eleven o'clock to the Broken Needle Memorial Service.

I decided to make my own coffee that morning rather than have it at Giulia's so I'd be able to check in by phone with Michael.

After we'd exchanged greetings, he got down to business. He said that Mrs. Taki had reviewed the tape of what I'd said in Japanese, and the context of "erasing" was not what I'd thought.

"But the general manager wasn't at the store yesterday," I said, after listening to Michael's explanation.

"Did you ask anyone where he might be?"

"No. I didn't want to arouse any suspicions."

"Hmm. I suppose he's likely to be meeting with the staff at another one of Mitsutan's stores. You haven't heard any sound from his bug?"

"That's right. I'm not sure why." I hoped it wasn't because he was dead.

"I'd like to know if he has anything to say about Jimmy DeLone. You know the guy's still in Tokyo?"

"I—I guess so. I haven't been reading the papers." Now I felt embarrassed. Here I was, the agent on foreign soil, and my boss was telling me about a development I should be informing him about.

"Rei, you need to keep up with the news, and fax or e-mail me things of importance. All right?"

"I'm sorry. I will get back on track. But first, there's something I've got to tell you." In as neutral a language as I could muster, given the situation, I told my boss that three of the executives who had been at the retreat were attempting to meet me privately.

"What the hell? What did you do, internationally expose yourself?"

"Well, there was exposure of a sort, but not the kind that you're thinking of." Rather shakily, I explained about following Mrs. Okuma's directions to meet her in the women's section of the *rotenburo*, and the mix-up I'd made by going into an open section, where I was unfortunately joined by Masahiro Mitsuyama, plus Kitagawa, Yoshino, and Fujiwara. I'd been recognized, and I'd beaten a fairly hasty retreat, but not before they'd gotten a glimpse.

"I understand," Michael had answered after a pause. "These are older guys away from home, perhaps already half sloshed. They get a glimpse of you, an attractive junior employee, in a bikini, and they start to fantasize—"

"But I wasn't wearing a bikini. A *rotenburo* is an outdoor bath, not a swimming pool."

"You mean to say . . ." Michael's voice trailed off. "Oh, my God."

"I was naked! They were naked! That's why I got out of the water. If I'd stayed a moment longer, I might have been raped."

Michael had been silent.

"Are you there? Please understand that I did the best I could, under the circumstances."

"I've got to go." Michael's voice was curt.

"What would you suggest that—" But I never finished my sentence. He had hung up, leaving me to stew.

It was eight-thirty, and I really had to get out of the apartment, if I was going to retrieve the kimono from Norie in time. There was a Japanese expression for the way I was feeling: *hari-no-mushiro,* sitting on needles, anxious and uncomfortable.

I picked up the bedside phone and punched in a number I knew by heart, that of my relatives in Yokohama. My aunt Norie was in the process of serving her husband and son their breakfast, but she sounded delighted to hear from me. She promised that after breakfast, she'd open up the *tansu* chest where she kept four dozen kimono neatly stored, and pick a good one for me to wear to the temple. Of course she asked me with whom I was going; I said a few friends, because I couldn't figure out how to mention my connection to Mrs. Ono. Fortunately, my aunt believed the story; she knew I loved folk festivals and temples. She only asked me to pick up some incense for her while I was there.

Hearing my aunt's voice, so normal and warm, made me feel human again. I rolled out of bed; took a shower; and dressed in a warm sweater, jeans, and my favorite black rain shoes. I decided not to do the elaborate eye makeup until later, because it would startle my aunt. She knew nothing about my cover, my job at Mitsutan, or my fancy apartment in Hiroo; she thought I was staying with my old roommate Richard while I was job hunting.

My feet felt great in the flat-bottomed rain shoes, I thought an hour later as I splashed up the hill to my aunt's house in the Minami Makigahara section of Yokohama. If only I could get away with wearing the rain shoes with the kimono, rather than the high-heeled wooden sandals that were de rigueur. My aunt always kept a pair in my size handy, because during my visits one of her favorite things was to take me, properly dressed, to events hosted by her cultured women friends.

"Welcome home, Rei-chan! Won't you please stay for a while?" she said when I'd called my greeting and stepped in through the front door.

"I'm so sorry, but not today, Obasan. I'm meeting someone at Asakusa at eleven." I was already taking off my wet coat and shoes. "What do you think I should wear?"

"Well, I'm sorry to say you can't wear pink anymore—because of your age, you need something *shibui.*" *Shibui* expressed a kind of subtle elegance, which until this point, she'd always said was too old for me. "I was thinking of this lavender and olive silk—it's not too bright, but look at the pattern of wisteria, how delicate it is." She smiled nostalgically. "I wore this to the birth ceremony for Chika."

"Vintage kimono like this are becoming very trendy among young women," I said, fingering the silk moiré with appreciation. It was thick, yet incredibly supple—much better quality than any of the sexy but flimsy silk blouses that I'd been thinking about buying in Young Fashion. Nobody wove silk like this anymore—it was too expensive.

"Well, popular or not, I'm not giving them up to any kimono salesman. Can you imagine, a dealer came through the neighborhood last week, knocking on doors and asking housewives if they had any old kimono to sell? I told him no, thank you. I'm sure the price he'd offer would be even less than what my parents paid thirty years ago."

My aunt took me into a side room, where she drew closed the *shoji* screens and I undressed down to my underwear. The first step was putting on the thin silk socks known as *tabi*, which have a separated big toe, because once I was dressed, with a thick, stiff sash around my middle, I'd be physically unable to lean over and pull the socks on. So I put on the *tabi* first, then a half-slip, then the light cotton under-kimono, then a succession of cotton sashes designed to make my middle as flat as possible, and finally the kimono itself. I knew how to dress myself in a kimono—I'd taken a six-month course—and I could even tie the thirteen-foot obi sash in a fancy bow; but it was much nicer—and quicker—to be helped by my aunt. As she worked, she chatted about whether we should tie a double butterfly bow or something else.

"If it's a date with a man, you should definitely have an extravagant bow," she said leadingly.

Irately, I asked, "What kind of a man goes to a memorial service for sewing needles?"

"A tailor, or perhaps even a fashion designer. I know you enjoy fashion. I noticed that you were wearing a lovely new cardigan today. What's the label?"

"Agnes B," I said.

"You're spending more on your clothes, since I've last seen you." My aunt sounded approving but curious.

"Well, I earned some decent money in the United States before I came over, so I guess I'm treating myself." It was hard to resist clothing at Mitsutan, especially when I had no expenses for food or housing, plus a generous salary paid by the government. I was spending more on clothes than my weekly pay from Mitsutan, that was for certain, but it was part of the character I was supposed to be. It was like a little party, a party that would come to end in a few weeks; I might as well enjoy it, before I returned to my secondhand lifestyle.

And secondhand clothes could be very elegant, if you kept them nicely, as my aunt had preserved the kimono I was wearing. I felt fresh when I set off, holding my uncle's golf umbrella over me. I was wearing a special mauve brocade kimono raincoat—a bag-shaped garment that would protect most of the kimono from the rain, and I'd let Aunt Norie apply light makeup to my face, although she did nothing around the eyes except for covering my under-eye circles and applying light mascara. The goal was to look very natural, to harmonize with the traditional garment. If I had time, I told myself, I'd do the eye makeup on the train. I'd seen lots of women doing things like makeup and eyebrow plucking on the train; it was a strange exhibition of private behavior, given that people were too embarrassed to speak on their cell phones in public places. Perhaps it was because exposure of a person's inner life was considered more dangerous than taming one's eyebrows or cleaning one's teeth.

Ultimately, I decided against redoing the eye makeup on the train. Wearing a kimono was a form of exhibitionism; I saw everyone looking me over, the way people in the West can't help stopping to look at a bride. Women looked because they were interested in the fabric design and the intricacy of the bow; men looked to figure out whether you were a respectable housewife going to a tea ceremony, or a less respectable but more exciting woman working in "hospitality." Elders looked because they were nostalgic; children looked because they were seeing their fairy tales come to life. No matter who you were in Japan, a kimono turned you into a cultural icon, and I wasn't going to ruin my image by fussing with my eyes. I could do it in the women's restroom at Asakusa Station.

I got out at Asakusa, and in the wet, smelly restroom did my eye makeup as quickly as I could; took off the rain shoes; and put on the high, tricky geta. Then I carefully made my way up the stairs and out to the street, where the rain had lessened slightly. Every tenth woman I saw was wearing a kimono—a high proportion, no doubt because of the festival.

Mrs. Ono was already waiting underneath Kaminarimon, the famous bright red gate with a 100-kilogram lantern hanging in its center. To the left were old carved wooden statues of the gods of wind and thunder, who had done a bang-up job with the day so far. As usual, people were taking shelter under the gate's tiled roof, while young tourists relentlessly photographed the gate and each other with digital cameras. I spotted a news crew with a camera, first photographing the scene at the gate and then heading in the direction of

Sensoji Temple. The needle memorial service was a feel-good story that might lead off the night's broadcast, if it turned out to be a slow news day. I made my way to Mrs. Ono, trying to stay away from the camera crew.

"I'm sorry I'm late," I said, though by my watch it was one minute to eleven. "You must be very inconvenienced and tired, waiting here for me all this time."

"It was just a minute. And look how pretty you are in that purple, like a real orchid."

I flushed at the unexpected compliment, which I knew I'd better deflect fast, to show her that I wasn't arrogant. "Oh, it's very old and out of style. But it's a rainy day, so my mother didn't want me to ruin anything of hers that was nice."

Mrs. Ono smiled at that. "I arrived early to make a lunch reservation for us at the pork cutlet place, but unfortunately they are full."

I made a sorrowful face but was inwardly relieved. There was a very famous *katsu-don* restaurant in the area, but I didn't eat meat. "Perhaps we can find another traditional restaurant after the ceremony. There are so many in this area. I know a wonderful place for sushi—"

"Yes, yes, but we are in kimono. We must be careful with the fabric; shoyu stains are almost impossible to remove. By the way, that's an attractive raincoat. Few young women possess the right cover garment." She nodded in approval at the traditional garment Aunt Norie had tied over me.

"Oh, it's quite old. From my mother's closet," I said.

"The old silks are the best. How I'd love to work with those instead of cheap Chinese fabric."

"You could. I mean, I noticed that there are all these little boutiques springing up around the city, where young women are buying old kimono to wear themselves."

"Really?" Her eyes widened with interest.

"Yes," I said. "And since Mitsutan sells some antique furniture and china, it would make sense for the store to get in on this trend. I'd be happy to put together a proposal, if you could put the idea upward in the company."

"I'll think about it," Mrs. Ono said, in a voice that told me she thought the idea would never fly. "Come, it's wet. Let us visit Sensoji, and then we shall have time to talk."

We hurried through Nakamise-dori, the 300-year-old shopping

street, where vendors still sold Japanese goods, and on to Tokyo's oldest temple, founded in the seventh century. The temple's copper tiled roof had been replaced many times, but nevertheless, the current tiles were oxidized to a gorgeous green. A delicious smell of incense wafted out as Mrs. Ono and I managed to find a place on the ground to leave our sandals, and then stepped up on the rain-spotted wooden steps that led to the tatami-floored house of worship.

The floor was heated. That was the only source of warmth in the open-air space packed with women dressed like us, either standing in front of an image of Buddha or kneeling in prayer. There were two large pans of plain white tofu lying in state, studded with what looked like hundreds of pins and needles: sewing pins with colorful ball tops, regular needles with thin eyes, and even hospital syringes, which I fervently hoped weren't used.

Mrs. Ono spoke briefly with the priest, while I bought incense for my aunt and then spent some time studying the needle display, trying to figure out where I could stick the unbroken needle I'd brought with me.

"Are you ready?" she asked me, taking not just one but ten needles out of a strawberry pincushion in her purse. When she saw me look at the needles in awe, she added, "I'm making offerings for the whole alterations department."

"Why is there tofu?" I asked.

"As you know, tofu is very soft. It's easy for the needle to pass through. So it's a good place for us to insert our needles."

"What happens to all of it?" I noticed the priest carrying away one tray, and another ceremoniously kneeling to place a new tray of the soybean curd in its place.

"The priest recites a sutra that expresses a prayer for the needles passing from active life. After that, the tofu is burned."

I paused. "Wouldn't the needles survive the fire?"

"Yes, of course. They are kept in a sacred place in perpetuity. It is like a cremation for a person; here, they receive respect and a peaceful place to rest forever." As Mrs. Ono spoke, she neatly stabbed each needle she'd brought into place. I followed suit with my needle, which slid softly into the tofu.

"Very good. Now I shall pray."

Mrs. Ono knelt before the altar for a long time, her grayish-black head bowed. I had to squeeze in between some other women, because the space was so tight. As I tucked my feet under my thighs in the classic *seiza* position, I thought about the meaning of the day; how interesting it was that in Japan the instruments of work, such as needles, were honored rather than people. No matter how intently the seamstresses and nurses around me were praying, I was sure that their working lives would continue to be tough. I'd been working for only a week at Mitsutan, and already I was exhausted; I could imagine the situation of people like Mrs. Ono, who had spent almost fifty years on a craft. I'd seen how gnarled and rough her fingers were when she'd clasped her hands in prayer.

"Will you be my guest for lunch? Please, I insist," I said twenty minutes later, as we reentered the rainy streets of Asakusa.

"We must take care of our clothing," Mrs. Ono fretted. "I can't imagine what we can safely consume."

After some looking, during which time the rain picked up, we decided that our best bet was a sandwich shop on a lane that ran parallel to Nakamise-dori. It was so warm inside that the windows were steamed up, and the air was rich with the scent of good coffee. We each ordered a lunch set; a set of finger sandwiches, a cup of corn soup, and a cup of tea. It felt odd to me to eat nouvelle western food while wearing a kimono, in a casual restaurant with a television mounted close to the ceiling, but Mrs. Ono ate quietly and zealously.

"Have you had a very busy year in the alterations department? Is this the reason you brought the needles?" I asked.

She shrugged, her small shoulders barely rising under the stiff kimono. "Not especially. These days, there are so many special sections, like Daisy and Rose, for ladies who don't fit into the standard clothing. Not so many alterations for us to do these days, but still, we are employed, and the store continues to profit. I'm quite lucky."

"Is that so?" I had no idea how to judge the high profits that I'd seen reported when I'd glanced at the K Team's computer each day. I kept notes and sent the figures by e-mail to Michael, nevertheless. The OCI wanted numbers; the analysts in Virginia were supposed to be able to understand what they meant.

"Just a minute. The news!" She lifted her chin toward the television, which she was facing. I turned my chair to look, because my obi was so tight that I couldn't twist my body. By the time I turned around, the television was showing a long delivery truck bearing the Mitsutan name surrounded by ambulances and police cars. It was parked in the alley that ran behind Mitsutan—the area I passed through to get to the locker room each morning.

"Oh, it can't be!" Mrs. Ono exclaimed as the film footage showed next the store's general manager, Enobu Mitsuyama, bowing and greeting customers.

"But it is," I said with a growing feeling of dread. "That's our *sha-cho*, Mitsuyama-san."

"Sssh," she said, despite the fact she was the one who'd started talking. Now they were showing another shot of the van, and another Mitsutan employee—a man I didn't recognize, wearing a dark suit, standing at a podium before a crowd of journalists clicking cameras.

I listened as hard as I could, but the din of the lunch customers, plus the fact that Japanese wasn't my first language, made it impossible for me to understand what had already had been said. There was news at Mitsutan, and from what Mrs. Ono had already expressed, it wasn't good.

When the show switched to a commercial, Mrs. Ono turned to me. Her mouth was trembling. "I can hardly believe it. And just after we prayed."

"Is the store being sold? What was the news?" I was tripping over myself to learn what I hadn't been able to understand.

"It's very bad news." She dropped her gaze downward, in the same manner she'd done in the temple. She was praying. After a minute, she spoke again.

"I'm especially sorry for you, Shimura-san. I know that Fujiwara-san was a mentor to you and all the new salespeople who just finished customer training."

"Something happened to Mr. Fujiwara?"

"I'm afraid so. He was found dead in one of our store vans. And the police are saying that he may have been the victim of foul play!"

22

On the way home from Asakusa, I found myself shivering with a mixture of sorrow and fury. It wasn't that I cared at all about Mr. Fujiwara personally—in fact, I had considered him the ringleader in my harassment in the *rotenburo*. But I had known, through my eavesdropping, of a probable murder—and I had not figured out that he was at risk.

But I'd assumed after listening to the conversation that the silent person on the other end of the phone was Masahiro Mitsuyama's son, Enobu. I'd chosen to believe that the tense conversation was a family matter; the *sempai* father talking to his *kohai* son. But of course, Masahiro Mitsuyama would have felt free to rail against anyone in the store.

I needed to tell Michael as soon as possible what had happened. On my subway ride home, I whipped out the cell phone and began patiently pressing the combination of keys that allowed me to text-message in English. It was a cumbersome procedure, but it was the only way. I wrote CUST SERVICE BOSS FUJIWARA MURDRD MOR LATR, then sent it.

I was too strung out and shocked to go all the way to my aunt's house, so I went straight home; took off the kimono by myself; and sat on the edge of the bed in my underwear, still shaking, while the tub filled in the bathroom.

I was no stranger to death, but that didn't make things feel any easier. For the first time, I had actual knowledge of a crime in advance of its occurrence; and if nobody believed me, well, I had the recording on file.

There was something else I had to feel bad about: Mr. Fujiwara's phone call, the one to me that I'd avoided answering. If I had answered, I probably would have found out his plans for the evening, maybe even the person he was going to see.

The call he'd placed to me, however, was a danger in itself. Both Miyo and Mrs. Okuma knew he'd called. Miyo had been the one to give me the handwritten message, with his phone number. Miyo might tell a lot of people; I remembered how quickly she'd ratted on me to Mrs. Ono about my taking my uniform home.

I went into the bathroom, turned off the taps, and sank into the hot water. It was almost too hot, but I felt I deserved to suffer a bit. After a minute, my muscles began to relax, and I slowly traced over everything I remembered about Mr. Fujiwara. He'd been married; I remembered his little story about his wife as a typical housewife shopper. Maybe his wife knew he was after younger women, and she'd gotten revenge. That—or he had been the person being threatened by Masahiro Mitsuyama.

I wondered about all this as I lay back in the bath, fragrant with Hakone bath salts that had been in the vanity, most likely left behind by an earlier spy. It was the nicest leftover I'd found; there were also less savory things, like some dirty sweat socks, an opened box of condoms, and two porn magazines. I decided these things had belonged to Tyler Farraday, not Michael.

The phone hanging on the wall near the toilet rang. I eyed it, wondering if it was Aunt Norie. I'd left her a quick message that because the weather was so bad, I wanted to come to dinner a day later. I hoped she wasn't calling to protest.

I let the phone ring until it stopped, and then it began ringing again. Growing weary of the noise, I stood up in the tub, reached for the cordless receiver, and clicked it on.

"I got your message," Michael said. "Can you talk?"

"Yes! Have you gotten in touch with the police?" I asked, stepping out of the bath and beginning to dry myself—awkwardly, since the receiver was cradled uncomfortably between my ear and shoulder.

"No way, nohow," Michael said. "Agency rules."

"But you cooperated with the Japanese government before. Remember? I was there with you—"

"Not the police. We dealt with their department of state, and that's who they thought I was, too. And that was a secret matter, as is this one."

I took a deep breath. "I know I signed secrecy agreements, but I can't help feeling this is really serious, us knowing what we do and just standing by."

"It boils down to this: the integrity of this project will be ruined if anyone in Japan learns you planted bugs. Not to mention that you'd probably go to jail."

"And what if I don't talk? How can I keep working in the department store, knowing that the guys on top are responsible for a killing?"

"We don't know that yet." Michael's voice sounded strained. "Still, you've convinced me that the risk has elevated."

"Which means . . ." *Please, not that I'm being sent home.*

"I'm flying over to join you ASAP. It's been cleared, and I'm just waiting till morning, when I can get my airline tickets and some orders from State."

"So you're coming to bring me home?" Now my anguish was turning to anger. "Because I'm inexperienced and I screwed things up, or because you're afraid of what I might say?"

"No to all three," Michael said. "I wish I could tell you more, but you'll have to wait until we meet face-to-face."

"And when you're here . . . what's going to happen? Are you moving into the apartment?" Now that I knew Michael wasn't sending me home, I couldn't help feeling relief, tinged with anticipation.

"No," Michael said crisply. "I'll book myself into some lodgings nearby and will make the contact after I arrive. Don't find me; I'll find you."

"But—how are you going to pull it off? What are you going to do, go to the store and pretend to be a customer? I can't possibly keep a straight face if you come into the K Team office."

"The store's your territory. I wouldn't dream of encroaching, and I'll steer a wide berth around you as well. I'll explain my story once I'm there."

"So you'll text-message me or something about when to meet?"

"Or something." Michael's voice was tight. "Be careful over the next few days, okay? More careful than you've been."

"How so?"

"Watch your back. Suspicious vehicles, people following you, the kind of stuff you learned in Surveillance 101."

Michael sounded like a broken record or, to be more up-to-date, a skipping CD. I thought about the recording that held the voice of Masahiro Mitsuyama talking for just a few minutes, but that had not, since then, picked up any more sound. This situation made me wonder if he'd simply stopped wearing that pair of shoes—or if he had detected the bug.

I'd thought I'd done a good job with the bugging, but there were a lot of things I'd done that I'd thought were good but were turning out to be all wrong.

23

While putting on my black uniform jacket the next morning, I found the note with Mr. Fujiwara's message, which I'd wanted to forget. Now, as I looked over the message, I realized that the phone number was not from inside the Mitsutan store; it was an outside number, with an area code, 090, typically used for cell phones. Mr. Fujiwara could have called from the building, using the cell; or he could have been somewhere else. I went inside one of the toilet stalls at the far end of the locker room and shifted the message from my jacket pocket to the inside lining of my purse. This number would be something to follow up on later.

I came out of the stall, washed my hands and regarded myself in the mirror. My overly made-up face looked back, its paleness exaggerated even more by the austere black uniform.

In the West, the color of death was black; in Japan, it had once been white, long ago, when Buddhist beliefs were more prevalent, but it had changed to black over time. There was an entire department on the fourth floor devoted to women's mourning suits with prices starting at 49,000 yen. I didn't own a mourning suit; to buy one, I thought, was to be a real pessimist. But thinking over my life patterns in Japan, I had to admit that I probably should have my own, instead of always borrowing from Aunt Norie.

I still needed to return her kimono. When could I do it? I made up my mind to do it right after work. During my lunch break, I made it out to the street and used my cell phone to call Aunt Norie to double-check about supper that night.

"We're very excited to see you, but I apologize for not being so well prepared," my aunt said. "I'm a bit busy, so I'll stop in at one of the *depaatos* to pick up some of the meal."

I cringed at the possibility that she could catch me in uniform, but then realized that she was probably talking about a department store in Yokohama. But if she was busy, she shouldn't have to shop for food at all.

"Let me bring something from Tokyo, to save you the trouble," I offered.

"No, you won't know what to buy. If you do bring something, don't get it from Mitsutan."

"Why?" I asked cautiously. Had she gotten wind of where I worked?

"One of the store managers was killed. I heard on the television news this morning. That means the store workers will be very distracted. And with a police investigation going on, fresh food deliveries may be delayed. We could suffer food poisoning."

"I would gladly pick something up at Mitsukoshi," I suggested, wanting to change the subject.

But Aunt Norie wouldn't be deterred. "It's a terrible situation, really. The *yakuza* have their fingers in everything."

"Oh? Have the police said that gangsters are responsible for the executive's death?" I could never possibly catch all the news that my aunt did.

"Well, what they said is, it appeared to be the work of violent ones, and you know what that means."

I finished the call, in the end agreeing to my aunt's request for me to stay overnight. Since dinner was going to be served at nine-thirty, the plan made sense. I remembered Michael's order for me to watch my back. That was a lot easier to do if I moved between cities during the day than at night.

As I walked the Ginza, watching everywhere for spies, I thought more about my aunt's casual mention of the link between organized crime and department stores. I did recall reading about gangsters in the historical overview of Japanese retailing that Michael had given me. Apparently many department stores still paid off gangsters around the time of their annual stockholders' meetings, mainly to suppress any hard questions that the shareholders might ask of the company. Any shareholders who did ask questions would be shouted down or threatened by the bad guys in suits. It seemed remarkable to me that *yakuza* could walk brazenly into a stockholders' meeting; but the fact was that many *yakuza* had offices with their emblem on the door and gave huge, publicized charitable donations in times of trouble, like the Kobe earthquake.

Perhaps Mitsutan was paying gangsters off to be able to do business as usual; gangster involvement might even have something to do with the sky-high profits. I supposed there could even be gangsters at the store working within the management and sales force. I knew the store had a slight shoplifting problem; what if it mostly came from a few employees, who were, say, filching the latest handbag in order for it to be copied and sold on shady backstreets?

My thoughts flitted for a second to Miyo. There was a stereotype that the *yakuza* were among the few Japanese institutions that had warmly welcomed Korean people—but it might be just a story. There were conflicting stories: for instance, that the *yakuza* were descended from samurai: my family's social class.

Yakuza and labor—now that was a combination worth pondering. According to the news I'd seen on television that morning, Mr. Fujiwara had been rolled up in a quilted blanket used for padding crates, to keep them from scraping against elevators and walls as they were transported through the stores. The choice of the blanket and van would seem to indicate that the person doing the work was involved in a cruder job at Mitsutan, surely not one of the executives or someone in the sales force. But the loading dock was adjacent to the building holding Mitsutan's annex, which housed the employees' locker rooms and cafeteria, plus many administrative and storage rooms. Closest to the front was Personnel, the place where I'd started my brilliant career a little over a week before.

I looked at my watch. I still had fifteen minutes of my break. Impulsively, I left my post at Wako and turned the corner into the alley that ran between Mitsutan and the annex. The van that had held Mr. Fujiwara was gone, although the area where it had stood was roped off with tape. This meant that traffic into and out of the parking garage was proceeding slowly, at the direction of numerous sign-wielding store security officers.

I walked into the annex building, swiping the slot next to the door with my employee ID. Then, instead of going to the restroom or cafeteria, I walked into Personnel.

Miss Yamada, the secretary who had helped me before, looked at me blankly.

"Do you need to make an appointment?"

"No. It's—I'm Rei Shimura. You were kind to me a couple of weeks ago, when I came here for the interview."

Her hands flew to her mouth. "I'm sorry. Of course it's you! I just—I guess I didn't recognize you in the uniform."

Wearing Mitsutan black, with our hair in a minute range of shades, with one ring per hand and pale pink polish, we all looked the same. I smiled at her, thinking that my cover was a total success.

"It's good you came, actually. I have something for you that would have gone upstairs by interoffice mail, but I'll just get it for you. I'd set it aside because your file is gone." She jumped up and rummaged around in a cabinet.

"What do you mean about my file?" I asked.

"Someone came by and said her boss requested it. I was going to make a photocopy, but she wanted the original."

"Really?" Who had wanted my file, and what was he looking for? "Do you know the secretary's name, by any chance—"

"No, but don't worry about it. It's not your boss, Mrs. Okuma— that's the important thing." She went into an office and came out with a small brown envelope. "I just remembered where Aoki-san said to put your *meishi*. And I thought the spelling was right, but now I see your name tag, I'm afraid I made a mistake."

She was talking about business cards, with the Mitsutan three-diamond crest on the top, and my name on the center of the card, with the K Team phone and fax numbers below. How exciting to have my own business card, but as she said, my first name was spelled wrong: it was the more ordinary form of "Rei" that meant bow, not the unusual "Rei" my parents had chosen for me, a *kanji* character that meant a crystal-clear sound.

Rei who bowed, though, was perfect for a department store. I could live with it, for the time being.

"Please don't worry about the business card. It's no problem. In fact it will be easier for the customers to read," I said.

"Great. And by the way, is everything okay? Is there a reason you need to see Aoki-san?"

"Oh, my job with the K Team is fantastic. I'm very happy there," I said quickly.

"I'm glad you're comfortable. I wasn't sure if there was a problem when you came in. As you have heard, there's been no girl before you lasting longer than six months."

"Why do you think that they left?" I asked.

"I'm not sure. They are temporary contract jobs, to begin with, but I also think it is hard overseeing the tax rebates. If you make a mistake with a rebate, the foreigners get really upset."

I nodded, thinking how ironic it was that Mrs. Okuma made mistakes herself, all the time.

"Or maybe it's working with the other K Team member. I've heard she's a bit territorial."

"That's true, but I'm working on getting along better with her." I paused. "Actually, the reason I stopped by was just to say hello and offer my condolences to you. I know that you knew Mr. Fujiwara pretty well, because he came into this office to do all the training talks."

Miss Yamada nodded. "Yes, it's really sad. And scary. To think some evil street person reached into one of our trucks and put Fujiwara-san inside it."

It was an odd way to reconstruct the circumstances around the murder—especially since I'd never seen a homeless-looking person walking along the Ginza—but I considered it. "Do you mean that you think he was on his way to work and he was just killed and shoved inside?"

"On the news, the announcer said it was a violent one, and you know what that means." Miss Yamada shuddered. "It's a tragedy. His wife has called several times already, anxious to find out what benefits she and the children still have."

"That poor woman. I can't imagine what she's feeling, to have lost her best friend and life support—"

"Heh? I'm talking about his wife, not his friend."

I blushed, realizing that my comments were showing my western bias. I'd better shut up.

"Well," I said, gathering up my bag, "I'm off. Just wanted to say thanks for all the help you gave me at the beginning."

"Don't mention it, Rei-san." She beamed at me, and I felt a flash of comfort that I didn't understand until I'd left. Miss Yamada had been the first person at Mitsutan to use my first name.

• • •

Five foreign customers were waiting in the K Team's office when I returned. Miyo was missing in action—presumably on the floor with another customer group—and Mrs. Okuma was trying to process a tax rebate for an elderly woman in a sari while dealing with a couple of impatient younger women from Hong Kong—I'd learned to recognize them, from the accent and shoes—who were demanding an accounting of the Japanese designers available who had collections *not* in black. There was a European couple, too, sitting against the wall; from their grim expressions, I could guess they were last in line.

"Take the Germans, they just want to buy a kimono," Mrs. Okuma said to me in rapid-fire Japanese, mid-sentence, then swung back into Mandarin.

"Hallo?" I ventured to the German wife, whose husband seemed to have fallen asleep against her shoulder. And the bench for waiting, a few feet from the desk, wasn't a very comfortable place at all.

"We are hoping to find someone to show us kimonos. Upstairs everything is packaged in plastic, and we were told we are forbidden to it open up. How can we find the sizes this way?"

"Ja, ja, that's a shame," I said, then stopped myself. I was such a mimic that I was inadvertently picking up the speech patterns of my customers. "Come, I'll take you and we shall open them together."

I was just handing them my new business card when yet another woman walked into the office. She was a real looker, with fine facial features and waves of perfectly highlighted red-brown hair flowing around her face. Unlike most of the Caucasians who used our shopping help, she was both skinny and chic; in a split second I'd identified her jacket from the Issey Miyake section—the section within designer sportswear that was more expensive than the ME line, which I bought—and her Comme des Garçons trousers, studded with plenty of straps and snaps. Both garments were inky black, and between them, she had a multicolored silk chiffon tank top, designer unknown, but just the kind of thing that I liked. But the pièce de résistance was her shoes—open-toe stiletto-heel suede pumps, patterned in stripes and swirls of gold, black, gray, and brown. I hadn't seen those shoes in any of the designer collections in the store.

Was she a celebrity? I wondered. Foreigners who came to us for help rarely looked so sleek. She couldn't be someone who was traveling; her heels were too high, and the only thing crumpled on her was the Issey Miyake.

"Shimura-san!" Mrs. Okuma hissed, cutting off my reverie. "A VIP just came in! I'm giving her to you."

"But there are others—" I began, but my voice trailed off as Mrs. Okuma jumped to her feet and started bowing. "Kravitz-san, how happy we are to see you!"

"It's a sad day for you all, I heard," the woman said in a breathy, baby-like voice, pulling down the sides of her mouth. She looked completely phony.

"Ah, I'm sorry you were burdened with our news." Mrs. Okuma gave me a warning glance, but I'd learned my lesson earlier that day. I stayed quiet, just watching.

"You owe me two thousand yen, isn't it?" Mrs. Okuma's Indian customer interrupted.

"Right away, madam. And Mrs. Kravitz, our newest consultant, Rei Shimura, will help you straight away."

"Rei Shimura." Melanie Kravitz turned emerald-green eyes on me—eyes that looked as if they'd been enhanced with color contacts, a trend I'd thought had come and gone. Apparently I was wrong about that—just as I'd been wrong about her age, at first impression. Her skin wasn't quite taut enough, and there were tiny laugh lines around the emerald-green eyes. She was over forty, for sure, and my hat was off to her for avoiding plastic surgery.

"Rei Shimura," she repeated. "I know that name, somehow. Are you famous?"

"If only."

"Your English is great. So colloquial. Where did you study?"

"California. But, Mrs. Kravitz—"

"Melanie, please! Mrs. Kravitz sounds like my mother-in-law." She rolled her beautiful gem-like eyes.

"Melanie, then. I know that you're a very special customer to the store and I'm delighted to have the opportunity to work with you. Would you care to take a cup of tea while I handle—"

"Shimura-san, no! Kravitz-san takes precedence!" Mrs. Okuma was speaking Japanese, but her tone was so vehement that the Germans practically jumped in their seats.

"I'm sorry, I've been called away," I said to the Germans, who were already standing up, getting ready to go. "I'm really sorry—"

"The Japanese, they're just—two-faced!" one of them said to the other, in English, not German, so I'd be sure to understand.

"Touchy," Melanie Kravitz said, opening up her Kelly bag—authentic, I was sure—to remove a hot-pink telephone. I hadn't heard it ring before, but now I heard its chirp.

"Hi, honey, what is it?" she asked, totally focused on the receiver.

I watched her listen to whatever was coming over the line, her red-brown brows drawing together for a minute, then relaxing. "Okay. I promise. And the red, yes, I understand about the red being crucial." She made a kissing noise and then closed the phone. "My dear husband. He just returned from a three-day business trip and was checking in."

"Oh, really? You mean a trip outside Japan?" I asked, steering her out of the office.

"No, just Osaka. Winston Brothers has a branch office there."

"That's nice," I said, thinking that this meant Warren Kravitz hadn't been under anyone's surveillance on Monday, the night when Mr. Fujiwara had died. "So, what are you in the mood to shop for today?"

"Well, I need to pick up a few things for my husband—he's put on a few pounds and he could use a few new sweaters."

"There are some sales on sweaters in men's, this being February."

"Price isn't an issue." Melanie winked at me. "Why would I cheap out on him when I plan to treat myself to a really great dress?"

"What's the event?"

"The Tokyo Children's Relief Ball; I'm chairing it. And while I'm at it, I want to pick up some undies, casual stuff, and some makeup. It's time to stock up."

I knew from the K Team records that the last time Melanie had stocked up was thirteen days earlier, to the tune of $1,500.

"You need to—shop for a lot of different items," I said.

She nodded happily. "The way I normally do it—when Miyo or Yuki takes me around—is just from floor one, accessories, right up to the top."

I didn't realize who Yuki was at first, until I realized she meant Mrs. Okuma. The fact that Melanie had called my boss by her first name made me almost shudder at the impropriety. But what seemed more significant, when I thought about it, was what Melanie Kravitz was apparently doing: going floor by floor, as if she were casing the place.

Was Melanie Kravitz spying on behalf of her husband, just as I was doing for Michael and his bosses? I thought about how she'd said my name easily and acted as if she'd heard it before. Did she know my name from last year's tabloids, or was it because Warren Kravitz knew exactly who from OCI was involved in researching Mitsutan? My missing personnel file might not really have been taken by someone in Mitsutan's management. It could have been taken by one of Warren's own people.

As my doubts grew, I realized that my smile had frozen. Frantically I worked to make myself look normal and happy again. "What a delightful idea! I can't imagine anything more wonderful than going through every single department of the store looking at every single thing."

"Are you kidding me, Rei? Not everyone likes to shop. That other girl in the office, Miyo, I think she runs at the sight of me," Melanie said, handing me the heavy Kelly bag to carry.

"This is my job, and I love it," I said, gripping her bag tightly between my hands, knowing I was on the verge of a really good idea.

24

I had never met a woman like Melanie Kravitz before. My mother loved to shop—and looked it—but she never would have run through the equivalent of $3,000 in two hours, just on clothes. But then, my mother was old money, which often came with a bit of frugality; Melanie Kravitz's money had to be almost as new as her Miyake jacket.

"Your husband must be the greatest. Wish I could get one like that myself," I said after we'd spent half an hour in lingerie looking for a bra to fit under the red satin Carmen Marc Valvo gown she'd chosen for Saturday night. Melanie was thin enough to fit easily into standard Japanese sizes, but she was too big for most of the bras, which came in European sizes designed for Japanese bodies. I wore size 75, which, judging from the chatter in the women's locker room, was the most popular bra size in Japan. Melanie wore size 90, and it took three lingerie salesclerks to help me locate a pretty strapless bra in that size.

"You know, you really should try on some things. I'd love to see how they look," I said when we'd finished in lingerie and were passing by a series of designer denim boutiques, ranging from special-issue Levis to the new power brands: Lucky, Citizens for Humanity, Earl, and Evisu.

"Oh, I prefer to try things on at home, where I have more room and a really good mirror. If it doesn't fit, I'll bring it back."

"Of course," I said, suddenly thinking about that. Maybe Melanie spent thousands but returned thousands. Customers' returns weren't tracked in the K Team registry—just their initial spending.

"Don't worry, I'm not like those women who buy an evening gown, wear it once, and then dump it on the store again. Haven't done that since I was a teenager." She laughed lightly. "I choose very carefully. My closet is large by Japanese standards, but not by mine."

"Where do you live?"

"We have a condo in Roppongi Hills. It's a cliché, I know, but the firm really is close by. Not to mention the Iron Grill for my husband, and all the other restaurants he and his cronies seem to live in." She shuddered. "I send him out to dinner by himself. If I ate the way he did, I wouldn't fit into my clothes."

"So you were saying your husband works at Winston Brothers' Tokyo office?"

"Yes. He's head of the Japan investment banking division."

"Wow," I said admiringly. "That happened fast. I mean, you're so young, I wouldn't expect it."

"Warren's just forty-two, a couple of years younger than me. But sssh." Melanie winked. "He worked hard for it, though. He's had a lot of success bringing in foreign investors."

"Really," I said, thinking back to the paperwork I'd seen on Kravitz. It had mentioned that he'd overseen the acquisition of many distressed properties in Japan, but it hadn't said anything about foreign investors.

"Yes, actually, if you're in the market for something . . . I mean, someone," she winked at me, "maybe I could facilitate an introduction."

"That would be super," I said, though after suffering the indignities of life with an expat lawyer, the last thing I wanted was an expat banker.

"Yes, well, that girl you work with is always asking me to fix her up, but she just doesn't have the language skills. Can you imagine how hard it would be for her to fit in?"

I nodded as if this were a very serious issue indeed.

"Well, back to work!" Melanie said cheerfully. "I'd better not forget to buy something for Warren."

"That's right. You said something about sweaters. Do you know if he tends to like things from Papa's Pocket or the other men's departments?" I was trying to be discreet about seeing whether he needed a plus size.

"He's not that bad off. I like him in Paul Smith." She sighed, trailing her hand along a row of jeans. "God, I hate to leave this department. Those jeans are really cute, though I'm not sure if they're the right length—"

"It's the new Evisu jean," said a salesgirl, who'd been hanging at the edge of the conversation. "We have only one in each size. That pair will be gone by tonight, after the office ladies come to shop."

"That's the only size six, though you look, to me, like you should also try the four," I said, translating and adding on a compliment that I hoped would lead her toward the changing room. "Both of them might be worth trying on, since the clerk said when the young girls come in tonight, after getting off work, she's sure they'll be gone."

Melanie licked her full lower lip, as if considering the point. "You're right. I could bring back the jeans, but I might not be able to get the right size."

"You're lucky that you can even wear Japanese sizes," I said.

"Don't I know it. Half my friends are going to Korea next week, just hoping to find spring wardrobes that fit. And the clothes here are great, exactly the same labels you'd get in New York or L.A."

I thought the clothing sold in Japan was a lot better, but I wasn't going to correct a customer. Instead I said, "There's a dressing room right here, and I'll stay right outside in case you need anything."

"Great." She plopped her bag into my lap.

"By the way, I've got a favor to ask." I smiled at her. "May I make a quick call on your phone to my boss? I want to tell her that we'll be a while."

This was great, I thought, as I seated myself on the velvet bench just outside the booths, the place where husbands usually sat. Under the cover of a pair of size-2 jeans folded over my lap, I used one of the tools from inside my jacket to pry off the hard plastic plate that covered the exterior of the phone. I slipped one of the last few bugs I had inside the phone, and fit the plate back on. I nestled the phone in Melanie's Kelly bag, next to an envelope labeled "Warren," which I would have loved to look into, had it not been closed with a red wax seal.

"I think these are going to work." Melanie stepped out of the booth and slowly revolved, showing off how snugly the jeans hugged her perfect butt. If this was what forty-four could look like, I thought to myself, bring it on!

"I like them with your pumps. I was wondering where you got those shoes?"

"Fendi. The boutique on Omote-Sando."

Hmm. We had a Fendi department in the store, but I hadn't seen the shoes. Maybe they were from last season. I asked, "Are you sure you don't want to try the four? You're so slender that, well, I can't help thinking those might suit you, too." I'd picked up a few of Miyo's tricks of flattery by now.

"Don't need to. But I'm not thrilled about the length." I followed her gaze to the bottom of her jeans, which barely grazed her ankles.

"I see what you mean." I paused. "You could take a pass on them, or we could see whether Alterations could actually take out the hem. But that would be if you were really interested, you know, not planning on returning them—"

"Do you mean, leave the bottoms unfinished and frayed?"

"Exactly. It's kind of trendy; it might not be what you want." I could never, in my mind, imagine a banker's wife dressing like this.

"My Seven for Mankind jeans are like that." Melanie nodded. "It's a good look. Might work. Tell me, what's the cost of a typical alteration?"

"Alterations are free," I said, although Mrs. Ono might never let me off the hook for forcing her to do something as sacrilegious as pull out the hem of 70,000-yen jeans.

"One of the few deals around here, huh?" She laughed lightly, but I sensed, all of a sudden, that she was storing the detail. Something for her husband to chew over with her after he came back from dinner at the Iron Grill. Or maybe she'd call him directly on the phone. I was eager to hear what she was up to, once I got home and checked in with my listening station.

Melanie Kravitz left the store three hours later, loaded down with beige-and-black shopping bags that contained merchandise worth 300,000 yen. Because she was a resident foreigner, she didn't qualify for the tax rebate. At the cashier's station, she paid for everything in 5,000- and 10,000-yen bills that she pulled from the "Warren" envelope. It was an unconventional way to shop—using small, worn bills instead of antiseptic new ones, especially when the worn bills came out of a sealed envelope. I picked up the halves of the broken seal, which had fallen onto the cashing counter, and tucked them in my pocket with a look of apology at the cashier. The cashier, though, was counting the money intently. There was more risk of a mistake with small bills, and if it turned out that she had done something wrong, it would be her nightmare—and, Melanie being such a valued K Team customer, in turn, mine.

Riding home that evening on the subway, I wondered why I hadn't heard from Michael. Maybe he was having trouble getting in from the airport. I hoped that he'd had the foresight to exchange dollars for yen in advance, rather than arrive broke, as I did.

It wasn't the middle of the night; the currency exchange booth would be open. I reminded myself, as I opened the apartment door, that Michael Hendricks was experienced enough to handle these things.

I moved around the apartment, doing the security checks, and then scrubbed off my stage makeup and packed my aunt's kimono to return to her. I also packed another bag containing different clothes to wear to and from work the next day. I'd decided not to go overboard dressing up for Mr. Kitagawa. I'd chosen an asymmetrical black cowl-neck—Comme des Garçons, on sale—and a below-the-knee straight gray skirt, which I would wear with matching tights. I wanted as much of me covered as possible, this time.

It seemed crazy to be heading out for a nine-thirty dinner, but that was actually the reality in many Japanese households. People didn't think of Japanese as having hard lives, but it was things like this—working all day long, mostly on my feet, and having a very late dinner at the end of an hour's commute—that made me think this wasn't the promised land.

Good smells of steaming rice and simmering soy and garlic wafted up the stone walk from the house as I approached its sliding doors, which glowed welcomingly behind translucent glass.

"*Tadaima!*" I dutifully called out the news of my arrival after I slid the door open. Until my aunt went to bed, the door stayed unlocked, no matter how many warnings I had given her about the changing nature of Japan.

"*Okaeri*, Rei-chan." My aunt emerged from the direction of the kitchen, wiping her hands on the apron she wore over her silk sweater and tweed pants. "You're the last one to arrive tonight."

I could hear male voices in the dining room—Uncle Hiroshi and my cousin Tom. I wondered about my youngest cousin. "Is Chika around?"

"Hi, Anego!" Chika called out from the dining room, where she was at the computer, doing something or other. Chika had recently graduated from Kyoto University, and had managed to find a non-office lady job: a traveling sales position for a cell phone company that took her from Kansai to Hokkaido practically every week. I missed my cousin, but I couldn't help thinking that this kind of travel was a big improvement over her recent involvement as a camp follower to a British rock band.

"What did you call your cousin?" Norie came between the two of us. She was frowning at Chika.

"Anego," I repeated. "It's a way of saying big sister, and you'd use it for the oldest, leader kind of woman in the group—"

"It's gangster talk," Norie said. "It's a word for a *yakuza* mistress or wife. How can you call your cousin such a terrible thing?"

I gulped because I hadn't known that the cute salutation came out of organized crime.

"Obasan, you're so—unfashionable. But if it means that much to you, I'll call her onee-san." Chika bowed, giving a false show of humility.

"Rei's fine," I said, giving her shoulders a light hug.

"You and Chika will share her room tonight," my aunt continued. "But first, let's eat."

The food my aunt had selected from Mitsutan's Yokohama store was identical to what I knew from the food basement at the flagship store in Tokyo. There were tiny, plump *gyoza* dumplings filled with garlicky pork; nobody batted an eye when the self-proclaimed vegetarian quietly took a few. There was a bowl of spinach steeped in rice wine and ginger, and a plate of smoky grilled eels. On the side were a carrot-sesame salad and shrimp and cheese croquettes. The rice Norie had prepared herself in the trusty old Zojirushi rice cooker, and the warm soy-garlic smell turned out to belong to a heated noodle dish.

Everyone ate heartily, though Uncle Hiroshi made some sexist protests about wives who were too busy with outside activities to do their real job. And buying food like this cost a fortune! What had Norie spent, he wanted to know?

"Not in front of the children," Aunt Norie said, smiling at us. I felt a stab of guilt because if I had bought the food, it would have been ten percent off. But my aunt hadn't wanted to buy food from the store where the murdered man had been found.

Everywhere I went, I couldn't escape the impact of Mr. Fujiwara's death. I hadn't taken his call on Monday—his last day of life—because I wanted to avoid speaking to a man I was certain just wanted to proposition me. But, as Michael could have told me himself, I hadn't known his intentions for sure. I thought back to my job interview in Mitsutan, when I'd told Ms. Aoki that my greatest skill was listening; but when the time had come for me to listen, I hadn't been there at all.

25

Michael had been on my case about keeping up with the news in Japan, which I'd hardly been doing the way I once had done in Washington. I resolved to reform myself, starting first thing in the morning at my aunt's house. It was easy, because my aunt kept the television in the dining room, and it was always turned on. It was easier for me to follow the voices of television announcers in a quiet house; the only problem was that the NHK morning news was flat-out boring.

I thought about asking my aunt if she minded my switching to one of the tabloid "wide shows," because I knew programs like that would probably spend a lot of time reporting details on a murder like Mr. Fujiwara's. But my uncle Hiroshi, who worked in a bank, seemed very interested in a report on economic recovery. He speared pieces of tofu and seaweed from his morning bowl of soup, his eyes not leaving the numbers on the screen that told the story of the nation's GDP.

My patience was unexpectedly rewarded when the screen showed a rail-thin Caucasian in a business suit and cowboy boots walking along the Ginza flanked by a court of Japanese attendants.

In rapid-fire Japanese, the announcer was talking about Supermart's interest in acquiring Japanese department stores. Jimmy DeLone had made an offer for Wako—flash to a shot of the famous store's clock tower—but had been rebuffed.

There followed a one-on-one interview of DeLone by a journalist in NHK's studio. It must have taken place after the offer was refused, because Jimmy DeLone didn't look as jovial as he did in the shots where he was walking into Wako's building.

"We have a sayin' in English, bah low and sayell hah." His accent made him sound like a cowboy in an old Western; Uncle Hiroshi's brow was furrowed in confusion until subtitles suddenly appeared. "The prahs of Japanese retail is too hah fer what it's worth. In mah explorations, ah found almost every store in this country has not only decreased sales, but plenty of bad loans. Nobody's willin' to make the hard changes necessary to pare down and profit. Ah'd have liked to help out, but taking on that kind of debt, with a high purchase price, makes about as much as sense as going deer hunting in June."

I was stunned by DeLone's unguarded, undiplomatic remarks—and longed to hear more. How disappointing that the camera returned to the news announcer's desk.

"On the other hand, the retail climate in the United States is suffering," the announcer intoned piously. "James DeLone's Supermart empire is under questioning for hiring illegal foreign workers and denying health benefits to the legal ones. Most of the merchandise comes from China, and while those items are inexpensive, they are frequently found to have caused consumers to complain."

Tit for tat, I thought, as the camera went back to Jimmy DeLone, walking on the Ginza again—this time through the doors of Mitsutan, where Enobu Mitsuyama and his father Masahiro stood at the door, bowing their official welcome.

"What do you think about that fellow?" I asked my uncle during the commercial.

"Hmm," he said. "DeLone-san seems to be very frank. On the other hand, he seems a bit crazy, since he has all those troubles of his own. What do you think? Is he a typical American businessman?"

"He's definitely one of the most successful we have," I said slowly. "But don't think that I, or most people in the country, would consider him a role model. Please!"

The ride from Yokohama added an extra forty-five minutes to my commute, so I used the time, balanced with my back against one of the grab-poles, to text-message Michael about what I'd learned from the newscast.

The store's morning pep talk was about triumphing after tragedy. Enobu Mitsuyama stood on the podium, wearing a plain black suit, the kind of suit sold in the men's funeral boutique on the sixth floor. He would be at a memorial service for Mr. Fujiwara that evening—a service to which, Mrs. Fujiwara had said, all past associates were welcome to pay their respects. However, the services started at six, which might make it difficult for employees working a full shift. Therefore, he would offer sincere condolences, on behalf of all of us, to Mrs. Fujiwara and her two grown sons, one a college student and the other a salaryman.

Then Mr. Mitsuyama launched into a brief history of the great contributions of Mr. Fujiwara to the store's growth and his dedication to training the sales force. Mr. Fujiwara had worked at Mitsutan for twenty-seven years; in the last ten years, when he'd been the director of customer services, he had personally trained over 1,200 salespeople.

"Fujiwara-san may have left us in body, but he will never leave us in soul. His enthusiasm and attention to detail will live on in each one of you. As you go through your day, listening to the unspoken desires of your customers, Mr. Fujiwara's wisdom remains with in you, as a guide. Do not betray him by forgetting to work hard, beyond the extent of what you think a good salesperson or manager must be. I recall that one of Mr. Fujiwara's favorite sayings was that if a customer has to ask you for something, you have failed; to anticipate the desire, before it is voiced, is our duty."

Enobu Mitsuyama wrapped up his speech by cautioning us against gossip, against anything that might tarnish the store's reputation. Nothing was to be said to customers, though if anyone offered condolences, a gracious thank-you would be appropriate. After that, salespeople were requested to change the subject back to shopping. That would be the essence of good customer service, which Mr. Fujiwara would have wanted.

There had been no discussion, I thought as I went upstairs, of the fact that a crime had been committed. There had been no talk about safety precautions people should perhaps be taking when they traveled through the alley to reach the annex building after dark—as we all did, after closing time. Maybe Enobu Mitsuyama understood that there was no risk, that the death had not been the random act of a street person or gangster.

I asked Mrs. Okuma if she'd heard, internally, whether there was more information from the police about the murder. It was a quiet moment, when a Finnish tourist had just left the office with her rebate, and Miyo was out on the floor with two Australian rugby players who needed help buying shirts.

"Well, yesterday I needed to take some papers to Mitsuyama-san's office, so I asked him that same question." She sighed. "I shouldn't even be talking about this; you heard what he said about gossip at the morning talk."

"You're right. I don't mean to be a bother, but my parents are worried about my security. They might not let me continue working here unless that criminal is caught."

Mrs. Okuma sighed. "I understand that. My husband is worried as well. So I don't know if this will make them feel better, but I have been told that Mr. Fujiwara's body was in the van for at least twenty-four hours before discovery."

"And the van was parked out in the alley for all that time?"

"No, the thing is, it was traveling. It went out to several of the warehouses of the manufacturers that supply clothing to us."

"Consigners?" I asked.

"Yes. I think it was a lot of clothing."

"Really? Which brands?"

"We can't even ask that! If people knew—that clothing had been present in the same vehicle as a dead man, it would be a terrible scandal. It could tarnish the store's reputation."

"Why not just pull that merchandise, send it back? I hear the consigners greatly accommodate the desires of the store."

"They don't want it back, either." She shook her head.

"Was he—was he killed because he suffocated or something like that, in the van? Or killed beforehand?"

Mrs. Okuma didn't answer my question. Instead, she brought up what I'd been hoping she never would recall: the fact that Mr. Fujiwara had left a phone message for me.

"That's right, Miyo took the message." I was trying my damnedest to sound blasé.

"What did he want?"

To lie, or not to lie? I paused. "I'm sorry to say that I never found out. I forgot to return the call."

"You forgot?" Mrs. Okuma's tone made it clear she didn't believe me.

"I did. I'm sorry. It was only the start of my second week, and I was frankly exhausted by all that had happened."

"I see," Mrs. Okuma said, and that was it.

I hung my head the way I'd seen the others do at morning exercises. It seemed clear that I'd screwed up in not saying anything—but I feared that if I did make something up, even something innocuous, Mrs. Okuma might tell someone. And it was my own damn fault, really, that she'd asked the question; I'd talked too much. I reminded myself of what Mr. Fujiwara had counseled: the importance of listening, even to things that weren't said.

The wine bar in Hiroo was crowded, but that made me feel secure as I walked in exactly half an hour after getting off work. Mr. Kitagawa was nowhere to be seen, and that was even better. I supposed I could wait fifteen minutes, then leave; I'd have the perfect excuse, that he hadn't arrived.

Although this wouldn't end things, I knew; he would probably request that I meet him again. After all, Mr. Kitagawa hadn't responded to my plea that my boyfriend wouldn't approve of my meeting him.

Fourteen minutes after I'd arrived, the door opened and I saw a tall man with gray-and-black hair stride confidently in. He wore a gray business suit, which looked like one of the Paul Smith collection that was so popular at the store; male employees at Mitsutan didn't have to wear uniforms like the women, just suits. I noticed that he had a red tie, but he'd tucked it in the front pocket of his jacket, leaving his collar open.

Date mode. My stomach jumped with anxiety, and I actually put a hand on my belly to steady it. I felt the presence of my navel ring underneath, hard and reassuring. I would survive this.

"Shimura-san?" The executive looked me up and down, and his expression seemed to falter slightly at the sight of my clothing.

"Yes, it's me." I bobbed my head, understanding that my outfit had done exactly what I'd hoped: turned him off.

"I suppose we'd better get a table. I like this place because it has wine by the glass, you know, so you can try different things. They have a lot of wines from Europe that are quite good."

"American, too," I said as we squeezed into a tiny table just being vacated by a group of tipsy office women. I'd noticed some California reds that I liked, Rosenblum and Duckhorn—a nice surprise in Tokyo.

"Ah, American wines aren't as good as the European. At least— that's my opinion." He gave me a patronizing smile. "Shall I choose something for you?"

"Could you choose between Ebisu and Kirin?" There would be almost no chance that he could poison me with Rohypnol if I had a bottle with a tiny opening that I could keep a finger on, casually, at all times.

He frowned, but gave the order to the waitress when she arrived. For himself, he chose a whiskey.

"Well, really, I've called you here to apologize," he said heartily, after the drinks had arrived and we'd toasted each other.

"If you're talking about last weekend, there's no need. Really, I shouldn't have been there in the first place."

"It certainly put a smile on everyone's face," he said.

"I'm glad you all had a good meeting," I said. "It seems like a very long time ago, doesn't it, since Mr. Fujiwara has died."

"Yes, yes." He shook his head. "A tragedy. I would have gone to the memorial service, but the timing was wrong."

Mr. Kitagawa was a top executive in the store; he should have been able to leave for a colleague's memorial service. Instead, he'd kept to his original schedule of meeting me for a date.

"Did you ever meet his wife?"

"No, I'm afraid I didn't. We keep our work and family lives pretty separate at the store. I knew him very well, of course; he trains all the sales force in our department."

"Yes, and Young Fashion is so huge—what is it made up of, thirty-nine individual boutiques?"

"Thirty-nine at the moment, though we hope to add a few more. That's one of the things we were discussing at the meeting." He smiled at me. "What kind of clothes do you think we should add to attract the attention of girls like you?"

"Oh, I'd better not say! I've gotten into plenty of trouble over-spending there already."

"I see you like Comme des Garçons." He was looking at my blouse.

"Yes, but I don't do it justice," I said. "It's a great label. Really original."

"It's not my favorite, because it's rather—architectural. But of course I can't say that I only want to stock clothes that make women look sexy. I instruct the buyers to choose what women want to buy."

"You're right," I said, thinking. "Women don't necessarily buy clothes to please a man's eye. We buy them, I suppose, because we're afraid of seeming out of step with other women," I added, thinking of Melanie Kravitz and her cool-kid jeans.

"My wife, for example," Mr. Kitagawa said. I'd been waiting for this; within the space of a few minutes, he'd told me how his wife was nothing like the girl he'd married, how her fashion decisions were based on whether things were machine-washable. No matter how many times he offered to take her shopping for something bright or sexy, she always demurred, saying that at her age, she felt self-conscious.

"Tell me, how old are you, Shimura-san?"

"Twenty-three."

"Funny," he said. "Girls your age usually don't speak in such—such a strong and confident manner." And with that, his hand clamped on my thigh.

"I suppose you bring it out in me. I mean, it's very unusual to have such attention from a senior executive," I said, removing his hand. "I want to make the most of this learning experience."

My maneuver must have shut him down, because he shook his head. "Sorry, I don't know why I'm here."

"I thought—because you phoned me—you did this kind of thing all the time." Even though he might think I was encouraging him, I had to know. Had he called me because he wanted a *furin* or because he wanted to figure out for sure that I wasn't a genuine employee?

His face flushed. "Not at all. Fujiwara-san, now, he was one who had plenty of girlfriends, but I've always been faithful to my wife. Not always happy, but always true."

"That's impressive." I studied him, not sure how much I could believe. "Literally thousands of girls walk through Young Fashion every day. Not to mention that you know many girls who work at the store."

"I'm not on the sales floor. I'm in the annex most of the time, dealing with management issues." He sighed. "I don't know why I invited you. I guess it was because I knew the others would."

"The others? You mean Mr. Fujiwara?"

"Not just him. Yoshino, too. It was Mr. Mitsuyama's idea."

"What was the idea?" I had a growing feeling of dread.

"To see who would get you first. Since you'd offered yourself, as he said."

"Offered myself? I'm sorry, but I was in the bath first. Alone!"

"It's ridiculous," Mr. Kitagawa admitted. "From the moments we've spent together, I can tell you're not exactly the mistress type."

"Do the managers at Mitsutan do this kind of thing on a regular basis? I mean, make bets about taking on mistresses, or other kinds of games?" Total decadence, I thought to myself.

"Retreats bring out some silly behavior," he said. "I apologize. I shouldn't have told you so much."

"It's all right," I said, putting down my half-finished beer, no longer fearing that it would be poisoned. "I'd rather be forewarned."

"I felt bad about it, you being a target." He sighed, then glanced at his watch. "Excuse me for being rude again, but I think I'd better go."

"Not at all. And I thank you for being—so polite about things." I stood up and bowed, relieved that the date had taken less than an hour and exacted no blood.

"Don't mention it." Mr. Kitagawa put a 10,000-yen note down on the little tray the waitress had left containing the bill, and followed me out of the restaurant. There we parted; he went toward the subway station, and I went toward my street.

It wasn't until I was about to step inside that I thought about what had been so strange. Mr. Kitagawa hadn't gotten change for our drinks. But I knew from the menu board I'd studied before he arrived that our drinks couldn't have cost more than 5,000 yen.

And in Japan, only foreigners left restaurants without taking their change.

26

WR R U? H2O.

The text message flashed across my screen when I took my phone out to check it, killing time as I waited for the light to change. I thought for a few seconds before figuring out who H2O was. Brooks!

GNG HM. R U IN TOWN? I pressed the keypad awkwardly, then hit send. I was more used to talking on the phone than typing on it.

Michael flashed back a message to me. AT HOTL. NEED TO C U.

RNT U TIRED? I wrote.

NOPE. AT H STA, LOCATE TALL BLK SOLDR WITH DFL BAG. MAKE EYE CONTCT THEN FOLLOW. HE'LL BRING U2 ME.

Cloak and dagger, I thought, stifling a yawn as I replied in the affirmative and Michael finished the conversation with his usual sign-off, OAO, which meant over and out.

Having me follow a soldier was quite an example of paranoia, I thought to myself as I turned around and went back to Hiroo Station. Michael should simply have given me the address; I'd attract less attention going by taxi or foot by myself than following in the wake of a tall African-American in uniform. Most Japanese didn't like the military, especially since the new war; and the armed forces' reputation for stealing Japanese women was a legend that was still going strong after sixty years. Right after arriving in Tokyo this time, I'd noticed some graffiti scrawled on Tengenjibashi Crossing near Hiroo Station: U.S. SOLDIER STAY AWAY FROM OUR WOMEN. I'd been disturbed not only by the message but by the fact that Tokyo's usually zealous cleaning squads had left the message untouched.

The soldier was standing outside the station exit by the bakery called Kobeya Kitchen. His eyes were on the crowd coming up the station stairs. He was a handsome guy, well over six feet tall and close to 200 pounds, but not tough-looking, I thought, as our eyes met briefly. I wasn't sure if he knew what I looked like; but he turned out to have been prepared, because after a minute he shouldered his bag and started walking, at a relaxed pace, down the street.

A hawker waved packages of promotional tissues at me, and I took two, nodding thanks and zipping them into my bag. You never knew when you'd find no toilet paper in the restroom.

I set off along the same path as the man. There were still a good number of people and bikers on the street, but the soldier was so tall that he was easy to keep track of as he passed the Hair and Meke beauty salon, a children's clothing boutique, an art gallery and an Italian restaurant. At Tengenjibashi Crossing, which still bore the graffiti warning, he made a sharp left turn. I did too, after making a quick check behind me to be sure that nobody who'd been walking behind me at the station was still there.

Two more blocks, past a few clothing boutiques and a patisserie and wine bar, and then a large slate-tiled building flying an American flag. Not the embassy; that was a couple of miles away. The building had a sheltered driveway and guideposts, which he disappeared into after several salutes were exchanged. I hesitated, and a Japanese guard walked a few steps toward me.

"Your name?" he asked in Japanese.

"Shimura Rei."

He checked a paper, then looked back. "Photo identification?"

For security reasons the only form of ID I carried was my Mitsutan employee card, which worked as a photo ID, time-clock card, and credit card all in one. It wasn't as official as a Japanese driver's license, but at least the guard would be able to read it.

"Enter, please."

I walked into a large lobby lit by chandeliers and gleaming with acres of new polished rosewood paneling. A reception desk staffed by Japanese men in navy blue suits was crowded with a throng of casually dressed Americans. They were not backpackers, but more the kind of crowd I was used to seeing in suburban Virginia—men with short hair wearing jeans and sneakers, and American-looking women in similarly simple, comfortable clothes. Could they all be military? I wondered, putting together the flag, the soldier, and the strict security.

"Over here." The soldier appeared again and led me through the lobby and through a set of doors marked Embarcadero Lounge. It was a cocktail lounge, I realized, lit mostly by televisions showing a football game somewhere in the United States. Small groups of short-haired men clustered at tables, talking; there were only a couple of women in the room, both of them middle-aged and drinking wine, with shopping bags around their feet—Mitsukoshi, I noticed, not Mitsutan.

My gaze went to the far corner of the room, where a white man with short black hair, wearing wire-rimmed glasses and a business suit, was shaking hands with another westerner, also dressed in a suit, who was leaving. As the older man left, the younger one raised a hand to me, and I was shocked to realize that this was Michael.

"You colored your hair!" I whispered after the soldier had saluted Michael and moved off to a table closer to the entrance. "And the glasses. You look like a freshly minted MBA. Harvard, Wharton, or Stanford?"

"It's a light disguise, no big deal. But you look like—" Michael shook his head. "I don't know. I just can't get used to that Japanese makeup. I like the turtleneck, though. It looks like some kind of Halloween costume."

"It's fashion as architecture, Comme de Garçons," I said brightly. "And with regard to the makeup, I'm pretty used to it by now. Only takes ten minutes to slap on the paint. But enough of that. How was your flight?"

"Perfect. Join me for a drink?"

If Michael was drinking on company time, it was obviously to maintain cover—that we were a man and a woman socializing. Well, I didn't mind this bit of subterfuge at all, I thought as I studied the menu, which was in U.S. dollars and outrageously cheap. "I'll have a glass of the house white. By the way, should I be speaking English in a Japanese accent here?"

Michael cocked his head at me. "Only if you can keep it up all night long, which would give me a headache. If anyone asks, you're my interpreter, okay?"

Michael placed the order with a Filipina waitress—a glass of California chardonnay for me, another Bud Lite for him, plus a platter of oily-looking nachos I would have warned him against, if I hadn't been trying to stay in cover as a polite Japanese interpreter.

When we were by ourselves again, I asked Michael about the setting. "I didn't see a hotel name outside," I said. "And I never, ever heard of a hotel where you have to show your photo ID and be on a list before you get inside. It's something to do with the U.S. government, I guessed from the flag that's flying—is it an embassy outpost, or something?"

"This is the New Sanno Hotel," Michael said. "It's an American military installation meant to shelter DOD personnel passing through and those on vacation from nearby bases. Believe me, this is a fantastic improvement on the old place in Akasaka where my family sometimes stayed in the seventies. You would not believe the bakery here; they make everything in house, napoleons and éclairs and—"

"Sugar on an empty stomach gives me the shakes," I said.

"Okay, I won't give you a bag to take home. I'll just give you my room number and phone number here." Michael scribbled on the back of a business card he took out of his wallet, that of Jonathan Lockwood, a security attaché at the American embassy in Japan. I imagined this might be the distinguished gray-haired man who'd left as I arrived.

"What would your girlfriend think about my having your room number?" I joked as I looked it over the information he'd written down.

"What girlfriend?" Michael looked away from me to sign the check the waitress had brought along with the drinks.

"The woman in the photograph. You know, the one you have in your office?" I'd decided to challenge him directly, while I still had Chardonnay courage.

There was a long pause, then Michael said, "That was my wife. Jennifer died ten years ago."

"Oh, Michael. I didn't know. I'm really sorry." I gulped, thinking that this was something I should have figured out myself. It had been inexplicably strange that Michael, so obviously straight and gorgeous, did not date. I longed to know why she'd died—disease, car accident, or something more sinister. She could have been an agent too, for all I knew.

"Thank you," Michael said crisply. "And while we're on the subject of relationships, I want to ask whether you've been in touch with Hugh?"

"No," I said, wishing I'd never brought up the topic of girlfriends at all.

"That doesn't sound very convincing," Michael said.

"Well, you know, I Google him every now and then. It looks like he has been through Tokyo recently with a girlfriend or fiancée or something of the sort."

"I'm sorry," Michael said.

"Thank you," I replied, consciously using the same words he'd said to me. "Now, then, those things are settled. Tell me more about what you're doing here. Is your cover just that you are a government wonk?"

Michael smiled, appearing relaxed again. "A State Department wonk on temporary duty over here, with orders attaching me to the embassy. It's the fully backstopped cover under which I originally met you."

I nodded and tucked the business card into my backpack.

"You should burn the card after you've memorized the data about my lodgings. I believe there are matches and candles in the apartment bathroom, second vanity drawer."

"You've been in my apartment?" I looked at him in alarm. I hadn't made the bed that morning and there was hand-washed laundry—mostly lingerie—draped all over the dining room furniture.

"No, but I have a key because I stayed there in the past. I know where things are."

I nodded. "So when did we meet each other? You know, as the State Department wonk and his humble interpreter?"

"My last visit to Japan, which was five years ago." He paused. "And don't bring that up unless it's absolutely necessary. People who see us together tonight will just assume the obvious. And in the future, if we need to transfer information to each other that can't be accommodated through our cell phones, we'll need a meeting place. Any ideas about a sheltered place near the store?"

I sipped the overly oaky chardonnay, and said, "How about the Kabuki Theater? It's about four blocks from the store, right on Ginza-dori. Because kabuki plays last a whole day, the theater has a walk-in policy. You pay a thousand yen and get access to this little gallery up on the fourth floor, where you can stay for a single act—though you can go in and out at any time. Foreigners and Japanese go there, though not large numbers of either. And everyone's focused on the play; they'd never see you or me sit down in the back row. We could transfer the information right under the seats."

"Taped under a seat, because I'd come in a little bit later than you." Michael sounded thoughtful. "That's a great idea. So that's our day-time MO. For night, we'll have to think of something different. But now, since you're here in the flesh and we don't have to censor our conversation, I'd like to hear exactly what's been going on."

I told him about what had happened at work: the phone calls I'd received, and who knew about them. I spoke briefly about my date with Mr. Kitagawa, and what I'd learned about Mr. Fujiwara's life-style, and also about Mitsutan's possible ties with the *yakuza*. Michael listened carefully, taking notes as I told him about Warren Kravitz's wife Melanie coming in to shop: our floor-by-floor trip through the store, and my suspicion that she might be reporting things about the store to Warren.

"We'll know soon enough what she's up to," I said cheerfully. "While she was trying on jeans, I slid a bug into her phone."

Michael gaped. "You wiretapped her?"

"Sure. I figured she's worth listening to, as much as anybody. I've been thinking about what you said earlier—that we don't have solid evidence that Mr. Mitsuyama ordered Fujiwara killed. A death or-der could have come from Warren Kravitz, if he really wanted Mit-sutan's stock to dive—which it did yesterday, according to gossip I overheard in the cafeteria. And come to think of it, Melanie Kravitz also told me her husband was away from home during the time that Fujiwara was killed."

"You bugged an American citizen," Michael repeated, as if all I'd said had been meaningless. "Don't you know that it's against the law for our agency to spy on American citizens?"

"Many people in our government would disagree. And if you're so idealistic, then why did you wiretap me last year?" I fired back.

"The phone in question was registered to a noncitizen. Besides, I needed to know I could trust you, before I hired you." Michael put his head in his hands. "Oh, God. I cannot believe the situation you've put us in."

"Opportunity knocked. She was in the dressing room, and I got the idea and there was no way I could call you. I'm very sorry. If I see her again I can find a way to remove the damn thing—"

"I'll reset the frequency of that part of the listening station. It's rather complicated, so I'll come over and do it myself sometime tomorrow." Michael yawned outright, covering his mouth with his hand. "I'm beat."

"Yes, drinking surely heightens the postflight effect." I put down my empty glass, feeling no buzz, unless I counted the vibrating feeling of anxiety in my belly.

"The beer's going to help me sleep till six without waking. Or so I hope," Michael added gloomily.

I nodded. "Everyone has a personal method of overcoming jet lag. If you're up early, give me a call. You can stop over and do what you need to with the listening station."

"I don't want to be there when most of the tenants are there." Michael yawned again. "Don't worry, I've still got a key. And I want to hear what's been taped over the last few days. Before we say good night, do you have anything else to mention?"

"Every time I'm home I've listened for a few hours," I said. "There's plenty of chatter from the bugs I set up in the store, but nothing that seems like a highlight. I haven't yet caught anything about Mr. Fujiwara's death, but that's probably because it's improper for store employees to talk about things like that on the sales floor."

"And the shoe bugs?"

"I haven't heard a peep, not since that night."

"Maybe something's wrong with the listening station," Michael said. "I'll check that unit, when I'm there."

"Those shoes are at position number nine," I said. "And Melanie Kravitz is seven."

"What have you done with the data you've listened to so far?"

"Sent it back to Mrs. Taki, just like you requested."

"From this point on, I want you to do the translations yourself, if you're up to it. It makes more sense for me to analyze the info as fast as it comes in."

"Of course," I said, not knowing whether I should feel cheerful about Michael's trusting me to do translations, or wary about the amount of work it would entail. When would I ever sleep? Blearily, I watched Michael signal for the waitress and asked him what was on his agenda for the next day.

"I'm going to report to the embassy and get settled in my tempo-rary office. As soon as possible, I'm going to call Winston Brothers and see if I can catch up with Warren Kravitz."

"And that's not considered spying on a citizen?" I challenged.

"It's an up-front information interview. Using my State Depart-ment cover, I'll tell him that I'm still in a pre-investigative stage. He won't know I already have someone in place at the store."

"Maybe you'll find out what his real interests are," I said.

"I'll try to be objective," Michael said drily. "As for you, what's your game plan?"

"I work a full day at the store on Thursday, and that evening I'm seeing Mr. Yoshino. And the days following—Friday, Saturday, and Sunday—I have duty at the store."

"Mr. Yoshino—are you talking about the accessories manager? One of the guys who went to the corporate retreat?"

"Yes. I don't know exactly what he wants, but I'll handle the situa-tion just the way I did with Mr. Kitagawa tonight."

"Be careful," Michael said as the waitress approached with the bill.

When she'd departed with his crisp twenty, no change required, I said to Michael, "I don't think she heard anything."

"That's not what I mean. I want you to be very careful tomorrow night. There's something I've got to tell you about what happened at the hot spring."

"What?"

"A couple of days ago, I double-checked the English-language ver-sion of the *ryokan* map. You didn't make a mistake about entering the men's section of the bath."

"How do you know?"

"I'm positive. I checked the map out in Japanese with Mrs. Taki, just to be sure. You were definitely in the women's section of the *ro-tenburo*, and they invaded it."

I sucked in my breath. "I suppose it could be an honest mistake. In any case, I should feel vindicated, but—"

"Those guys crossed the line." Michael's face was tight with an emotion that I couldn't place. "You were right to get the hell out of there. And if you weren't gathering such good information, I wouldn't want you anywhere near them at all."

27

"Where are you going, the beatnik coffeehouse?" Miyo asked.

Thursday had been a long, exhausting haze of a day; I found myself wondering about Michael's activities, and whether Melanie Kravitz had detected her phone bug, at all kinds of inopportune times, like when I was trying to calculate rebates and actually blanked on the meaning of several kanji characters that I had studied many times. Mrs. Okuma had been nearby and said something that made the kanji snap back into context, but she'd looked at me sympathetically and asked if I was getting enough sleep.

The short answer was no. And now, as I changed clothes in the women's locker room with Miyo watching me, I decided that the workday I'd just endured seemed easy in comparison with what lay ahead that night. First would be the meeting with Mr. Yoshino. And after that, I'd have to recap it all to Michael; prove I'd done the job and had gathered useful information.

The section of the women's locker room where I was dressing was almost deserted; saleswomen tended to change their clothes quickly at night to flee for the good times. I was surprised that Miyo was still around.

"Where are you going?" she repeated.

"Just out," I said shortly, snapping the tight low-waisted jeans closed. I'd had the foresight to remove my navel ring at home that morning, so Miyo couldn't report to anyone about it.

"It's a very *casual* look, I'd say. My boyfriend wouldn't care for it at all." Miyo was critically examining her profile in a cherry-colored lace bra and a Stella McCartney white denim mini. It hit me that Miyo was purposely delaying putting on a blouse, to rub in that she was not only taller and prettier but bustier—at least size 85.

"If your boyfriend's so serious, why doesn't he ever stop by at lunch to say hello, like all the other gaijin?" I said as I slipped my new T-shirt over the head, pale pink cotton with the message I'M MAR-RIED TO THE MAHARAJA spelled out in rhinestones. I'd found it on sale in a section of Young Fashion called Park Avenue Princess, and decided it would be a subtle way to nudge Mr. Yoshino into really believing what I'd told him: that I had a boyfriend.

Miyo was glaring at me when my head emerged from the T-shirt. "At least I don't sleep with old businessmen."

I had thought I'd kept the details of my forthcoming meeting with Mr. Yoshino private, but she'd obviously deduced that something was going on.

I sighed and said, "What's so great about an expat boyfriend? Please tell me. I really don't know."

"You're trying to trick me with that question." Miyo looked uncertain.

"Sometimes I wonder," I said, sitting down on the long wooden bench and patting the space beside me. "Maybe the British investment banker boyfriend you mention needs to be traded in for a better model. What are his teeth like?"

"What?"

"His teeth, Miyo. If you want a guy with good teeth—children with good teeth," I added, remembering her interest in marriageable customers, "go American. If you'd lighten up a little bit, I would be happy to introduce you to a few guys I know."

"As if I'd be so stupid! You and your great English, like Kravitz-san said. You'd all have a good laugh at me—"

So I'd guessed right. She felt competitive with me because she thought I'd snag the eligible expatriate customers. And the way I'd seemed to suck in the senior male executives could only feed her belief that I was a man-hungry slut.

"Miyo, I have something very personal to tell you. Just between us." I motioned her to sit closer.

Miyo remained in place but, from her expression, seemed warily interested.

"As you know, I've grown up around the world. Because of what my father has seen of gaijin lifestyles, he will not permit me to marry a foreign man. I'm not even allowed to date a foreigner, after . . . after some trouble I ran into, a few years ago." That would cover any tabloid photographs, should Miyo stumble across one.

She blinked rapidly. "What are you, a girl in a box? I wouldn't have guessed."

I nodded enthusiastically, then realized that I should seem depressed. "I'm in this job because they're hoping I'll meet someone respectable, totally Japanese, preferably older. For me, the assignment to the K Team, well, it's been a setback. My parents don't want me around foreigners."

Miyo sighed, and for the first time she spoke naturally. "I know what you mean. My parents, they'd prefer for me someone Korean. But when you think about the choices you have with gaijin . . . I've heard they're not only good in bed, but they make beds, too."

"Could it really be true?" I asked and forced a laugh. She laughed too, and I found that encouraging.

"Let's go out after work sometime, Miyo. I'll introduce you to that kind of guy, if you like."

"I meet plenty of them here—"

"But it never goes anywhere. We need to go out and meet someone who's ready to have a good time. I'll teach you some casual phrases ahead of time, so your English sounds really good. I won't talk much at all."

Miyo looked at me doubtfully. "When?"

"You're probably busy Friday, but that's a good night in Roppongi."

"We could go out right after work." Miyo paused. "But why would you do something like this for me? I haven't been very nice."

Looking her straight in the eye, I told her the truth. "I can't afford to have you as an enemy."

"But you could afford new clothes."

"What do you mean?"

"You're not going anywhere with me looking like a beatnik. Between today and Friday, I want you to look around the store and put some new outfits on hold. I want to approve any of your future purchases before you put them on your card. Got it?"

Was this the start of friendship, or was it something else—a kind of spying of her own? I was being paranoid, maybe. I nodded, pushing down my uneasiness but resolving not to forget it.

● ● ●

Thirty minutes later, Mr. Yoshino was helping me off with my coat and goggling at my rhinestone T-shirt. The place he'd suggested, Aladdin's Cave, was a subterranean cocktail lounge overrun by long-haired young Japanese guys in vintage-looking silkscreen shirts. For the most part, their female companions wore chiffon and silk tops over low-slung jeans. It was rather like a beatnik coffeehouse; my outfit was totally appropriate.

The stereo was playing neo–Middle Eastern music—not authentic Arab music, but Sting, sounding Middle Eastern. But the cushions made from hand-knotted rugs looked authentic, as did the hookah pipes people were smoking, and the low, elaborately carved and in-laid wood tables set along the far wall and screened by heavy embroidered curtains.

This probably was Mr. Yoshino's fantasy of a den of iniquity, in every sense of the word. I gently declined the offer of a shared hookah, but felt I couldn't protest against the curtained booth to which the waitress led us, no matter how nervous it made me feel.

After our order had been taken—a bottle of Kirin for me, since they didn't have Sapporo; and a double vodka martini for Mr. Yoshino—she lit a candle in a pierced iron holder on the table between us, and closed the curtains.

"So glad you came," he half whispered.

"Actually, I'm on a tight schedule. My boyfriend and my parents are expecting to see me in a little bit." Don't even think of slipping a drug into my drink, was my unsaid warning.

"Your father is a banker, *neh*?"

Could he be the one who'd pulled my personnel file? "Yes. I didn't think I mentioned that."

He looked at me unsmilingly. "You seem nervous. I'm so very sorry. I thought you were happy to come here tonight."

"I know it's my duty to be here," I said carefully. "You said you had something to show me." I eyed the heavy black briefcase next to him. What could it be?

"Yes, indeed. But why rush to business? Let's have a drink first."

The waitress rang a chain of bells hanging outside the closed curtains—as if she was afraid of interrupting something—and waited for Mr. Yoshino to tell her to come in. As she served the drinks and a plate of pita triangles, I wondered how many times Mr. Yoshino had come here before. Knowing about a place like Aladdin's Cave, so clearly out of his age demographic, gave me the feeling that he was following tips from some younger person, or maybe even a men's magazine.

When the curtains closed again, Mr. Yoshino made a gesture, trying to pour my beer into the glass the waitress had brought alongside. I said, "Please don't. I prefer the taste from the bottle. It's just so—clean."

"Ah, drinking from a bottle is like an American." He nodded sagely. "You must have learned that habit during your time abroad."

He *had* read my file. "Yes. Aoki-san hired me because she thinks I'm a *kokusaijin*."

"And are you?"

"I love Japan, but there are things about California that I miss. The weather, for one."

"Was it in California where you had your navel pierced?" He lowered his voice.

"Yes." It wasn't, but I didn't dare reveal that I'd spent any time near Washington, D.C.

"Your navel ring was quite a vision. I have seen many thousands of accessories and pieces of jewelry during my career at Mitsutan. But I'd not seen a thing like that before on a real woman I know." He sipped his martini, then closed his eyes, and I imagined he was summoning up a vision of the past.

I pressed my lips together, trying not to show any reaction. So it was the navel ring that had aroused him. Not the breasts, not anything but the queer, exotic ring of gold-plated steel.

"You inspired me," he said at last. "Your beauty, and style leadership, has inspired me with an idea that I think will bring our accessories department to the forefront of Japanese retailing."

"Are you considering selling navel rings in the accessories department?" I was giddy with relief at the change of topic. Maybe he'd pulled my file, read it, and been impressed by my retail background in the United States. Maybe I'd been overreacting about everything the whole time.

"Sssh!" He put a finger to his lips. "We want to surprise Japan, not give our secrets away."

"But in order to sell the navel rings you need to have customers who already have a piercing," I explained in a lower voice as he opened the case and began laying out various pieces of gold, silver, and stone-studded body jewelry on the table. "How can we sell to the girls if they aren't already pierced?"

"An advertising campaign. We'll hire a famous foreign actress with a navel piercing, put her on some posters and TV commercials."

"Great idea. You used a foreign male model for a men's accessories shoot recently, huh?"

"Tyler Farraday." He shook his head. "We had to pull that ad campaign, actually. How did you hear about it?"

"Fashion gossip," I said. "It's a shame that you had to pull those ads, because I saw Tyler, and he was pretty hot."

"You like gaijin, then?"

I hesitated. I wanted to throw Mr. Yoshino off from thinking I wanted to sleep with him, but I didn't want to totally quash the evening. I winked and said, "Sometimes."

He smiled, seemingly relieved. "The problem with gaijin is they have no understanding of when to hold back. Farraday was just a model, but he wanted to act like an executive—to be on the same level."

"I feel like you're giving me a special opportunity, to give you my opinion about this new jewelry campaign. I'm very grateful," I said demurely.

"Yes, yes, tell me more about what you think." He leaned so far across the table that I could catch his breath, heavy with a mixture of alcohol and mints.

"Well, I wonder where girls can go to get the piercing done so they can wear the jewelry you're going to sell. From what I understand, tattoo and piercing parlors are pretty much the province of gangsters, which would make many women—me, for instance—too nervous to go."

"I've already spoken to the director for beauty services. She is investigating getting a license to perform piercing in our store beauty salons. It'll take some trouble, and maybe even side payments to get the licenses and so on, but if we are the first *depaato* to run with this trend, we'll gather quite a bit of publicity."

Side payments reminded me of what my aunt had said about the *yakuza*. "Won't the gangsters be upset if you try to do something that's their province? I mean, there's a good reason department stores haven't taken on the *pachinko* industry."

"Don't worry about it. I know how to handle things."

"Really," I said, taking a sip of beer and studying him.

"Truly. Don't worry your lovely head about it. Now, the favor I must ask you?" He leaned over the table again until his breath ruffled the edge of my hair. "While we're here tonight, I'd be very grateful if you would examine the jewelry I've had sent to me by some of the jewelry companies."

"Sure!" All he wanted was my good judgment. I inspected the pieces, asking him questions about the metal and pricing as I went along. It was imperative, I said, that whatever navel rings Mitsutan sold were not the kind that would sound off at airport metal detectors.

Mr. Yoshino had done a thorough canvassing of the market. He'd provided a wonderful assortment of belly jewelry, ranging from costume pieces with artificial turquoise to eighteen-karat gold. There were even some special pieces, with diamonds, that would appeal to a customer like Melanie Kravitz, if she ever decided to get pierced.

"I like these," I said at last, laying aside eight navel rings. I explained each choice. I had selected several because the stone decorations would appeal to young women; others, in heavy silver, because they had a sexy, edgy quality; and finally, some in gold and platinum, for the girl who cared about Gucci and Prada and other high-priced labels.

"What about the diamond? It's half a carat, and it would retail for just under one hundred thousand yen. A nice price point, don't you think?"

"A limited market, though," I said, picking up the piece, which to me didn't look like a solid stone. It seemed to be a faux solitaire made up of many tiny diamond chips that had been glued together. Still, it glittered and looked very Hollywood. "It's hard to know, because navel rings are still kind of underground in Japan. Can you take some diamond pieces on consignment, rather than pay wholesale?"

"Hmm, I usually handle that wholesale. In any case, I'd like to see the diamond on you."

"Very much agreed! Maybe I'll get one once they're in store, though I hear we don't get to use our fifteen percent discount on jewelry or cosmetics."

Mr. Yoshino's face went pink. "I meant to say, Shimura-san, I'd like you to keep the diamond navel ring, at the end of this evening."

"Excuse me?" I didn't think I'd heard him right.

"It's just a sample; nobody cares. After you try on all eight that you already told me you like"—he lowered his voice from a whisper to something barely audible—"please put on the diamond. It will be my little present to you, for your kindness to me."

"But I—I!" One of my hands flew to my navel, protectively.

"I humbly request." Mr. Yoshino's voice cracked with emotion.

I swallowed hard. This wasn't going to be fun, but at least it wasn't like stripping or sleeping with him. And come to think of it, if he was so busy navel-gazing, I might be able to sneak in a few questions.

I took a deep breath, not only gathering courage but putting my famous abdomen at its best advantage. Then I rolled up my sweater until it grazed the bottom of my rib cage, tugged down the already low waist of my jeans an extra inch, and began the show.

28

It was almost ten when I finally was released from duty at Aladdin's Cave; Mr. Yoshino had wanted a good-night kiss, which I deflected to my cheek before I made a quick escape, mentioning my waiting boyfriend and parents.

When I was securely hidden by the hubbub of the crowd at Shinjuku Station, I clicked open my phone to see what was waiting for me. A message from Michael.

C U AT APT. LMK WHEN U RCH STA. H2O.

So Mr. Brooks Brothers was in my apartment, fixing things so I couldn't eavesdrop on Melanie Kravitz again. I would have thought simply not using that particular circuit would have been okay, but apparently that wasn't thorough enough. At Hiroo Station, I realized that I was starving. I hadn't had more than a single pita wedge at Aladdin's Cave, because Mr. Yoshino had kept me so busy. It was a shame that I hadn't been able to get much gossip out of him; he had been totally distracted by my navel. I could imagine the nightmare ahead for any models, should the store ever mount the kind of advertising campaign he wanted.

I stopped into Kobeya Kitchen and bought a spinach croissant for myself and then, thinking of Michael, added another, and two chocolate cream puffs. I'd give Michael the cream puffs for the road, because who knew how long he'd been waiting for me in the apartment, where I'd not refilled the fridge since my initial grocery run. I'd been too busy to eat take-out at home, let alone cook new things.

Just before I stepped out of the bakery, I phoned the apartment.

Someone picked up, but there was no sound on the other end. For the first time, I felt a prickling of unease.

I'd thought it would be safe to call my apartment, but why wasn't he answering me? "Moshi-moshi?" I said.

"Sis," Michael answered. "Are you en route?"

"Yep, just passing by Kobeya Kitchen."

"That's a bakery, isn't it? I don't suppose you could pick me up something—"

"I already have, H2O. See you." I clicked off, smiling. It felt good to be going home to Michael. Really, really good.

I turned the key in the vestibule door and hurried up with a bounce in my step, and when I unlocked the apartment door, I heard the sound of music. Michael had gotten into my CD collection, and he was playing the new disc from My Morning Jacket.

I slipped out of my heels and went into the kitchenette, where my boss was crouched by the dishwasher, working. His plano glasses were off, and he was wearing a black turtleneck and jeans, which made him look more like Cary Grant in *To Catch a Thief* than a State Department bureaucrat.

"In the mood for sweets?" I said, holding the bag of croissants aloft.

"That's quite a way to greet your repairman," he said, turning and giving me a broad grin. "By the way, I've swept the place already. You can relax."

He meant sweeping the site for evidence of bugs, using the hand-held detectors. I nodded and said, "I like your outfit. I'm guessing . . . Prada?"

"REI Outfitters." He winked at me.

"I should own that company, but instead, I work for you," I said. "Now, I can hardly wait to tell you about my evening."

Michael raised his eyebrows. "Drinks first?"

"Sorry," I apologized. "I don't have anything in the fridge. I've turned into more of a cocoa person, since I've been here."

"I picked up wine at Meidi-ya," Michael said, going to the fridge. "Pinot grigio from California, although it's not from one of those special little vineyards you were so revved up about."

Thank you very much for understanding about California wines, I thought, taking the glass he handed me and clinking it, very lightly. He patted the seat next to him on the apartment's small sofa.

I settled down next to him with a plate of pastries in front of us, thinking that this was just like old times in the office, eating our meals while we worked. "Well, it turned out to be a trunk show—with me serving as the model."

"What's a trunk show?"

"It's a kind of fashion show, where a vendor brings a lot of goods to be examined, and hopefully ordered for purchase. But I'm actually making a bit of a bad joke, because it turned out that Mr. Yoshino brought many samples of different navel rings for me to try on."

"What?" Michael put his glass down and sat bolt upright.

"He insisted at the end that I take one home—the most expensive one, of course."

"Show me," Michael said.

Feeling mellowed by both the company and the small amount of wine, I turned toward him, shifting backward so that he could see the diamond navel ring glittering just above the low waist of my jeans. But as he stared at my navel, his eyes narrowed.

"I guess you don't like it?"

"It's very sexy," he said, but his voice was like lead. He put his finger to his lips and turned his head from side to side. It was a code that any moron could understand: shut up. Trouble. I followed his gaze around to the windows. All the blinds were closed.

I hadn't heard anything outside the apartment. What was he, clairvoyant? Quietly, Michael went into my bedroom, then came back out, a pad of paper and pencil clutched in one hand and the handheld bug-sweeping gizmo in the other.

He sat down beside me again and quickly scribbled a note. He held it out to me.

CD B A BUG.

I shook my head at him, realizing that Michael had slipped into another paranoid episode. At least I hoped he was overreacting.

"Time to go to the bedroom," Michael said loudly, the warmth restored to his voice. He scribbled again and showed me the paper: TO COVR NOISE, WE'LL SIMULATE SOUNDS OF SEX.

I shook my head. He was not only paranoid but silly.

"When you show me a trinket like that, well, it's asking for it, isn't it?" Michael waved his arm frantically, indicating that I walk with him into the bedroom. I trailed after him, thinking that the only thing worse than participating in this humiliating pretense was the chance that someone actually was overhearing it.

I'd had the foresight to make my bed that morning, thank goodness. I lay down stiffly and unbuttoned the waist of my jeans. Thank God I was the kind of girl who always wore underwear—and these days, really good underwear, purple silk bikinis by Tsumori Chisato.

Sorry, he mouthed at me. Aloud, he said, "I can't wait to make love to you."

I made a nasty face at him; if it turned out I'd opened up my jeans for nothing, I'd kill him.

I watched my boss scan the handheld detector across my navel, and its steady green light turned to a blinking red signal. Positive.

"Wow," Michael said. "I've been waiting for this all night. And you've been driving me crazy, going out with this other guy, and now you're wearing jewelry he's given you, I'm going to have to take it out with my teeth or something—"

"I dare you," I said, trying to sound breathy and tempting while I felt with my fingers to where the gold ring screwed into the side of the diamond. I turned the screw attachment, but it was solidly stuck.

"I'm having a little bit of trouble here getting my, um, bra off. Can you help me?"

"God, you're hot," Michael said, turning the bedside light on full blast, over my stomach. Under the harsh light one could see everything, even the return of a few tiny hairs that Dora had waxed three weeks ago.

Michael was no better at it than I. He kept trying, but it seemed as if the ring was screwed permanently closed.

"Oh, again and again!" I said, trying to make up for the inadvertent yelp I'd made at his last attempt to pull metal from flesh. Quickly, I scrawled a note: MY COUSIN CAN HELP, HE'S A DR.

Michael shook his head vehemently. Without his saying a word, I traced the probable trajectory of his thought: that we'd give ourselves away if we asked anyone for help.

Michael spoke, his voice almost rough. "So which way do you want it, Rei?"

"I don't really care," I said, utterly frazzled. Trying to make it sound like we were still in bed together, I rustled the sheets as Michael hopped out of bed and started quietly picking through his backpack.

"Come on, tell me, honey, while I get a condom!"

"Anything. Seriously, anything!"

Michael was back on the bed, with condoms from the bathroom and a tiny wrench. "Mind if I put on some music, help us relax a little?"

"Sure," I said, looking at the tool with interest. I hadn't been issued a piece like that.

Michael reached for the clock radio next to the bed. Puffy blared out, the supersweet duo, and he grimaced.

"Let me find something." I groped for the remote on the bedside table, and soon Jack Johnson filled the room with his soft crooning and slack-key guitar. I motioned for him to give me his tool, but he shook his head and began to pry gently with a miniature wrench at the connection between the edge of the diamond and the ring. His tugging had hurt a little before, but this time around, he seemed to understand what he was doing. To my surprise, I was starting to become aroused.

There was a change in the atmosphere, similar to the way the air pressure alters right before a storm. I opened my eyes and discovered that Michael was leaning over me.

He took my hand, which was still ineffectively working at the navel ring, and touched it to his face for a minute. Then he stretched it out against the bed, pinning me under him as he lowered his head and kissed me.

Michael Hendricks was kissing me; slowly, deliberately, perfectly. Once or twice back in Washington, I had thought about what it would be like to maybe kiss him, maybe come up to him from behind, graze his neck and shock him away from the center-column article of the *Journal*. This was not what I'd expected; it was better. Michael's breath was heaven, a mix of mint and sugar, all that sugar he was always consuming. His tongue curled around mine, and I lost it; I forgot all about being under surveillance and used my thighs to slam his body down on top of mine. As I shuddered at the delicious impact of this, and what would happen next, abruptly, Michael lifted himself away.

I'd gone too far. But I could hardly make an apology, with a microphone plugged into my navel.

"Wow," Michael said. But he wasn't smiling; in fact, he was regarding me with an expression I couldn't understand. He didn't say anything else as he dug into his backpack again, halfway across the room, safe from me.

Then he returned. I watched him make a thick layer out of condoms from the vanity drawer, stacked against my skin. Then he showed me the tool he'd brought out: a multibladed Leatherman. He made a quick, decisive snip with the gadget's pliers. A spark flew, and we both jumped.

"Oh!" I said, surprised by the brief electric shock. Michael turned the contraption so I could really see into the ring itself—which contained a black electrical wire.

"You're amazing," Michael said, hopping up from the bed and heading for the bathroom. "I got a little carried away. I hope you weren't hurt?"

"Not at all. But the ring came out of my tummy, can you believe that?" It was a stretch for me to keep the game going, because someone might be listening in.

"Very sorry. I wish I could buy you another, but I'm afraid I can't afford it." Michael's voice was soft.

I got to my feet and snapped my jeans closed. "Let me put the ring somewhere safe. I've got to get it repaired; it was a gift from one of my bosses at work, a simply wonderful gentleman. He would be so upset if he knew what happened!"

Michael rolled his eyes and put a finger to his lips. Obviously, I'd gone too far.

Michael dropped the ring into the toilet, and we both watched it whirl away in the company of some lipstick-stained toilet paper.

I turned to Michael, ready to heave a great sigh of relief, but instead, he was running around the apartment with the handheld bug detectors again. I went to the drawer, picked up my own device, and ran it over my purse and my coat, just in case anything else had been dropped in.

When I finished, Michael was sitting on the edge of the bed, with his head in his hands. "I think everything's normal again."

"Actually, everything's different now. Isn't it?" Since Michael and I had touched each other, the blurred outline that was Hugh Glendinning, the man who broke my heart, had faded even more. What did this mean, though?

Michael nodded absently, but didn't speak.

"Why did you kiss me?" I asked, thinking that I was the one who typically did stupid things—but this time, the mistake had started with Michael.

"Oh, I don't know." Michael glanced at me quickly, then looked away. "Jet lag, I guess."

"What?" This was both the most bizarre and the worst excuse I'd ever heard.

Michael continued, "My body clock's out of sync, which really screws with the endorphins. I'm always like this."

"So mean you've had the impulsive kissing problem for a while?" I asked sarcastically.

"Yes. I mean, no! I haven't done what I did in—a long time."

Because of Jennifer. I thought about his long-gone wife, and the desire that had flared in me subsided.

"Well, if you're as exhausted as you're saying, you'd better get back to the New Sanno and take care of yourself. Get a good night's sleep. It's already almost midnight."

"But you," Michael said. "What about you? I don't know what to do."

"In what regard?"

"I can't figure out if Yoshino was acting alone," Michael said. "You met Mr. Kitagawa the day before. From what you told me, they both seemed familiar with details that could have been gleaned from your personnel file."

"Maybe. But personal spying is a kind of national passion," I said, following Michael back into the living room, where he sidled close to the wall and gently lifted the edge of the drawn blind to look outside. "This is the nation that created the X-ray camcorders that people use to see what others look like undressed. This navel ring bug is probably something he gave to me because he wants to be able to hear me pee or something—"

"So you think it's just a matter of his prurient interest in you?" Michael shook his head. "And you think this prurient, pathologically obsessed accessories manager is sharp enough to run his own listening station? And by the way, where might it be located?"

"Not too far away, five or ten miles," I said.

"Agreed. It was a very low-power bug, judging from the fact that I didn't kill you when I removed it."

"Was there—a chance of my being electrocuted?" I held my breath.

"No." Michael sounded tired. "That was just a joke."

"Oh." I flushed, because before he'd answered I was starting to put it together in my mind that Michael had kissed me because he thought we were on the edge of death—that it was the one and only chance he had to show me how he felt. What a sentimental fool!

"We were talking about the listening station," Michael continued. "As I was saying, the bug was low-power, so the receiver would have to be very close to this apartment"

"Or what about the annex?" I asked. "That's where his office is, and I'm right across the alley from him, almost fifty hours a week. Maybe he's interested in what's going on in my life over at Mitsutan."

"Another possibility. I wonder if he's acting alone or at the request of someone." Michael turned back to the room and studied me. "How can we find out?"

29

I had trouble getting to sleep, although Michael had assured me by phone, after he reached the Sanno, that he had inspected the street and had seen nothing to indicate anyone was watching the apartment—at least, from the sidewalk or parked cars.

He'd left the apartment in heavy disguise, looking exactly like a working-class Asian man. He'd swapped the cat-burglar black for clothing from the disguise closet—a red baseball jacket with a Jinglish slogan, "Number One Fan," embroidered across the back; and a pair of plain khaki trousers and vinyl loafers. I'd watched with interest as he'd applied his makeup: a heavy foundation that turned his face and the backs of his hands a light gold; several eye shadows that he blended, in the manner that I did, to minimize the eyelid crease. He pulled a pair of glasses out of the disguise drawer: round, wire-edged frames that looked Asian. The only Japanese male accessory that he lacked was a man-bag, but the government stylists who had stocked the disguise closet had failed in this department. So Michael picked up the same plain black briefcase he'd arrived with and was off.

I wondered how he'd gained admission to his hotel looking like that, but it had happened. Maybe he'd wiped off the makeup at the guard station, or just explained himself brilliantly. Michael had options.

I, on the other hand, didn't. I turned on my bedside clock, and saw that it read two. It was Friday morning already, practically time to pull myself together for work at Mitsutan. My game plan was simple: avoid engaging in risky behavior. No pointed questions, no more planting of bugs. I was to maintain my holding pattern at the K Team desk until I was cleared to leave.

I flipped my pillow over, thinking that I'd never get to sleep. Of course I understood that my personal security was at risk—the fact that I'd so naively stuck the navel ring in my middle made me sick each time I thought of it—but I couldn't stand doing nothing. What was my job? Listening. Now, more than ever, I needed to know what was being said.

Since I couldn't sleep, I decided to do some listening. Michael had been confident that the apartment was bug-free, but just to be on the safe side, I slipped the first microchip of the department store recordings into my cell phone and crawled back into bed with a notepad and pen.

It took a good hour to transcribe everything from the first two bugs. I decided to type up my translation on the PC right away, in case I became too sleepy before I finished listening to all the tapes. I didn't want to leave my handwritten notes around; my plan was to send the translations right to Michael, then purge the evidence.

Lulu, one of the first consignment boutique departments I'd bugged, had a lot to transcribe, and it wasn't as boring as I'd expected. I was able to hear the tough circumstances for the independent designers operating a business under the Mitsutan roof. There were calls back and forth between Mr. Kitagawa and Miss Akai, the Lulu manager, not only about clothes sold but about which clothes had been tried on or rejected that day. He discussed at length the plight of some spring separates that hadn't sold well. Miss Akai offered to mark down the garments by twenty percent. Kitagawa agreed, with some stipulations: the sale merchandise had to be displayed discreetly, and it would be allowed to remain on the floor for only three weeks before Lulu would have to remove it. Finally, Mitsutan would collect eighty percent of the price of sales merchandise, rather than the normal sixty-five percent, as compensation for the vendor's inconvenience to the store. Miss Akai accepted her orders, sounding subdued.

I remembered hearing about similar situations in the United States, where some prestigious department stores had demanded a kickback from their wholesalers after the stores had to put the merchandise on discount. It was against the law, and the American stores had paid high fines. Given the power Japanese department stores seemed to wield over their consigners, I doubted that Mr. Kitagawa's demand was illegal. At the same time, I felt secretly lucky to know in advance that Lulu was going to have a surprise sale. I'd return to the department and maybe be able to buy myself a pair of pants as cool as Melanie Kravitz's.

After I was through listening, I realized that during all the time I'd spent eavesdropping on the accessories department, I had not heard Mr. Yoshino at all. He hadn't called in hounding the manager about her daily numbers; nor had she telephoned him for any reason. Maybe it was because the department was doing so well, or because Mr. Yoshino was so far removed from the sales team; he was so high up, in terms of status, that perhaps he didn't think daily communication with the accessories section manager was necessary. But Mr. Kitagawa—whose rank was similar—did make daily contact with his people. I'd heard him.

So maybe Yoshino was a hands-off manager; or else, I thought darkly, he'd planted bugs in his department so he could learn what he needed without having to call anyone.

I finished my notes, took a walk around the apartment, and did a few yoga stretches. It was just after three-thirty, and I was nowhere near ready to sleep. I seated myself in the lotus position, clapped the headphones on again, and began listening to the third recording, which came from the bug in Masahiro Mitsuyama's shoe. An argument with his wife started his day; then there was more grumbling as he was driven to work and made calls on his cell phone to various colleagues. The high point was a tirade against the food basement's sushi chef, because Mr. Mitsuyama was offended by the color of the tuna. I wrote it all down, imagining Michael's reaction. Utter boredom.

The fourth recording started out at the K Team, more or less with conversations I'd heard because I'd been there. Midway, I heard a new voice: a whiny woman's voice speaking in English. Melanie Kravitz.

I pressed "pause." I had the Kravitz recording, the one Michael had said was unethical. I'd assumed that Michael had taken the microchip with him, but he had left it in place, no doubt forgetting it after the chaos that had taken over the evening.

Now I had it, and whether I was going to listen to it or set it aside was my decision. I didn't take long to decide. I had to listen, because the fact was, that there was likely to be K Team business following

Melanie's voice. Or maybe she'd been using a K Team phone—she could have returned while I was on my break.

"Warren?" Her words left no doubt who she was talking to. "Warren, did you just call my cell? I can't get a signal, so I'm calling you back from a landline."

"Yeah, you got a minute?" he responded.

"Not really, but what is it? Did you forget to tell me something you needed?"

"It's about the party Saturday. See if you can catch a ride with the Abbots, or somebody, because I'm not going to get there till late."

"You mean—you won't get there at all." She laughed shortly. "Not again, Warren. Do you realize how annoying this is for me? It's not like Tyler's around any more to take me places. What do you want me to do, recruit one of those cute young boys from your department?"

"You're a big girl, Melanie. You can show up by yourself."

"But why? You've known about the orphanage ball for the last two months. You're chairing it with me."

"It's new business. Hot new business."

"Oh, come off it—"

"Shut up for a minute. Jimmy DeLone wants to spend some time when it's quiet, and the media aren't crawling all over him. His people say that it's got to be Saturday, and to block off the whole day into evening, just in case."

"The whole day into evening? Please!" Melanie shrilled. "I can't believe you'd leave me to chair this ball alone, after you were the one who pressured me to get you on the committee."

"Multibillion-dollar deals don't come along every week, Melanie. Imagine the year-end bonus."

There was an intake of breath. "Why not bring him to the party with you?"

"I'll ask what he wants to do," Warren said. "From what I hear, he's an oddball, and he's media-shy, like I said, because of the negative coverage on NHK."

"Did he bring his wife to Japan?" Melanie asked.

"He doesn't have one."

"Are you going to get him a girl?"

"What am I now, some kind of pimp?" Warren sounded exasperated.

"Not that kind of girl, Warren, just a pretty Japanese girl. Unless he's one of those confirmed bachelors. How old is he?"

"Pushing sixty, Melanie, and I have no idea whether he's gay. But there's a sexual harassment policy in our office. I can't pressure any of the OLs to spend time with Jimmy DeLone. And after the way he spoke to me, I think he'd scare most Japanese women off within ten minutes."

"I have an idea about a girl," Melanie said.

"I don't like the sound of that—"

"Never mind, honey. It was just an idea. I'll let you take care of your own business."

"Thank you, honey. You know, it's not just for me, it's for—"

"Us," Melanie finished. "Love you, Warren. Bye-bye."

I was laughing to myself by the end of the conversation. Melanie and Warren Kravitz certainly had a unified marriage. So their lives might be devoted to shopping, social climbing, and making the money to pay for it all.

Melanie's casual mention of someone named Tyler was interesting. Had Melanie Kravitz used good-looking young Tyler Farraday as her occasional escort? I wondered how they'd met, since I couldn't recall any mention, in the Tyler Farraday file, of the Kravitzes. Maybe the situation had come about because Warren wanted Tyler to keep tabs on his wife . . . or maybe because Tyler was attempting to cultivate ties with Melanie or Warren. Tyler had to have known that Warren was the man who'd instigated the whole American investigation of Mitsutan.

After I finished transcribing the rest of the recordings—business as usual between Mrs. Okuma and her contacts in the cashier's office—I decided to call Michael. It was five, which was early, but not too early for someone with jet lag.

"Hendricks," Michael answered after the hotel operator had patched me through to his room. His real name: how novel.

"Were you awake?" I asked.

"For hours," Michael said. "What's up?"

"Well, I did the transcriptions, and I'm about to send you something—"

"Don't. I have no Internet access in my room, and the situation with public computers downstairs isn't secure enough."

"That's a drag. You've simply got to hear what I've got on Warren—"

"This is a nonsecure line," Michael interrupted me.

"Well, then, I want to give you a transcript. Can you meet me right now?"

"I'd rather not. Too many people around."

"But you have to know what I heard before you go off to Winston Brothers today."

"I see. Well, then, why don't you make a drop at the place we discussed a while back?"

He was talking about the Kabuki Theater. I answered, "Sure. After I get to work this morning, I'll text-message you when I'm going on break, and see you over there."

"Try to send the message in advance, Rei. Even if I take a taxi, it could be a while till I get there."

"Okay, I understand. Over and out—"

"One last thing?"

"Yes?" I answered.

"Write it in code, on the off chance it's intercepted."

"Which code?"

"Two."

30

Michael and I had worked out a variety of codes together back in Pentagon City, on one of the icy days when the government was closed and there was little else to do. Today, because there wasn't much time for me to fuss, Michael had requested one of the easiest systems, which meant replacing each letter with one that was two farther along in the alphabet. Thus Warren became YCTTGP, and Mitsutan was OKVUWVCP. I just hoped Michael would have time to sit down privately and spell things out for himself before his one o'clock meeting with Warren Kravitz.

After my shower, I dressed for work, slipping the coded note inside a pink-and-orange Tsumori Chisato bra. Tonight was the night I was going out with Miyo, and I imagined she'd be checking me out critically as we dressed in the locker room, so I made sure everything matched. I pulled on a pair of Nice Claup khakis and an older Agnes B sweater just to get to the annex, but in my bag I was carrying better clothes for the night ahead of me: a slim-fitting Anna Sui purple corduroy skirt; a delicate chiffon-and-ribbon blouse from Rachel's Diary; and raspberry fishnet stockings that I would layer over flesh-toned hose, since the weather was still chilly. I remembered Mrs. Taki's warnings about fishnet stockings sending the wrong message in Japan, but I wasn't going to be courting any Japanese.

Mrs. Taki remained in my mind as I rode the subway to work. She'd bombarded me with e-mail messages that I barely had time to read: reminders that I needed to keep up my grooming with frequent appointments; that she hoped I was practicing my kanji; and that if

I had time, I was to go to Mitsutan's book department to find the novel she had asked me to bring. It was a good thing I hadn't told my parents I was abroad; who knows what they would have asked me to buy?

I put away my thoughts of the future as I stood at attention during the Friday morning *cho-rei*. Mr. Morita, general manager of the credit department, was expounding on the need for every salesperson to suggest that customers using cash should open store credit accounts. In Japan, he explained, credit cards were used for only eight percent of all spending—far less than in other countries, a situation the manager was deploring. If underlings were allowed to speak up at *cho-rei*, I would have told him the reason: Japanese credit cards didn't offer the chance to substantially delay payment, which was the crux of why most people used credit cards in the United States. Japanese creditors—whether they were responsible for Mitsutan's own private shopping card or a national card like Saison or J-Card—registered your bank account number when you signed up. Once or twice a month, the credit card would suck the payment due right out of your bank. If you were caught in a bind and didn't have enough funds in your account, the credit card company wouldn't allow you to roll over the balance to the next month; you'd have to pay within days. Most people did this by taking out a loan from a private lending company. The private companies charged horrifically high interest, and would send *yakuza* after you if you couldn't promptly repay them.

It was no wonder that people preferred to stay away from credit cards; the only incentive was a card that offered a discount. Big spenders at Mitsutan qualified for a Titanium shopping card, and thus could receive a five percent discount if they spent 800,000 yen within a six-month period. Mr. Morita pointed out that while 800,000 yen sounded like a lot of money, it really wasn't, if customers chose to buy foodstuffs and electronics at the store as well as clothes. Everyone benefited from using credit cards; it was our task, that day, to ponder how we could best increase the number of users.

"Boring," Miyo said when we'd started work a few minutes later in the K Team's office.

"Are you talking about the *cho-rei*?" I asked.

"No, the day itself. I wait so long for Friday and then I have to get through the whole day. We're still on for tonight, aren't we?" Miyo asked.

"Of course. And about the daytime schedule, when are you taking lunch?"   .

"Well, I'd like to go around one, if that's okay with you."

I blinked, surprised at her new politeness. "Sure. I was hoping to go early, around eleven."

"Don't worry, I'll say something to Okuma-san if she wonders where you are. She seems distracted, anyway; I'm sure she won't care. I bet you're looking for something to wear tonight." She beamed. "I hear there's going to be a sale in Comme des Garçons, but those aren't exactly clothes for dating."

"Agreed." I thought about Mr. Kitagawa's and Michael's reactions to the CDG top I'd worn a few days ago. "For tonight I brought an outfit already."

"You promised to let me see what you were thinking about!" Miyo sounded hurt.

"I know, but I can't spend too much. I think you'll approve. I tried to copy your style a bit," I added.

Miyo was right that Okuma-san was not going to notice what I was doing at eleven. She had not even sat down at the desk, but went right away to the PC in the back of the office, her fingers flying over the keyboard. At ten-twenty, I briefly excused myself to go to the women's room, saying something about drinking too much coffee; in the privacy of a stall, I opened up my phone and text-messaged Michael that I'd be inside the theater gallery by eleven-fifteen.

When the first customers of the day came in, an Italian husband and wife looking for a gift for their dog, I led them to Fifi and Ramone, the pet fashion boutique. They cooed over the cashmere dog sweaters, but ultimately settled on a blue-and-red vinyl raincoat. Excellent choice, I thought, not pricey enough for them to get the rebate, which meant that I could send them on their way and pop into the K Team's office briefly to sign out for my lunch.

Two customer groups were waiting. Mrs. Okuma was still on the computer, looking consumed. Miyo waved me off. "Go, Rei-san! I've got the situation covered."

I rushed over to the annex to get my coat, because I couldn't go to the Kabuki-za with my Mitsutan uniform showing. As I approached the building, I looked at the windows on the higher floors. Mr. Yoshino worked on the fifth floor, as I knew from the information on the business card he'd pressed on me at Aladdin's Cave. I thought I saw a figure looking down at me, or at the alley itself; however, I didn't have time to stand around counting up to see which floor the window belonged to.

The women's locker room was completely empty. I would have welcomed that a week earlier, when I was shy about joining the group. Today I felt differently; it spooked me to be here alone, when nobody would troop in to get a coat or anything else for at least an hour. As I opened my locker, I thought I heard the door I'd come through creak open, but there were no footsteps following.

I opened my locker, which, according to company rules, could not actually be locked, and slid my coat off the hanger. As I slipped my arm into one sleeve, it got caught in the lining. I pulled it out, irritated, then saw the cause; the lining had actually been slit. The same was true of the other sleeve, and there was also a slit along the hem at the coat's bottom.

Surely, Miyo wasn't mad at me anymore; we were going out that night. I couldn't think of anyone else who would do such a thing, and when would anyone have had time to do it?

During *cho-rei*. The only people who didn't have to attend *cho-rei* were senior managers, the people who worked in the annex. I hadn't seen Mr. Yoshino or Mr. Kitagawa at the morning lecture.

Now I was so nervous that I practically ran out of the building, slowing my pace only when I was out on Ginza-dori. I wondered if I'd done the right thing in wearing the damaged coat; all the cutting was in the interior, so I didn't look as if I were wearing rags, but I wondered about the integrity of the coat. I half wondered if there was a bug inside it.

I didn't like it. I popped into a rival department store, Mitsukoshi, got myself lost in a throng of women shopping for cosmetics, and rode an elevator up to the third floor, where I dumped the coat in a trash can in the women's room when the coast was clear. I did it with regret, because the Persian lamb jacket dated from the 1970s and had belonged to my mother. True, it was starting to get worn in many places, but it still had sentimental value—and it looked cool.

I took the store's stairs down to the food basement, where my Mitsutan uniform drew a few glances from shoppers and the Mitsukoshi staff, but I was quickly out the Harumi Street exit. After that, it was just a matter of crossing the street to the Kabuki-za.

A handsome black-haired foreigner with tortoiseshell spectacles and a cashmere overcoat was already at the small ticket window to the left of the main entrance. Michael, much more recognizable than usual.

I dawdled until he'd bought his ticket and gone inside. Then I drew close to the sign above the ticket window and studied it, trying to seem as if I were deciding which act to see. After a few more customers had bought tickets, I approached the same window and bought mine.

"There are only two rows of seats, at the back of the fourth floor. It's the highest place in the theater." The ticket clerk looked at me doubtfully.

"That's fine," I said quickly, handing her a 1,000-yen note and struggling to keep myself from grabbing the ticket she eventually gave me.

I ascended four steep flights of stairs, trying not to look rushed. Another day, I would have slowed my pace, because the theater, rebuilt in the style of the original 1924 building, was a beauty. But Michael was already inside, waiting for the drop.

I shook off my fantasy because a suited man was asking me for my ticket. I gave it to him, and he broke off the stub and returned it to me.

"Would you like to rent earphones?" he asked me in Japanese.

"No, thanks." I knew the play, *Bancho Sarayashiki*, the story of a quick-tempered lord who falls in love with a lady-in-waiting. I certainly didn't need expert commentary.

"Please go ahead. This side is less crowded." He waved his hand toward a curtained entryway. I walked through it carefully and, in the semidarkness, looked for Michael. Of course, he was sitting on the other side; in the seat closest to the aisle, with a briefcase laid over the empty seat between him and a couple of elderly Japanese women. This was bad manners, given that there were so few seats; but since he was a foreigner, nobody was going to test him. He had a pair of earphones on, I noticed, even though the show hadn't started; his gaze was downward at the English-language program.

I went out of the gallery again, and ignored the look of the ticket-taker as I entered through the other curtained doorway, which was closer to where Michael was sitting.

"*Sumimasen*," I said, and he looked up at me briefly, frowned, but removed the briefcase so I could sit down. I wondered if the frown was just for show, or if he was actually annoyed. I had been supposed to arrive there first, and have the message taped under his seat. Now I'd come late and would have to pass him the message without being noticed.

I jumped at the sharp sound of wooden blocks being struck together, the signal that the curtain was about to open. The audience leaned forward, drinking in the spectacle of a springtime scene complete with cherry blossoms. Soon we'd see the actors in spectacular robes.

Without the cover of a coat, getting out the transcript was going to be tricky. Thank goodness Michael had chosen a seat in the back row, I thought as I undid the three buttons of my work jacket so I could reach into my bra. The information packet had slid practically down to my ribs, so I had to unbutton a bit more to get it out.

Once I had it in hand, I waited for the right moment to drop the three stapled papers to the floor, then used my heel to shoot the papers in Michael's direction.

Unfortunately, I overshot the distance. The plastic-wrapped papers landed a few inches out from Michael's seat, in the aisle. Michael swiftly picked up the packet under the cover of a theater program already inside his hand.

Wordlessly, he handed me the program; the plastic-wrapped papers had already disappeared from sight.

"Domo sumimasen deshita." I made an elaborate, whispered excuse in Japanese for the sake of the woman on my left, who was looking at me first with annoyance, and then with shock, when she saw my open jacket.

I started buttoning myself up, embarrassed that I hadn't taken care of this before shooting Michael the papers. A couple of minutes later—when I'd ascertained that the prim woman was looking at the stage again—I glanced over to see what Michael was doing, but it turned out that he'd already left.

31

"So, what did you do for lunch?" Miyo asked when I returned to the department.

I paused, thinking over my answer. "Looked around at coats."

"Good idea," Miyo said. "That old furry thing you wear is really too shabby. I know you like vintage clothes and everything, but it's better to have something nice and new."

I watched her face, wondering if there was a chance she'd been the one who'd cut the coat up, perhaps in an effort not to have me go out with her while I was wearing it. After all, she had slid into place near me during *cho-rei* about five minutes later than me; she could have done the job.

"Did you go to the Nicholas de Gesquierre section?" Miyo continued. "There's a great coat there."

"I went all over, but I couldn't make up my mind." Now I realized that I had a problem—no coat whatsoever in the locker room. How would I explain that to her when we went out?

"Mmm," Miyo said. "Well, I haven't taken my lunch yet. I'm looking for a jacket myself, so if I see anything that would suit you I'll have it put on hold."

"That's really very kind—"

"It's not kind. I don't want to be embarrassed by you, that's all."

Touché. But I'd decided that Miyo's bark was worse than her bite, because she returned from lunch smiling and eager to talk. However, I was busy with a trio of Dominican baseball players who needed to be guided to the Super Men clothes department. When I was through with them, Mrs. Okuma wanted me to work with a Danish woman who was wheelchair-bound. That assignment turned into a very long expedition, since we needed not only to catch elevators but to ride in ones where there was enough room for the chair. Today was busier than usual, and I noticed that more O.L.s were around, as if they'd left the office early. Many of them were carrying boxes of chocolates. Valentine's Day fell on Sunday, so these would be last-minute gifts to the men in their office—delivered this afternoon.

I toyed with the thought of getting Michael some chocolates, but found myself fantasizing about feeding the chocolates to him with my fingers, so I discarded that idea. Anyway, the Dane didn't want to look at chocolates; she wanted to see books about Japan. I showed her some of my favorites and also managed to find the book Mrs. Taki had requested. I bought it discreetly while the customer was browsing. Now that was multitasking, I thought as the clerk wrapped my book in a specially sized brown paper cover.

The coat that Miyo wanted me to buy was going to be a magnet for dirt. It was the palest cream boiled wool, a wasp-waisted trench with a shearling collar that reminded me an old saying Hugh used to use: mutton dressed as lamb. Here I was, thirty years old and pretending to be twenty-three, in a coat that was utterly impractical. Not only was it white; it had no buttons or zipper. It just crossed elegantly across the front, so the effect with a tightly tied belt was quite slimming.

"Miyo, I can't go into a bar in this coat. It'll be stained within minutes." We had stopped into Designer Coats on the sixth floor, during the last thirty minutes the store was open. We were officially off duty and in our civilian clothes, so shopping was permitted.

"Yves Saint Laurent," Miyo said. "From the tag, I can tell it arrived in the store two months ago. I can't believe it didn't sell; guess it's because it's a large size."

"How nice of you to remember my size," I said drily.

"I'm not trying to be unkind," Miyo protested. "You're lucky you wear a size that isn't so common; it means you can find marked-down clothes. It looks fantastic on you, Rei-san. And it's reduced from 90,000 to 60,000. Fifteen percent off makes that 51,000 yen plus 2,550 yen for tax."

I'd been in the *depaato* world so long that $530 for a coat seemed reasonable.

"I'll take it." If OCI wouldn't cover the cost, I'd sell it on eBay.

"Good decision," Miyo said. "And it looks great with what you're wearing underneath.

"We'll take it to the cashier ourselves," Miyo said cheerily to the smiling salesclerk. I'd learned that it was store etiquette for shopping employees not to make the working salesclerks do too much. Miyo and I were lucky to have our schedules end an hour before closing, a K Team precaution against the embarrassment of having to rush a foreigner.

I handed the cashier my charge card and rested my elbows on the counter while she went into the backstage area to run it across the scanner. She spent an unduly long time, I thought, and when she came back her face was pink.

"I'm sorry, your card was—it can't—I'm sorry!" she ended in a torrent.

I blinked. "Do you mean the charge was not accepted?"

"I'm afraid so."

"You've been here two weeks, and you've already gone over your limit?" Miyo's voice held a mixture of admiration and disbelief. "How can that be? It's payday today, so you should have received a week's salary."

"That's right! And it's ridiculous that there's such a low limit on a store card. I mean, we should be encouraged to shop, not have our hands slapped this way."

"It's not Mitsutan's decision, but the decision of your bank," the cashier said quietly. "When I went back, I checked the record, and it shows that your Citibank account was already overdrawn."

"I'm sorry to hear that," I said, utterly mystified. My OCI consultant fees, including a hefty retainer for daily expenses, went straight into Citibank, as did the salary from Mitsutan. With two salaries, how could I have gone so swiftly into the red?

"Do you want me to charge the coat to my card?" Miyo offered. "I can do it. I've been here so long that my limit's really high. You can pay me back next week."

"No, no, it's okay—"

But Miyo insisted, and privately, I was relieved that I'd have something to cover me on a thirty-five-degree night.

It was seven-thirty, and we should have been hurrying out to the station to catch a train to Roppongi, but we were riding the escalators downward in the store, with Miyo still brooding. "I can't believe you shopped so much you depleted your bank account. It's my nightmare, but it's never actually happened to me. How weird that it happened to you, a banker's daughter."

"You know that about me?" I thought suddenly about the missing personnel file. Maybe Miyo wasn't really such a great new friend after all.

"Sure. Okuma-san told me. Now, I'm wondering about something," Miyo said. "Maybe the fifteen percent discount hadn't kicked in yet for you, and they're still only taking off ten percent. If you were cheated out of the discount, that's a serious problem, something for the union to hear about!"

"My receipts looked fine," I said, thinking that Miyo was the last person I'd ever imagine as a union supporter. "Seriously, I admit I've been spending too much. I need to cut back."

"I've got an idea, and it's only going to take a minute. Won't delay us much at all," she said, motioning for me to follow her off on the fourth floor, back to the K Team's office.

"What is it?"

"Let's check something on the computer." Miyo led me back into the empty department, sat at the desk that I usually used, and turned on my PC.

As it booted up, I said, "We could get into trouble for this."

"For working extra time? I doubt it. What's your ID number?"

I hesitated. If she learned my ID number, she could use it for any amount of mayhem. "I'll put it in."

Miyo grumbled and stood aside as I typed in the password, then I switched seats with her so she could do what she'd planned.

Miyo tapped the keys. "Here's the date you started, your home address and phone number. . . . I'll go into the next screen to see your credit card account."

All the clothes and accessories I'd bought were spelled out clearly in the phonetic alphabet katakana, each followed by a dollar amount. At the lingerie department, six Tsumori Chisato bras had cost me 52,000 yen. I winced; that was almost as much as the cost of the coat. Matching panties for each bra rolled in at 30,000 yen, total.

The Anna Sui skirt I wore was 33,000; the top was 22,000. I'd known

I was spending a lot . . . but not quite this much. I winced again as I tabulated the totals for Earl Jeans, the Issey Miyake jacket, trousers from Agnes B, slacks and a cowl-neck top from Comme des Garçons, and the Coach backpack. I had become, for all intents, a junior version of Melanie Kravitz, but without a husband to pay the bill.

"I shopped a lot," I said to Miyo.

"Not really. Everyone shops a lot here."

"My dad's going to kill me when he realizes I've spent all my salary and savings in less than two weeks." I was thinking about Michael Hendricks. Maybe I should buy him chocolates after all to soften my request for more money, immediately, in my Citibank checking account.

"I've never gone into an account like this, so give me a moment." Miyo tapped some more. "There is no breakdown here that shows the employee discount. Do you think it was factored in?"

"Yes. I remember seeing the discount marked on my own receipt. I'm sure it was there."

"Check the receipts," Miyo said as the printer started chugging out a paper. "This paper I'm printing out is for you to take home to compare."

"I will do that. Thank you." I'd given a lot of receipts to Michael during our meeting at the New Sanno, but I knew I had the slips from my most recent purchases in an envelope on my bedside table.

Miyo turned off the computer and stood up. "After this nightmare about the coat, I should be buying you a drink."

"Not at all," I answered, folding the paper into my purse. "I have plenty of cash, and I invited you. Besides, after the first drink or two, I don't think we'll have to cover many expenses at all."

32

The ride from Ginza to Roppongi on the Hibiya line was supposed to take thirty-two minutes, but it went much faster with Miyo at my side. Every now and then, a subway car is noisy; and our particular car, filled with lively young people going out on the Friday evening of Valentine's weekend, was buzzing. People were even using their cell phones, a violation of subway policy.

Normally I would have used the time to text-message Michael—I was consumed with curiosity about his interview with Warren Kravitz—but with Miyo at my side, that was impossible. So I talked to her.

As I'd suspected, the British boyfriend was not exactly in the picture. From what I could gather, she'd dated an Englishman a few times, but things hadn't gone well on their shopping trip, and he hadn't called her since. She was at loose ends, because she had no interest in dating Japanese or Koreans.

"*Tsumaranai*," she said; by now, I'd realized that "boring" was her buzzword for anything she didn't want. In Miyo's worldview, Asian men were boring because they didn't treat women well enough; they expected women to do all the housework, to defer to men's authority, and so on.

I was about to point out that there were many American men like that, too, before remembering that I had promised to help her meet an American guy—not just any guy, but one who was handsome, single, and high-earning. I lectured, "The thing about American men, which you might not understand, is that abroad, they sometimes lose a good bit of charm."

"How?" Miyo sounded skeptical.

"They become arrogant because of the way so many Asians seem to cater to them. It doesn't matter that it's not even sincere admiration—just regular politeness. " I paused. "You don't want to live with a man who acts this way. Believe me."

"But I don't want my family's life. Japanese like Koreans as long as they're acting in television soap operas or operating barbecue restaurants. They don't want to work under Koreans, in companies or stores. I've told you before how I'm trapped as a contract employee at Mitsutan. I'll never be a salaried, lifetime worker."

"So marriage is an escape—"

"Exactly. And if I get a foreigner—a really good foreigner—I can just leave this. Go away, like you did, to another country, where race doesn't matter."

Race did matter, in every country that I'd been in. But I didn't correct Miyo, because I felt that I was finally starting to understand her bitterness. And her marriage plan did make sense, in a warped kind of way.

As we strolled down Roppongi-dori, I further explained the classic problem with cross-cultural dating. I told Miyo that although she was beautiful, she wouldn't be able to take a relationship past the proverbial one-night stand if she couldn't talk to a man properly.

"And when I say talk, it's not just *hai-hai-hai*," I said. "Flattery is important, but not the only thing. You must carefully tease them."

"You mean—like bullying in schools?" Miyo sounded shocked.

"No, not exactly." I was rambling, because this was not my usual arena of expertise. "It's like insulting them, but with a smile."

"Maybe we should go somewhere less public while we're talking about this." Miyo had lowered her voice, as if she was worried that I was about to give away state secrets.

"Sure," I agreed. "Let's sit down and have a drink somewhere in Roppongi Hills. There are so many places." Roppongi Hills housed at least three major foreign investment banks, perfect fishing grounds for Miyo—and not a bad spot for me to keep an eye out for the men I was interested in: Michael, Warren Kravitz, and Jimmy DeLone.

Under the soft golden light at the Iron Grill, I coached Miyo. Her English was not going to be transformed, but at least she now had some sample conversational openers to interest men, so she didn't come off as a stereotyped Japanese girl: the kind of girl western guys were delighted to sleep with a few times, until the next beautiful girl came along.

"Can you ride a bicycle? I mean, a bike?" I asked Miyo in English, keeping an eye on the door. Where were the guys, anyway?

"Yes, I can ride a bike." Miyo sounded bored.

"Any other sports?"

"Well, I've been kick-boxing and snowboarding this winter, and I scuba-dive in the spring and summer."

"That's fantastic," I said. "I had no idea you're so athletic! It totally goes against the stereotype of the delicate Japanese blossom."

"You have to take up hobbies when you have your free day in the middle of the week. Certainly, men aren't available to go out."

I'd noticed small groups of men coming in for dinner together—colleagues, it was clear, some of them probably entertaining international visitors. I was hoping to find a twosome or threesome, possibly including women; that would make our efforts seem less like a cold, hard hit, so I asked the bartender if it would be possible for Miyo and me to move to a centrally located table and consider the menu.

Of course. We were pretty girls, and pretty girls usually got visible seats in restaurants. I glanced over the menu, which was classically western, but with mostly regional ingredients: pork from Kagoshima, beef from Tokachi, and so on. There was some seafood, too; I could survive, if we were going to have dinner later, as I hoped. In the meantime, I ordered sizzling Hokkaido scallops and Miyo took the prawn cocktail. We practiced English conversation as we nibbled, and finally, I was convinced I'd seen the right pair. They'd come in with their ties off and jackets open; one was blond, tall, and looked all of twenty-two years old, though I knew he was probably at least old enough to have earned an MBA. The shorter man with him had longish dark hair and an olive complexion: South Asian, I guessed.

In Monterey, I'd sometimes gone by myself to the historic old Regency Theater on Alvarado Street to watch the Indian movies screened there on Sunday afternoons. The young man resembled a younger version of one of the most popular male romantic heroes, Salman Khan. But this Indian sitting in a Tokyo restaurant was not a film star; he was something even better, I realized as I took in the gym bag with a Winston Brothers logo near his feet.

"They've probably got girls arriving," Miyo said, because the table was a four-top.

"Not likely," I said, although that was a possibility. By now, the restaurant was packed with girls dining with girls and guys with guys, all stylish young Japanese. "I'm sure our boys were given the good table because they're regulars. They're just having their usual supper, and then when it's almost eleven, they'll head back to their office to talk on the phone with their bosses back in New York," I said, watching the two sip Cokes.

"But westerners aren't supposed to work very hard, not like Japanese."

"They have to report in at night, when the stock markets are just opening in the morning in New York. Only after they've touched base with their colleagues will they hit the clubs, and that's where our competition will be. We can't let them get to that point."

"I thought you were going to introduce me to someone you knew," Miyo said.

"Unfortunately, the ones I knew are abroad at the moment," I said. "But I think I have the skills to carry this off. Just watch."

"Well, I want the blond one," Miyo said.

"Sure." I preferred exotic foreigners over Americans, anyway. But I said, "Remember, I'm trying not to get involved with a westerner; my parents would kill me. I'm only here to help make an introduction."

The plan was simple. I called the waiter over and ordered two dirty martinis to be sent over to the boys' table. I included a note, which said in English, "Too much work makes Jack a dull boy. See ya! Miyo and Rei."

"It's pretty forward," Miyo said, not wanting to look up from her plate after the waiter had gone off, smirking a little. I was sure the note was an oddity; an expensive restaurant like the Iron Grill wasn't exactly a pickup joint.

The restaurant was really jumping now, so it took ten minutes for the drinks to get to the table. I instructed Miyo to join me in looking steadily at the two young men, until they'd established our identity. I waved as cheerfully as if we all were old friends.

The blond stood up and waved back. That made it official, I thought; we were welcome to join them.

"Let's carry our drinks over. I already left money for the waiter," I told Miyo.

"I'm so nervous. I know I won't say anything, and you'll get all the attention—"

"You walk ahead of me and you say the first line, remember?" I said under my breath as we started walking. "And after that, if you get tongue-tied, I'll speak Japanese to tell you what to say."

Miyo performed brilliantly. The fact was, that a girl as beautiful as she was needed to say only a few friendly things to make a man feel successful—and if there was a teasing quality to the talk, as I'd said, it was all the better. Miyo asked the blond if he was the snowboarder who'd fallen on his face in Hokkaido the previous week. After he was done laughing, he said that no, he hadn't been there, but skiing in Hokkaido was something he hoped to do. The season was almost over, I said, mentioning that Miyo and I were getting ready for a scuba-diving vacation in Izu.

The blond one was called Archibald Weinstock and the dark one Ravindra Shah—Ravi for short. They'd both earned MBAs at Penn. Archie had been at Winston Brothers for two years, Ravi for one year. Their lives were so busy that they hadn't had a moment to study Japanese; they couldn't believe how good our English was.

"Have you had dinner yet?" Archie asked, smiling.

"Actually, we've just had a few appetizers," I said. "But we intend to eat. Miyo loves steak, so I'm taking her out tonight because it's her twenty-first birthday."

A round of happy birthdays ensued. Before we knew it, Archie and Miyo were both ordering Japanese flat-iron steaks, and I was wavering between grilled asparagus and macaroni gratin.

"So little to eat?" Ravi asked, looking concerned.

"I'm a vegetarian," I confessed.

"Really! I am, too. I just came here with Archie tonight because it's close." Ravi Shah had a nice accent—New Jersey tinged with something else. I had to smile at his dinner order; sautéed spinach, broccoli, asparagus, pumpkin puree, and the macaroni gratin.

"Why not add the mushrooms, potatoes, and onion rings?" I raised my eyebrows. "Then you'd have it all."

"Ah, but I cannot eat anything that grows underground," Ravi said. "That's the problem."

"Not to mention meat or fish," Archie said. "Ravi has a hard time staying alive in Japan."

"Are you a Jain?" I asked.

Ravi blinked. "Yes. I'm surprised you've heard of my faith."

I bit my lip. It was a little unusual for a Japanese to know much about foreign religions. For someone from San Francisco, it was par for the course, but I wasn't supposed to be American tonight. "In our jobs, we help many foreigners. Some are Jains."

"Yes, I just helped a kind lady named Jane last week," Miyo said.

Quickly, I explained to Miyo a bit about the Indian religion that held all forms of life reverent—even small insects, which could be accidentally killed if vegetables were pulled from the earth.

"You're quite the interpreter," Archie said, grinning. He was loosening up nicely, thanks to the martinis. But I had to watch myself, and give more talking time to Miyo.

"Just as Archie is to Ravi, Miyo, you're my *sempai*. Please explain our job; you'll make a much better effort than I can, as I have a lot to learn."

"We help foreigners buy things," Miyo said. "Everything from underwears to umbrellas."

Both men laughed appreciatively, and I winked at Miyo. I'd taught her the line earlier, wanting her to sound both suggestive and innocent, at the same time. It had all come off seamlessly.

"I guess you could say we help people buy things, too," Archie said, leaning a little closer to her. "Not underwears, but bonds."

"How exciting! You must be very smart," I purred.

Ravi looked at me a bit longer, and more skeptically, making me feel a bit uncomfortable. Obviously, my knowledge of Indian religions didn't jibe with my charming naïveté.

"We have a customer from your firm, what is his name, Miyo?" I said, screwing up my forehead. "Kravis-san?"

"Kravitz? Are you talking about Warren Kravitz?" Ravi rubbed his hand across his chin, which was developing a very attractive five-o'clock shadow.

"Yes, that's it. Miyo-chan, you said you met him, right?" I waited, half hoping Miyo would say something inflammatory, like he was a pain in the ass to take shopping.

"Oh, yes. He is actually our number one foreign customer!" Miyo smiled at me, almost making me forget how snippy she'd been when I'd asked about the Kravitzes before.

"Warren Kravitz does so well that he could shop all day and night, if he had the time," Ravi said. "He's head of the Japanese investment banking division. The year-end bonus he gets is the stuff of legend."

"How much?" Miyo asked, and I quickly kicked her under the table. We didn't want to give the impression that we were after the men for their money.

"How much time do you have to work at the firm to become a partner? That's what Miyo was asking," I said.

"Oh, God, I don't know. Ten years?" Ravi said. "For Kravitz, it was faster."

"And they usually recruit guys from the outside to take the really sweet spots. There's a lot of movement within the banking community," Archie said.

"You'd think that somebody working loyally within the company would be rewarded. That's our Japanese thinking," I said.

"You know what gets rewarded?" Archie said.

Both Miyo and I shook our heads.

"Dumb luck. A guy makes a risky trade or purchase, and it pans out nicely—well, he gets the bonus at year's end. And then the whole gang goes to Seventh Heaven or Climax to celebrate."

And Russian strippers would lap-dance all over them, but of course I wasn't going to give away my knowledge of the seamier side of their lifestyle. It didn't pay to sound jealous.

"I know better clubs than Seventh Heaven and Climax," Miyo said, and the two bankers exchanged amused glances.

"We'd like to take you girls out after dinner," Archie said. "The thing is, I have to go back to the office to make a call at nine. You two can come with us, if you wouldn't find it too boring."

"What do you think, Miyo?" I asked.

She blinked rapidly, as if unable to believe this wasn't a dream. "I think it sounds—awesome."

The guys smiled at her use of the phrase, and inwardly, I cheered.

33

I could barely keep my eyes open when I rolled into bed six hours later. We'd done the Winston Brothers office, where Miyo and I spun around on office chairs, trying to make Archie crack up while he made his serious phone call to the big boss in New York. Then we'd gone out to a rave at Cube 326, and after we'd all been thoroughly over-heated, I led everyone out, pointing to a place I'd noticed in a nearby lane: an old-fashioned games parlor in Shinjuku, a place where you could sit and play go for hours, drinking sake and surrounded by a totally Japanese crowd.

It had done the boys good to get out of their element, to go to a couple of places that must have felt edgy because they were almost completely devoid of gaijin. Miyo had said a few things earlier that gave me reason to suspect she was excellent at go—in Korea, they call it *baduk*—so each of us paired with one of the men, trying to teach them the basics. But it was pointless. No matter how many times we explained the rules of how to capture the opponent by surrounding him, they missed good opportunities: Ravi because he seemed a bit distracted, and Archie because he was getting drunk.

As Ravi and Archie swayed their way into a cab, Archie declared that they'd never had such a wild evening with Japanese girls. In return, he insisted that the two of us come with them the following evening to the Tokyo Children's Aid Ball.

I couldn't have been more pleased, but I acted regretful, reminding Miyo that we both had plans. Her face fell, but then she caught on to my game. We let the boys plead long and hard, and I made a call on

my cell phone, a call that I made sound like a social date I was cancel-
ing, though I was actually just talking to my answering machine.

"I thank you for this special time," Miyo had said, doing everything but hug me when we were saying good night at Shibuya Station. The boys had long since packed off in a taxi to their apartments
in Ark Hills.

"I was happy to help you meet someone, Han-san. I think Archie
really likes you."

"Oh, call me Miyo, from now on. And, Rei-san—I'm sorry about the
beginning we had. I just didn't understand who you really were."

If she did really know, what would she think? I shuddered, thinking about it as I took off my smoky clothes and jumped into the
shower, because I didn't want to contaminate the bed with the aromas of everywhere I'd been that night.

When I got out, the phone was ringing, and I picked it up as I tow-
eled off.

It was Michael, sounding anxious. "You've been out of contact for
hours."

"Sorry, I thought I told you I had plans for the evening." Guilt flashed
through me, because I hadn't messaged Michael when I'd stepped into
the women's lavatory several times that evening. But I'd been eager to
get back, not to miss a bit of information the boys might spill.

"Are you alone?"

"Of course I'm alone." I struggled into my nightgown double-time
and heard the ominous sound of tearing silk. "What are you insinu-
ating?"

"Nothing. I just wanted to—thank you for what you gave me earlier today—it was quite interesting. Since you're alone, I'll be able to
talk about what I learned in the interview."

Michael recounted how Warren Kravitz had jump-started Winston
Brothers' rise in Japan during the 1990s, owing to his talent at lo-
cating distressed properties and then matching them to rich American clients who needed a guiding hand overseas. The recent slight
rebound in the Japanese economy had raised his antenna, Michael
said; it had caused his sharp eye to focus on Japanese retail patterns,
whereupon he noticed the problem with Mitsutan and duly reported
it to our government.

"Why did he even complain in the first place?" I demanded. "I can't help wondering if it's because he wanted to start a bad rumor about Mitsutan, ruin the company's value, and then help Jimmy DeLone buy it cheap."

"There's no indication, from my conversation or your tape, that Warren's association with DeLone isn't completely new business. DeLone's been having trouble with the bank he was originally talking with in Japan, which was why he switched to Winston Brothers."

"Really. And what motivation, then, does Warren Kravitz say drove him to tell tales to the government?"

"I think the exact word he used was 'patriotism.'"

"Excuse me?" I smoothed my nightgown over my hips with one hand, checking myself in the mirror. Yes, I'd definitely torn the side. What a shame!

"He's worried for our country. He sees Japanese companies engaged in unscrupulous business practices take over so many markets that once were ours—cars, cameras, televisions, videos. Now with China on the rise, Japan is more desperate. I have to agree with him."

"But what's the actual threat to our nation? Mitsutan's not trying to take over Saks Fifth Avenue—or Supermart, for that matter." I paused. "What did you make of Melanie's mentioning Tyler?"

"I was startled," Michael said. "I brought Tyler's name up casually—one of the reasons I told Warren that I was in Japan, at the embassy, was to make sure all of Tyler's possessions had been removed from his apartments, his bills paid, and so on. Warren chimed in that he'd met Tyler a few times because Melanie had used him as an extra man at some dinner parties, and so on."

"And?"

"Well, he said that the kid talked to him about moving out of modeling and into investment banking, and Warren gave him a lecture on the academic qualifications needed. Of course, he had no idea Tyler was actually well educated."

"Really? Where?"

"Princeton."

"Oh!" This did surprise me, because I'd assumed, since he was so handsome, that he wasn't very smart. I'd been guilty of prejudice. "Well, if Tyler had this conversation with Warren, and these dinner parties or whatever with Melanie, why wasn't that all in the reports?"

"Probably because it happened quite close to the time of Tyler's death. He might not have had a chance to report it—or perhaps he was embarrassed to, because he actually did want to make a switch. Civil servants don't make that much, as I'm sure you know."

I was actually making more, per month, now than I had ever made in my life—but of course, it was not a twelve-month-a-year job, just a temporary contract. And my last, if I didn't succeed. I offered, "Perhaps Tyler thought there was something bad going on at Warren's bank, and that's why he wanted to go in. He might not have been as bad an agent as you and I have been thinking."

"I'm doubtful of that," Michael said. "After all, he got himself killed."

"Because he was killed, he must have been stupid? Is that the way you think things work?"

There was a long silence. Michael finally said, "No, of course not. You're right that Tyler gave his life for this investigation. I stand corrected."

In a gentler tone, I said, "I think it makes us feel safer about our own situation here if we say the reason he died was that he made an error. But the fact is, there are unidentified people who are suspicious of me already, and God help you if you're on their radar screen as well."

"Don't worry so much. I'm here to watch over you, okay?"

"Well, don't do it too closely," I said. "Tomorrow night I don't want to see you, because I'm going to be in the vicinity of Warren and Melanie and even Jimmy DeLone."

Michael interrupted me. "Sorry, but they're not on your turf."

"But it'll blow my cover if I change my plans for tomorrow evening." I explained how Miyo and I had met up with two young Winston Brothers employees who had asked us to accompany them to the charity ball.

"I got the feeling it was to save face with their boss. Apparently, Melanie wants a lot of Winston Brothers employees at the event. The unmarried ones are supposed to bring dates."

"If you go, it's purely social. Right?"

"I'm sure that I'll enjoy myself, but I'll keep my ears open." I desperately wanted to go. If I canceled, Miyo might flounder; and besides, I was curious to meet Warren Kravitz.

"You're not on assignment. I didn't send you there. In fact, I don't really want you to be there."

"It's just a double date. The guys think I'm a mild-mannered salesgirl."

"Oh, really! Have they seen your navel piercing yet?"

"No, but that reminds me that there are some things I need to tell you." I described the slashed coat in my locker and the sorry state of my bank account.

Michael sounded fairly subdued at the end of my recital. "Are you still wearing the coat?"

"No. I threw it away, just in case there was a bug in it."

"I would have liked to examine it," Michael said. "But never mind. I presume this means you're going shopping again?"

"I didn't mean to spend as much money as I have," I apologized, "but I guess it goes with the territory. Fortunately coats are on sale, and Miyo lent me the money to buy one yesterday because I was short. I don't have the receipt, but I do have the price tag. Can I use that in my expense report, minus the discount, of course?"

"Are you asking me for a cash advance?" Michael asked, instead of directly answering me.

"Well, yes. I want to pay her back as soon as possible."

"So you just need money for the coat?"

"No," I admitted. "Other clothes purchases are bound to come up, plus transportation, and I should really pay something toward all these bar and restaurant outings with Miyo and the guys, which should continue, because I'm forging important alliances, don't you think?"

There was a long silence. Then Michael said, "I've given you the right to manage your expenses, because you've been very trustworthy to date. I never imagined how high the totals would be. I don't know how I'm going to even start to explain your ridiculous lingerie bill to our accounting head."

"Did you forget our conversation about where I needed to be carrying the bugs? As you know, there's a closet full of disguises in the apartment, but it did not include any bras, nor the right kind of pants with lots of pockets, and—and you know the rest. Everything I've worn has a purpose," I protested.

Michael sighed and said, "I'll have two thousand dollars wired to your bank account, but it probably won't get there till sometime tomorrow. You may use whatever's needed from that to pay for the coat. And as far as tomorrow evening goes, please understand that you are not on assignment. This means, don't even think of asking me to recoup the cost of an evening dress."

34

"Hungover?" Miyo whispered when we saw each other in the K Team's office at ten o'clock sharp on Saturday morning. Mrs. Okuma was already at her desk, looking rather sourly at both of us, as if she'd figured out that something had changed in the K Team, but not for the better.

I whispered back, "A bit. You?"

"Couldn't help it. What a good time!"

"And it was so nice of you to lend me the money for a new coat. I should have the money tonight to repay you." I didn't need to tell her that at home the previous evening, I'd run the bug-detecting equipment over every inch of the garment, just to make sure Miyo hadn't slipped anything into it. The coat was cleaner inside than out, where—as I'd predicted—I already had a small stain from an over-turned Kirin beer at the go parlor.

"Don't worry about it." In her next breath, she said, "What are you wearing tonight?"

"I have a black Azzedine Alaia bandage dress. I think I'll wear that." Thank goodness I'd packed the trusty old friend in my luggage.

Miyo winced. "A bandage dress? But that's so old, like from the time when we were children—"

When *she* was a child. I merely shrugged and said, "American men don't read *Oggi* or *25 Ans*. It's a nice, sexy dress; they're bound to think it's cool. And even if I had the money, there'd be no time to shop with just the two of us covering the desk."

It was true; this was a very busy day, with a Swedish tour group coming in, assorted Chinese and Koreans, and what seemed like a representative of every Eastern European country. Miyo was willing to take the Korean customers around, I was glad to see. I was getting faster on the computer; by now, I knew most of the kanji that came my way, as I oversaw sales transactions and handled tax rebates by myself.

I was just giving 2,500 yen to a jubilant Thai woman—it never failed to thrill the foreign customers that they could get a fraction of money they'd spent back from the store—when Ravi Shah walked in. He was wearing khakis, a rugby shirt and Top-Siders, looking every bit the Indian preppie. His gaze swept over Miyo and me, and he smiled.

"What are you doing here, stranger?" I smiled back at him, thinking that, except for the matter of age, Ravi would be quite appropriate for a rebound romance. I was also feeling relieved that Mrs. Okuma was at lunch and wasn't around to listen in to this particular conversation.

"Oh, just wanted to check out if you two really worked here." His smile was ingratiating, but I felt myself cringe slightly under his alert gaze.

"Of course we work here. What do you want, shopping help?" Miyo giggled. She had been the only one to jump up and give him the mandated welcoming bow; I'd been too stunned by his appearance to remember my etiquette.

"I already bought something for tonight." Ravi held up one of Mitsutan's to-go garment bags, which I deduced was hanging over a formal suit. "This has to be the only country in the world where I can buy a suit without needing to alter the trouser length."

"What about India?" Miyo asked.

"Everything there's custom-sewn by tailors. You can get an exact copy of a Savile Row suit hand-stitched in less than forty-eight hours, and I can't begin to tell you at how low a price."

"You'll make me cry." I'd already unzipped the garment bag and examined the inky-black Christian Dior tuxedo. "I hope you bought the tux using your Mitsutan credit card."

"I used Visa. Why?"

"Well, if you use the store card, your purchases are tracked. If you're a good customer, you get some money back at the end of the year."

"Ah, but *good* means spending a fortune, right?" Ravi raised his eyebrows. "And I'm not big on Japanese banks."

"Why?" I asked.

"No offense intended. I'm sure that this store's banking and credit division is fine." He leaned forward over my desk. "Actually, Rei, I was wondering if I could stash the suit here for about an hour while you show me around the store. You mentioned last evening something about an exhibit of antique Japanese games. And would you have time for lunch after that?"

"I wish I did, but there's just two of us on the K Team desk today."

"You can go," Miyo said. "And why not take Ravi-san to lunch using the house charge?"

"Are you sure it would qualify?" I asked.

"Look at what he's bought so far," Miyo replied in Japanese. "I'll enter him in the K Team book, saying you helped him with the tuxedo, and then, as far as Okuma-san goes, there will be nothing out of line."

Life was so much better, now that Miyo liked me. But I felt a bit uneasy, heading off with Ravi, who I sensed had something more on his mind than the games exhibit or lunch with me.

"The store has so many restaurants that we really have a lot of choices. I can help you figure out something vegetarian," I said to him from the back of the elevator, where we were jammed in along with many housewives, all headed up toward the restaurant floor.

"Don't worry about that. I'm actually not that hungry. But I'd like to see the games."

We exited on five and entered Musée Mitsutan, which was twice as crowded as it had been the last time I'd stopped in. This must have been because it was Saturday. Fathers were around, holding their children's hands and explaining the intricacies of the different games. A few of the children got really excited and tried to pick up the old agate and crystal pieces; one toddler started screaming when a Mitsutan staffer tried to intervene.

I couldn't help smiling, and Ravi said to me, "That's quite a cool game. But it's really Chinese in origin, isn't it?"

I turned to him. "It's a matter of debate. Each country wants to claim to be first. I tend to believe great games can develop spontaneously in different places."

"Games also traveled quite a bit. I know India's supposed to be the original place for a lot of games, like snakes and ladders and chess—which actually seems a bit like that game over there." He pointed at a footed *shogi* board with eighty-one square places marked on its surface; on it were little pieces of lacquered wood inscribed with words for gold and silver generals, knight and lance. I explained the strategy of *shogi*, and its various playing pieces, to Ravi.

"Is this the most important game in Japan?" he asked.

"Probably. It's such a great game of strategy. I know it's tough to play the first time around, but I'm sure you'll get the hang of it, if you're interested."

"You said it was a game of siege when we were talking yesterday."

"That's right. But in order to win, you need to develop a skill we call *taikyoku-kan*."

"Which means?"

"The ability to view the entirety of what's going on, all the time." I looked at Ravi, who seemed befuddled, so I went on. "The way it works, I think, is by constantly surveying the progress of the game, always imagining different outcomes. A player who gets really excited by a partial victory could be defeated at the end; that's what kept happening to you and Archie last night, I think."

"Archie didn't care," Ravi said.

"But did you? Did it bother you that two girls were taking the lead, telling you what to do?"

Ravi's voice sounded guarded. "Are you asking me this because you think I come from a conservative culture?"

I hesitated, remembering who I was supposed to be. Quietly, I replied, "I suppose so. As an Asian woman, I know there are some things I'm not supposed to say or do in order to keep things harmonious."

My mind on this, I picked La Mer, Mitsutan's Mediterranean restaurant, for lunch. I figured there would be some kind of pasta or salad that would meet Ravi's standards, but unfortunately, just about everything contained some form of meat or fish. The waitress shook her head when I asked if the spaghetti bolognese could be served just with olive oil. So much for catering to the customer's needs. Also, we hadn't gotten a good table up front; we were in the back, next to the kitchen door.

"I'll order the fruit cup; I'm not that hungry anyway," Ravi said.

"I'll have the salmon salad, then, if you don't mind seeing fish on my plate."

"It's okay. I'm used to being close to things I don't like."

"You seem a bit stressed," I said. "Is there anything I can do to help?"

"A bit stressed," Ravi repeated. "What an interesting phrase."

"What do you mean?" I said, laying out the napkin on my lap. It was a treat for me to eat in a Mitsutan restaurant while in uniform; the only reason that it was happening was that I had a customer, and I was determined to enjoy my meal, whether or not the customer was surly.

"Your English is very good for a Japanese store clerk," Ravi said, and from the expression in his dark, hooded eyes, I finally understood that he knew. I couldn't play the acquiescent Asian anymore; I'd have to match his aggressive moves with a few of my own.

Lowering my voice, I said, "I wonder how many people have said the same kind of thing about your English?"

"English is the national language of India," Ravi said stiffly. "I attended English schools until I arrived in New Jersey, at the age of ten. Yes, I speak Gujarati at home with my parents, but English is what I've always spoken, most of the time."

"Of course. But there's the matter of how you look. And how I do, as well."

"You're not really twenty-three years old," Ravi said.

I shrugged. "Maybe not. I didn't say anything when Miyo was telling you my age because I didn't want to scare you young darlings off."

"I believe you're thirty years old," Ravi went on, "and you're not a graduate of Waseda University, but of Johns Hopkins in Baltimore."

We were staring at each other when the waitress interrupted us with the fruit cup and my salad. She left the bill prominently at my side. It was because I worked for the K Team, of course; but Ravi didn't know. He stared at the bill as if it were dirty.

I picked it up. "I'm paying this, and I can do it right now and leave if that would make you more comfortable. Obviously you've done a Google search or something like that on me, and I'm not to your taste. That's fine—I understand it completely—"

"Don't go," he said. "I just want to know why you're pretending to be someone else."

I gazed into the eyes of this bright, energetic young man, knowing that what Michael feared most was happening: my cover was on the verge of being blown. The only consolation was that he didn't work at Mitsutan; but even as a friend, he was a danger to me.

"I don't know if you can possibly understand what it's like to grow up in two worlds." I spoke slowly, formulating my words as I went along. What I was going to say was based mostly on truth, and that was what made it so difficult. "I was educated there . . . but I'm supposed to fit in here. That's why I'm at Mitsutan. It's the perfect place for a woman in her twenties, and, well, my twenties were a lost decade, I'm sure you already know, if you read about all the things that happened." I paused. "Did you?"

"Well, actually, what I did was follow a hunch and go to the website for foreign alumni of Waseda. It tells what everyone did after the junior year abroad. You, I believe, went to Hopkins and Berkeley and then over here, to sell antiques? That's a far cry from what you're doing now."

I shook my head in dismay. "There is a Japanese-language website for regular Waseda alumni, with a different Rei Shimura listed, with all the correct biographical data. I'm sure of it!" Michael and Mrs. Taki had slipped the information about me into the existing web page.

"Yeah, but because I don't read Japanese, I wound up in the foreigners' section, like I always do." He was talking about a section I had never bothered to search, and hadn't even known had listed me.

"Well, during the last few years in Japan I've faced—some discrimination—so I've decided to go completely native. You've heard of born-again Christians? Well, I'm a born-again Japanese! That's about all I can say for myself."

"Why do you pretend to have a Japanese accent? It kept coming and going last night; it was ridiculous. Don't even use it tonight."

"I don't know whether I should come with you. I'm a bit anxious, now, about it. I just thought it was going to be a good time, dancing and that kind of thing—"

"Why did you hit on us last night?" Ravi asked abruptly.

"Miyo and I were just out—enjoying ourselves. We saw two cute, friendly-looking guys and sent over a couple of martinis. We didn't mean to cause you any concern."

"Listen, I have enough phony shit going on all day long," Ravi said. "The last thing I need is more of the same."

I would have loved to hear what he considered phony shit, but I didn't want to press my luck. So I sliced off a wedge of salmon and chewed it instead of answering.

Ravi spoke again. "I must marry an Indian girl."

I looked up at him, and saw how agitated he had become. This twenty-four-year-old guy, who I'd thought was happy-go-lucky the previous night, seemed on the verge of tears. I said, "Is that a big problem?"

"Sometimes I wonder if anyone will have me."

"Of course someone will. You'll have your pick, I'm sure."

Ravi closed his eyes for a long moment. "My parents worked so hard for this . . . for me to go to Penn, then to get a chance at a place like Winston Brothers . . . but it's just rotten. I wish I could quit."

I nodded, not having to fake sympathy. "What's going on at work, exactly?"

"It's—the things we do, the corners we cut." He shook his head. "Our business practices are no better than the worst stories I hear from my uncles in India. Maybe it's because we're in Asia. But then again, I'm working for a hundred-year-old American firm, supposedly perfect."

"I left America for a reason," I said, feeling treacherous as the words left my mouth. Surely Michael would never make comments like this, even if he were a prisoner of war threatened with torture. But I felt that I knew exactly what Ravi was talking about.

"I don't know where I belong." Ravi sounded bleak. "You know, I'm supposed to be going back next winter to choose my bride."

"Lucky girl." I tried to smile.

"Nobody's fortunate to have to come with me into this life." Ravi ran a hand across his unlined, damp brow. "You saw us on Friday night, when it was over. Basically, we work about one hundred twenty hours a week, sitting on our asses, shouting into telephones. How is that any different from the life of my cousin, sitting in Mumbai answering phone calls from people with effed-up computers?"

"You're making a lot more money than your cousin, I bet."

"Yes, it's all about money." Ravi sighed heavily. "That's what Warren Kravitz said."

Warren Kravitz, who Michael thought was great. I said, "I would love to go out with you tonight. But only if you want me there."

"As long as you understand the situation." Ravi looked at me intently. "Don't expect anything from me, and I won't expect anything from you."

35

"You recruited me, back when I was down and out. Why can't I recruit him?"

I was arguing with Michael Hendricks through my bathroom door while getting dressed. The chic bandage dress that had fit so sleekly when I was twenty-seven now was sadly overtaxed. I tried to tell myself it was because of all the muscle I had developed, but that was only part of it.

"You're not a case officer; you're an informant. Only COs and administrators in the Directorate of Operations can do the recruiting." Michael's voice was patient. "And at this point, nobody new is joining our game."

"OCI is supposed to be a street-smart, creative agency. Why can't I use my street smarts where it really would count?"

"Leave it alone, Rei. And come out of the bathroom. I'm sure your makeup's fine, and it's almost time for you to meet Miyo."

"All right, but I'm having a problem with the dress." I came out in the square-necked dress, with openings at the midriff that were punctuated by diagonal bands of black. The dress fell to mid-thigh, and I'd accented it with a sheer black stocking with a diamond pattern. On my feet, I wore Jimmy Choo satin-and-rhinestone evening sandals, which my mother had passed down to me after one season.

"Whoa. That looks pretty—severe. Severely pretty," Michael amended when he saw my hurt expression. I hadn't intended to look like a dominatrix.

"I can't close the zipper." I turned around to show him.

Michael shook his head. "I'll count to three while you suck in."

I did, and unbelievably, the zipper lurched upward.

"Thanks," I said.

"No problem. I had to do that kind of thing for Jennifer, occasionally. I guess I haven't forgotten one skill, at least."

I turned to face Michael. "If it's not too intrusive . . . I was wondering if you'd tell me what happened."

"You want to hear how she was killed?" Michael sounded startled.

I nodded, startled by the word. Most people would have said "died."

"It happened when I was in the navy. We'd had a long separation, almost a year, when I was deployed on an aircraft carrier in the Persian Gulf. After that, I was sent TDY to a small destroyer out of Rota."

"TDY?" I hated to interrupt him, but I didn't understand.

"Temporary duty, which meant I could go only if unaccompanied. That meant Jenny and I would be apart six more months."

"No wonder you left the navy," I said, feeling indignant.

"Jenny couldn't tolerate the extended separation. She raided our savings and booked an apartment for us in a small Spanish village. I wanted her to fly on a military plane, but she was always lowest priority, a spouse traveling alone, without any moving orders."

"Could she take a commercial flight?" I was beginning to have a sinking feeling.

"No, she couldn't." Michael paused, and when his voice came out, it was a croak. "I don't quite understand why she wound up on that particular Pan Am flight."

"Oh, my God." Now I understood that he was talking about the flight that had exploded into a million pieces of shrapnel over Europe, killing everyone aboard. People all over the world had mourned the event, but nobody seemed to realize it was just the beginning of many more bad things to come.

"After Jennifer was killed, I resigned from the navy at my first opportunity. I felt like it was pointless to spend my life just—reacting—to bad things that had happened. I wanted to identify dangerous situations as they started to emerge, and halt them before they got out of control. I never wanted anyone else to suffer what happened to Jennifer and to me." He paused. "Don't cry, Rei. It's going to ruin the mascara."

"I'm so sorry about what happened to you," I said as I hurried to the bathroom to check what had happened to my eye makeup.

Michael followed and leaned against the door. "I haven't told many people about what happened. I don't want pity."

We looked at each other in the shining surface of the mirror, and I nodded. "I won't talk about it with anyone." Not even Mrs. Taki, who would have dearly wanted to know the details about the woman in the picture.

"Now, getting back to what we were talking about: Ravi Shah." Michael's voice was brisk.

"Yes," I said, collecting myself. "Obviously, he's got a lot he can tell us."

"Instead of recruiting him, I'd say, wear a wire and record him, but I don't see room for electronic equipment inside that dress."

"So you are interested in what's going on at Winston Brothers," I said.

"Yes, I admit I'd like to know more—although I doubt it has any bearing on the situation at Mitsutan. You may continue your contact with Ravi. You did say he was born in India, right?"

"It's what he told me. What's the significance?"

"If he's still an Indian citizen, that gives you a legal basis to collect information without revealing yourself. Try to find that out, will you? And by the way, did you get his cell number yet?"

"Yes, but—"

"If you give me the exchange, I'm pretty sure we can tie his calls into the listening station."

I hesitated, then said, "I don't want to do anything to hurt him. It's not like he's one of the bad guys."

"Or so it appears. Be careful tonight."

"And in this case, careful means?" I was tired of finding out too late that I'd screwed up on OCI procedure.

"Don't ask any questions of the big two, Kravitz and DeLone. Try to maintain your cover. And above all, don't bring anyone home. If you have a problem, I won't be lurking around the dishwasher to save you."

The party was at the American Club, the longest-running, highest-class gaijin hangout in Tokyo. I'd been here years ago, wearing the same dress. I remembered how excited I'd been, that young girl in borrowed clothes on the arm of a much older man—someone who eventually became a good friend. Tonight, I was again with a platonic male acquaintance, someone who'd brought me, I understood, only because Archie was bringing Miyo. Ravi knew that I was older and American and full of lies; I imagined he'd tell Archie sooner or later when they were having their guy talk. At the moment, Archie was treating me normally, greeting me with a bear hug at the entrance.

Things looked very good between Miyo and Archie—I was quite pleased with the success of my matchmaking. Archie was straight-shooting and happy-go-lucky, the opposite of Ravi. Miyo, absolutely stunning in a Behnaz Serafpour floor-length turquoise silk crepe gown, was starting to gain confidence with her English; she even made a little joke to Archie about his appearance in the tuxedo, some-thing about blond penguins. Miyo's grammar was almost perfect, I realized; all she needed was a bit of vocabulary expansion and some coaching on pronunciation.

While Ravi and Archie and Miyo stood in a long line at the bar that was serving mojitos, I sipped a glass of club soda and walked around the fourth-floor ballroom, which was decorated in an all-white theme. The crowd was made up almost entirely of American expats, with a swirl of wealthy Japanese thrown in; fortunately, I'd never run with this crowd, so I doubted that I'd be recognized.

One of the people who might recognize me—Melanie Kravitz—didn't seem to be around, though I expected her to appear soon, since she was chairwoman. The format was standard: cocktails, a seated dinner, and then the dancing. I couldn't imagine how it would go, because there was actually a shortage of women. The crowd was almost all middle-aged couples, about half of them white-white, the others white-Japanese. These Japanese wives and I exchanged nods, and I could imagine the calculations going on: Japanese girl, nobody's wife, who is she with?

I realized that I was attracting more notice because I was alone, so I returned to my small posse, who had merged with more men. Miyo was nodding to everyone, beaming with her joy at being there, sur-rounded by so many objects of her desire.

"Don't you want a cocktail, glass of wine, something?" Archie asked me. He was looking almost worried, as if his beautiful butter-fly might flit off.

"Oh, I'm still reeling from last night." The fact was that starting a long night of supposed fun with a date who was glowering at me made my comfort level pretty low. I never drank anywhere that I didn't feel safe.

"Let me introduce you around, Rei," Ravi said. "Meet Bill and Andy and Carter and Nick. And their dates are—where?"

"Only about half of us could get dates," the one called Bill said. "The girls who are here are in the ladies' room planning their escape."

Miyo looked alarmed, and I had to quickly explain to her in Japanese that this was a joke. She laughed, and Archie beamed, putting his arm around her slim shoulders.

"I just love this girl. Just met her last night, but can you believe, she's a snowboarder? We're trying to get a plan together for Hokkaido. Are you in, Rei?"

"Impossible. We can never both get the weekend off. In fact, Miyo-chan, I'll work an extra Saturday so you can have the whole of next weekend off."

"But don't you want to go sometime, Rei?" Andy asked.

"I doubt she does," Ravi said curtly. "Rei is about as poor at sports as I am."

"Really? But you look like you work out." Andy was appraising my arms, which I'd pumped up with a few sets of push-ups before getting dressed. I always did, if I was going sleeveless.

"My muscles come from carrying lots of clothes," I said.

"Come on, Rei, I want to get another drink." Ravi practically yanked me out of the circle of beaming young men.

"I didn't say a word, so why are you so upset?" I said under my breath as we went out toward the hallway.

"Archie's all right, but most of those bastards are—are totally amoral," Ravi said.

"You picked a fine field to work in if you have so many problems with morals. Why didn't you go into something nice and neutral like medicine?" I asked. "You could have joined the public health service and gone to Appalachia."

"Not allowed," Ravi said tightly. "My father's an ear-nose-throat doctor, and he says there isn't enough money in any subspecialty to make medicine worthwhile anymore."

"You do sound like you need a drink." I swiped one off a tray being walked around by a waitress, all the while thinking that although I'd done all right fixing up Miyo, I'd done miserably for myself.

"I don't know where we can go to talk without being overwhelmed by buffoons," Ravi said, practically inhaling the glass of white wine.

"How about the hallway? There's some bench seating there. Let's just take a little while to talk while we're waiting for dinner to be served."

As we were seating ourselves, a group swept into the hallway. A portly Caucasian man in his fifties with a hawkish profile, wearing a perfectly tailored black business suit, was walking with another gaijin, a tall man who was actually wearing a cowboy hat with his suit, an off-the-rack polyester blend. A tiny woman in a familiar red gown trailed them, talking at the top of her lungs on a cell phone. It was Melanie Kravitz, at last; and I deduced that the men with her were the ones Michael had called the big two: her husband, Warren; and Jimmy DeLone.

Melanie was practically spitting into the phone. "We're here, and I've already heard about the problems people are having getting a drink. You need to get more waiters on the floor immediately—yes, I know about the total we ordered, but I happen to see dozens of employees standing around this club, doing nothing—"

I was trying to make myself small behind Ravi, but that was a challenge, because he was small himself. In any case, Melanie caught sight of me. She didn't stop talking on the phone, but she beamed and fluttered her free hand hello.

I fluttered my hand back weakly. Warren didn't seem to notice me at all. He was holding Jimmy DeLone by the elbow and speaking to him in a low voice.

As they passed by, Ravi jumped to his feet. "Hello, sir, I'm Ravi Shah from fixed income. I left a few messages in your voice mail last week."

I cringed, first because it was bad form to talk business at a party, and second, because I remembered Michael's warning to stay away from Kravitz and DeLone.

"Shah. Well, are you having a good time?" Warren Kravitz's cold gaze slid over me, and I shivered. How could Michael have thought this man gave a good up-front interview?

"Yes, but—"

"If I don't get inside there, my wife'll kill me. We can catch up on business in the office."

The group blazed along into the ballroom, and I turned to Ravi. "They seem to be in a bit of a rush."

"It's always that way," Ravi said. "If that fool in the cowboy hat is joining our company, I'm ready to jump out a window."

"He's probably a client, someone to whom Mr. Kravitz needs to give his utmost attention." I paused. "What did you want to tell him that was so pressing you would bring it up at a social gathering?"

"I didn't mean to say anything in front of the client," Ravi said tightly. "I was hoping to introduce myself, just so he knew who I was. I'd sent him e-mail which he hasn't responded to, and I thought it might be because he didn't know who I was."

"What kind of e-mail?" I asked.

"Why do you want to know?"

"Because—" I hesitated, then remembered how much Ravi had on me. The only way I could gain his trust was through honesty. "Because, from what I know about that guy, he seems a bit—tough."

Ravi looked at me for a long moment, then finally spoke. "It's about these bonds we're selling to people over here who want to make investments in the American market. Do you know much about bonds?"

"What I understand is that the Japanese have always bought many American treasury bonds. Japan has been financing our deficit for years."

"Yeah, but I'm talking about different kinds of bonds, ones that are pure profit for us."

I'd been thinking on too large a scale, and not about the immediate business at hand. I tried again. "I didn't know you had the responsibility to sell directly to Japanese clients—do you speak to them in Japanese?"

"No, we have Japanese employees who do that—some of them are inside that room. They handle the Japanese clients, and also other Asians—guys from Korea, China, and even India. A lot of them buy using cash." Ravi looked disapproving.

"Well, isn't that normal, to some extent? Doesn't financing a bond purchase require a credit line? And it's really hard for people to get credit in Japan, especially foreigners."

"Yes, but to buy things like bonds, it's supposed to be done with a bank transfer from a normal, recognized financial institution. Or, if it's not a wire transfer, there should be a personal check drawing from the account of a known bank. But I see messengers coming in with these big envelopes full of old bills. And they don't even bother to wait for a receipt from anyone, just drop it off."

I nodded, remembering the envelope I'd seen in Melanie Kravitz's bag. "What do they look like—the envelopes?"

"They're big, I don't know, the standard kind of envelopes used for business. And they're always sealed with wax. No name on the envelope, just that wax seal."

"I don't suppose it looks like this?" From an old beaded Judith Lieber evening purse that once belonged to my mother, I withdrew the two halves of the red seal that had been on the envelope Melanie had broken. I'd transferred the seal from my Mitsutan uniform pocket to the makeup case inside my Coach backpack earlier in the day for safekeeping, and the makeup case had naturally been packed in my evening bag for quick touch-ups.

Ravi looked at me suspiciously and said, "Yes, this might be the same. How did you get it?"

"Melanie dropped it when she was opening an envelope in the store." I paused, letting the significance sink in. "Now, the question I have is what the emblem on the wax means."

"I don't know," Ravi said, his forehead furrowed in concentration. We examined the seal together; it looked like a tree, with some strong lines emanating from it. Suddenly I remembered all the *yakuza* reference books in my apartment; one of them had a section on gang symbols. I would look at it later on.

"I know that to accept an envelope like this, without any kind of deposit slip, let alone identification, is wrong. I've reminded the Japanese guys I work with of our policy, and they just keep smiling and saying yes, yes, yes! The deliveries, I think, are now coming whenever I take my lunch; I'm not supposed to know it's still going on."

"So you want to talk to Warren Kravitz about this?"

"Yes! As I told you, I sent him an e-mail to which he never responded, though I know he at least opened the message. We have a way of checking that—"

"I see. Did you try again?"

He shrugged. "I called him on the phone. My computer crashed last week, and the idiots from the tech department are taking their time fixing it. I'm pretty powerless without that computer. That's part of the reason I was out with Archie last night; I had nothing to do."

I studied Ravi for a minute and asked, "Does your bank have anything to do with Mitsutan?"

"You mean, are they our client? No. They have their own bank and credit division, I understand."

"So there's no relationship whatsoever?" I paused. "I heard that a guy who was modeling at Mitsutan wanted a job with your bank."

"You knew Tyler Farraday?" Ravi's voice was low and urgent.

"No, I just heard some scuttlebutt. What happened at the bank?"

"Well, from what I heard, he used to take some of the bankers' wives around—which didn't make a whole lot of sense, given the age gap."

I smiled, thinking how very traditional Ravi was when it came to certain things.

"Some of the guys were, like, trying to impress him, so they shot some salary talk around. I gather after that he showed up at personnel with a résumé, but it never went anywhere, and then, a few weeks later, he died. I feel pretty bad about it," Ravi said.

"It wasn't your fault. Sounded like he had a lot of drugs in his system, and he drowned."

"I could have stepped in, not let the others make him so crazy with jealousy over money. Maybe he had a sense of failure, and that's why he died."

"Maybe," I said, wishing I could reassure Ravi, but that would be saying too much. "Getting back to your own work problem, I wonder if perhaps you should stop trying to talk to Warren Kravitz. What you know could be a matter for that new Japanese government agency that is trying to wipe out money laundering."

"So you think it sounds like money laundering, too." Ravi's voice had sunk to a whisper. "Surely the proper thing is to tell my boss first. Don't you think?"

The sealed dirty-money envelope had Warren's name on it. I shook my head vehemently at Ravi. I said, "No! You should be careful. Why do you suppose your computer's still out of order?"

"I have no idea, because the guys from tech support don't speak much English at all."

"Maybe someone wanted to make all the evidence of your outgoing e-mail disappear. And there could be an interest in other messages you've sent and received, too."

Ravi blinked. "You mean—someone's spying on me?"

"I don't know." I paused. "Did you keep a printout of that e-mail?"

Ravi shook his head. "Too much clutter. And I knew it was on the computer, so I could always pull it up again."

"Ravi, after your computer's working again, don't send any important messages to anybody."

"Archie said the same thing. He recommends that I should just lie low and let the company business go on as usual."

"If you want to tell someone, like I said, there's a Japanese agency that handles these matters. You can find them on the Internet, and the website's in English as well as Japanese." I thought some more. "Since it's an American bank, and you're a little—unfamiliar—with Japanese ways, you could, as an alternative, contact someone in the American government. What would you think of that?"

"I wouldn't know where to begin," Ravi said.

"Well, there's a specific group called Fincen that investigates banks that break laws," I said. "You can even find them on the web."

"Really." Ravi looked at me speculatively. "Who are you really, Rei Shimura, that you know these people?"

"Think of me like the big sister you never had." I patted his shoulder. "Let's go back to the others, and don't worry anymore."

36

The party broke up around one—early by my usual standards, but late for me tonight. I said good-bye to Miyo, who was riding in a taxi with the guys over to Roppongi Hills, where, presumably, she'd continue her evening with Archie. I warned her not to do anything too fast; coming from me, this advice was actually quite ironic.

In the taxi, I watched the meter tick upward, feeling relieved that I had the money to pay for it. Earlier that day, I'd gone to my bank's ATM and discovered I had funds galore—not just the expense account advance, but my latest biweekly pay check from the Department of Defense.

The whole mishap with the credit card, I'd figured out, was the result of a fourteen-hour time difference between Langley and Tokyo. My paycheck was deposited in the Citibank account every other Friday morning. During the time that Mitsutan's credit card company had attempted to withdraw money, it was actually still Thursday in the United States, so my paycheck hadn't been deposited.

I was glad the funds were there, because I could quickly pay back the credit division in cash on Monday, and—I hoped—avert any further negative attention. Bad credit was the kind of complication that could lead to an investigation of who I really was—surely not a banker's daughter, after all.

My taxi had stopped outside the apartment building in Hiroo. I asked for a receipt and reached into my bag for money to pay the driver. I glanced through the window at the building, where all the lights were out, save the one in the vestibule. Then I hesitated.

The vestibule light shone over a car parked in front of the building, in the no-parking zone. This wouldn't be remarkable except that four people were inside, waiting, judging from four faint pinpoints of light from the interior: cigarettes.

"I'm sorry, but this isn't the spot. Can you drive on?" I asked the driver.

"Heh?"

"I just realized I don't have my key, I'm so sorry."

"Can't your parents let you in?"

"No, I want to do something different. Can you make a U-turn and head back toward Hiroo Station?"

"Of course." He made a quick three-point turn and we went sailing out of the alley. I turned around and saw that the other car had sprung to life and was backing up in the alley.

This was exactly what I hoped wouldn't happen. My options were so limited. I couldn't go to the Japanese police; nor could I lead whoever was tailing me to the embassy. It was hard to think of where I could disappear safely.

"How about Roppongi Hills?" I said to the driver. I scrambled in my purse for Miyo's cell phone number. She'd be able to tell me the exact address of Archie's apartment, and if she and Archie were otherwise engaged, maybe they could give me Ravi's address.

"Roppongi Hills is a large area. Do you know where you want to go?" The cabbie sounded wary.

"Isn't the mall open?"

"Not at this hour. Please be more specific."

"Um, I'm sorry to say, but I don't like the look of the car following this vehicle. Do you think you might be able to lose it on the way?"

"How? I don't understand."

"Drive fast, take some turns, go backward—you know!"

"This isn't a movie," he said stiffly. "I'm not a stunt driver. If there's a problem, you should go to the police box."

The man was hopeless. Abandoning my plan not to call Michael, I rang his cell phone, which he answered with a yawn.

I began, "I'm sorry to wake you, but there's a problem."

"What is it, Sis?" He sounded more alert.

"I saw a car outside the building, and I had my taxi drive me away from it, but they're following us."

"Have the taxi shake him."

"The driver can't do it. He's very timid!"

"Where are you?"

"Well, we're heading toward Roppongi Hills. My hope is that he could get up on the Shuto Expressway and, at a higher speed, escape the tail, but this is kind of guy who clearly does not want to break the law."

"There's a chance he's working in cooperation with the tail. Rei, this could be really bad."

Michael was clearly upset—so upset that he'd forgotten not to say my name aloud. I was scared, but Michael's being scared for me was even worse. I tried to reassure us both. "It can't be. He was a regular driver I saw outside the American Club dropping off a couple going in. I only take taxis under those circumstances, just like you taught me. And he's nervous himself; he even suggested going to a police box."

"Of course you told him no—"

"Of course!"

"You'd better come to the New Sanno."

"But that's—American government territory! That'll blow the cover—"

"Not exactly. I want you to pass by, and I'll create a distraction with a vehicle or something so that you can get away. But right now, get him to drive around a while longer in brightly lit, busy parts of town. I'll need at least fifteen minutes to get into position. And right now, I need a full description of the car behind you and the taxi itself."

I did that as best I could. The sedan was dark—it was hard to tell the color at night—and there was no license plate on the front. About my own vehicle, I could at least give the license number, which was displayed on interior paperwork along with the driver's picture, and I mentioned that there was an advertisement on top of the taxi for DoCoMo telephone.

"Excellent. Now, I want you to phone my cell as you're approaching Tengenjibashi Crossing. Okay?"

"I will." I clicked off, feeling even more nervous than when I'd first picked up the phone.

Fifteen minutes felt more like fifty as we drove on. I'd spent over 10,000 yen on the cab ride so far. The driver was distracted by now; I could see him glancing in his rearview mirror continually, at the car behind us.

"What did you do, to make these people follow you?"

"Long story," I said, glancing at my watch. "If we took a turn back toward Tengenjibashi Crossing now, how long do you think it would take us to reach there?"

"If we go a back way, five minutes; the long way, ten—"

"Go the long way, please! I mean, whatever way is well lit and has lots of people."

"*Hai, hai.* I'll do that. Though I still think we should visit the police box—"

"No! We'll be fine," I barked, too distracted to focus on anything else beyond getting to Tengenjibashi Crossing and praying that whatever plan Michael had in place would work.

Finally, the pedestrian bridge with its anti-American graffiti message loomed up ahead. I punched redial and got Michael on the line.

"We're approaching the crossing, about to turn left toward the hotel—"

"Get his speed down to thirty kilometers an hour, and pass the tractor-trailer sticking out in the road. We're waiting for you." He shouted at the end, presumably to someone other than myself.

My heart felt about to jump out of the tight dress as my driver made the left turn and decreased his speed. He drove up the divided street where the New Sanno lay ahead.

The heavy gates leading to the delivery area were open, and I saw a tractor-trailer halfway out of the driveway, its cab edged into the first lane. A group of men—one of them Michael, I realized; the others part of the hotel's security force—stood in the shadows of the gate.

"Keep going, the tractor-trailer's waiting, it won't hit us!" I urged the cabdriver to pass the idling vehicle, and in the split second after he'd passed the driveway, the tractor-trailer charged into the street, across all three lanes, so that the car behind us was cut off.

"Go, go, go!" I shouted at my driver. "Up on the Shuto Expressway, please."

"North or south?"

"Doesn't matter! Just go. Please!" There was no need to panic, I knew, but all the adrenaline surged so fast I couldn't help raising my voice. And the driver, to his credit, finally was driving fast.

I picked up the phone and said, "Thank you."

Michael laughed into the receiver. "You know, I actually wanted to be the one driving the truck, but union regulations precluded that."

"I'm glad you were the one watching out." I felt my pulse slowing. "What happened to the guys who were following me?"

"Well, they reversed the car all the way back to Tengenjibashi Crossing. Don't know where they're heading now, but I suggest you forget about going back to the apartment. I'll get over there tonight with armed backup, and we'll pack everything out that we need to."

Michael didn't carry a gun, ever; nobody was supposed to do that, in OCI. It was one of the things that had reassured me about working for the agency. But now I felt secretly relieved that he did have people to help him, who could protect him in what had to be a very dangerous situation.

"Any idea where you think I should go?"

"I've already decided on the Grand Hyatt. We have a corporate account there, and you liked that place last time you were here."

"Yes, but isn't that a bit—extravagant?"

"After we finish this call, I'll make a reservation. The room's going to be under the name Michael Flynn. And don't go directly there; have Robert DeNiro leave you at one of the Roppongi Hills restaurants and make your way to the hotel after he's gone."

The new task had me panicked. "How can I check in under an American man's name? And I don't have my charge card with me—"

"I'll book it using my credit card over the phone. I'll lead them to think you're my wife, and that I'll be joining you there shortly."

"But you're not really going to do that," I said, feeling the way I often did around him: a sickening mixture of anticipation, nerves, and despair.

"I'll be there, but I have to handle some business first. Just go to bed. I'll be a while."

Even though the Grand Hyatt was a very popular hotel, its reception area always seemed deserted, an illusion created by the height of the ceiling and the sparse furniture in the granite-floored space. It looked even deader than usual when I arrived at two. As always, there was a small, alert team of employees waiting at the desk. The same woman who'd courteously welcomed me when I'd last stayed there, in the fall, didn't seem to recognize me this time. Maybe I looked very different, or she was being the soul of discretion. In any case, she greeted me courteously as Mrs. Flynn, and after ascertaining the obvious—that I had no luggage, save for a small purse—had a bellman escort me upstairs, down a long, golden corridor to the room Michael had booked.

It was much bigger than the room I'd had before: a suite, which was as minimally chic as every other space in the hotel. The bed was king-size, not queen-size, and there was a large bathroom and a modern, armless sofa that could serve as a bed in the living room. The bellman pointed out the illuminated Tokyo Tower, which could be seen from the sitting-room and bedroom windows; but the minute he left, I closed the shades electronically.

I was glad that Michael had given me the go-ahead to sleep, because I was thoroughly drained, and the thought of heading off to work at Mitsutan in a little over seven hours was making me even more exhausted. As I unbound my tight dress and slid between luxuriously thick cotton sheets, something Ravi had said niggled at the edge of my mind. What was it? I knew it was important . . . but it was just out of my range.

37

Michael was kissing me, but this time, not my mouth. He was going along every inch of my body, as if he were memorizing it for an exam, while all I wanted to do was throw away the book. I ran my fingers through his short, razor-cut hair, whispering to him how he'd changed my life forever, and for the better. Then a siren started to blare. The police were coming, all because I'd dragged him into breaking OCI rules . . .

I blinked my eyes open and saw that the alarm clock on the table next to me was buzzing. I shut off the clock and rolled over on my stomach, pressing my legs together. I was still hot from the dream, but now I felt overwhelmingly guilty. I was in rebound mode, that was all it was. I knew that at some point and time I would find someone to take Hugh's place, but I was vastly upset with my subconscious for suggesting that the man could be Michael.

I raised myself on my elbows and peered into the suite's living room, where the object of my lust was sprawled across the couch, a blanket half fallen revealing a flash of checked cotton boxer shorts. Michael did not want to make love to me. What had happened that strange night in the apartment had been a case of method acting gone wild. I would never again allow myself to forget that Michael was the consummate spy, who would do anything needed to keep our covers intact.

I sat up, wrapping the bedsheet close around me, and surveyed the suite through the soft light filtering through the window shade. The bedroom and living room had been pristine when I'd come in, but now I saw my carry-on bag, as well as a hodgepodge of boxes and electronic equipment that had come from the apartment. I couldn't remember hearing Michael come in. Then I had a second, horrifying thought: that I might have talked in my sleep. And how many dreams might I have had over the night? It wasn't the first time I'd dreamed about Michael. I'd dreamed about him back in Washington, too, but tried to forget it because I was still in love with Hugh.

Not anymore. My feelings for Hugh might never completely disappear, but they felt blurred, the way objects in the hotel suite had appeared when I'd first opened my eyes.

I wore the sheet around me like a toga as I picked some clothes out of the carry-on, embarrassed that Michael had handled my dirty laundry as well as the clean clothes, and went into the bathroom for a hot shower. I shampooed, shaved my legs, and moisturized, all with the hotel's fancy organic toiletries. After I'd blown my hair dry and put on my standard Japanese makeup, half an hour had passed. I stepped out of the bathroom, fully dressed, and heard the sounds of NHK news. I peeked into the living room and saw that Michael was awake, wearing a T-shirt and shorts and watching the news on a large flat-screen TV.

"I think you finally slept through the night," I said. "Congratulations."

"Not really." Michael yawned. "I only got in at three, after Brian and I packed out the apartment completely and moved everything over. I see you found your clothes?"

"Yes, thanks. I'm sorry I wasn't up when you came in. I wanted to ask you—did it look as if anyone had gotten inside the apartment?"

"Yes. But the listening station didn't appear to be detected. We took it out, as a precaution, in case anyone comes back." Michael yawned again. "What time is it, anyway?"

"Ten after seven. I have a bit of time before I go to work, if you want to have coffee and talk some more." I'd spied the coffeemaker and was already filling the carafe with water in the bathroom.

"You're not going to work."

"What do you mean? I have a cover to maintain—"

"You are in hiding," Michael said, stepping into the bathroom behind me. "And if by now you don't understand the reason, you'll never survive as an agent."

"But if I don't show up at the K Team, I'll be in trouble. And that will bring attention to me."

"Mrs. Taki has orders to telephone Personnel when it opens. She'll pose as your mother calling in for you because you're too ill to speak. Miyo will believe it, given that you partied the night before."

I shook my head. "All I drank was club soda, and I left the party early. She'll know something's wrong."

"Who cares? I'm more concerned about whether this hotel is secure enough or if I should move you to the New Sanno until you can fly out, but I don't think they'd do a good job with your hair."

"What do you mean about my hair?" I touched it. Had my blow-dry been that bad?

"I can't risk you leaving the hotel to buy a wig somewhere. Inside the hotel spa, you'll be able to get a cut and color change. Back in the States, you can reverse it to whatever you want."

So he really didn't want me to be recognized. And I was really going home. I said, "I wonder if you would treat a male agent this protectively."

"The order came from Len Novak, back at Langley," Michael said. "If you go against my boss's order, you'll probably get us both fired. Is that what you want?"

"Of course not." If I were to lose my career at OCI because I'd blown my cover on this job, I'd regret it heartily—and if I screwed things up for Michael, I would feel just as bad. He was a spy, pure and simple; it wasn't as if he could fall back on selling antiques the way that I could.

"Now, let's move on to the rest of the discussion." He pointed an accusatory finger at my carry-on. "That bag contains most of your recent purchases. You can take it all back to the States to wear there if you like, but not in this town. The clothing you're wearing now—it's new, isn't it?"

"The Comme des Garçons pants are new." I gestured toward the strap-and-buckle pants; I was wearing them with a peach ruffle-edged chiffon blouse from Rachel's Diary that I'd bought at Matsuya a few years back. Underneath it all was one of the infamous Tsumori Chisato bras, which I supposed I should count as well because the blouse was semitransparent.

"The forty-thousand-yen Comme des Garçons purchase, I remember that well."

"Hold on. Those pants were twenty-five-five with my discount," I said.

"Thirty-eight thousand plus five percent tax was the total I saw on a printout that I packed up in your room. Do you know what that means? Almost four hundred dollars for a pair of cotton canvas work pants that I could have bought for you at a military uniform shop for thirty dollars!"

"Show me the data." I folded my arms and stared him down, because I knew what I'd paid. I'd given Michael the Mitsutan sales receipts a few days earlier, along with the filled-out governmental expense account form.

This conversation was ridiculous. I'd never, ever gotten flack from anyone before. My former lovers had been spendthrifts, in fact, and never would have suggested my buying clothes at a military supply store. But then again, Michael was an aristocratic Yankee, which meant cheap.

"Here!" Michael crowed, holding aloft two sheets of paper he'd removed from a box. "My proof. And once we settle this, let's get back to the business you're evading."

He handed me the printout Miyo had ripped off the computer just before we'd gone out to Roppongi Hills on Friday night. I hadn't looked at it before, because that would take too much time: it was neatly typed in katakana, not English.

"You read this?" I looked at Michael in shock.

"Did you think I can't read Japanese? Come on, I'm director of OCI's Japan division."

"I know, but you always asked me for translated transcripts. And I've hardly heard you speak."

"Speaking Japanese doesn't come easily to me, and I wouldn't trust myself to handle translations. But I can read the hiragana and katakana alphabets; I learned in elementary school, when my dad was stationed at Yokosuka."

I returned to the paperwork. Unbelievably, it said that the pants were almost 40,000 yen. My bras were also several thousand yen more expensive than I'd thought—apiece. My Issey Miyake crinkle-cotton jacket was 29,200, not 22,250, as I'd recalled seeing on my sales receipt at the time of purchase. And the Coach backpack I thought I'd paid 34,000 for was actually 46,000.

"I don't understand it," I said slowly. "It's more than the price tags said at the time—I'm almost certain."

"Soldiers throughout Iraq don't have armored vehicles, and our government is spending more than four hundred fifty dollars on a fashionable backpack! Thank God we don't have anyone from the press corps embedded with us who could expose this—this Backpackgate!"

I shook my head. "You would never hit me with this garbage if you really knew me. I'm a bargain shopper. I lived in vintage clothing and my mom's hand-me-downs for my entire twenties. I would never lose control of the amount of money I'm spending. Something's fishy about this. I just—I just didn't spend this much. Ever." I stabbed at the paper with a fingernail that badly needed a manicure. "The paper you're looking at is an internal computer record at Mitsutan. It's not like the receipts that I signed and took away with me. Those signed receipts are the real evidence that I can use to fight the charges."

"If it's an internal computer record—how did you get it?" Michael's expression had turned from anger to curiosity.

"Miyo messed around with my computer at the K Team desk one night and printed it out. She was concerned because my credit card had been rejected when I tried to buy a coat on Friday night."

"A coat which she bought and you reimbursed her for."

"That's correct."

Michael poured a cup of coffee and handed it to me. He'd forgotten the milk. "These records might actually be significant. If I could just get another one, compare it with another cardholder's receipts . . ."

"We need mine first," I said. "Will you go back to the Sanno today to pick them up?" I picked up the printout and looked it over again. "I'm not a mathematical genius, as you know, but it looks as if this record shows there was no subtraction of the employee discount, but actually an addition of fifteen percent to the regular retail price—plus the corresponding sales tax. I'd like to see if everything I bought was inflated in the same pattern—that would be interesting, wouldn't it?"

Michael was no longer looking scornful, I was pleased to notice; he was just attentive.

I continued to explain my theory, which was slowly evolving. If Mitsutan's internal records, with inflated amounts of profit, were the official data shared with the public, Mitsutan would seem more profitable. And why would the government suspect anything? Mitsutan was paying its taxes, and it was reporting numbers that would prove the prime minister's economic reforms were working.

"Tell me, who runs the accounting department at Mitsutan?" Michael asked when I was through.

"A Mr. Sato does now, but Enobu Mitsuyama did until he was appointed general manager of the Ginza store."

"So it could be that Mr. Sato created the corruption—"

"Or that Enobu Mitsuyama rigged the accounting and then switched out of the job so he would never be subject to blame if the scheme was exposed. The profits started surging about three years ago, when he became general manager," I reminded my boss.

"It would be in his interest to do it at that time," Michael said slowly. "If anything were to be uncovered, he could argue that he couldn't be held accountable—since it was Sato's department. Of course, the senior Mitsuyama couldn't be blamed either, because he's just chairman of the board. It seems awfully risky, though—"

I shrugged. "Lots of people are willing to take risks. I never spoke a word to Warren last night—per your request—but I found out about some rather extraordinary risk-taking of his own. Ravi told me about a pattern of cash deposits of small bills being funneled through Winston Brothers. No return address, but the Japanese workers there, and Warren Kravitz, seem to know exactly who it comes from."

Michael folded his arms across his chest and studied me. "Our second mystery, the one totally unconnected to what's going on at Mitsutan."

"Maybe, maybe not. But it's definitely intriguing," I said. I rummaged through my purse and picked out the halves of the wax seal, which I'd been keeping carefully in a handkerchief. I put them down on the coffee table in front of Michael. "This was the seal on the envelope of cash Melanie used for her shopping. I didn't think much about it at the time, but when I showed it to Ravi, he confirmed that this wax seal is just like one he saw on big envelopes of money he'd seen coming into the bank."

"Really." Michael was staring at the seal with a horrified expression.

"I want to know whose seal this is. Maybe, if you brought some of those *yakuza* books from the apartment, we could take a look—"

"I can tell you whose seal it is." Michael swallowed hard. "It's the symbol for Kanazawa-kai, one of the upcoming gangs. I know about them because of a case I worked on, a couple of years back, that dealt with drug trafficking through Asia."

"Are you sure?" I'd hoped that the seal would mean something, but this was almost too scary to comprehend. No wonder Ravi's attempt to alert his boss to money laundering was being stonewalled.

"Yes," Michael said shortly. He rummaged through a box and came up with one of the *yakuza* books. He flipped through it and showed me an illustration.

"I'm amazed that they would leave such a blatant sign of their identity on an envelope. I mean, they are breaking the law—"

"Rei, I've seen *yakuza* walking around with lapel pins. They're part of the established infrastructure of Japan."

I sucked in my breath. "So Warren is friends with gangsters, which means that gangster money is coming into a major American bank, which means that our economy is already tainted."

"Please don't make me feel any sicker than I do already." Michael put his head in his hands. "I don't know what bearing this has on the Mitsutan investigation. Obviously, the Kanazawa-kai aren't involved in Mitsutan, because if Warren's cooperating with this gang, he wouldn't dare do something to hurt their interests."

I thought for a minute, then said, "But he might want to do something to help them."

"I don't follow." Michael looked up at me.

"The Nozumi-gumi, a much older *yakuza* organization, has been historically linked with Mitsutan."

"Yes. It was in the background history of Mitsutan I gave you to read on the plane from California to Washington."

"What I remember is the part about the Nozumi-gumi being involved in the rebuilding of Mitsutan after the war. The gang was able to procure luxury goods like stockings and chocolate from the black market, which they in turn sold to the store, and the store in turn sold the goods to customers. Later on, after there were no more shortages of luxury goods, the Nozumi-gumi expanded into different arenas— construction projects, *pachinko,* and so on."

"That's right. But those construction scams, some of which involved Mitsutan and other big companies, were exposed, fines paid, and so on."

"But what if the Nozumi-gumi were still entrenched within the store? What if, somehow, they're involved in the profits?"

Michael shook his head. "But we've just figured out that Mitsutan's profits aren't *real*. I don't follow your logic."

"Well, according to basic knowledge—I mean, stories I've read in the papers here—Nozumi-gumi and Kanazawa-kai are competitors."

"I've read those stories, too. Kanazawa-kai isn't as powerful as Nozumi-gumi, but wants to be. There are lots of turf battles, minor-league gangsters getting shot, and so on. It goes back at least five or six years—"

"What if the Kanazawa-kai figured out a way to run a totally discreet war, using Americans as pawns instead of their own people?" I paused, because my thoughts were so far ahead of my words. "If the Kanazawa-kai could, using their friend Warren Kravitz, expose Nozumi-gumi's secret operations within Mitsutan—it would smash that operation. And their hands would be clean."

Michael stared at me for a long moment. When he finally spoke, his voice was husky. "Rei, have I ever mentioned how glad I am to have hired you?"

"A few times." I flushed. "Thank you. It's kind of a stretch, my hypothesis—"

"I want to believe it," Michael said slowly. "But we don't know all the pieces. What's the evidence that the Nozumi-gumi are still operating within Mitsutan? What are they doing there? What can we prove?"

"I'm not sure," I admitted. "And as you said, I can't go back. But if you let me work from here, I'll do my best to figure it out."

Michael smiled. "I'm going to the Sanno right now, for those receipts. And yes, you do have clearance to keep working. As long as you stay in the hotel."

"Don't worry." I went to pick up my laptop, which was lying on one of the boxes he'd brought. "I may have the situation figured out by the time you return."

"Great. Just don't forget about getting your hair cut and colored."

I threw a stiletto pump at him, but it missed.

38

Once you've gone Japanese, it's hard to go back.

This saying was often repeated by western men to explain their obsession with Japanese women, but I was finding it apt with regard to my hair. The Japanese straightening technique I'd undergone a few weeks earlier wasn't quickly reversible. At the hotel salon, the hairstylist told me that only the passage of time—specifically, five or six months—would convert my ramrod-straight hair back to its looser natural state. If I shortened the pageboy to chin length, I was going to look like a Japanese kindergartner.

So I whispered in the stylist's ear what I wanted her to do. I was almost embarrassed to say it aloud. But she understood. Lots of women in Japan did it, and she had the products to pull the whole thing off. Once the decision was made, it felt exquisite to lie with my head back at the edge of a stone bowl, then get an invigorating head massage that was part and parcel of any Japanese grooming. And as my head was pummeled, it took me away, for a few minutes, from all that I needed to do.

I had to get in touch with Ravi. Before Michael had left, he'd told me he was willing to meet Ravi later that day; but the call I'd made to set up the meeting with Ravi had gone unanswered, and I was too worried about my friend's security to leave a voice mail message. I was using public telephones with a telephone card now, instead of my cell phone, because Michael was worried about the gangs' tracking my whereabouts through the cell phone towers. I kept my cell phone in my pocket, though, on vibrate mode, just in case Ravi called in.

Time to take off the towel, rinse the head, and see the hair. I kept my eyes averted from the mirror intentionally, until everything was cut and dried. It seemed like a reprise of my time at Dora's beauty salon, when I'd turned so dramatically Japanese.

I looked at myself finally, and it was all right—not the awful, harsh greenish-blond that was the usual result when black hair was colored, but something more subtle and honey-colored. I looked almost like a young version of my mother, Catherine Shimura, circa 1970. Going Caucasian was extreme, but it was the most dramatic way I could think of to divorce myself from my identity of the past few weeks.

I put the hefty salon charges on the room account, and went upstairs, trying to find clothes that didn't look like Rei Shimura, K Team girl. From a box, I pulled out some of the athletic gear I'd brought to Tokyo—a long-sleeved nylon shirt, my old Levis, and the Asics sneakers. Then my cell phone buzzed. I hesitated, then went to pick it up. It could have been Ravi, but it was Miyo.

"Hello, Miyo-san." I croaked my greeting, trying to sound as if I had laryngitis.

"Anego, you let me down!" Her voice was angry.

"I'm sorry, but I have—laryngitis."

"You have enough voice to speak with; I understand you perfectly. How could you be gone today?"

"I'm really, really sorry that my mother wouldn't let me go to work because of my illness—"

"Forget that excuse. I don't believe it, anyway." Her voice broke. "It's about Ravi-san."

"Ravi Shah? Did he come to the store to see me again?" If he was out shopping, maybe that was why he'd missed my call. Although it had been a cell number, hadn't it?

"No, he . . ." She paused to make a great, gusty sob. "He was supposed to have brunch with Archie at Wolfgang Puck, but he wasn't there. Archie went to his building, to try to see if he'd overslept, and . . ."

My body was suddenly cold, despite the room's warm, even heat. "He was gone?"

"Ravi-san fell out of his living room window." Miyo's voice broke. "Archie-san says that our good friend has died."

• • •

Ravi had been a Jain—someone who believed so deeply in the sanctity of every life, no matter how small, that he wouldn't touch a vegetable that had been uprooted from the earth. Ravi had seemed worried, but not suicidal. He had been concerned that bank rules were being broken. This, I was certain, was why he'd been killed.

Of course, I didn't say a word about it to Miyo. We talked a few more minutes about how awful the situation was, and then she returned to her customers.

As I hung up, I realized that I was sliding into a state beyond shock and close to rage. This death was as much my fault as anyone's. Sure, I'd warned Ravi to be careful; but I had never understood just how dangerous his situation was. I shouldn't have let him go home after the party at the American Club. I should have protected him.

I turned on the television, and at noon when the news came on, his death led the report. An unnamed foreign banker had jumped from Roppongi Hills, a suicide. It had caused a lot of messy cleanup for a city sanitation crew. His employer, Winston Brothers Asia Headquarters, was not available for comment.

Tears streamed down my face as I made myself as small as possible, curling into a ball in a corner of the suite behind the sofa. I had known Ravi about forty-eight hours, but he'd made such a strong impression on me that I knew I'd never forget him—and never erase my own feeling of guilt for not doing more when I had the chance.

I must have been in the corner for a long time, because the light had changed, behind the room's translucent blind, when Michael finally came in. I heard the sound of the door clicking open, then his voice.

"I've got the receipts, and you were absolutely right, Rei! You paid less than what the internal store paperwork recorded—oh, wow!" He paused, as if taking in the situation. "You're a blond. It's not what I would have expected."

I couldn't answer, just dug my face deeper into my knees.

Michael crouched down close enough that I could feel his body heat. "Okay, I didn't mean to cause any offense. And I'm sorry I had to ask you to make the change. You can get your natural color back the minute you touch ground in the United States, if you hate the color so much—"

I breathed deeply, desperately trying to take control. "Michael, something—happened."

"It's not about your hair?"

"Ravi Shah was killed." I said it slowly, because I still didn't want it to be true.

"You mean—he's the investment banker who suicided? I saw something on the little TV screen on the subway—how did you find out the identity?" Michael was peppering me with questions so quickly I could hardly answer them.

"Miyo has my cell phone number. She called a—a while ago. He supposedly jumped out—his window. But I don't believe he did it voluntarily. He never would have, I know him—" I'd used the wrong tense, and that made me cry. I didn't know Ravi anymore; I'd known him. And now he was gone.

"Oh, Rei. I'm so sorry." And then I was in Michael's arms, and he was holding me. His chest felt like a rock, I thought—the lifesaving security that I wished Ravi could have found before he fell. I cried on and on. And still, Michael stayed in place, no matter that I was soaking his oxford shirt.

"I shouldn't have let him tell me anything in public. Especially not at the American Club, with Warren Kravitz walking right by. He couldn't have heard the words, but he must have put two and two together—"

"But Warren Kravitz doesn't know about your real job," Michael said. "And what you told me about the e-mail and then the computer crash makes it clear that Ravi had already been a marked man."

"The *yakuza* make people jump out of windows. It's a favorite modus operandi. It was how they killed my favorite filmmaker."

"Don't," Michael said firmly. "Don't watch that same movie again. Believe me, it's a problem I have myself."

"Why didn't we bring him over to meet with us, first thing this morning? We could have protected him. Instead we were drinking coffee and arguing about clothing receipts."

"When there's an unjust, unexpected death, there are always what-ifs. Of course we're fallible. But we didn't kill him. Please remember that."

I ran my fingers through my new blond hair, wishing I could tear it out. "But we're going to stand by and let this thing pass as a suicide because Warren Kravitz is not under our jurisdiction. You told me that our mission isn't to catch bad Americans committing crimes abroad; it's only to catch bad foreigners—"

"Ravi Shah's an American citizen. I didn't know it, but I found out after a few phone calls I made from the New Sanno. This means that his death, if from unnatural causes, is an issue of concern for our country—"

"But according to all the lectures you've given me, we can't interfere in the lives of American citizens."

"It's true." Michael's voice was subdued. "Under the system with which we operate, the OCI cannot investigate crimes against American citizens, even if they're abroad. That is a matter for the FBI."

"I'm sorry to sound skeptical, but the system sucks. I can't imagine when the next FBI team is going to rush over to investigate the suicide of a foreign-born male banker. It's not like a case of a murdered blond hostess or English teacher—"

Michael grabbed my biceps so tightly I flinched. But the move worked; I finally raised my face to look at him.

"We'll work the system, together, Rei. Haven't I said this to you before?"

Michael's eyes were shining with something odd, and I found myself wondering to what—or whom—he truly gave his allegiance.

39

I was still in the hotel a day later—and it wasn't good. I felt as impotent as a woman could feel; all I could do with myself was order room service and talk on the telephone.

"My mother's driving me crazy," I confided to Miyo in the middle of Monday morning, when I'd phoned in to the K Team desk, using a brand-new cell phone Michael had bought me. It was a standard spy procedure, changing cell phones, especially at times when surveillance was suspected.

"Really?" Miyo said. "Well, you'll have plenty of time to spend with her, talking about it, since you've given up your job."

"I haven't formally resigned. You know I'm not feeling well."

"Well, in any case, your chance to work here is gone. I heard Okuma-san talking about you on the telephone this morning to the secretary at Personnel, who wants to confirm your home phone number, because she wasn't able to reach you."

"I can't imagine why." Only that the phone was in the cleared-out apartment in Hiroo—unless Michael had taken it with him. "How are you doing with—the news about Ravi?"

There was a pause. "I'm still very sad about it, and Archie's just—devastated. We spent all last night just holding on to each other, crying. Archie said the family is arriving soon; people are coming from America and also India. Many people."

"And how is the situation at his bank?"

"Archie says that everybody is shocked and sad. Archie said someone's coming in from New York to do an investigation, and he's sure it's because they think Ravi might have been doing something wrong, you know, to have taken his own life."

"It figures." So the crimes of Warren Kravitz's division would all be pinned on Ravi Shah. How convenient for everyone!

"Rei-san, I have to go in a minute, but there's one thing I want to ask. Are you really at home?"

"Why?" A prickle went up my back. I'd started to really trust Miyo, but who was she working with, that she was pushing for this information?

"Mrs. Okuma wants to know. She said there's no answer at your home, not even from your parents."

"I am on the Izu Peninsula for a bit, to recuperate," I fabricated. "The air is better for me there, and the hot springs are part of my doctor's recommended treatment."

"Well, please feel better," Miyo said, but there was an edge to her voice that made me think she hadn't believed a word that I'd said.

Now I understood that Michael had been correct about the danger of my remaining at Mitsutan. Still, I felt terrible that a man had been killed and nobody was close to being implicated in his death. All I'd figured out was the method by which Mitsutan was inflating its numbers.

I was trapped in my high-gloss box of a hotel room, without even Michael around to keep me company. At the moment—I checked my watch—he was supposed to be talking to a liaison at the American embassy who was close to the Japanese national police and might be able to persuade that organization to send detectives to inspect Ravi's apartment for evidence of a break-in.

Michael was doing something, at least; I could do so little. I thought about calling Personnel myself, since they were trying to find a way to officially fire me; no, I thought, Michael would hate that. Everything should be done through Mrs. Taki.

Her number had to be among the documents Michael had dumped into a box and brought to the hotel. I rummaged for twenty minutes before finding my little address book, which had her office, cell, and home phone numbers.

None of the calls were answered. I shook my head, wondering what she was doing. It was one thing if she was under a bubble-dryer at the beauty salon, but it was too late in the day for that.

I started the routine of calling her numbers one more time, and felt rewarded for my persistence when she picked up her home phone.

"Ah, Rei-chan. Is that you?"

"Yes, I'm sorry to disturb you. Were you sleeping?" I flinched at hearing her use my real name—she'd never been told my code name, or Michael's; but it would be pointless to try to explain these things to her now, over the phone.

"Happy Valentine's Day, though for you, it's already over," she said. "And how did you and Michael celebrate?"

I'd forgotten that the previous day—the day of Ravi's death—was the holiday of love. It didn't matter at all. And what was she doing, hinting around that Michael and I were involved in a romance? For the first time, I understood exactly what Michael had said about how a relationship between us, sexual or not, would be regarded by the rest of OCI.

"Happy Valentine's Day to you, and to answer your question, I didn't do anything special. He does his job and I do mine."

"Well, Rei-san, for what reason are you calling? Surely not to tell me you couldn't find that book before you left the store?"

"Oh, I've got your book, I'm sorry. I'll mail it to you today."

"Ah, thank you so much! If you don't mind sending it express, and to my house—you have that address, don't you?"

"Yes. Actually, I'm calling because I think you may need to call Mitsutan's personnel department and—defuse a difficult situation. Because I haven't been working, they've been trying to reach me by phone in Hiroo, and of course nobody is there to answer."

"Really! Did you move in with Michael, then?" Her question was coy.

Mrs. Taki's expertise in intelligence was showing, I thought, smiling to myself despite everything. "Okay, we're together, but not *together*. It's just a matter of security."

"You mean, *kusare-en*," Mrs. Taki said, using an expression for a kind of affair between people who were friends. It wasn't the Japanese ideal, more a relationship of convenience.

"No, please, it's nothing romantic at all." I had to get her off the romance track; it was embarrassing me beyond belief. "Taki-san, this is what I humbly request you to do. Remember the Mitsutan number you used to report that I was sick? Can you please call them back—ask for Aoki-san's secretary, Yamada-san; she won't give you trouble. You could tell her that you knew they've been calling our home phone, but the fact is we're away, so that's why there was no answer."

"Of course." Mrs. Taki's voice was reassuring. "But is there something else I can say? That message sounds a little strange."

"Actually, I'm afraid she'll want to tell *you* something—that I'm fired."

"Heh? Michael never said anything about you having trouble in your work—"

"Just let Personnel give you the bad news. I suppose you'll probably apologize a million times and tell her that I'm a terrible, irresponsible daughter."

"Are you sure? I could make an excuse about your illness again. Perhaps they'll take you back—we worked so hard to get you hired!" Mrs. Taki sounded more upset than I'd expected.

"Michael doesn't want me to return."

"Why?"

"An order from his boss. Oh, and getting back to Personnel, if they say something about my credit card bill, please let them know I'm aware of the problem, and there are funds to pay at my bank. They can run any charges through again. The last thing I want is to have my name go into a loan shark's database."

"That's a silly idea, Rei-san; you have no reason to worry about sharks in Japan. But the other things, like your clothing locker—I imagine Personnel might want to ask you to clean it out?"

She'd made a good point. The uniforms were there, and I probably needed to get them cleaned before returning them to Mrs. Ono. Thinking of Miyo, I said, "I'll ask a friend to do it for me."

After I'd finished speaking with Mrs. Taki, I moped about the hotel suite. It was one of the largest guest spaces in the hotel, but I felt that it was closing in on me. I thought about going to the fitness center, but Michael had thought it was too risky. He'd tossed me a travel jump rope, also confiscated from the apartment, and some light weights.

I jumped rope until a phone call came from the front desk. Someone in the room below me was trying to sleep. I apologized to the clerk and switched to 100, a series of fast abdominal Pilates exercises that one could do lying on the floor. When the phone rang again, I was exasperated. The 100 were quiet exercises; I couldn't believe I'd disturbed anyone.

It was only Michael on the other end. He told me the situation looked promising with the Japanese national police. Although Michael hadn't revealed his true identity—he had posed as a bureaucrat from the State Department—he had suggested that the police take a second look at the scene of the suicide, including dusting the apartment for fingerprints.

"What are you doing? Have you had lunch yet?" Michael asked when he was through telling me about his work.

"I've been exercising, and, no, I haven't eaten. I'm sick of room service. This hotel is packed with excellent restaurants, and I just feel so—confined."

"What about La Gola?"

"That great little Italian place on the street behind Kurofune Antiques?"

"Exactly. I'll stop there and look at the menu, give you a call, and you can order what you want. You'll hear from me by five at the latest, okay?"

La Gola had a marinated salmon that was one of my favorites, so I grudgingly thanked Michael. Only a few more hours to kill. I took a nap, and when I woke up, it was dark.

I got out of bed, went to the window, and opened the shade so that I could see the five-star view of Tokyo Tower, glittering skyscrapers, and boldly flashing billboards, including one for a *pachinko* parlor. *Pachinko* and other gambling games were almost entirely controlled by gangsters, but the games were so ingrained in Japanese society that there was even a large *pachinko* parlor right across from the historic Kabuki-za.

I switched on my laptop and started a search for references to the Kanazawa-kai and Nozumi-gun *yakuza* organizations. More than 3,000 hits. I scanned down for the newspaper articles that I trusted; and by the time I'd read the first forty, I had a good picture of the relationship between the two gangs, which had frequently tangled, with young gangsters on either side being the usual victims of shooting or stabbing.

Kanazawa-kai was one of the top *yakuza* organizations in Japan; it ran several loan-sharking agencies, in addition to the drug operations Michael had mentioned. Given its particular mode of work, I could see why the group had a need to launder money.

Nozumi-gumi was a different story. It was almost sixty years old, and it had diversified into many fields—including construction and real estate. But it did loan-sharking and debt collection, just like Kanazawa-kai. It had once filtered money through a bank, according to the news stories, but that bank had been shut down long ago.

Wait a minute. If Nozumi-gumi needed a bank, perhaps Mitsutan's credit division was the answer.

I jumped up from the computer and began pacing the room. If Nozumi-gumi left its own dirty money with someone in accounting at Mitsutan—it could, theoretically, match up with the inflated profits Mitsutan was reporting.

Yes, I thought with growing excitement. There might actually be a lot of money sitting around in the coffers of Mitsutan just because the Mitsuyamas had a secret deal whereby they took in money for Nozumi-gumi, and then rationalized its existence by means of the inflated profits being reported to stockholders, the media, and the Japanese government.

How clever Mitsutan's strategy had been! While most retailers involved in money laundering would have declared a financial loss and diverted unsold goods as payouts to their gangster friends, Mitsutan's board had instead proclaimed a profit, and used their own banking division to discreetly handle the distribution of dirty funds. It was a brilliant strategy, but perhaps one that Kanazawa-kai was aware of, and was attempting to shut down using Warren Kravitz as a whistle-blower to the American government.

And if this theory was true, the gangsters stalking me a few nights earlier couldn't have been Warren Kravitz's Kanazawa-kai friends. My stalkers had to be Nozumi-gumi, linked with the store that had become my second home. Someone at Mitsutan had deciphered who I was.

40

Michael had made me promise to refrain from going outside, but that didn't mean I couldn't call him. I did, every fifteen minutes, starting around five-thirty in the evening, because he'd talked about being back at five.

The calls I made went straight into his voice mail; he wasn't picking up. Maybe he was tied up in an important meeting at the embassy and just couldn't answer his phone. As I was hanging up my phone for the fourth time, I saw a message on its screen telling me there was an incoming call. I pressed talk and heard Miyo Han's voice on the other end.

Miyo! A prickle shot through me, now that I was thinking about who at the store had figured out my identity.

"They're getting a replacement for you," Miyo said, sounding as if she was about to cry. "I just wanted you to know, in case you're thinking of trying to come back."

"I'm sorry," I said. "I wish we could see each other, but I think it'll be a while till I can get out—"

"But I need to talk to you. The fact is, I've had a terrible day. Okuma-san nearly bit off my head!"

"Because you're feeling upset about—everything?"

"I am upset, but it's not just about Ravi. You see, this American customer came in, and he was asking me for an extra favor—okay, it was a bit unusual, and I probably shouldn't have done it. When Okuma-san walked in and saw the situation, she started yelling at me right in front of him and other customers who were coming in."

"What was the favor?" I asked.

"Well, this man was worried about how much money his wife was spending here, so he asked me to look for her record of purchases for the year, and as you know, it's pretty easy to pull that up, so I did. When Okuma-san saw what was on my screen, she actually sent him away from the K Team office. I've never seen her behave that way with any customer—it was awful!"

"What did this American look like?" I wondered if it was Warren Kravitz, trying to gather the same kind of evidence against the store as I'd found out myself. But Melanie paid cash, all the time—would the numbers, inside the system, also be fixed?

"His clothes weren't much—just khaki trousers and a white shirt without a tie—but he was really cute, somewhere in his thirties, I guess, dark-haired and with really cool glasses, though I bet he'd look better without them. The thing that really charmed me enough to do the favor, though, was that he spoke Korean."

"Did he give you a name?" I was so anxious that I could barely get the question out. She'd described exactly what Michael had been wearing when he left the hotel, minus the blazer.

"Jonathan, he said. Jonathan Lockwood, from the American consulate, which is why he spoke such good Korean—he said he had been posted to Seoul. I don't usually go out of my way for married male customers, but he was kind of—irresistible."

"Well, I agree that this customer sounds like a hard one." I remembered Michael mentioning a foreign service officer called Lockwood at the embassy. Michael had probably used Lockwood's name because he was married and had a wife whose record could actually be pulled and serve as evidence of number-tampering at Mitsutan.

"Okuma-san said I should never have gone as far as I did. She telephoned Security, right after he left."

"Did they call the police?" My God, how was I going to get Michael out of a Japanese prison?

"I have no idea. After the call was made, she just shouted at me, and you know, she gets mad sometimes but she never shouts. She said I'd once been a good employee, but you had been a bad influence. She said she knew you'd taught me to go into the computer to look for this kind of information, and it was wrong."

"Really?" Suddenly I felt a chill. I remembered how, the night that Miyo and I had looked at my spending record, I'd let her do everything, and I hadn't gone in behind her and erased the history of what we'd looked at. I knew how to do it; I'd been trained back in Virginia—but I hadn't wanted to do it, with Miyo looking on.

I'd returned to work the next day fully intending to erase the evidence of Miyo's credit investigation, but the visit from Ravi had thrown me off course. Mrs. Okuma had been in that day; she could have figured things out and called somebody within the store, who in turn could have sent gangsters to my doorstep.

"What is it, Rei-san?"

"Nothing." I'd been thinking that what had seemed like such a blessing—the hard evidence of financial lies—had also been my undoing, and in turn, had put Michael in danger.

"Ten more minutes and I'm done with work. Rei-san, I've got nothing to do tonight and I'm scared she might get me fired. Let's get together. Please?"

I was no longer fearful about Miyo's role in my life, but I was still on restriction. "I can't. Like I've been telling you, my own parents have me locked up for a while."

"I forgot. You're a girl in a box, aren't you?" Miyo's voice held a hint of the cold mockery that had once been her staple with me. But now I knew that the coldness was just a shield to hide her insecurity.

"You could say that," I said, looking around at the luxurious hotel room that had become my prison. "Listen, Miyo-san, if you see that same foreign guy as you're leaving the store tonight, will you call me right away?"

"I thought you didn't want to go out with a foreigner. Anyway, how can you think of picking up a married man with Ravi not even cremated yet?"

I thought quickly. "Remember how I told you about the way my father feels about me dating foreigners? Well, the truth is, I think the man who came to see you was someone who'd actually, um, hoped to see me. He is the one my parents are against. Oh, it's such a mess!"

"Because you're in love with a married gaijin?" Miyo's voice sank to a conspiratorial whisper.

"Yes," I said, after a beat. "I suppose I am."

By eight o'clock, Michael still hadn't returned. The store had closed at seven, which meant that even if Mitsutan's security people had kept him in their office, he would certainly have had time to get back to Roppongi Hills by this hour. Or at the very least, he would have phoned to tell me about the nightmare he'd gone through, and where he was heading next.

I abandoned the phone and went over to the low table near the sofa where Michael had slept the night before. The few possessions he'd brought from the New Sanno were neatly stacked; some folders, all marked "top secret"; and a small black address book.

Michael's black book! I opened it and saw a photograph of Jennifer pasted inside the cover. But I couldn't brood on that now; I was looking for contact information, ideally someone with whom he'd been working in Japan. I scrutinized the various embassy officers' cards. The only person I could remember him naming was Brian, the soldier who'd led me to him in the first place, and who'd helped Michael pack up the apartment. Brian was probably part of the armed backup group Michael had mentioned.

There was no business card for Brian Jones, but within the address book I found a handwritten line with his name and two telephone numbers in Tokyo.

I was going to break my promise to Michael—but only because I was worried. I dialed Brian's number, and he picked up on the second ring.

"Jones here."

"Is this Brian?"

"Yes, Sis. What's up?"

"How did you know it was me?" I was stunned by the fact that he'd recognized my voice, and also knew my code name. Michael obviously had included him in the intelligence loop.

"I've heard you speaking, lots of times." Brian sounded amused.

"I guess I didn't notice—"

"Pretty hard for a black guy not to get noticed in Tokyo."

"Well, of course I've seen you, and I know you've helped me—but I wasn't aware that you overheard me talking." I felt so flustered and embarrassed that I rushed on to my point. "Do you know where Brooks is at the moment?"

"Well, we spoke on the phone around one, and he said that by late afternoon he was going to an Italian restaurant in Roppongi for take-out. Said you were getting tired of room service food. I tell you, in all my years hanging with the guy, he never took the time to hand-deliver me meals—"

"He never arrived here. I think he might have encountered trouble at Mitsutan."

"You mean the store on the Ginza? Last time I talked to him, he was over at the embassy. He didn't mention Mitsutan."

If Brian didn't know about Mitsutan, he must not have known the specifics of the operation, so I was going to have to watch my words. "Yes, that's the place, and I know for a fact he was there. From what I understand, he was asking too many questions about things—and security may have taken him into custody, perhaps even turning him over to the police, or worse."

"That sounds bad." Brian's voice had changed.

"Do you have any connections to the embassy? Is there someone who could make a discreet inquiry to see if the police are holding him?" I would rule that situation out first before I panicked.

"I don't think there's a need to worry about the police," Brian said. "Michael's tight with the Japanese cops. He took a police chief to lunch today, right before that guy sent a detective crew over to that banker's suicide apartment in Roppongi Hills. Some concern of yours, he said. Do you think whatever he's gotten into is connected to that?"

"I don't think so. I think it's trouble relating to some—bad people—behind the department store."

"Rei, you're going to have to give me a for-instance, because I get the feeling you're holding back quite a lot of what's been going on. Not that I'm trying to pry, but this is my buddy. He'd take a bullet for me, and I would for him."

I shuddered at the image and said, "I think that he blew his cover and someone's got him."

"You mean—someone like the guys who were following you, the other night?" Brian exhaled sharply. "We don't know who those guys were. *Yakuza*, probably, but it was too dark to catch sight of their faces, let alone their tattoos."

"Probably it was Nozumi-gun," I said. "They're involved in Mitsutan, I'm almost certain."

"Okay." Brian's voice was crisp. "First thing I'm going to do is call Langley, to let them know he's MIA. Then I'll come to you, take over the surveillance. I'm sure Michael would want me to watch over you, in his absence—"

"Don't worry about me; worry about him," I said, trying to stifle my growing feeling of panic. "The hotel room's locked and I'm not opening for anybody. Just tell me where you'll be this evening. I may need to get in touch with you again."

"My plan was to meet a couple of friends over at the Sanno because they're broadcasting the Lakers game tonight on ESPN. But I can't possibly relax now."

I considered the situation. The New Sanno was in Hiroo, which was probably closer to the Ginza than his apartment.

"I think you should still go. Please. At least you're geographically close if I decide—if I decide I want you to come over."

"I'll give you my cell number, and don't hesitate to call about anything. Okay?"

It was the second number listed next to his name in the address book, but I wasn't about to tell him I'd been snooping in my boss's black book. Instead, I said, "Just one more question, Brian. You're not really an ordinary military grunt, are you?"

"I don't think anybody likes to think they're ordinary, and certainly not a grunt." The sarcasm in Brian's voice was clear.

"Sorry," I said.

"I can't tell you what I do," Brian said. "All I'll say is I've lived in that apartment in Hiroo before. And in Japan, you, Michael, and I are the sole members of a particular family—or should I say, trio?"

A triangle, I thought bleakly, with the point on top missing. I thanked Brian and hung up, resolute about bringing the last family member home, before it was too late.

41

The display windows at Mitsutan had changed. The Valentine's Day teddy bears were gone because White Day was ahead—the holiday on March 15 when Japanese men were supposed to give a return gift to the women who'd blessed them on Valentine's Day. In Japan, no *prezento* could go unreturned.

It was just after nine o'clock when I stood in the shadow of the building, trying to convince myself that I wasn't being watched. I glanced back and forth from the street to the interior of the window, where a young woman wearing blue jeans was altering a window display. She could wear clothes like this because she wasn't an official Mitsutan employee, but someone who worked for the creative agency that handled Mitsutan's window dressing.

The woman was clothing a faceless mannequin in a lacy white bra and panties; I knew the designers well enough by now to identify them as La Perla, the perfect brand to give for White Day.

The next window featured a completed display of white chocolates by Pierre Hermé, one of the chic international brands, like Anya Hindmarch and Akris, that I would never have known mattered if I hadn't worked at Mitsutan. I'd learned so many trivial things during my time at the store. What I really needed to know, I had missed completely.

I moved on, to the side of the building close to a window where another stylist was arranging a pure white handbag on a spotlighted cube, a handbag that was easily identifiable as Dior by the giant leather letters C and D hanging from the pockets in front. If the letters hadn't been there, the bag could have been made by anybody; but then nobody would pay $5,000 for it.

I couldn't imagine somebody feeling duty-bound to give this kind of thing to a coworker, unless she was a mistress. That made me, in turn, think about Mr. Yoshino; how Michael had feared that he'd been the one who'd figured me out, but I now believed that Mrs. Okuma, the only woman in the Mitsuyamas' inner circle, was the one who'd detected my identity. And I would bet my last 10,000-yen note that she was involved in the financial inflation, and knew why Mr. Fujiwara had been killed.

Mr. Fujiwara had to have played an important role in keeping the system running. He was the director of customer service, who would have been the ultimate authority over customers who might have questions or complaints about merchandise they'd bought, or problems with their charge cards. Mr. Fujiwara knew, and maybe he'd asked for more money in exchange for his cooperation. In any event, he'd done something to become the store's enemy.

Now Michael was caught up in the mess. Finding him would be a nightmare. He could be stashed in one of Mitsutan's dozens of warehouses scattered on the outskirts of the city; or in a store-owned vehicle; or in one of its buildings, like the main store or the annex. Or perhaps I'd never find him, because he was slowly hardening inside the cement foundation of one of Nozumi-gumi's many new construction projects inside or out of Tokyo.

I steeled myself, trying to remain calm enough to work. I would start with the obvious places first. The annex probably wasn't locked up tonight, since the stylists were working.

I approached the building—frequently checking behind me, to alleviate the sense I had of being followed. Nobody was there, so I looked resolutely ahead to the annex, where one window was lit. I counted upward five levels, and then from the left side toward the right, to ascertain that this was the same window from which someone had peered at me a few days before. This time, the curtain was closed.

I stepped through the door—which was open, as I'd expected—into a hallway lit only by the yellow light behind an emergency exit sign. The doors to Personnel and the locker rooms were locked. I looked up the grimy staircase, which vanished into black, and I wished I had something stronger to use for illumination than the mini-flashlight on my key chain.

Not wanting to make any noise on the steps, I bent to take off my Asics, and as I did so, something scratched against the floor. I winced at the sound, and as I picked up my left shoe, I discovered that I'd stepped on a pair of eyeglasses. They hadn't broken, though. I picked them up, and I didn't even need to look at the American brand name, Ralph Lauren, on the inside to know who they belonged to. They were Michael's, the ones he wore as a light disguise, with clear non-prescription lenses.

He'd lost his glasses. Had he left them for someone like me to find, or had they fallen during a struggle? Perhaps they'd been ripped off his face by someone hoping to make him less able to fight—no, I couldn't think about that. I just needed to find him.

I found an open storage closet, slipped in, and took out my telephone. I dialed Brian's cell number, which I'd programmed in ahead of time. He picked up immediately.

"I found his glasses," I whispered after he'd said hello.

"Come again?"

"His eyeglasses, the ones he uses when he pretends he's with State. They were lying within the entrance to a building behind Mitsutan, the store's annex. Since they're still here, I think he must have passed through not too long ago. He might still be here."

"You went to that store? Rei, what the hell are you doing?" Brian sounded alarmed.

"I had to do it. You can't expect me to stay in my box when Michael's missing!" It was hard to keep my voice to a whisper, because I was so upset; but I couldn't risk being overheard. "I've got to get off. I'll get back with you when I have a chance."

"Hold on. I'd like to come out there and be your backup. Where are you, exactly?"

I gave him the subway directions. "When you get here, come out to exit B12. It's one of the few exits that will be open at this time, and it comes right out on the street near the front of the store. The annex is behind the store, in an alley next to its parking garage. I should be out of the building by then, and I'll just hide in the alley, near the parking garage, until I see you."

"Do you want me to call you when I get there?"

"Better not. Even if the phone's on vibrate mode, someone could hear it, because the building's so quiet."

"Then you call me. One ring, and hang up, if you're in trouble. Two rings if you're still cool."

"Thanks," I said.

"Sure. And Rei? Don't try to be a hero, okay?"

I didn't answer, because I was tired of telling lies.

Ms. Aoki of Personnel had spent a little time telling my trainee group about the annex. This was where we would change our clothes, use the toilets, wash our hands, eat, smoke, and talk naturally: all forms of expression that were too human for us to reveal to customers in the main store. So I knew the places to do these things, and I also was dimly aware that the annex's third and fourth floors were storage areas, and the fifth and sixth floors were executive offices. Above that, I didn't know; the building was eight stories high, so there was a top level that I didn't know about, and perhaps this was where Michael was.

So many options; but I had to figure out plan A and plan B. My first temptation was to check every room, floor by floor, but I quickly nixed that. It would take too long to pick all the locks, and I might never find out who was in the lit-up office on the fifth floor. I had to discover the identity of the people in charge, because if I didn't ever find Michael, I wanted to know exactly who was to blame.

Keeping close to the wall, I climbed the stairs, which had the kind of grimy, sticky dirtiness that I could feel through my socks. Probably the stairs were never cleaned, just as the building was poorly lit and barely heated. I shone my mini-flashlight briefly as I reached each floor, looking for an obvious sign of an open door, but saw nothing. As I approached five, I slid the flashlight into my backpack again. Enough light for me to see where I was going seeped out of a half-open door located midway down the hallway.

I tiptoed along the hall, stopping two doorways down from that door, which I could see had Mr. Kitagawa's name on it. A woman's voice was speaking from within.

"Several customers were in the office when he was there. His presence could be remembered by them, if his photograph should appear in the papers." Mrs. Okuma's voice was not pitched politely, as it usually was with customers; it was lower and harder, befitting her status as a power player within Mitsutan's secret circle.

"There will be no photographs. Nobody will find him." Masahiro Mitsuyama's voice was firm.

"Excuse me," Mrs. Okuma persisted, "but Lockwood is a foreign service officer. Surely he will be a high-priority missing person for the national police as well as the American government."

"He can't be a real embassy official, because he was seen in Shimura's apartment—you know, where Farraday used to be. This new man must be the new spy." Mr. Kitagawa was speaking now, no longer using the friendly voice he'd used when he took me out. He sounded tough, almost as tough as Masahiro Mitsuyama.

"We can't get rid of him the same way." Masahiro Mitsuyama sounded thoughtful. "Well, our friends will have an idea."

"It would be difficult to do, without a lot of trouble," Mrs. Okuma spoke up. "He's listed in our database—"

Masahiro Mitsuyama said, "As a security precaution, you'll remove that name from your own records tomorrow. The record of the charge card will be erased. I'll get my son to go into the computers and fix it."

"But what if his wife tries to use her card when she shops here?" Mrs. Okuma persisted.

Mr. Kitagawa spoke up again. "Why would a wife bother to go shopping when she's worried about a missing husband? And you said you looked into the matter and found she wasn't a frequent shopper at all."

"It's true she didn't shop much," Mrs. Okuma admitted. "You might be right. I hope so."

"Both of you, enough," Mr. Mitsuyama said. "You're wasting time. All that matters is the gaijin is in the trunk and ready to go when Yoda-san arrives."

My head started pounding then, and I lost track of the whatever was said next. Car trunk. I'd had a very bad experience in a car trunk, some time ago; now it came back to me: the closed-in feeling, the terror. And Michael was in one, quite possibly dead.

I took several deep breaths and pushed myself back into the present, where I heard Mr. Kitagawa's voice rumbling about damage control. He said that the security officer who'd brought Michael to the office could be trusted, but would need to be watched. After a certain amount of time had passed, and if he'd remained quiet, he'd be re-warded.

I felt torn between staying to hear more and fleeing to grab Mi-chael. If only they'd say where the car was, but no such luck. I had a sense the car couldn't be far off, if they were waiting for someone, this Yoda person, to take it away. Remembering that there had been no cars in the alley, I had a sudden thought about where the vehicle holding Michael might be: the store's garage.

How much time had passed? I glanced at my watch. Twenty min-utes. The time was too short for Brian to have made it from Hiroo to the Ginza. I had to get to Michael before the car was driven away.

I tiptoed back down the hall and entered the stairway, again cling-ing to the shadows as much as I could. But midway down the flight of steps between three and two, I heard someone coming.

I turned and fled back up to three, where I took shelter behind a custodian's cart.

Two sets of footsteps were going up, both of them slow and mea-sured.

"Don't forget what I said, about being too—rough."

It was Enobu Mitsuyama, talking to someone.

"Why call us, then?" The voice was insolent, not the way anyone would normally speak to the heir to the Mitsutan chain.

"I didn't call you; my father did. I don't agree with what's happen-ing at all."

"Your father says one thing, you say another. What are we to do?"

"All I want is to—to remind you is to be human. If you—or any of your group—have any memory of what humanity means."

Enobu Mitsuyama's companion snorted in response, and their voices became too far away to hear as they continued upstairs. But I needed the breather, because I felt that I was finally fitting together the pieces of a very complicated puzzle.

Enobu Mitsuyama was a reluctant participant in the goings-on at the store, or at the very least ambivalent. Now I was wondering if he'd perhaps been forced by his father to tinker with the books in the first place. What Enobu had said to the gangster could have been about not killing Michael. This gave me a glimmer of hope.

The voices completely faded as they stopped at the fourth floor, and went down the hall.

42

They were high up enough not to hear me, so it was time to run. I emerged from my hiding place and quietly went down the remaining flights of stairs. I was about to head into the lobby when I caught sight of a security guard standing at the door. He was looking out the door to the alley, as if he was watching for possible interlopers.

Now I worried about Brian. I didn't think enough time had elapsed for him to reach the store by subway from Hiroo, but I needed to get out fast, not only to warn him but to ascertain if Michael was even in the garage. And this I'd have to do without being noticed.

I remembered the dim yellow emergency exit sign. It was situated in the back of the first floor, in a hallway that stretched out beyond personnel. This would be my only chance, I thought as I crept down the hallway, praying that the guard wouldn't suddenly turn around and scan the inside of the building, just in case. But when I reached the door at the end of the hall, I found that it was chained shut. Maybe I could have opened it with my tools, but chances were that I'd make so much noise I'd be caught before getting out.

What was my plan B?

In my head, I heard Michael talking. *If you create a commotion in the building, the guard will notice and leave the door. Distract him. Then get out.*

I had to create a distraction. I felt quietly through my backpack, my hands closing over the tool kit itself. If I threw the tool kit hard, in the hallway, perhaps he'd leave the door. But I'd need to hide myself somewhere outside the hallway, so I could make it out myself without being apprehended.

This time, there was nothing as helpful as the bulky custodial cart I'd found upstairs. The best hiding spot I could find was an unlocked door, which I moved to an angle where I could hide behind it. But as I did, it creaked—and instantly I understood that that the guard had heard it too, because I could hear him moving in the lobby.

I threw the bag as far as I could, down the hall, and held my breath from behind the doorway as the guard rounded the corner and spotted the kit lying at the end of the hall. He hurried by, and after he was twenty feet past me, I slipped out of my doorway and sped off, through the front of the building and the door.

I ran past the orange cones barricading the garage. Since it was after hours, I'd assumed that there would be just a few cars in the garage, but there were unfortunately more than I'd expected. The Mitsuyama Mercedes, with its fancy lettering on the door, was close to the exit; I didn't think it would be an obvious choice for carrying a body, but I thumped on the trunk anyway, calling Michael's name. Nothing. I ran along the first floor, which sloped up, shining around cars with the tiny flashlight and thumping trunks. There were nine floors to the garage, I realized as I glanced upward—too long a trek to do quickly on foot and check every car. And who knew how good a check I could do, anyway? If Michael was gagged, I'd probably be unable to find him.

I spotted an electric cart parked near an elevator. It would be quiet, and it might have the key inside the ignition. I slid onto the its seat and found out that the ignition went on with the turn of a switch, which was just as good. I started the vehicle, switched on the headlights, then turned them off. It was better not to reveal my presence to the people who'd be entering the garage at any minute. But I felt more powerful in the cart than I'd felt when I was on foot, and I steered straight up to the next level, where I found three more cars to check. All the cars, I was beginning to realize, had stickers on their windshields with a printed personal name, and the Mitsutan emblem.

It seemed that some employees were allowed to park overnight. Perhaps Michael was in an employee's car, the car of one of the people involved in the plot. I'd already checked out Mrs. Okuma's car on the first level, and the Mitsuyama sedan; I hadn't been looking for names on the other cars on the first level, so I could have passed the cars of others at the store without knowing it.

Who would want to run the risk of carrying a victim in a trunk? When I'd been kidnapped in Washington, there had been many traces of fibers from my clothing, and DNA from my body, left behind for police analysis, which fortunately had led to a quick conviction. I couldn't imagine the Mitsuyamas taking such a great personal risk with any of their family cars. Someone else would have to take the fall.

The fourth and fifth floors were devoid of cars; but on six there was a Toyota Windom parked close to the elevator. I put the cart in park and then hurried toward the car, which was parked nose forward, and read the name on the parking sticker: Fujiwara. Of course. Why not put a body in a dead man's car? The owner wasn't likely to notice.

As I drew closer I shone my flashlight around the edge of the trunk, and I saw, from the space in the wheel wells, how much lower the back of the car was sitting. Something was in the trunk. And as I laid my hand on the hood, I felt a slight warmth which told me that it had been recently driven.

I hurried around to the back of the car and pressed my mouth close to the car trunk. I called out Michael's name, and felt something knock hard, against the trunk, from inside.

I had no tools with me, because I'd stupidly thrown away my tool kit in the annex, but there was an easier, faster way to open a car trunk. From the electric cart, I grabbed a tire jack and used it to smash the window on the driver's side. This set off the alarm, but there was no time to fret.

I pulled the car's trunk-release button, and the trunk bobbed open. Inside I saw what looked like a package, a bulky shape wrapped in heavy brown paper. I tore at it with my hands, not caring about scratches or anything except getting to the inside, getting to the contents.

Dark brown hair matted with something sticky. Pale skin, and a blue eye looking up at me. It was Michael, still alive.

As I tore at the stocking that bound Michael's mouth, he said, "There's no time for that, just get me out—"

He was panicked, but he had a point. I started working on the ties that bound his legs.

"Can't walk—"

"Why? Tell me, what did those bastards do to you?"

Michael didn't seem to hear my question. "Roll me out and hide me somewhere, then get the hell out yourself. Call Brian—this was my stupid mistake, and you're not going down, too—"

I interrupted him. "I've got an electric cart."

Michael's eye suddenly looked less anxious, and I pushed down all my worries that I might not be able to enact the grand escape plan. At the outset, I was finding that moving a 165-pound man was quite difficult. I drove the cart to the edge of the car, and after I'd put on the emergency brake, slowly tugged Michael up and over. He let out a howl when he landed.

"I'm so sorry. I didn't mean to hurt you," I said, trying to wedge him into a sitting position.

"It's nothing compared to—"

Michael cut off his words as we both heard the sounds of shouting, a few floors below. They'd come over from the annex very quickly; the fact that I'd set off the Windom's car alarm had probably helped things along. Whether they were going to take the elevator up to seven or drive up from ground level remained to be seen.

"Let's go." I put the cart in gear.

"You're going to run straight into them, unless they're taking the elevator—" Michael craned his neck around to look at the elevators as I pushed the cart to its top speed of forty kilometers an hour.

"We have to get out." I started following the signs for the exit as we could hear the car below, purring its way up.

"Did they see you come in?"

"No, but I think they knew somebody was in the annex. I created a distraction." I slowed my speed slightly, because on the last turn Michael had almost fallen out.

"So they probably think I've got a helper, and they'll assume we're driving the car they stashed me in, because the alarm blew. They're probably blocking the exit ramp, to stop us."

"Then you think I should—" I was already turning the cart in a careful circle.

"Exactly. Turn around and go down the other direction."

I did it, keeping not to the left, Japanese-style, but the right, so that I could glance down over the edge, to look out for the oncoming car. And Michael pointed out to me that the elevator was in service, meaning that a second person or group was traveling upward.

"There!" I shouted to Michael, pointing. I could see the lights of a car traveling fast about a floor beneath us. It was traveling up the regular entry path, observing Japanese habit, despite the craziness of the situation. I'd been right and Michael wrong, but there was no time for blame.

"Through there!" Michael jerked his head toward a narrow gap between the garage's support pillars. I could only hope the cart was narrow enough to make it, as I edged through—it was, though the mirror on the driver's side broke off. A sharp left, and I was heading down the exit-only path.

I floored the accelerator, rushing downward, taking the curves so fast that Michael was again in danger of falling out. My cell phone was ringing in my lap, and Michael grabbed it and was suddenly shouting something to Brian.

We were heading into the first floor, out toward the pay booth, where there was no attendant, but still the wooden arm stretched downward, barring our way out. And as I slowed the cart so I could turn it to go out the way I'd come in, I saw Miyo Han. She was standing right next to the wooden arm barring our path.

Now I knew that I'd been right about someone following me outside. Miyo must have seen me slip into the annex and waited for me to emerge—at which point she'd followed me to the garage.

"It's a trap," Michael shouted at me. "You're supposed to slow down and stop and they'll get us."

"I can't run her over—"

"She's blocking our way. You will do it, Rei, you must—"

"I can't!" But I was going forward, hating myself, just as I saw Miyo's long, impossibly elegant leg flare out and kick out the wooden arm barring our path.

I surged forward, thanking God for sparing my friend, who'd jumped back so the cart could make it through.

We were out of the garage, free. But as I scanned the scene, I saw the headlights of a car turning into the alley, a situation that filled me with a fresh surge of panic until I realized that Brian Jones was jumping out of the passenger side. Within seconds he'd hauled Michael into the backseat and I'd jumped in right after him, just as the Mitsuyama Mercedes swerved out of the garage.

"Miyo!" I called out to my friend, but in vain. She'd run the other way, out of the alley. Well, at least she'd gotten away.

"They know we're in this car; we're sunk," I moaned as the car we were in took off.

"They're not going to follow us." Brian sounded confident.

"Why not?" I craned my head backward and saw that Brian was right: the car had stopped at the mouth of the garage.

"You didn't see what this car looks like."

I looked out the window and down at the side of the car. It was white and bore the emblem of the Tokyo police department.

I looked at Brian's smiling face, completely shocked by the situation. Michael had said that we weren't supposed to let anyone know what we were doing, and Brian had said himself that only the three of us were working on the project. And here we were, tucked into a Japanese police cruiser—

"For obvious reasons, this vehicle is seldom used in our fleet," Brian said. "I only take it out of the New Sanno's garage for special situations. The problem is, I don't know all the highways and by-ways, not to mention that I have an issue about being noticed. I had to ask Daisuke-san to help out—which is why we arrived a few minutes later than planned."

A Japanese man, wearing a very real-looking cap of the Tokyo metropolitan police, didn't turn around, but I could see in the rearview mirror that he looked concerned.

"Sir, would you prefer to visit a particular hospital?" Daisuke's voice was calm.

"It'll call too much—attention—and I'm not that badly off," Michael croaked. "I think my arm's broken, but that can wait."

A broken arm. Now I understood why he'd screamed with pain when I'd practically dropped him into the cart.

"But you can't walk, you said—"

"Your legs go to sleep, after a few hours of being shut up in a trunk," Michael said. "It's not a big deal."

"We can get you treated at Yokota Air Base," Brian said. "Daisuke-san, do we have enough gas to get out to Hachioji without stopping?"

Daisuke nodded and turned on his siren.

43

A day later, I was biting my lip, looking for the right move. And then I saw it.

"Checkmate," I said to Michael, moving my knight over his.

"How did you do that? Damn it," Michael said. "You're good."

"You're not so bad either," I said. "You won the last game."

We were playing chess in a hospital room, Michael in his bed, and me on a hard plastic chair drawn close. It was an American hospital, and the small library of games available for bored patients consisted of chess, checkers, and Candy Land.

Just as there wasn't much choice in playing materials, there had not been a private room available; Michael was sharing with a twenty-one-year-old airman who'd survived Iraq only to have suffered nine broken bones in a motorcycle accident at Yokota Air Base. During one of the times that this veteran was in the bathroom, being helped by a nurse, Michael had told me how lucky he felt. He'd had his arm broken by the chief of security, and he had multiple bruises on his face and body, but all of it would heal. He'd wanted to get out of bed and go for a fast-paced walk, since he couldn't run until the arm was healed—but the doctor in charge had given orders to rest until further notice.

"I should be out of here," Michael said. "In the States, I would have been out in three hours."

"You will get out. You're just being held for rest and relaxation. I know it's not the lap of luxury, but it's a lot better than the car trunk. That's what Len said, anyway." I was now on a first-name basis with

Michael's boss, the shadowy Len Novak. Len had called me on the phone many times, all night long, not only for updates on Michael but for all of the things I'd uncovered about the links between Winston Brothers bank and Kanazawa-kai, and Mitsutan and Nozumi-gun. I, in turn, had plenty of questions for him. Specifically, how could OCI, without revealing itself, ensure that the Japanese police would arrest Masahiro Mitsuyama for ordering the murders of Mr. Fujiwara and Tyler Farraday; for masterminding a money-laundering cover-up; and last but certainly not least, for kidnapping and attempting to murder Michael.

Len's response was short and simple. He told me that he thought the situation would naturally resolve itself. Of course we had our doubts.

"If Len wants to do something nice for us, he should have a car arranged to take us to the New Sanno. I know they have rooms; I called to check," Michael said.

"But that doesn't make sense. We're flying on a military air transport out of Yokota." I studied the chessboard, pondering what I'd do after Michael made his move.

"We certainly are, but after we debrief at the embassy. It makes sense for us to stay in the city."

"Okay, I'll push for getting us into the Sanno, though I wish you'd let me suggest Hotel Okura. It's much closer to the embassy and really charming."

"More expensive, and less secure," Michael said shortly. "By the way, what's going on with your friend Miyo?"

"Well, we've talked about some things, and she decided not to go back to work there."

"Did anyone see her help us in the garage?"

I shook my head. "She doesn't think so; remember, they were a few levels above us when she kicked out the gate."

"Excellent," Michael said. "But she shouldn't work there again. It's just not safe."

I looked at Michael steadily. "I had to tell Miyo some things in order to explain why I had to rescue you."

"You did?"

"I told her that you were my boyfriend." I flushed slightly, because it really was my secret fantasy. "I said you worked for people concerned about potential financial mismanagement at the store. I explained that I'd started working there to try to help you, and what she uncovered on the computer about my expenditures was evidence of internal corruption. That got her really upset and she wound up writing to the union representative for store workers, telling him to look at the difference between their purchases and store records of what they'd spent. And now the other salespeople think Mitsutan is somehow trying to cheat them out of their employee discounts, which is not exactly true, but is understandably wreaking havoc."

Michael smiled slowly, and said, "I'm all for labor agitation, but what about her future?"

"Well, she may be going to New York on a student visa."

"How so?"

"Archie's going back to Wall Street because he's left Winston Brothers and is interviewing at a bunch of other banks. He invited Miyo to accompany him."

Michael's eyes widened. "That's a fast operator."

"Who do you mean, Miyo or Archie?" I asked.

"Both, I suppose."

"Some people understand what they want and aren't afraid to go for it."

"Really," said Michael, not looking away as he moved his knight over mine.

The news on television in Tokyo was all about labor unrest at Mitsutan, but this was about all that was reported. It frustrated me, after what we'd gone through. There seemed to be no justice; I knew who'd ordered the murders of Tyler and Mr. Fujiwara, and I also knew the organization, at least, behind the murder of Ravi Shah. But there wasn't a thing Michael or I could do about it. And as far as our own government was concerned, our bosses at Langley had been pleased with the information we'd provided, and relieved that we were leaving Tokyo alive—but that was all.

"I bet that somebody in Washington advises Jimmy DeLone not to invest in Japanese retail," Michael said in the waning hours of our last night in Japan, as we sat at our regular table in the back of the New Sanno's Embarcadero Lounge. He was drinking a Bud Lite, and I was nursing a cup of coffee that had grown cold during the hour we'd been there.

"Back in D.C., that's what I told you I thought the mission was originally about," I reminded him.

"No, it was on the plane from California. You knew, even then. You always seem to know." Michael's eyes remained on me so long that I felt uncomfortable.

"I guess this means that Supermart shoppers, and our stock market, will be untouched by the *yakuza*. I only wish it were the same situation for the Japanese."

"They're entrenched, Rei." Michael shook his head. "We just have to accept that this is part of the way Japan operates, just as others put their loathing aside and accept that in our country, almost anyone can buy a gun."

My mind flashed back to Michael's suggestion that we had unfinished business to take care of in Tokyo. Maybe, in his mind, it had meant a drink in this place, when I'd thought we were going to do something to take care of what had been left undone.

I couldn't look at him another moment without breaking down, so I shifted my gaze upward, to the television screen over the bar. It had been fixed on the Pentagon channel, but now was flickering with the other channels that the Armed Forces Network beamed into the hotel. Apparently the bartender, a young Japanese woman, was looking for something to entertain herself, because there were no others in the bar except Michael and me, and we had been intent on each other, not the television.

A game show with Japanese dressed in silly costumes flashed by, as did a sign of a pirate holding a sword at someone's throat. Then I saw Warren Kravitz standing before a lectern, bowing his head, and then one of the Desperate Housewives locked with a hunky man in a kiss—

"Back to NHK news, please!" I shouted, jumping up and waving at the bartender, who looked displeased at my request, but switched back to channel eleven.

The television had no sound, but English subtitles ran across the bottom of the screen. Apparently Warren Kravitz, a vice president of Winston Brothers Tokyo branch, was cooperating with Japan's Financial Services Agency in an investigation of possible irregularities at the bank. Next, a photograph of Ravi's face flashed on the screen, followed by that of a Japanese government official holding a paper—a typed e-mail sent by Ravi from an Internet café in the early morning hours before his death. The letter categorized the irregularities at the bank, suggesting a possible involvement with the gangster organization Kanazawa-kai. It also mentioned the dates when Ravi had contacted Warren Kravitz with this information, and his boss's refusal to discuss the situation.

"Did you tell him anything about Warren?" Michael's eyes were fixed on the type going across the screen.

"Of course not! But I did mention Fincen, and tell him they were on the web. He must have done something the last night he was alive."

Michael lowered his voice. "The police think he was pushed into his own apartment, from the outside, by an intruder. Maybe he was caught on his way back from the café. It all makes sense now."

I shut my eyes to blink back the tears as the television ended its story and switched to breaking news about toothpaste. When I opened my eyes, I saw that Michael was watching me.

"I'm going upstairs, to turn on my own television, just in case there's more to the story later on." I had to get away from him, because I didn't want him to think that all I did was cry.

"There will be more news—but probably not tonight. What Ravi did changes everything, Rei, don't you realize?"

"I suppose it might cause some trouble for Warren."

"That's putting it mildly! The only way Warren will avoid being charged in your friend's murder, I bet, is if he can become an informant." Michael leaned over the table, so close that I could feel the warmth of his breath. "I think he's going to wind up spilling everything about the dirty money the bank took in, and perhaps even the orders that the Kanazawa-kai bosses gave him to publicize the money-laundering operation run by their rivals at Mitsutan."

"It could happen," I agreed, still feeling cautious. "Warren Kravitz is an American citizen, and I bet he'd do anything to enable himself to be sent home to a nice white-collar prison rather than be imprisoned in a Japanese jail."

"That's right," Michael said. "And to take your hypothesis a step further, if the Kanazawa-kai people go on the stand, they'd prefer to be charged with money laundering, I think, than murder. My guess is they'll reveal that Masahiro Mitsuyama himself was the one who ordered Fujiwara's death."

"I have the tape to prove it. What a shame I can't share it with anyone."

"Maybe you can. The tape could certainly arrive by special courier on the desk of a certain police chief I trust. They could do what they want with it, I'd think."

"I'd like that," I said.

"Good. I think I'll put together a small package and leave it with Brian before we go to the airport tomorrow. There will be no mention of our names or agency or how we made the recording. Just the evidence, pure and simple."

I tossed and turned in my bed that night, thinking about how I'd have to seem sharp for the debriefing at the American embassy the next morning, and immediately afterward head out to Yokota for what was bound to be a noisy, uncomfortable flight on a military plane back to the United States. And from that point, I'd have a few hours' rest before going with Michael to Langley to tell our story in more detail.

I wasn't even sure that I wanted to work at OCI anymore. Weeks earlier, I had been thrilled by the excitement and importance of spy work. But after what had happened in Mitsutan's annex and garage, I felt shaken. As much as I appreciated what OCI had given me—chiefly advanced language training and a steady paycheck—I couldn't see making a habit of close brushes with death.

Truthfully, what I'd loved most about my job at OCI was working with Michael. I stared at the ceiling, thinking about the many cozy mornings we'd read newspapers together in the office at Pentagon City, and the stolen lunch hour when we'd sat within touching distance of each other at the Kabuki-za, covertly passing information. I'd loved drinking with Michael, playing chess with him, having him zip me into a tricky evening dress.

No, I corrected myself. It wasn't that I loved working with Michael; I was starting to love him. But what could I do? If I quit OCI, I would probably never see Michael again. If I stayed on at the agency keeping my feelings hidden, life would also be unbearable.

The glow-in-the-dark alarm clock said it was one o'clock. I was never going to get to sleep, rolling around on my bed, alternately dreaming about Michael's mouth and punishing myself for my inappropriate thoughts.

He was the next room over, and probably still awake, because I

"But—don't!" Michael looked alarmed. "You're at the start of a very promising career. You can't give up intel. You're a natural."

"Well, the truth is, I sort of miss life in the antiques world."

"Really," Michael said. His expression had grown downcast. "So, you're going to leave?"

"I'm not sure." I wrapped my arms around myself, suddenly feeling naked. "Anyway, I sincerely apologize for embarrassing you with my—emotions. I will rein myself in, for the future, whether or not we continue to work together."

Michael studied me, and then said, "May I explain something to you?"

I nodded.

"When you came to work in my office—it was incredible. Not only did I have this brilliant and beautiful woman to work with, I had a real—friend. Of course I'm crazy about you. How could you doubt that?"

I didn't answer, because it was becoming clear to me that Michael was someone who was torn up by a combination of duty and memory—forces that I couldn't compete with.

"You've made me so happy," Michael continued. "Happier than I ever thought I could be, after Jenny's death. Not to mention safer. I will never forget the way that you risked your life to save mine."

Will never forget. It sounded like a brush-off. I nodded and went to the side of the bed, reaching for a tissue. Michael caught my arm on the way back.

"What are you going to do?" he asked.

"Well, I actually think I'm going back to my room to have a good cry. Then I suppose I'll fall asleep."

"Please stay."

"I don't think I heard you correctly," I said.

Michael looked down at the sheets for a moment, then back at me. "I can't stand to be alone the rest of the night. We could sleep together. I mean, just rest."

I looked at him, considering whether I could afford to put myself through this kind of nonsense. It would be painful, but being in such intimate contact, even just once, would be something I could always treasure.

Michael spoke again. "I've had a lot of insomnia during this trip. It's more than jet lag, it's anxiety: a lot of stuff I just can't tell you about yet. I was only able to sleep through two nights this trip: the first one at the hotel and then at the hospital. Both of these were times you were in the same room."

"That's nice of you to tell me," I said cautiously. "But I'm not sure things would go well between us in a room with just one bed—"

"If you stayed with me, I feel like it would—fix things. Please, Rei." There was a catch in his voice.

"All right," I said, because I didn't want to leave him, either. I slid between the sheets and lay with my arms around him, and my face against his back, feeling it gently relax into the rhythm of sleep.

I must have drifted off as well, because I had a strange dream. I was waiting for an elevator at Mitsutan; finally, it arrived and the doors opened. Inside, instead of the usual crowd of customers, there were just two men: young men, wearing beautiful hand-tailored suits, with their collars open. They were so deep in conversation that they didn't notice me as they stepped out of the elevator. But as they ambled past, the shorter, darker guy looked directly at me and smiled. It was Ravi, and I realized, a beat later, that his companion was Tyler Farraday.

I woke up and found tears in the corners of my eyes. I was weeping despite the fact that the two men had seemed serene, as if they were headed for someplace they didn't mind going.

It was all so poignant, I thought, as I reached out for Michael, and discovered that he was not there. I sat up and looked at the clock.

It was nine in the morning and Michael was gone—not just the man but his luggage, and every other personal item I'd seen in the room eight hours earlier. Trying not to become too depressed, I climbed out of bed and went into the tiny bathroom. I planned to splash water on my face to help me wake up to the fact that I was nothing more than a temporary security blanket. I'd served my purpose, and that was the end of it.

But as I reached for the taps, I noticed a note on the bathroom sink, clearly left for me to read. It was a spy joke just like the ones he used to send when we were on opposite coasts.

How many spies does it take to fall in love?

This was all that he'd written. I turned the paper over in my hand, looking for a clever answer, but nothing was there. Clearly, I was supposed to come up with it myself.

But as I folded the note to keep forever, I realized that I didn't know any words, Japanese or English, that could express how joyful I felt.